SIMPSONS™
COMICS

COLOSSAL COMPENDIUM
VOLUME FIVE

HARPER DESIGN
An Imprint of HarperCollins Publishers
www.hc.com

HarperCollins
PUBLISHERS
Since 1817

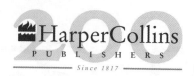

SIMPSONS COMICS COLOSSAL COMPENDIUM
VOLUME FIVE

Materials previously published in
Bart Simpson #85, Kang & Kodos #1, The Malevolent Mr. Burns #1, Professor Frink #1, Ralph Wiggum Comics #1, Simpsons Comics #208, #210, #220, Simpsons Summer Shindig #8, #9, Simpsons Super Spectacular #7, #15

FIRST EDITION

ISBN 978-0-06-256754-3
Library of Congress Control Number 2016958635

21 22 SCP 10 9 8 7 6 5 4 3

Publisher: Matt Groening

Creative Director: Nathan Kane
Managing Editor: Terry Delegeane
Director of Operations: Robert Zaugh
Production Manager: Christopher Ungar
Art Director: Jason Ho
Assistant Art Director: Mike Rote
Assistant Editor: Karen Bates
Production: Art Villanueva
Administration: Ruth Waytz
Legal Guardian: Susan A. Grode

Printed in China

D'OH-LICE ACADEMY

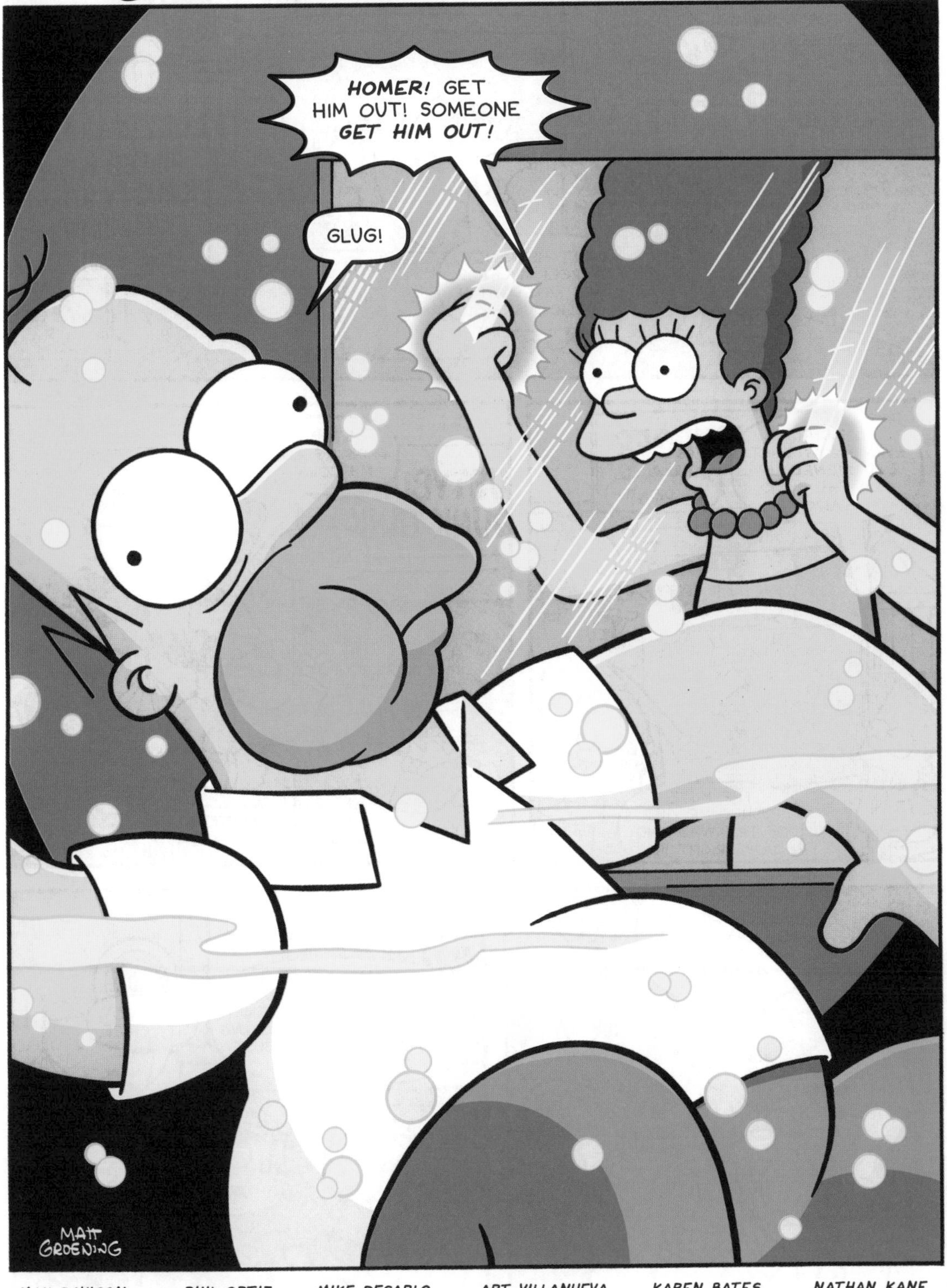
HOMER! GET HIM OUT! SOMEONE GET HIM OUT!
GLUG!
MATT GROENING

MAX DAVISON WRITER | PHIL ORTIZ PENCILS | MIKE DECARLO INKS | ART VILLANUEVA COLORS | KAREN BATES LETTERS | NATHAN KANE EDITOR

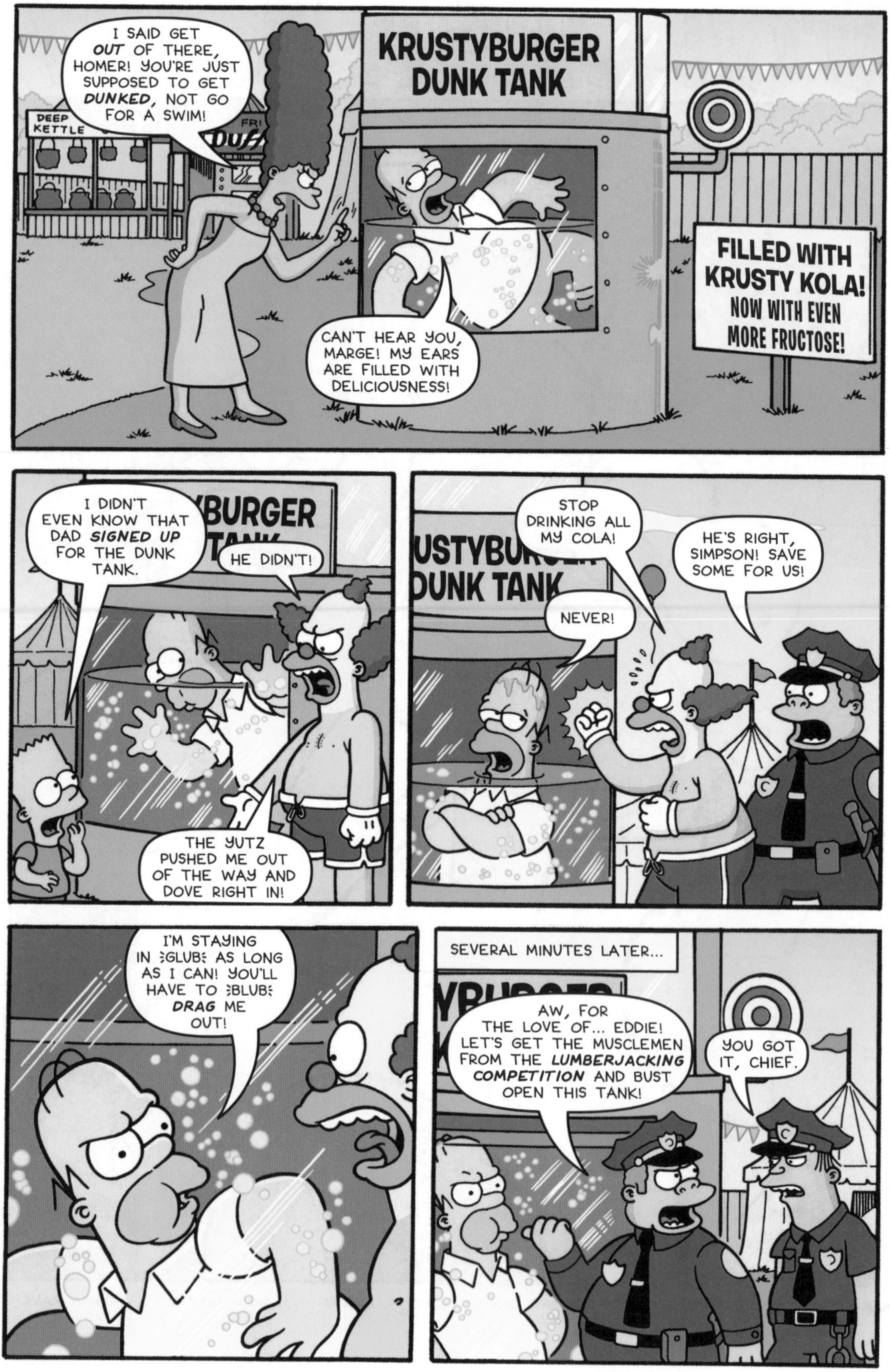
KRUSTYBURGER DUNK TANK
DEEP KETTLE
I SAID GET OUT OF THERE, HOMER! YOU'RE JUST SUPPOSED TO GET DUNKED, NOT GO FOR A SWIM!
CAN'T HEAR YOU, MARGE! MY EARS ARE FILLED WITH DELICIOUSNESS!
FILLED WITH KRUSTY KOLA! NOW WITH EVEN MORE FRUCTOSE!
I DIDN'T EVEN KNOW THAT DAD SIGNED UP FOR THE DUNK TANK.
HE DIDN'T!
THE YUTZ PUSHED ME OUT OF THE WAY AND DOVE RIGHT IN!
STOP DRINKING ALL MY COLA!
NEVER!
HE'S RIGHT, SIMPSON! SAVE SOME FOR US!
I'M STAYING IN :GLUB: AS LONG AS I CAN! YOU'LL HAVE TO :GLUB: DRAG ME OUT!
SEVERAL MINUTES LATER...
AW, FOR THE LOVE OF... EDDIE! LET'S GET THE MUSCLEMEN FROM THE LUMBERJACKING COMPETITION AND BUST OPEN THIS TANK!
YOU GOT IT, CHIEF.

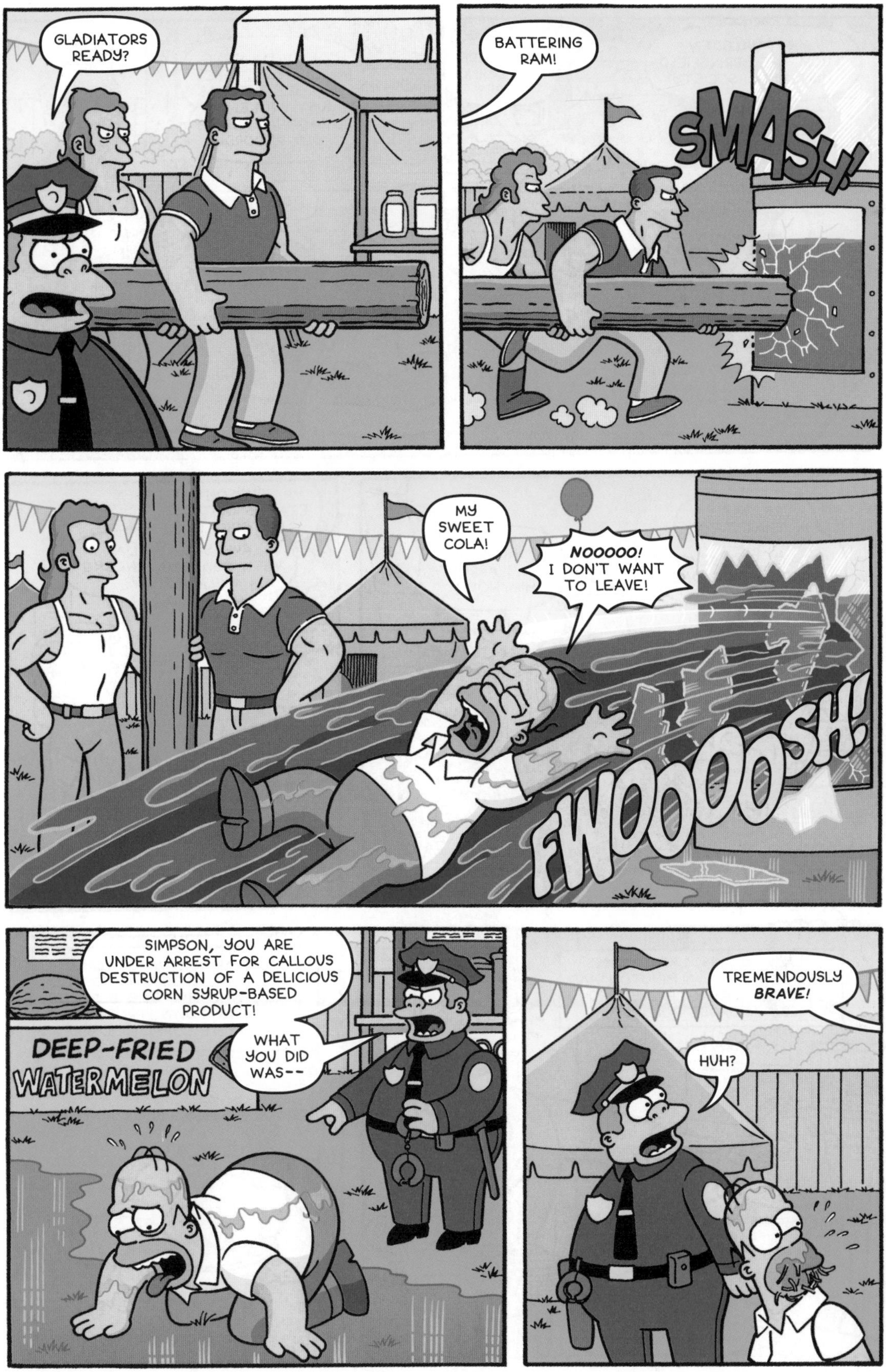
GLADIATORS READY?
BATTERING RAM!
SMASH!
MY SWEET COLA!
NOOOOO! I DON'T WANT TO LEAVE!
FWOOOOSH!
SIMPSON, YOU ARE UNDER ARREST FOR CALLOUS DESTRUCTION OF A DELICIOUS CORN SYRUP-BASED PRODUCT!
DEEP-FRIED WATERMELON
WHAT YOU DID WAS--
TREMENDOUSLY BRAVE!
HUH?

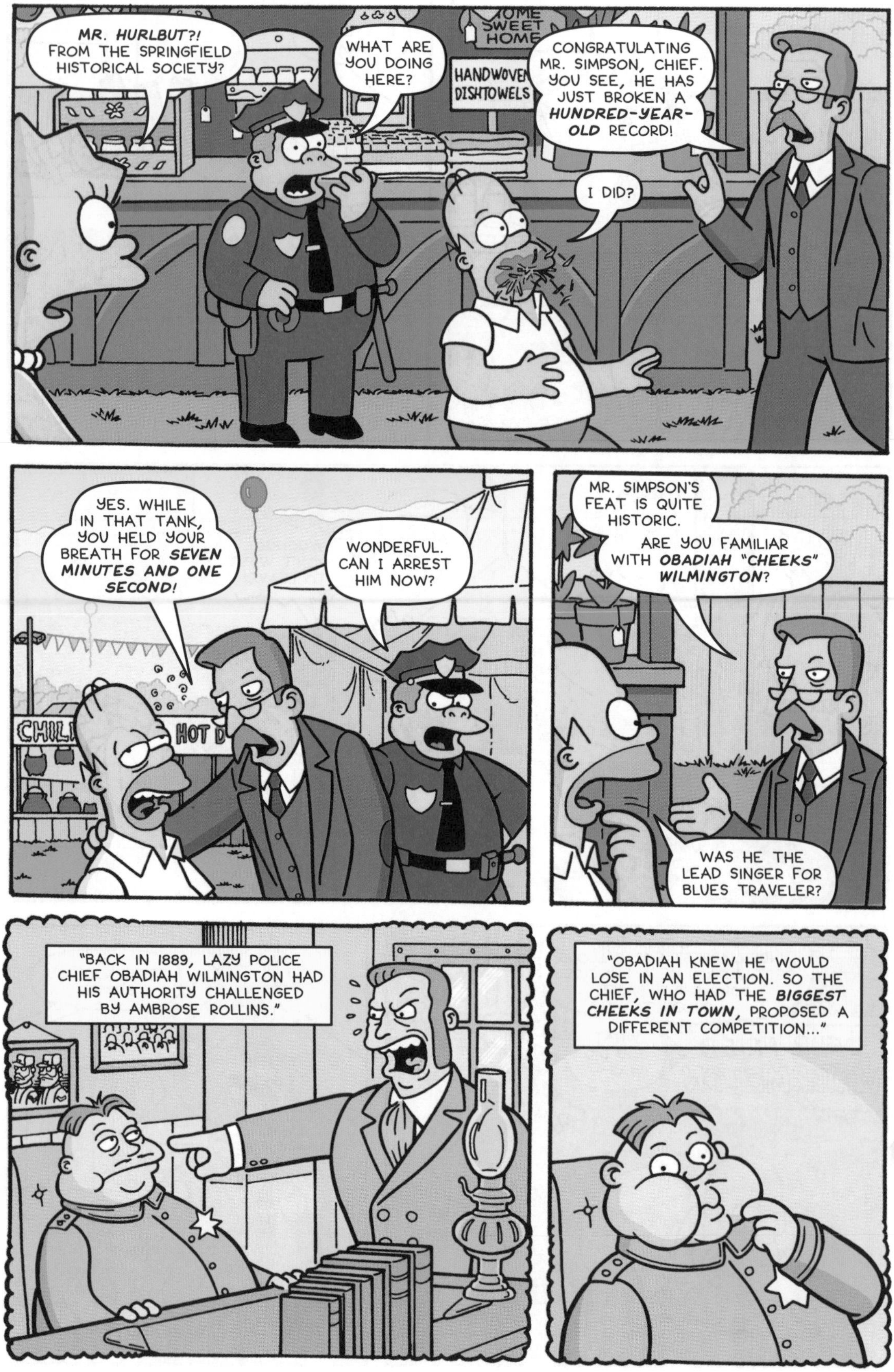
MR. HURLBUT?! FROM THE SPRINGFIELD HISTORICAL SOCIETY?
WHAT ARE YOU DOING HERE?
HOME SWEET HOME
HANDWOVEN DISHTOWELS
CONGRATULATING MR. SIMPSON, CHIEF. YOU SEE, HE HAS JUST BROKEN A HUNDRED-YEAR-OLD RECORD!
I DID?
YES. WHILE IN THAT TANK, YOU HELD YOUR BREATH FOR SEVEN MINUTES AND ONE SECOND!
WONDERFUL. CAN I ARREST HIM NOW?
MR. SIMPSON'S FEAT IS QUITE HISTORIC.
ARE YOU FAMILIAR WITH OBADIAH "CHEEKS" WILMINGTON?
WAS HE THE LEAD SINGER FOR BLUES TRAVELER?
"BACK IN 1889, LAZY POLICE CHIEF OBADIAH WILMINGTON HAD HIS AUTHORITY CHALLENGED BY AMBROSE ROLLINS."
"OBADIAH KNEW HE WOULD LOSE IN AN ELECTION. SO THE CHIEF, WHO HAD THE BIGGEST CHEEKS IN TOWN, PROPOSED A DIFFERENT COMPETITION..."

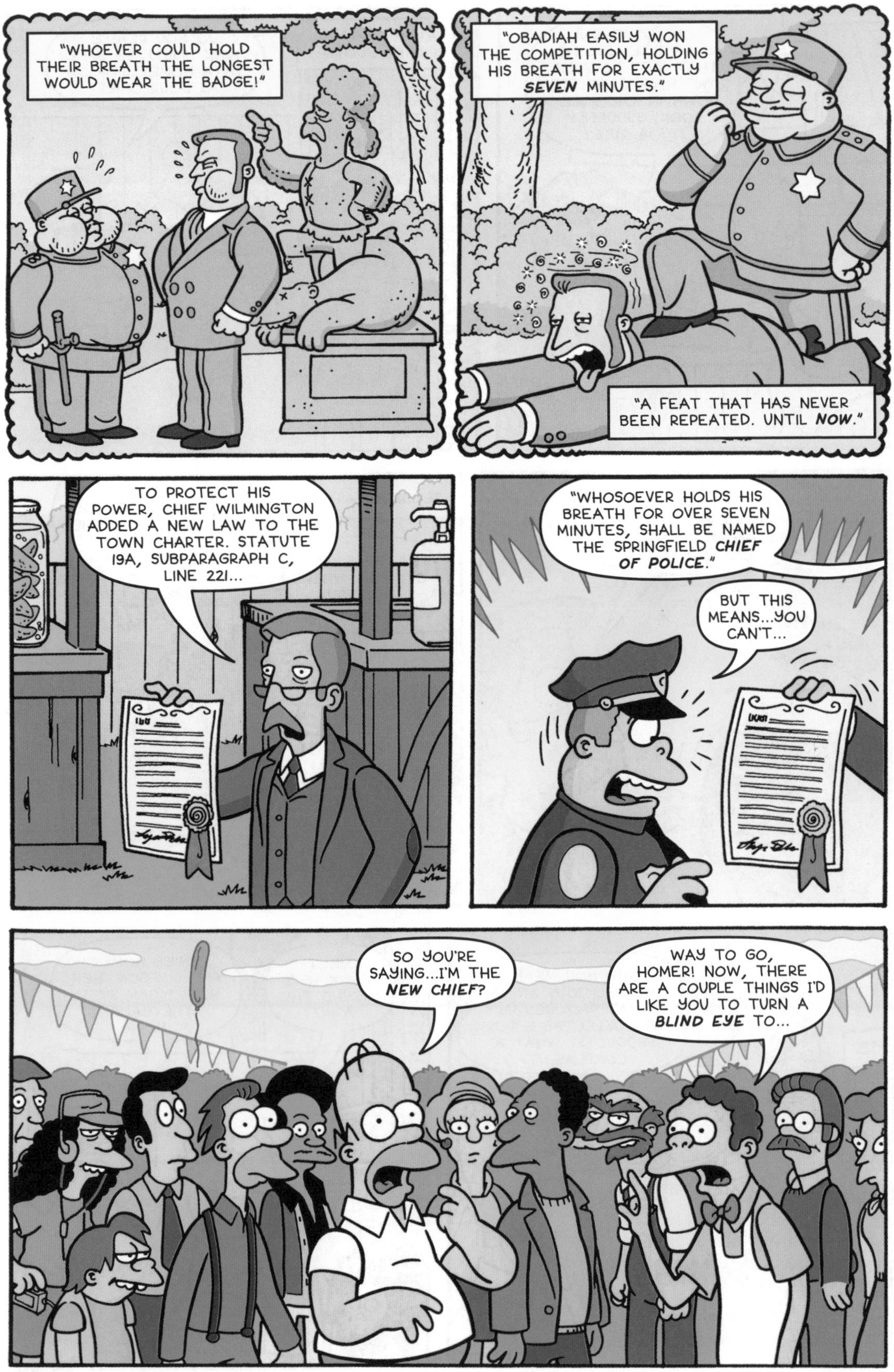
"WHOEVER COULD HOLD THEIR BREATH THE LONGEST WOULD WEAR THE BADGE!"
"OBADIAH EASILY WON THE COMPETITION, HOLDING HIS BREATH FOR EXACTLY SEVEN MINUTES."
"A FEAT THAT HAS NEVER BEEN REPEATED. UNTIL NOW."
TO PROTECT HIS POWER, CHIEF WILMINGTON ADDED A NEW LAW TO THE TOWN CHARTER. STATUTE 19A, SUBPARAGRAPH C, LINE 221...
"WHOSOEVER HOLDS HIS BREATH FOR OVER SEVEN MINUTES, SHALL BE NAMED THE SPRINGFIELD CHIEF OF POLICE."
BUT THIS MEANS...YOU CAN'T...
SO YOU'RE SAYING...I'M THE NEW CHIEF?
WAY TO GO, HOMER! NOW, THERE ARE A COUPLE THINGS I'D LIKE YOU TO TURN A BLIND EYE TO...

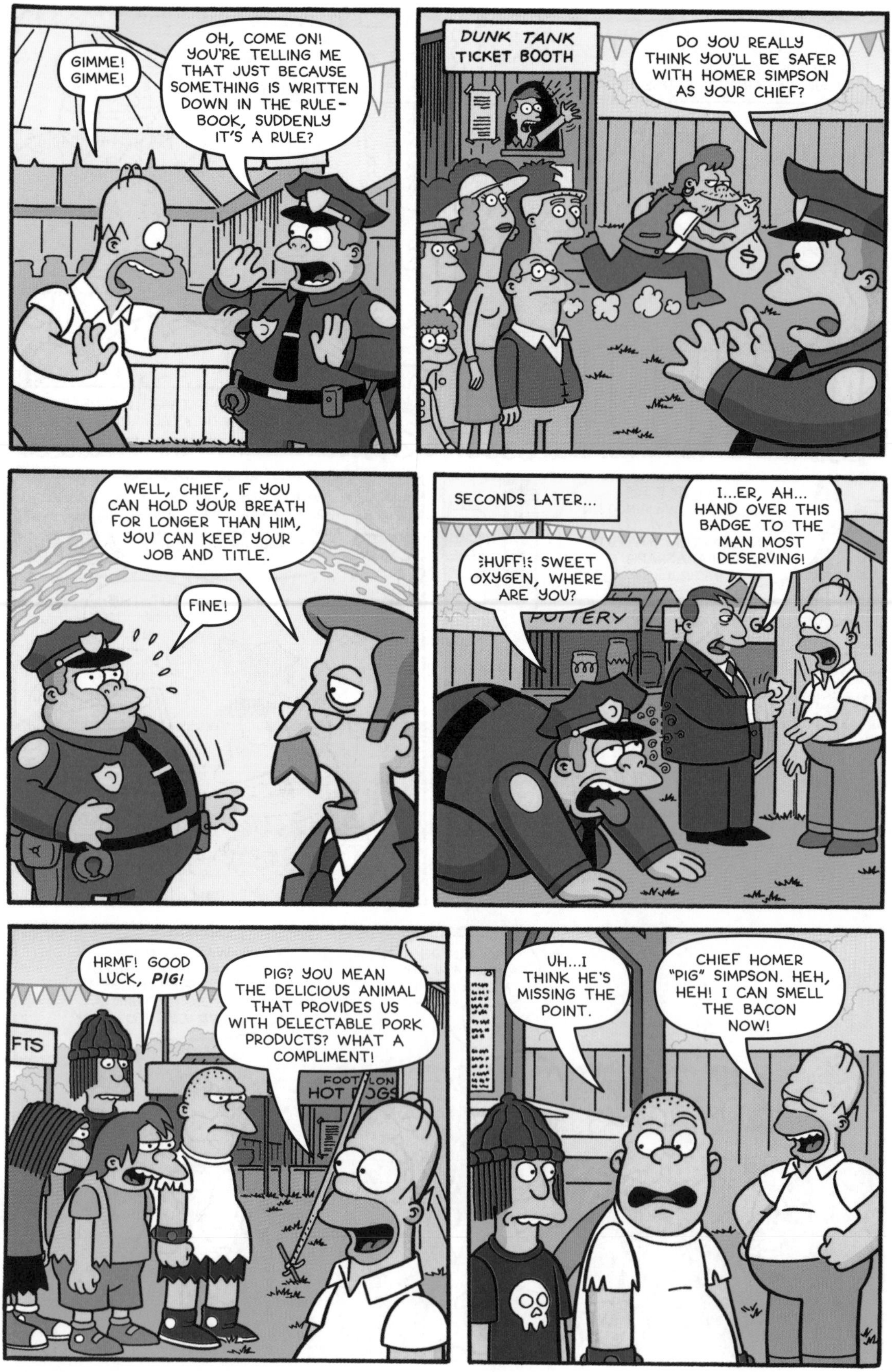
GIMME! GIMME!
OH, COME ON! YOU'RE TELLING ME THAT JUST BECAUSE SOMETHING IS WRITTEN DOWN IN THE RULE-BOOK, SUDDENLY IT'S A RULE?
DUNK TANK TICKET BOOTH
DO YOU REALLY THINK YOU'LL BE SAFER WITH HOMER SIMPSON AS YOUR CHIEF?
WELL, CHIEF, IF YOU CAN HOLD YOUR BREATH FOR LONGER THAN HIM, YOU CAN KEEP YOUR JOB AND TITLE.
FINE!
SECONDS LATER...
HUFF! SWEET OXYGEN, WHERE ARE YOU?
I...ER, AH... HAND OVER THIS BADGE TO THE MAN MOST DESERVING!
POTTERY
HRMF! GOOD LUCK, ***PIG***!
PIG? YOU MEAN THE DELICIOUS ANIMAL THAT PROVIDES US WITH DELECTABLE PORK PRODUCTS? WHAT A COMPLIMENT!
FTS
UH...I THINK HE'S MISSING THE POINT.
CHIEF HOMER "PIG" SIMPSON. HEH, HEH! I CAN SMELL THE BACON NOW!

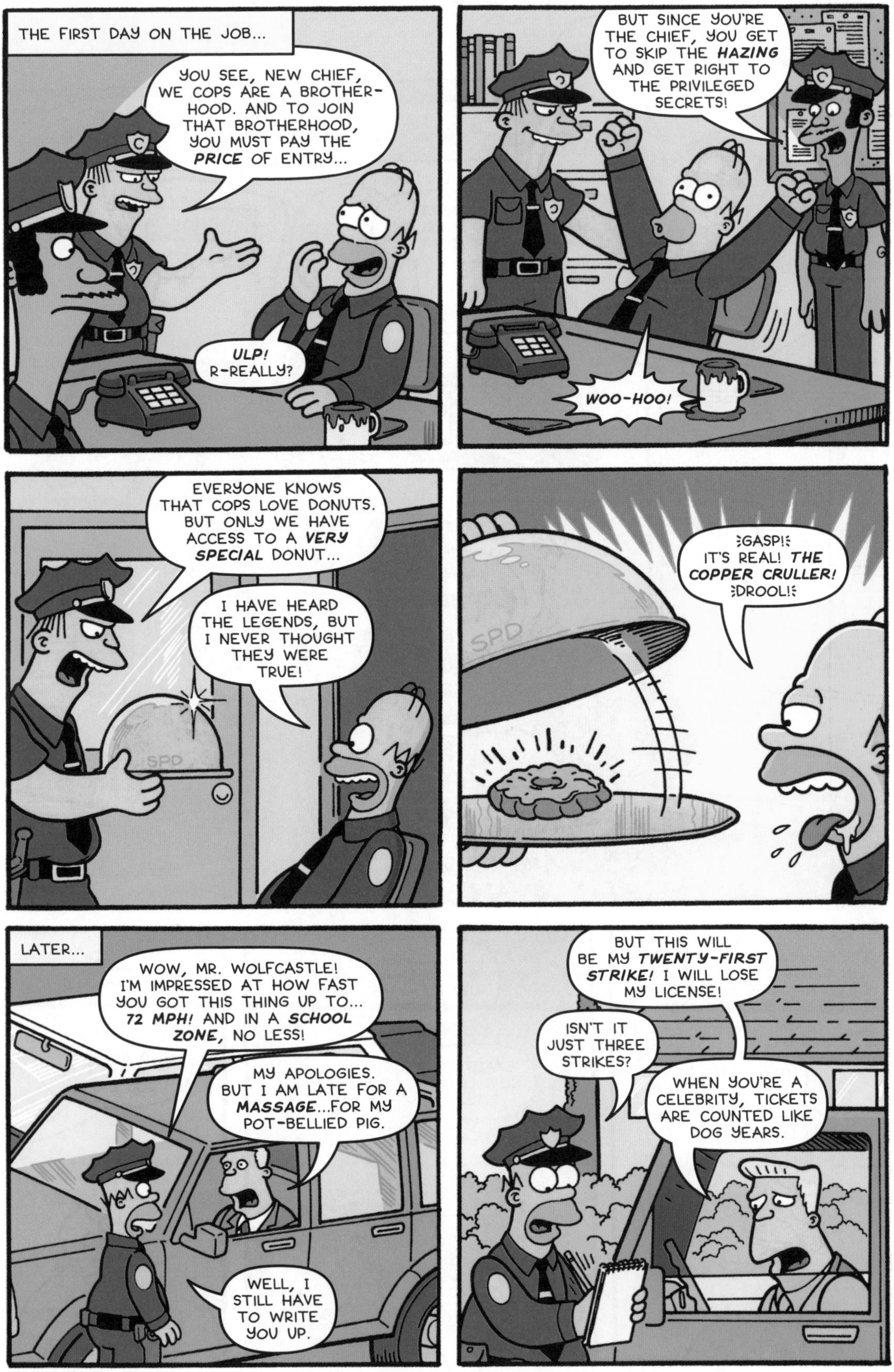

THE FIRST DAY ON THE JOB...
YOU SEE, NEW CHIEF, WE COPS ARE A BROTHER-HOOD. AND TO JOIN THAT BROTHERHOOD, YOU MUST PAY THE **PRICE** OF ENTRY...
ULP! R-REALLY?
BUT SINCE YOU'RE THE CHIEF, YOU GET TO SKIP THE ***HAZING*** AND GET RIGHT TO THE PRIVILEGED SECRETS!
WOO-HOO!
EVERYONE KNOWS THAT COPS LOVE DONUTS. BUT ONLY WE HAVE ACCESS TO A ***VERY SPECIAL*** DONUT...
I HAVE HEARD THE LEGENDS, BUT I NEVER THOUGHT THEY WERE TRUE!
SPD
SPD
GASP! IT'S REAL! ***THE COPPER CRULLER!*** DROOL!
LATER...
WOW, MR. WOLFCASTLE! I'M IMPRESSED AT HOW FAST YOU GOT THIS THING UP TO... ***72 MPH!*** AND IN A ***SCHOOL ZONE,*** NO LESS!
MY APOLOGIES. BUT I AM LATE FOR A ***MASSAGE***...FOR MY POT-BELLIED PIG.
WELL, I STILL HAVE TO WRITE YOU UP.
BUT THIS WILL BE MY ***TWENTY-FIRST STRIKE!*** I WILL LOSE MY LICENSE!
ISN'T IT JUST THREE STRIKES?
WHEN YOU'RE A CELEBRITY, TICKETS ARE COUNTED LIKE DOG YEARS.

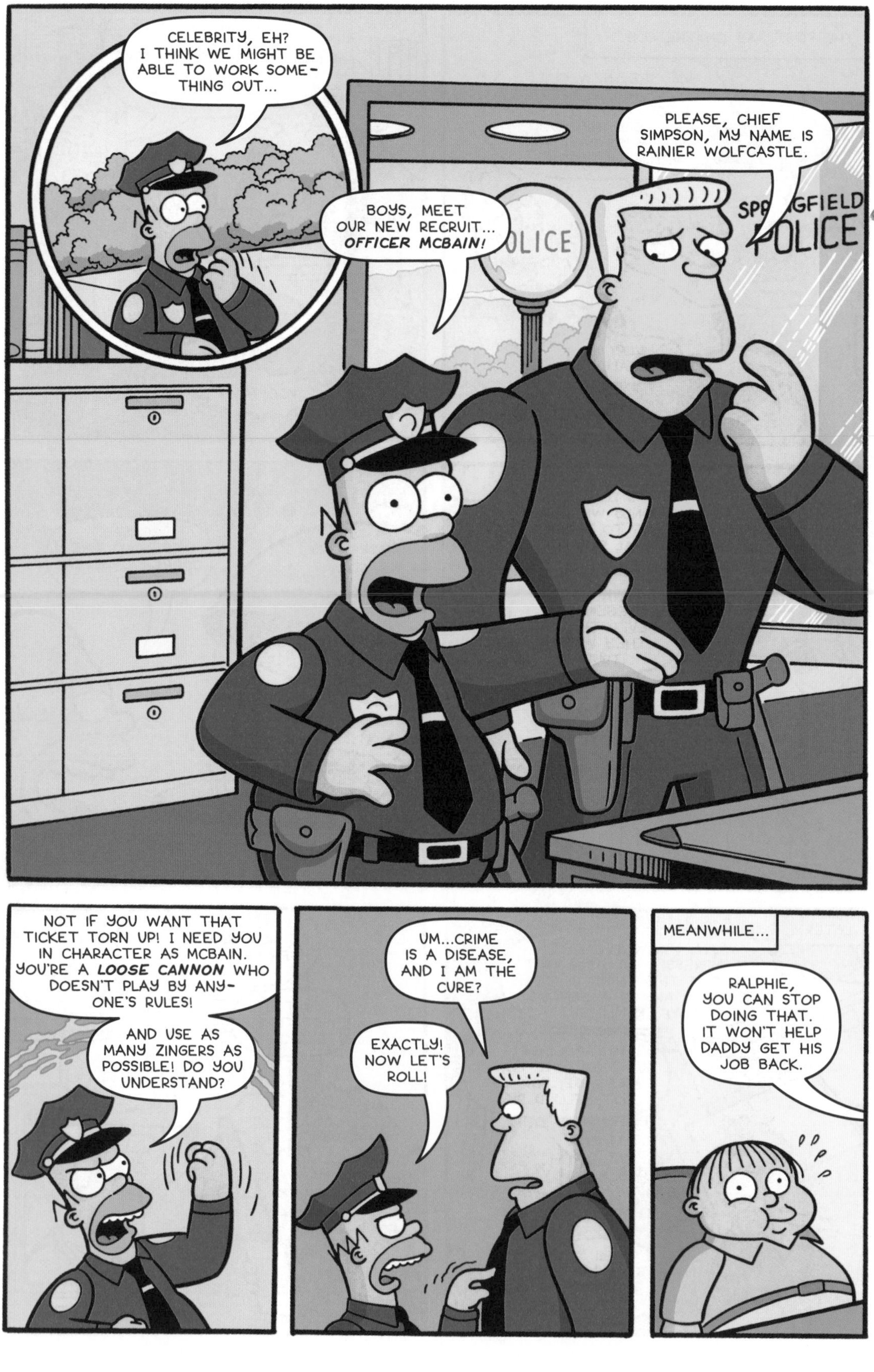
CELEBRITY, EH? I THINK WE MIGHT BE ABLE TO WORK SOME-THING OUT...
BOYS, MEET OUR NEW RECRUIT... **OFFICER MCBAIN!**
PLEASE, CHIEF SIMPSON, MY NAME IS RAINIER WOLFCASTLE.
POLICE
SPRINGFIELD POLICE
NOT IF YOU WANT THAT TICKET TORN UP! I NEED YOU IN CHARACTER AS MCBAIN. YOU'RE A **LOOSE CANNON** WHO DOESN'T PLAY BY ANY-ONE'S RULES!
AND USE AS MANY ZINGERS AS POSSIBLE! DO YOU UNDERSTAND?
UM...CRIME IS A DISEASE, AND I AM THE CURE?
EXACTLY! NOW LET'S ROLL!
MEANWHILE...
RALPHIE, YOU CAN STOP DOING THAT. IT WON'T HELP DADDY GET HIS JOB BACK.

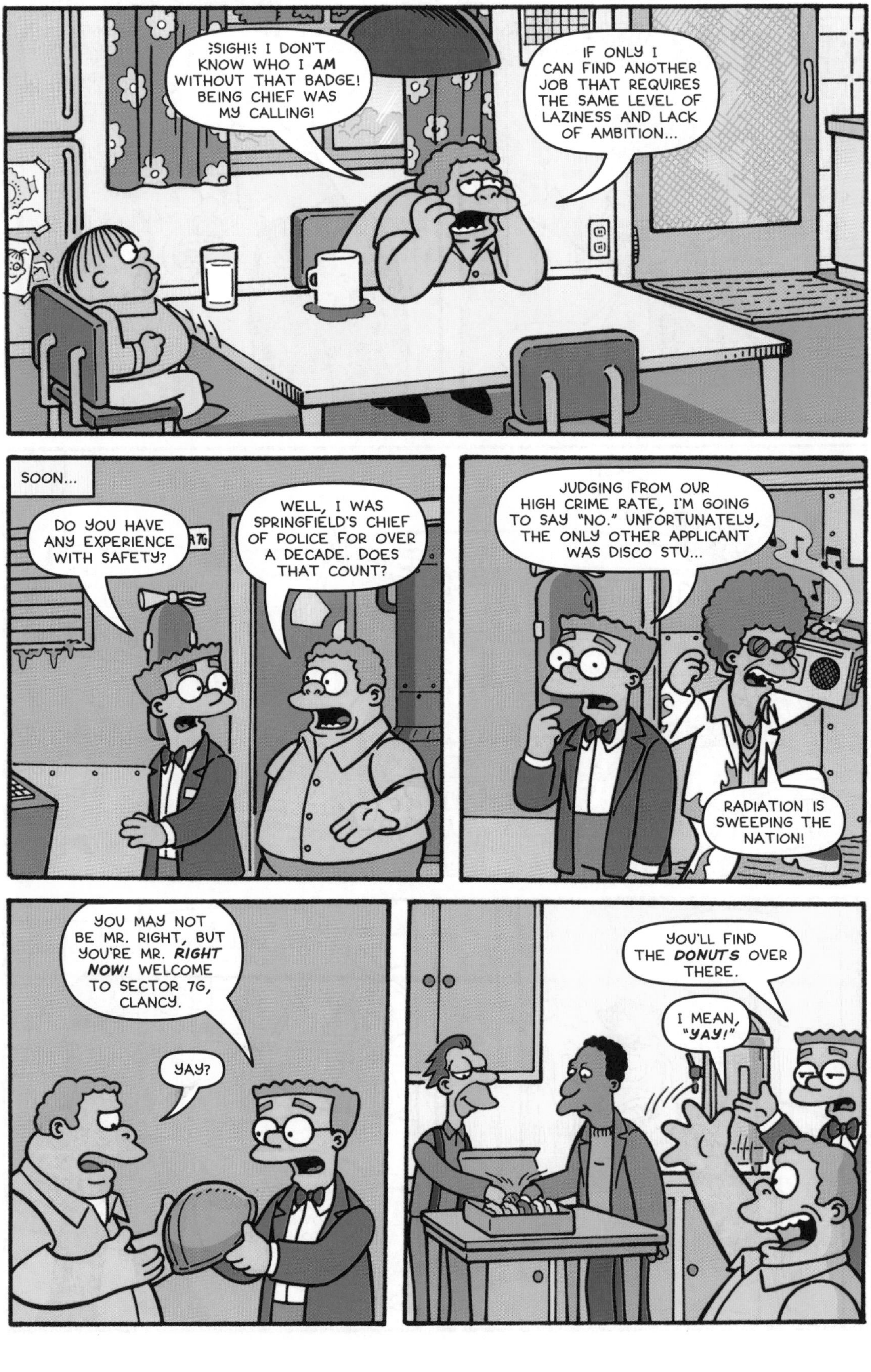
⁝SIGH!⁝ I DON'T KNOW WHO I **AM** WITHOUT THAT BADGE! BEING CHIEF WAS MY CALLING!
IF ONLY I CAN FIND ANOTHER JOB THAT REQUIRES THE SAME LEVEL OF LAZINESS AND LACK OF AMBITION...
SOON...
DO YOU HAVE ANY EXPERIENCE WITH SAFETY?
WELL, I WAS SPRINGFIELD'S CHIEF OF POLICE FOR OVER A DECADE. DOES THAT COUNT?
JUDGING FROM OUR HIGH CRIME RATE, I'M GOING TO SAY "NO." UNFORTUNATELY, THE ONLY OTHER APPLICANT WAS DISCO STU...
RADIATION IS SWEEPING THE NATION!
YOU MAY NOT BE MR. RIGHT, BUT YOU'RE MR. ***RIGHT NOW!*** WELCOME TO SECTOR 7G, CLANCY.
YAY?
YOU'LL FIND THE ***DONUTS*** OVER THERE.
I MEAN, "***YAY!***"

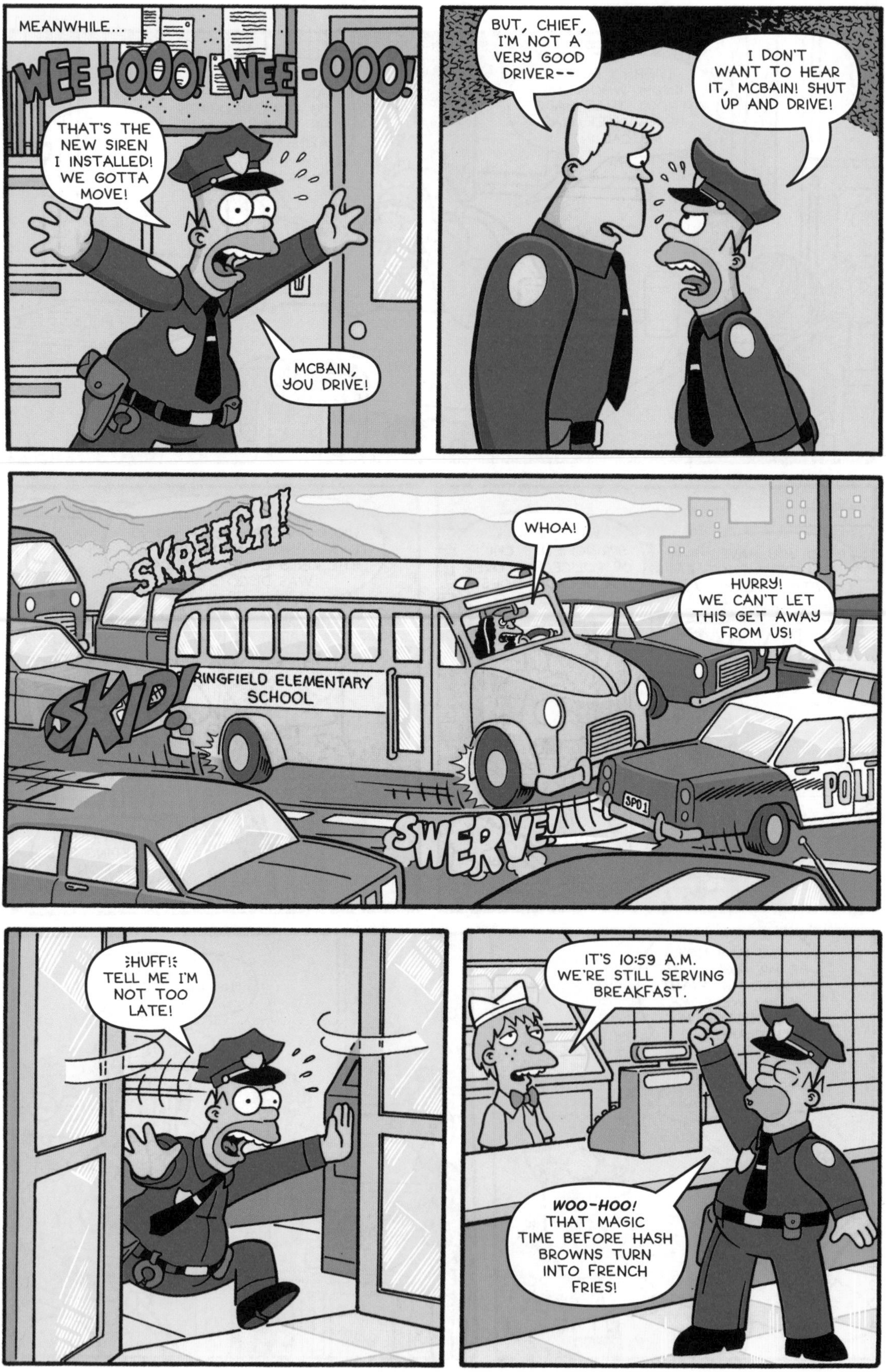

MEANWHILE...
WEE-OOO! WEE-OOO!
THAT'S THE NEW SIREN I INSTALLED! WE GOTTA MOVE!
MCBAIN, YOU DRIVE!
BUT, CHIEF, I'M NOT A VERY GOOD DRIVER--
I DON'T WANT TO HEAR IT, MCBAIN! SHUT UP AND DRIVE!
SKREECH!
WHOA!
HURRY! WE CAN'T LET THIS GET AWAY FROM US!
RINGFIELD ELEMENTARY SCHOOL
SKID!
SPD 1
POLI
SWERVE!
HUFF!
TELL ME I'M NOT TOO LATE!
IT'S 10:59 A.M. WE'RE STILL SERVING BREAKFAST.
WOO-HOO! THAT MAGIC TIME BEFORE HASH BROWNS TURN INTO FRENCH FRIES!

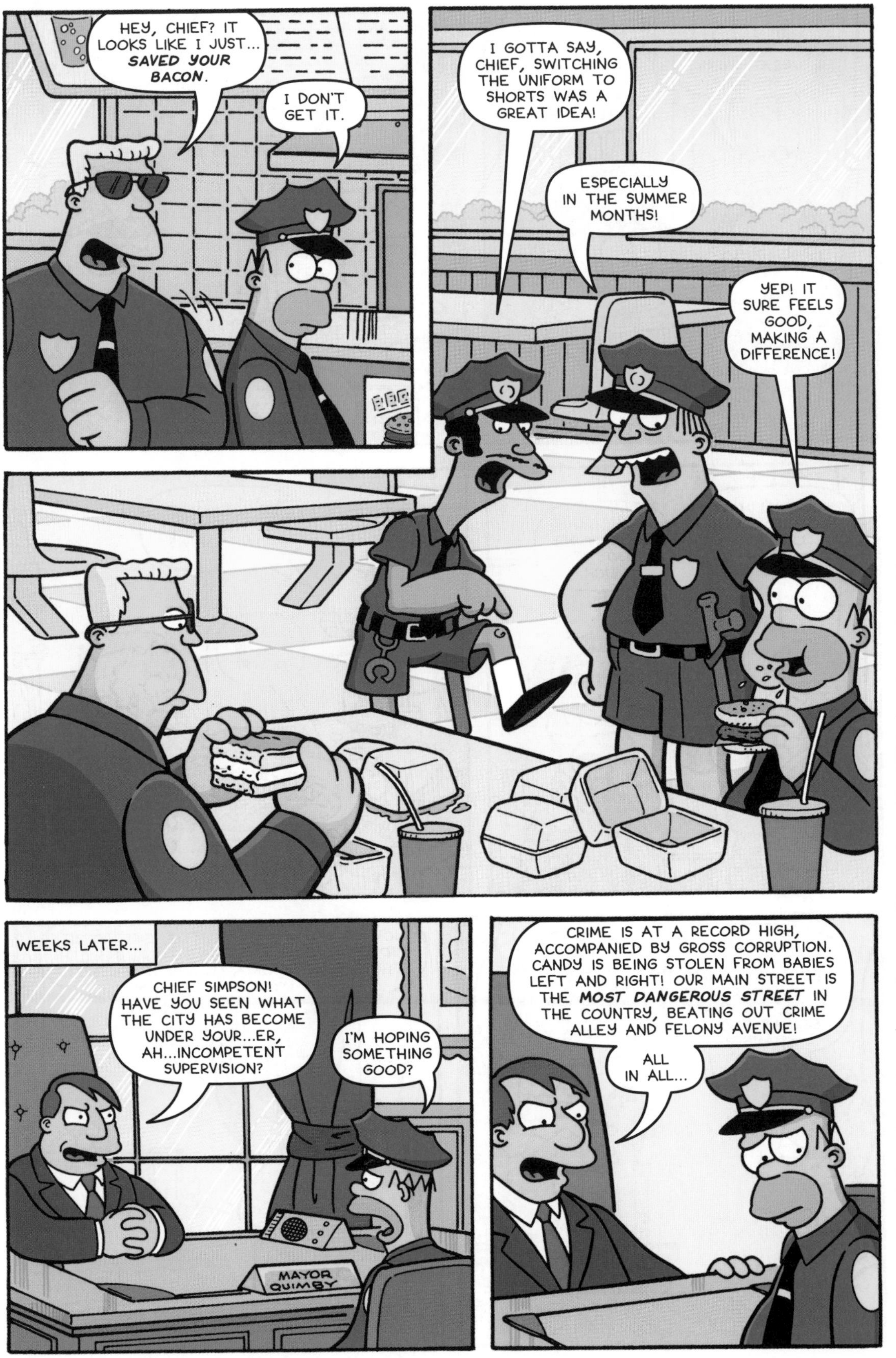
HEY, CHIEF? IT LOOKS LIKE I JUST... **SAVED YOUR BACON**.
I DON'T GET IT.
I GOTTA SAY, CHIEF, SWITCHING THE UNIFORM TO SHORTS WAS A GREAT IDEA!
ESPECIALLY IN THE SUMMER MONTHS!
YEP! IT SURE FEELS GOOD, MAKING A DIFFERENCE!
WEEKS LATER...
CHIEF SIMPSON! HAVE YOU SEEN WHAT THE CITY HAS BECOME UNDER YOUR...ER, AH...INCOMPETENT SUPERVISION?
I'M HOPING SOMETHING GOOD?
MAYOR QUIMBY
CRIME IS AT A RECORD HIGH, ACCOMPANIED BY GROSS CORRUPTION. CANDY IS BEING STOLEN FROM BABIES LEFT AND RIGHT! OUR MAIN STREET IS THE **MOST DANGEROUS STREET** IN THE COUNTRY, BEATING OUT CRIME ALLEY AND FELONY AVENUE!
ALL IN ALL...

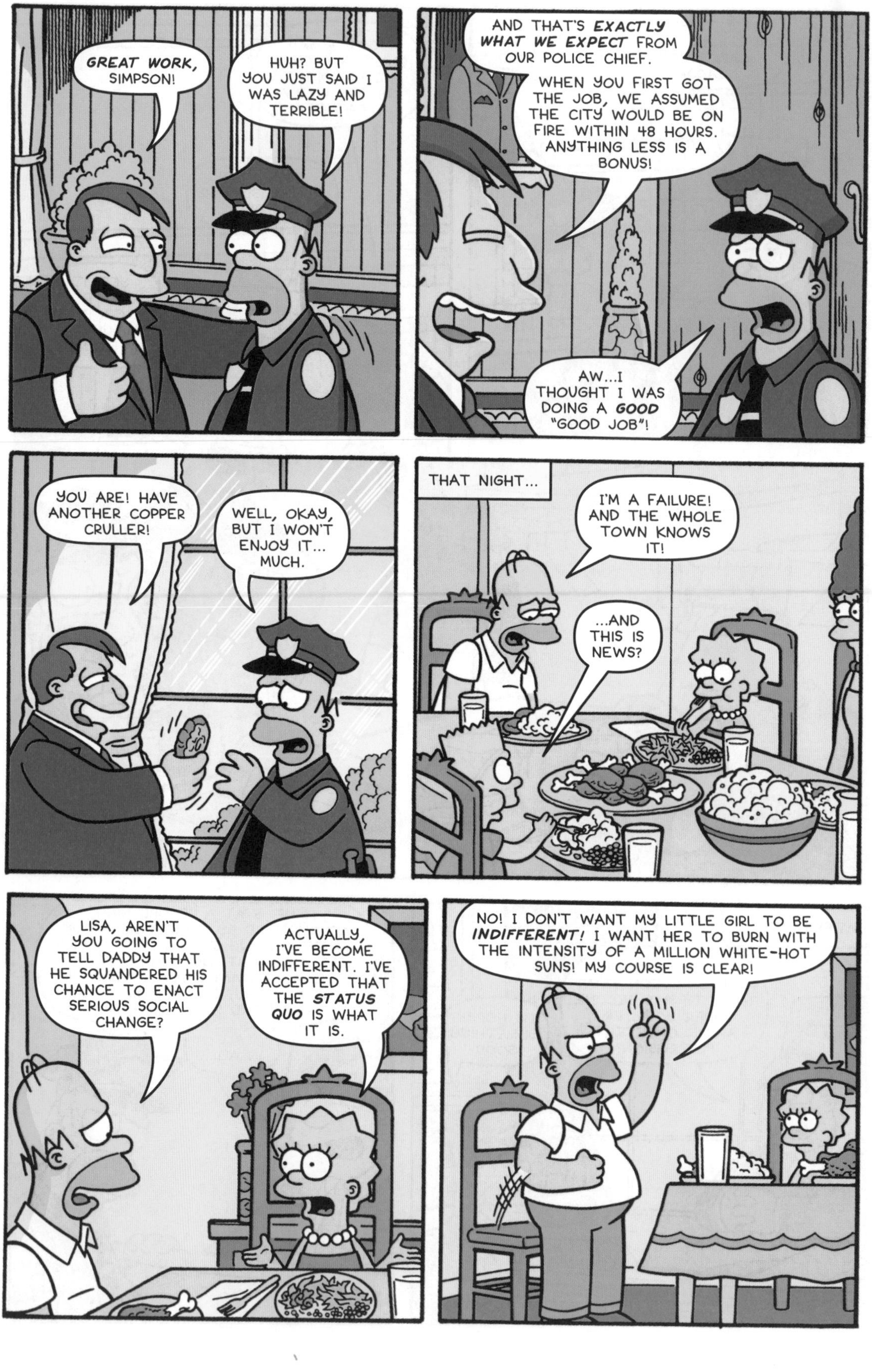
GREAT WORK, SIMPSON!
HUH? BUT YOU JUST SAID I WAS LAZY AND TERRIBLE!
AND THAT'S EXACTLY WHAT WE EXPECT FROM OUR POLICE CHIEF.
WHEN YOU FIRST GOT THE JOB, WE ASSUMED THE CITY WOULD BE ON FIRE WITHIN 48 HOURS. ANYTHING LESS IS A BONUS!
AW...I THOUGHT I WAS DOING A GOOD "GOOD JOB"!
YOU ARE! HAVE ANOTHER COPPER CRULLER!
WELL, OKAY, BUT I WON'T ENJOY IT... MUCH.
THAT NIGHT...
I'M A FAILURE! AND THE WHOLE TOWN KNOWS IT!
...AND THIS IS NEWS?
LISA, AREN'T YOU GOING TO TELL DADDY THAT HE SQUANDERED HIS CHANCE TO ENACT SERIOUS SOCIAL CHANGE?
ACTUALLY, I'VE BECOME INDIFFERENT. I'VE ACCEPTED THAT THE STATUS QUO IS WHAT IT IS.
NO! I DON'T WANT MY LITTLE GIRL TO BE INDIFFERENT! I WANT HER TO BURN WITH THE INTENSITY OF A MILLION WHITE-HOT SUNS! MY COURSE IS CLEAR!

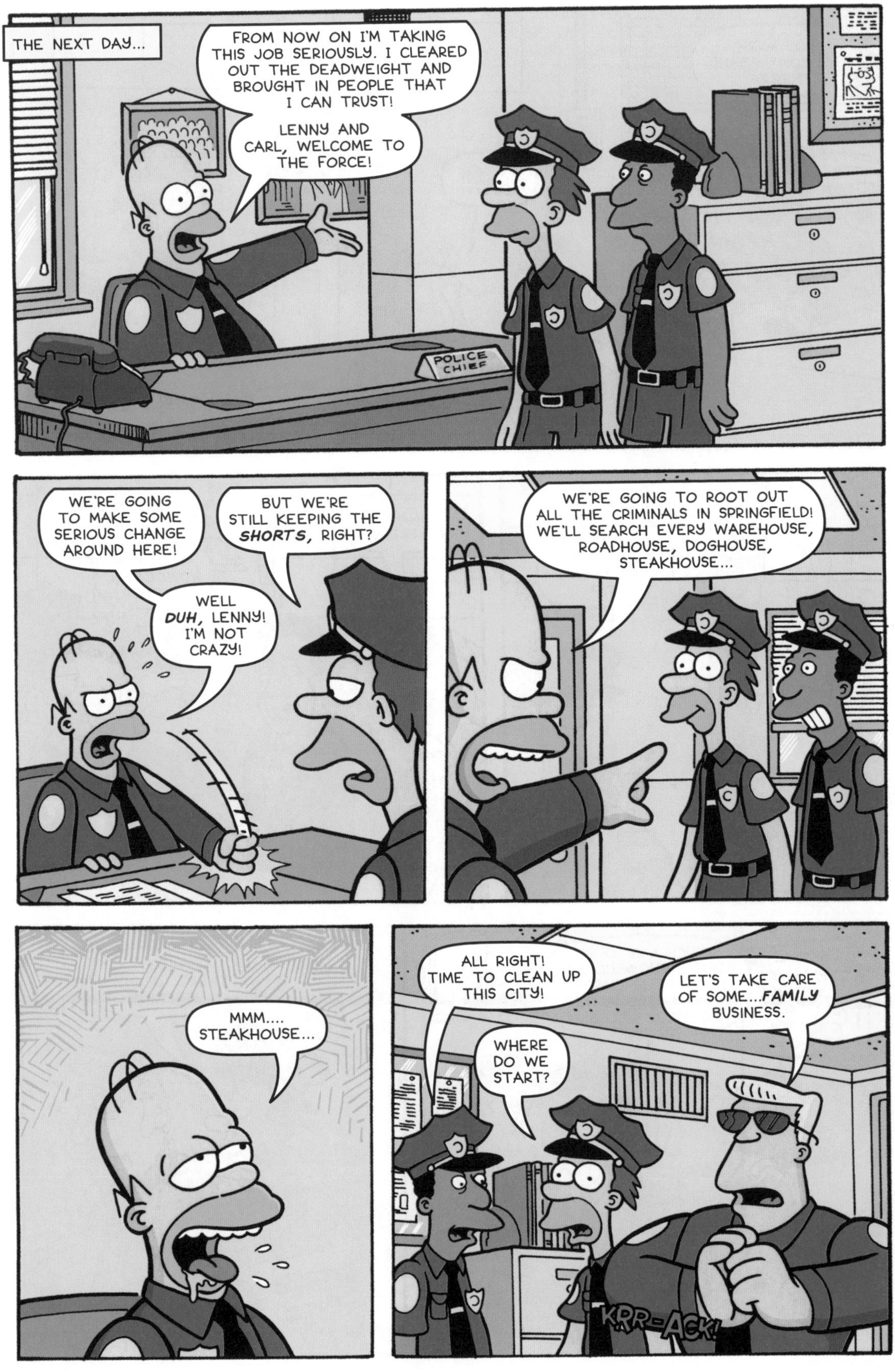
THE NEXT DAY...
FROM NOW ON I'M TAKING THIS JOB SERIOUSLY. I CLEARED OUT THE DEADWEIGHT AND BROUGHT IN PEOPLE THAT I CAN TRUST!
LENNY AND CARL, WELCOME TO THE FORCE!
POLICE CHIEF
WE'RE GOING TO MAKE SOME SERIOUS CHANGE AROUND HERE!
BUT WE'RE STILL KEEPING THE SHORTS, RIGHT?
WELL DUH, LENNY! I'M NOT CRAZY!
WE'RE GOING TO ROOT OUT ALL THE CRIMINALS IN SPRINGFIELD! WE'LL SEARCH EVERY WAREHOUSE, ROADHOUSE, DOGHOUSE, STEAKHOUSE...
MMM.... STEAKHOUSE...
ALL RIGHT! TIME TO CLEAN UP THIS CITY!
WHERE DO WE START?
LET'S TAKE CARE OF SOME...FAMILY BUSINESS.
KRR-ACK!

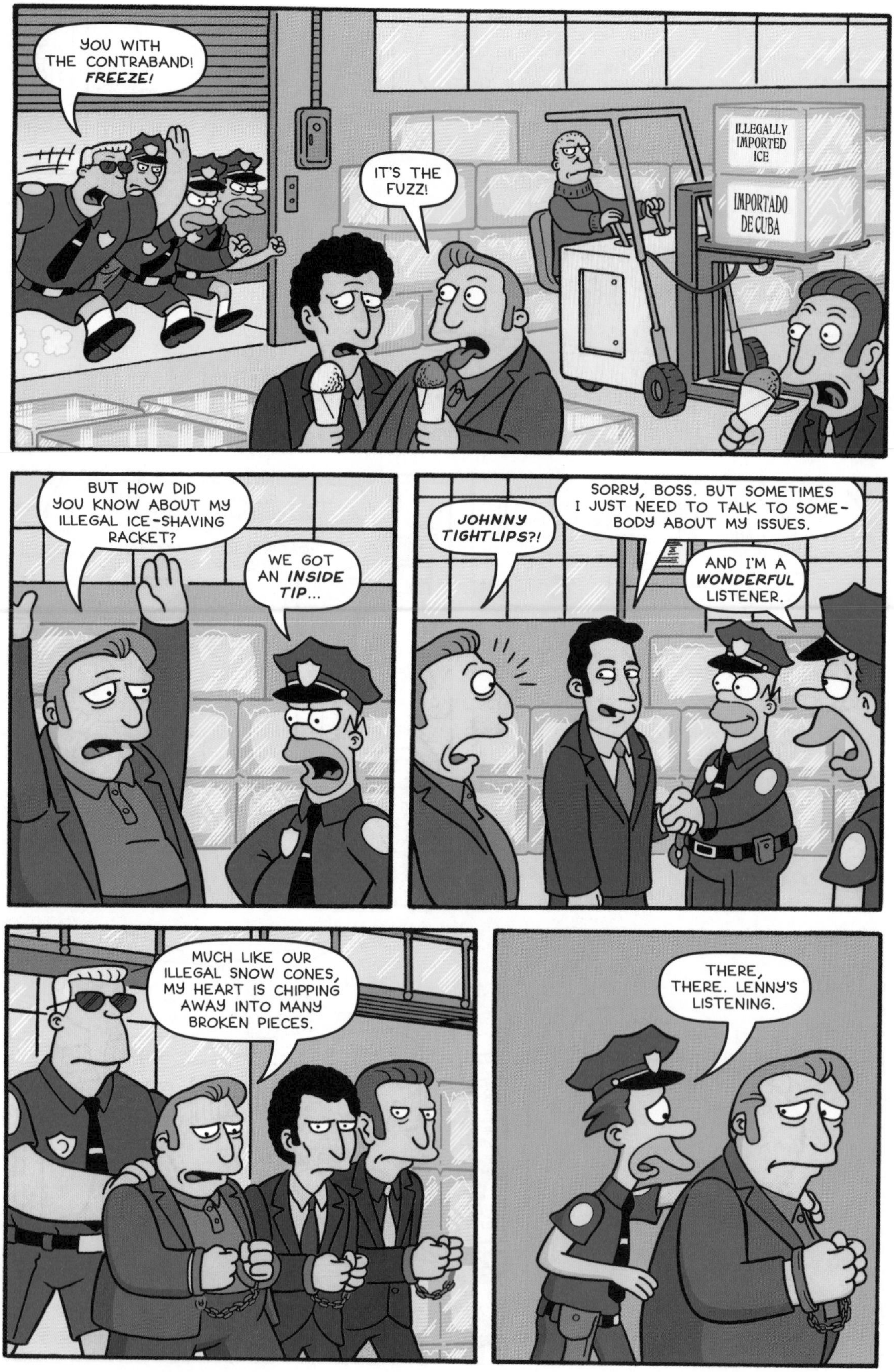
YOU WITH THE CONTRABAND! FREEZE!
IT'S THE FUZZ!
ILLEGALLY IMPORTED ICE
IMPORTADO DE CUBA
BUT HOW DID YOU KNOW ABOUT MY ILLEGAL ICE-SHAVING RACKET?
WE GOT AN INSIDE TIP...
JOHNNY TIGHTLIPS?!
SORRY, BOSS. BUT SOMETIMES I JUST NEED TO TALK TO SOMEBODY ABOUT MY ISSUES.
AND I'M A WONDERFUL LISTENER.
MUCH LIKE OUR ILLEGAL SNOW CONES, MY HEART IS CHIPPING AWAY INTO MANY BROKEN PIECES.
THERE, THERE. LENNY'S LISTENING.

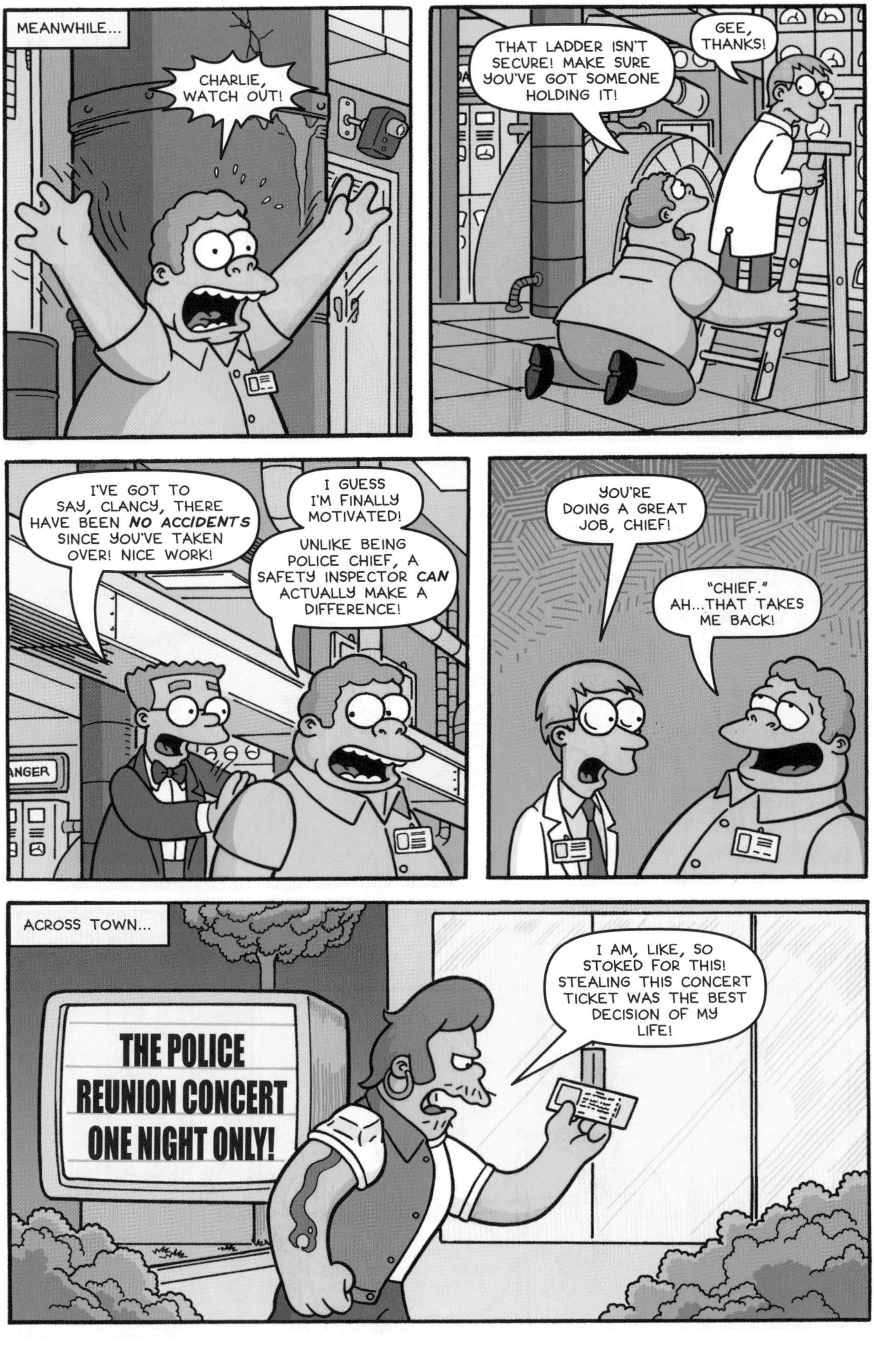
MEANWHILE...
CHARLIE, WATCH OUT!
THAT LADDER ISN'T SECURE! MAKE SURE YOU'VE GOT SOMEONE HOLDING IT!
GEE, THANKS!
I'VE GOT TO SAY, CLANCY, THERE HAVE BEEN NO ACCIDENTS SINCE YOU'VE TAKEN OVER! NICE WORK!
I GUESS I'M FINALLY MOTIVATED!
UNLIKE BEING POLICE CHIEF, A SAFETY INSPECTOR CAN ACTUALLY MAKE A DIFFERENCE!
ANGER
YOU'RE DOING A GREAT JOB, CHIEF!
"CHIEF." AH...THAT TAKES ME BACK!
ACROSS TOWN...
THE POLICE REUNION CONCERT ONE NIGHT ONLY!
I AM, LIKE, SO STOKED FOR THIS! STEALING THIS CONCERT TICKET WAS THE BEST DECISION OF MY LIFE!

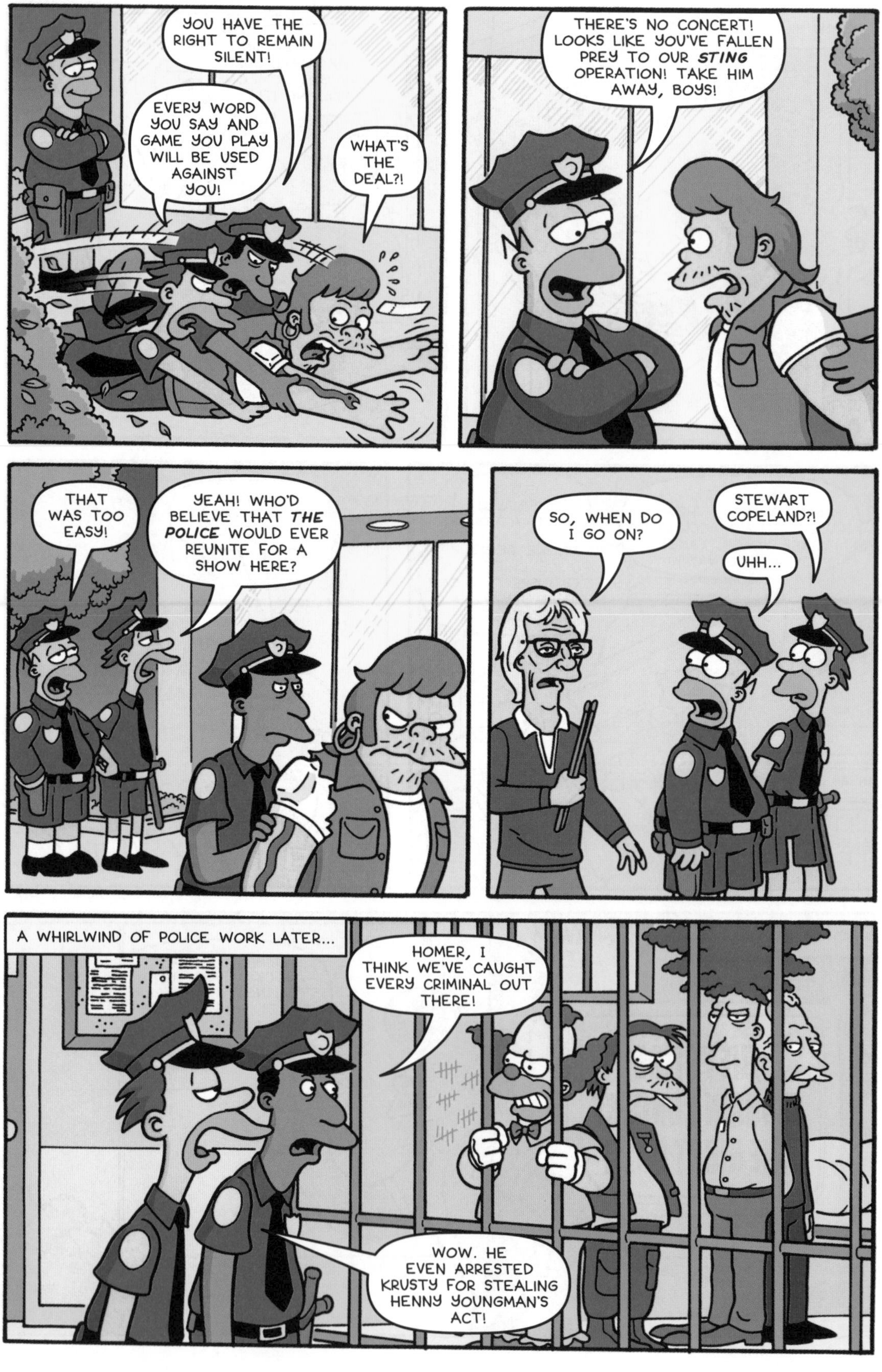
YOU HAVE THE RIGHT TO REMAIN SILENT!
EVERY WORD YOU SAY AND GAME YOU PLAY WILL BE USED AGAINST YOU!
WHAT'S THE DEAL?!
THERE'S NO CONCERT! LOOKS LIKE YOU'VE FALLEN PREY TO OUR STING OPERATION! TAKE HIM AWAY, BOYS!
THAT WAS TOO EASY!
YEAH! WHO'D BELIEVE THAT THE POLICE WOULD EVER REUNITE FOR A SHOW HERE?
SO, WHEN DO I GO ON?
STEWART COPELAND?!
UHH...
A WHIRLWIND OF POLICE WORK LATER...
HOMER, I THINK WE'VE CAUGHT EVERY CRIMINAL OUT THERE!
WOW. HE EVEN ARRESTED KRUSTY FOR STEALING HENNY YOUNGMAN'S ACT!

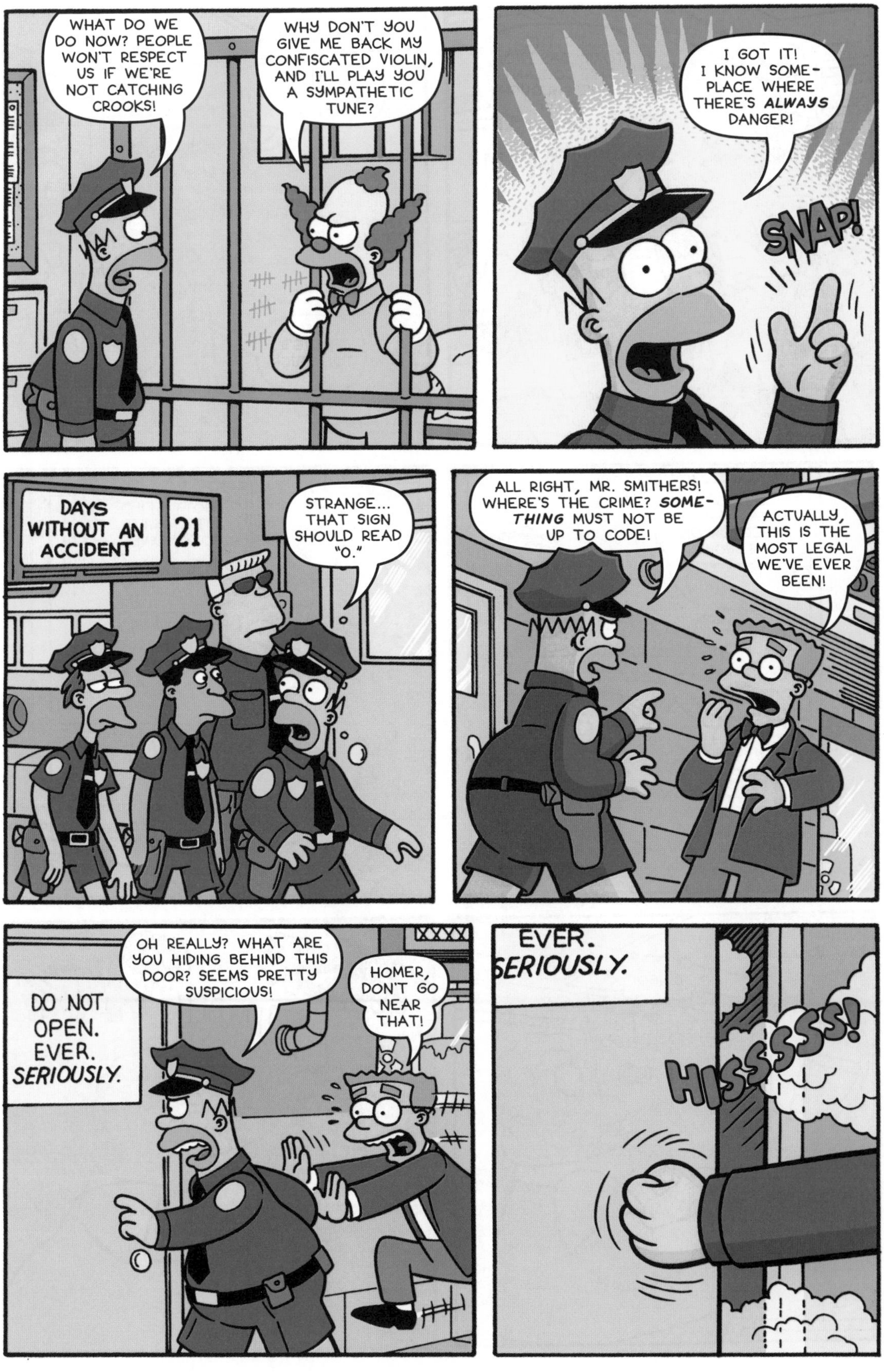
WHAT DO WE DO NOW? PEOPLE WON'T RESPECT US IF WE'RE NOT CATCHING CROOKS!
WHY DON'T YOU GIVE ME BACK MY CONFISCATED VIOLIN, AND I'LL PLAY YOU A SYMPATHETIC TUNE?
I GOT IT! I KNOW SOME-PLACE WHERE THERE'S *ALWAYS* DANGER!
SNAP!
DAYS WITHOUT AN ACCIDENT
21
STRANGE... THAT SIGN SHOULD READ "0."
ALL RIGHT, MR. SMITHERS! WHERE'S THE CRIME? *SOME-THING* MUST NOT BE UP TO CODE!
ACTUALLY, THIS IS THE MOST LEGAL WE'VE EVER BEEN!
DO NOT OPEN. EVER. *SERIOUSLY.*
OH REALLY? WHAT ARE YOU HIDING BEHIND THIS DOOR? SEEMS PRETTY SUSPICIOUS!
HOMER, DON'T GO NEAR THAT!
EVER. *SERIOUSLY.*
HISSSSSS!

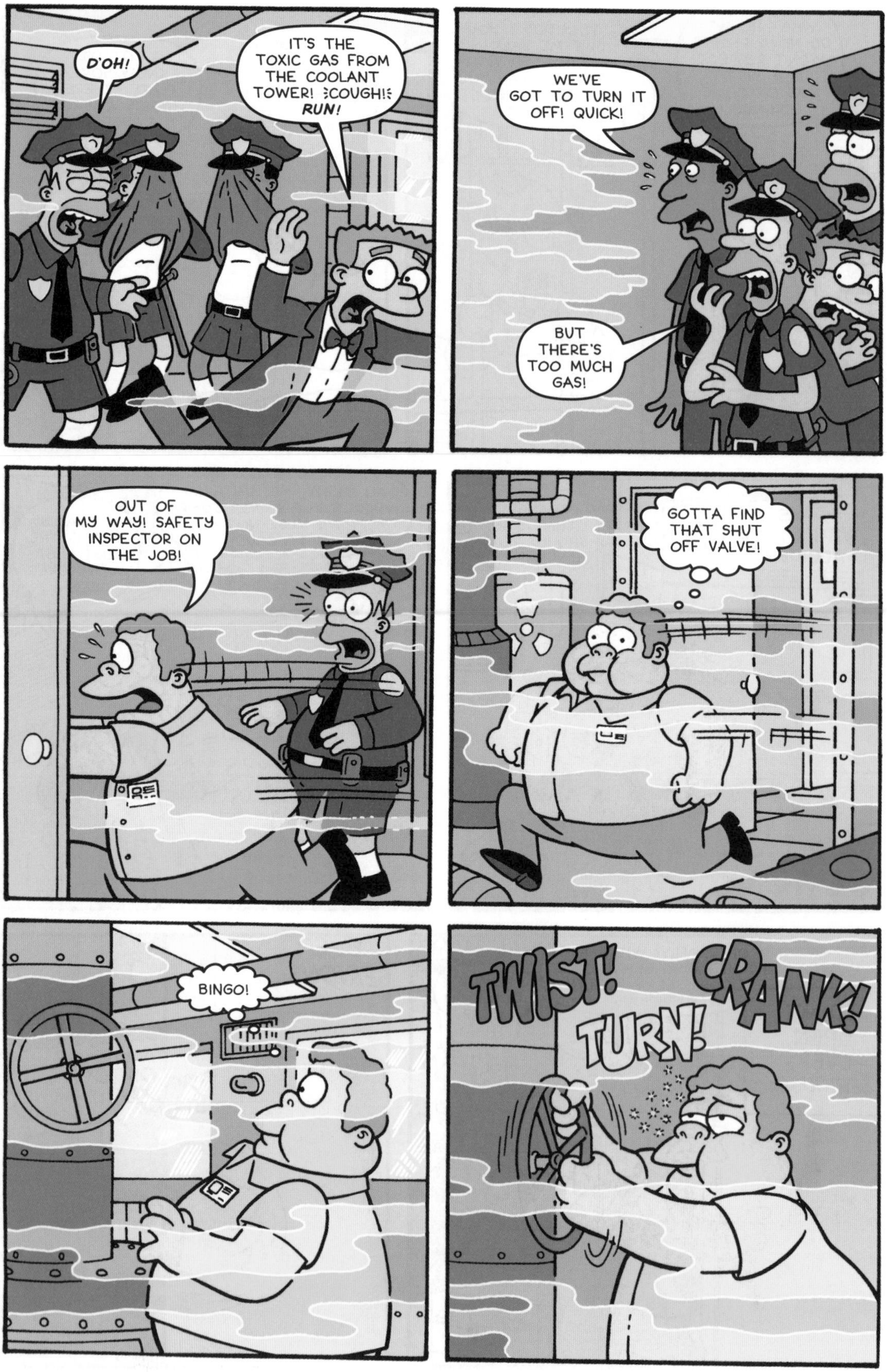
D'OH!
IT'S THE TOXIC GAS FROM THE COOLANT TOWER! COUGH! RUN!
WE'VE GOT TO TURN IT OFF! QUICK!
BUT THERE'S TOO MUCH GAS!
OUT OF MY WAY! SAFETY INSPECTOR ON THE JOB!
GOTTA FIND THAT SHUT OFF VALVE!
BINGO!
TWIST!
TURN!
CRANK!

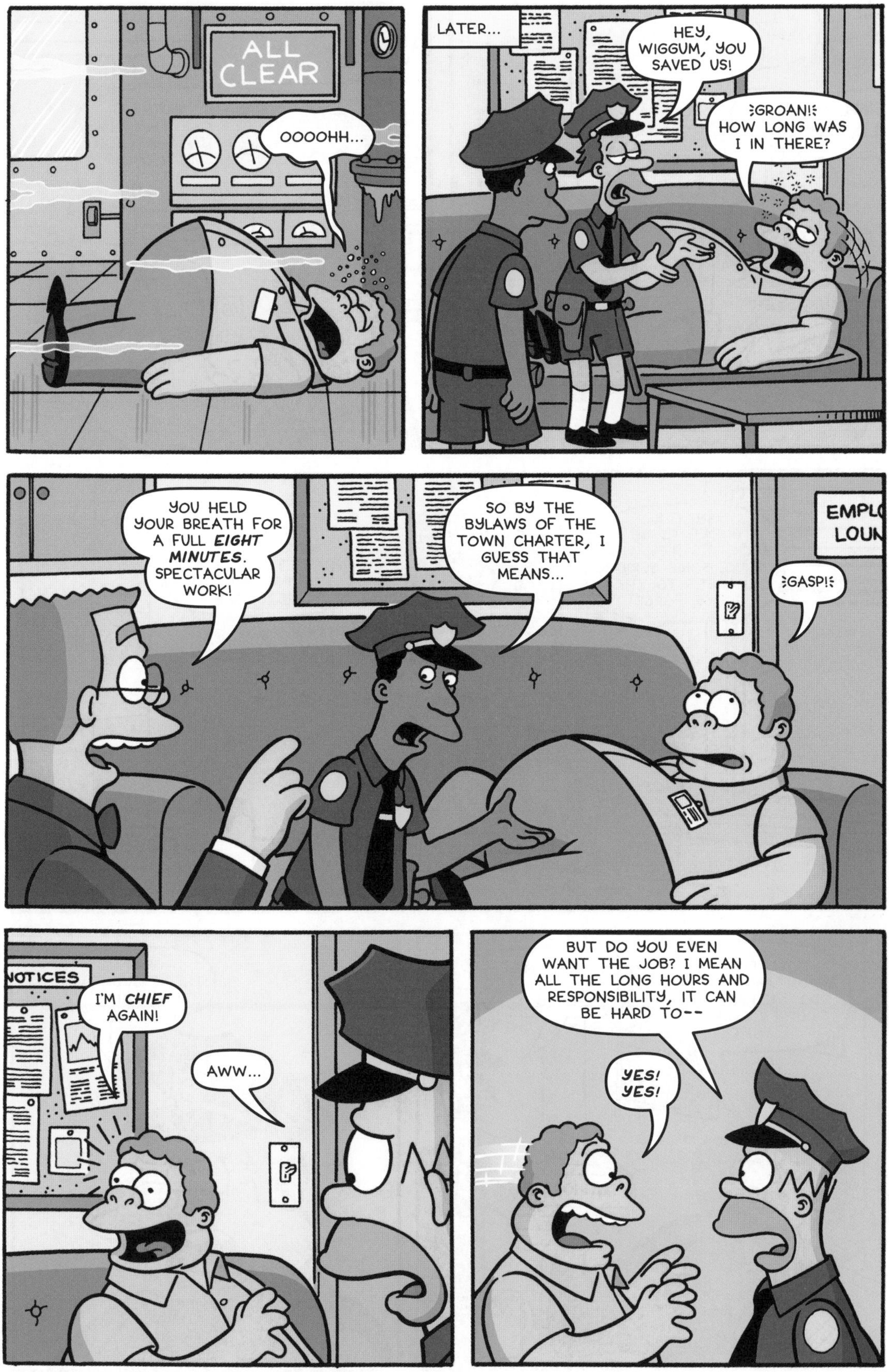
ALL CLEAR
OOOOHH...
LATER...
HEY, WIGGUM, YOU SAVED US!
GROAN! HOW LONG WAS I IN THERE?
YOU HELD YOUR BREATH FOR A FULL EIGHT MINUTES. SPECTACULAR WORK!
SO BY THE BYLAWS OF THE TOWN CHARTER, I GUESS THAT MEANS...
GASP!
NOTICES
I'M CHIEF AGAIN!
AWW...
BUT DO YOU EVEN WANT THE JOB? I MEAN ALL THE LONG HOURS AND RESPONSIBILITY, IT CAN BE HARD TO--
YES! YES!

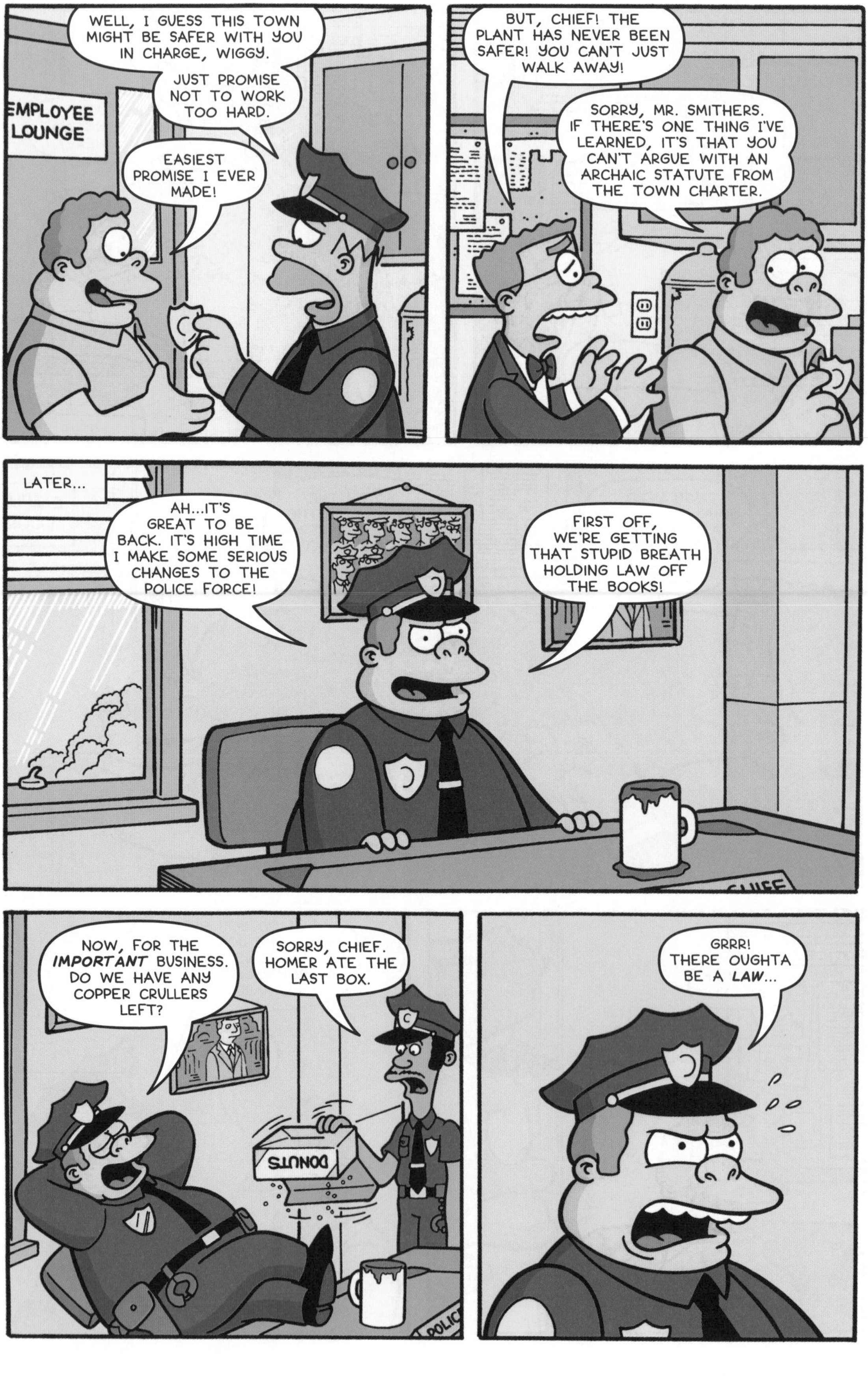
EMPLOYEE LOUNGE
WELL, I GUESS THIS TOWN MIGHT BE SAFER WITH YOU IN CHARGE, WIGGY.
JUST PROMISE NOT TO WORK TOO HARD.
EASIEST PROMISE I EVER MADE!
BUT, CHIEF! THE PLANT HAS NEVER BEEN SAFER! YOU CAN'T JUST WALK AWAY!
SORRY, MR. SMITHERS. IF THERE'S ONE THING I'VE LEARNED, IT'S THAT YOU CAN'T ARGUE WITH AN ARCHAIC STATUTE FROM THE TOWN CHARTER.
LATER...
AH...IT'S GREAT TO BE BACK. IT'S HIGH TIME I MAKE SOME SERIOUS CHANGES TO THE POLICE FORCE!
FIRST OFF, WE'RE GETTING THAT STUPID BREATH HOLDING LAW OFF THE BOOKS!
NOW, FOR THE ***IMPORTANT*** BUSINESS. DO WE HAVE ANY COPPER CRULLERS LEFT?
SORRY, CHIEF. HOMER ATE THE LAST BOX.
DONUTS
GRRR! THERE OUGHTA BE A ***LAW***...

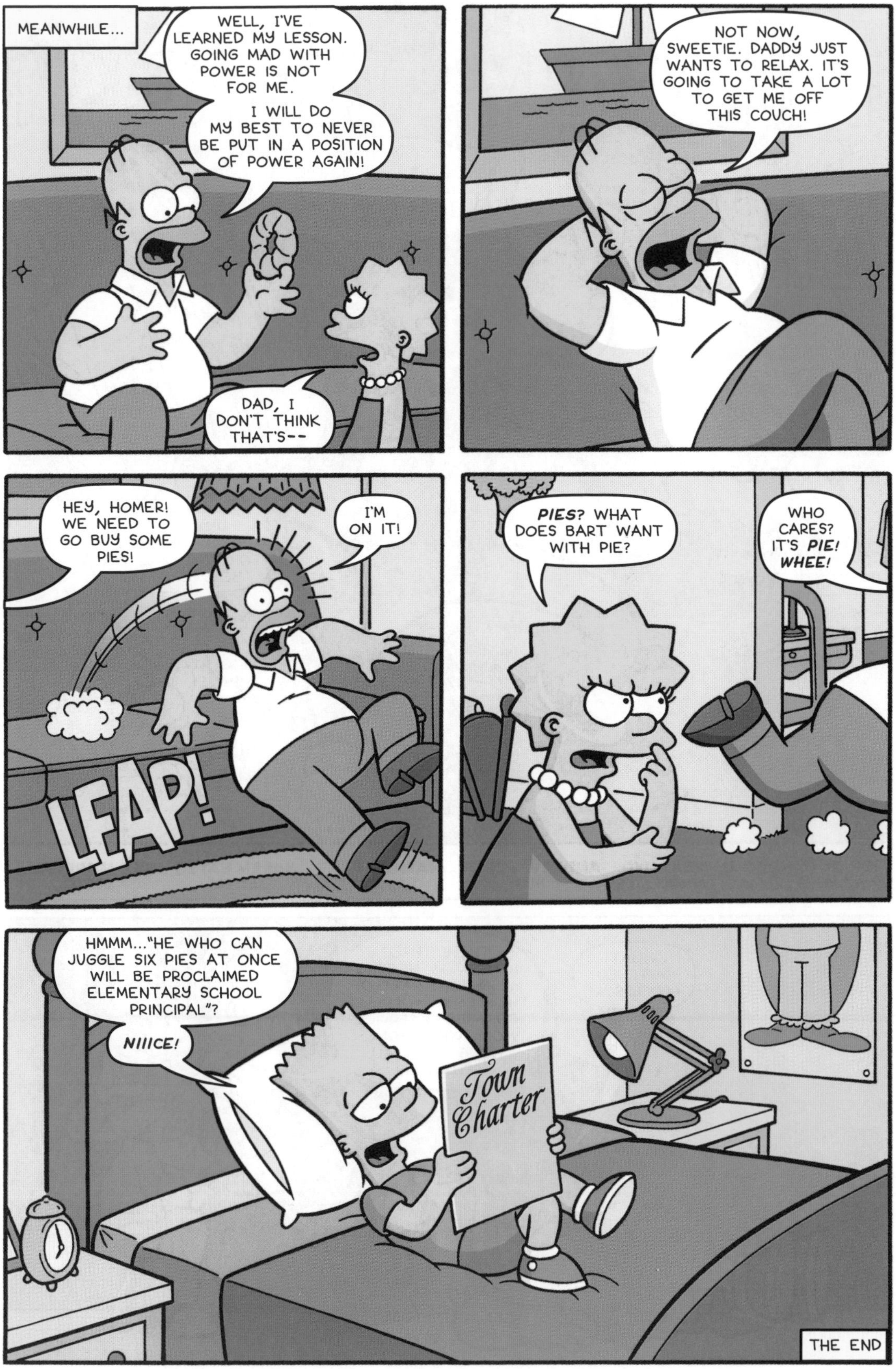
MEANWHILE...
WELL, I'VE LEARNED MY LESSON. GOING MAD WITH POWER IS NOT FOR ME.
I WILL DO MY BEST TO NEVER BE PUT IN A POSITION OF POWER AGAIN!
DAD, I DON'T THINK THAT'S--
NOT NOW, SWEETIE. DADDY JUST WANTS TO RELAX. IT'S GOING TO TAKE A LOT TO GET ME OFF THIS COUCH!
HEY, HOMER! WE NEED TO GO BUY SOME PIES!
I'M ON IT!
LEAP!
PIES? WHAT DOES BART WANT WITH PIE?
WHO CARES? IT'S PIE! WHEE!
HMMM..."HE WHO CAN JUGGLE SIX PIES AT ONCE WILL BE PROCLAIMED ELEMENTARY SCHOOL PRINCIPAL"?
NIIICE!
Town Charter
THE END

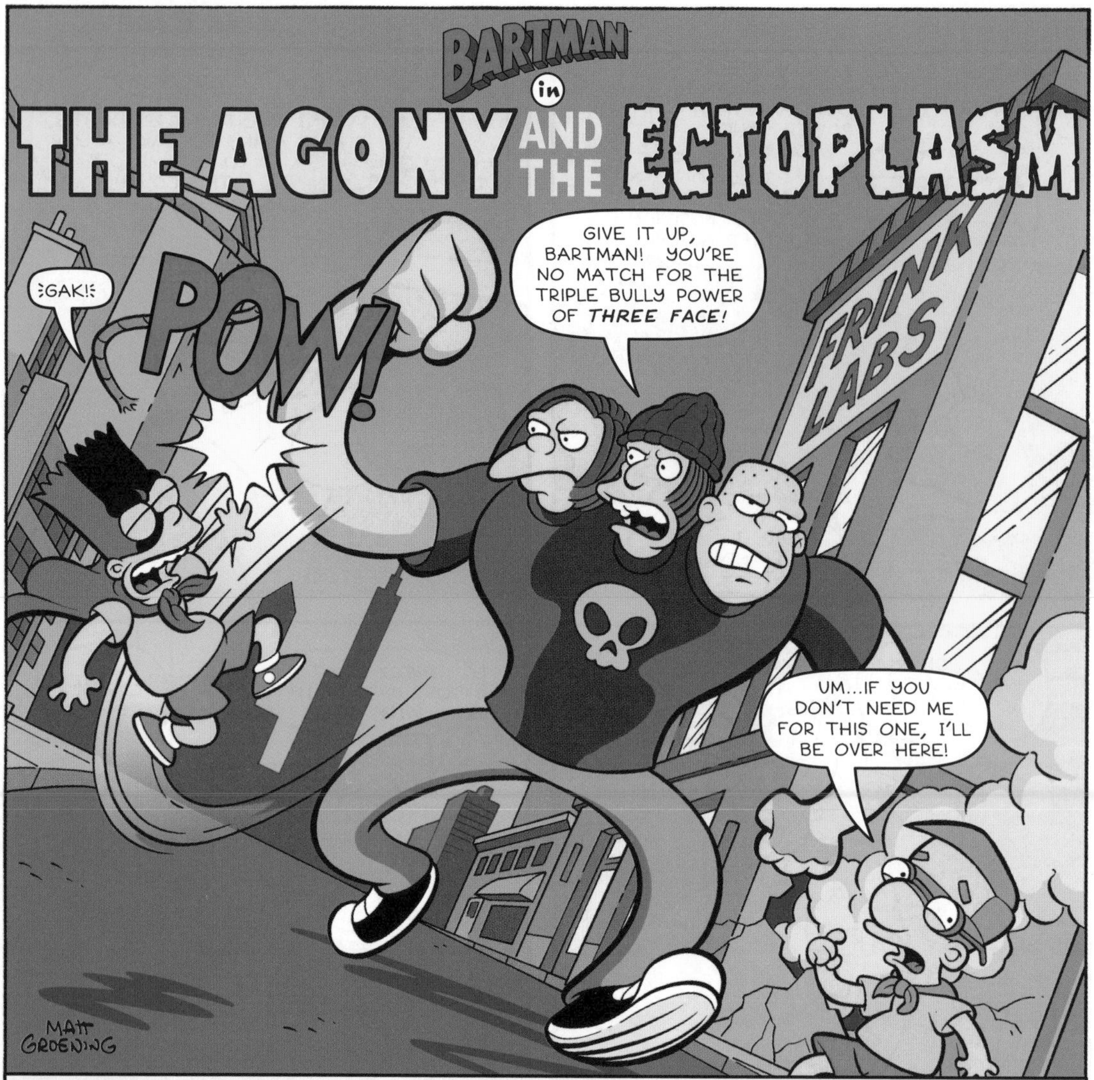
BARTMAN
in
THE AGONY AND THE ECTOPLASM
GAK!
POW!
GIVE IT UP, BARTMAN! YOU'RE NO MATCH FOR THE TRIPLE BULLY POWER OF *THREE FACE!*
FRINK LABS
UM...IF YOU DON'T NEED ME FOR THIS ONE, I'LL BE OVER HERE!
MATT GROENING

IAN BOOTHBY SCRIPT **JAMES LLOYD** PENCILS **ANDREW PEPOY** INKS **NATHAN KANE** COLORS **KAREN BATES** LETTERS **BILL MORRISON** EDITOR

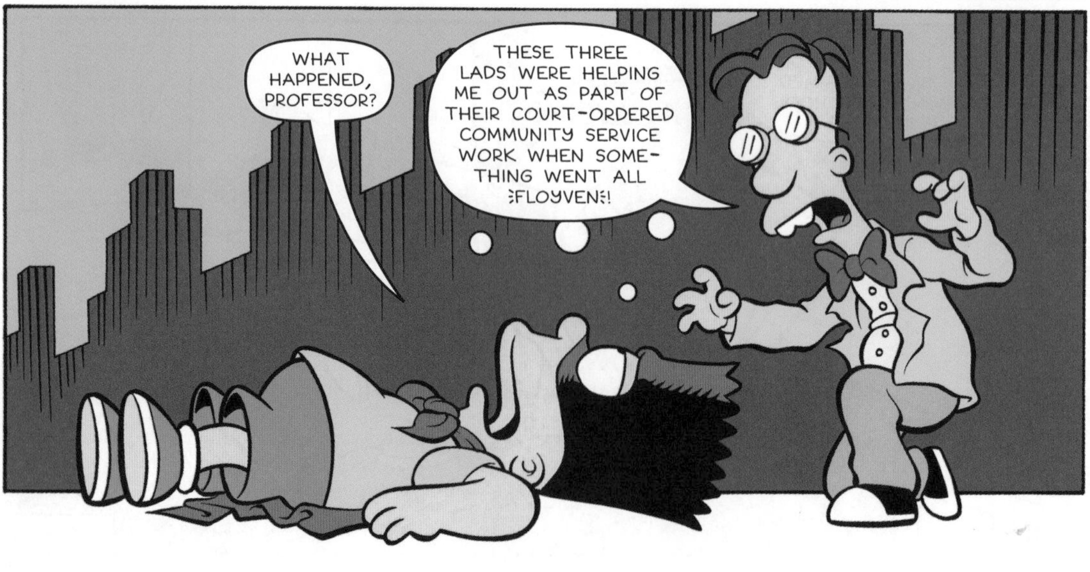
WHAT HAPPENED, PROFESSOR?
THESE THREE LADS WERE HELPING ME OUT AS PART OF THEIR COURT-ORDERED COMMUNITY SERVICE WORK WHEN SOMETHING WENT ALL FLOYVEN!

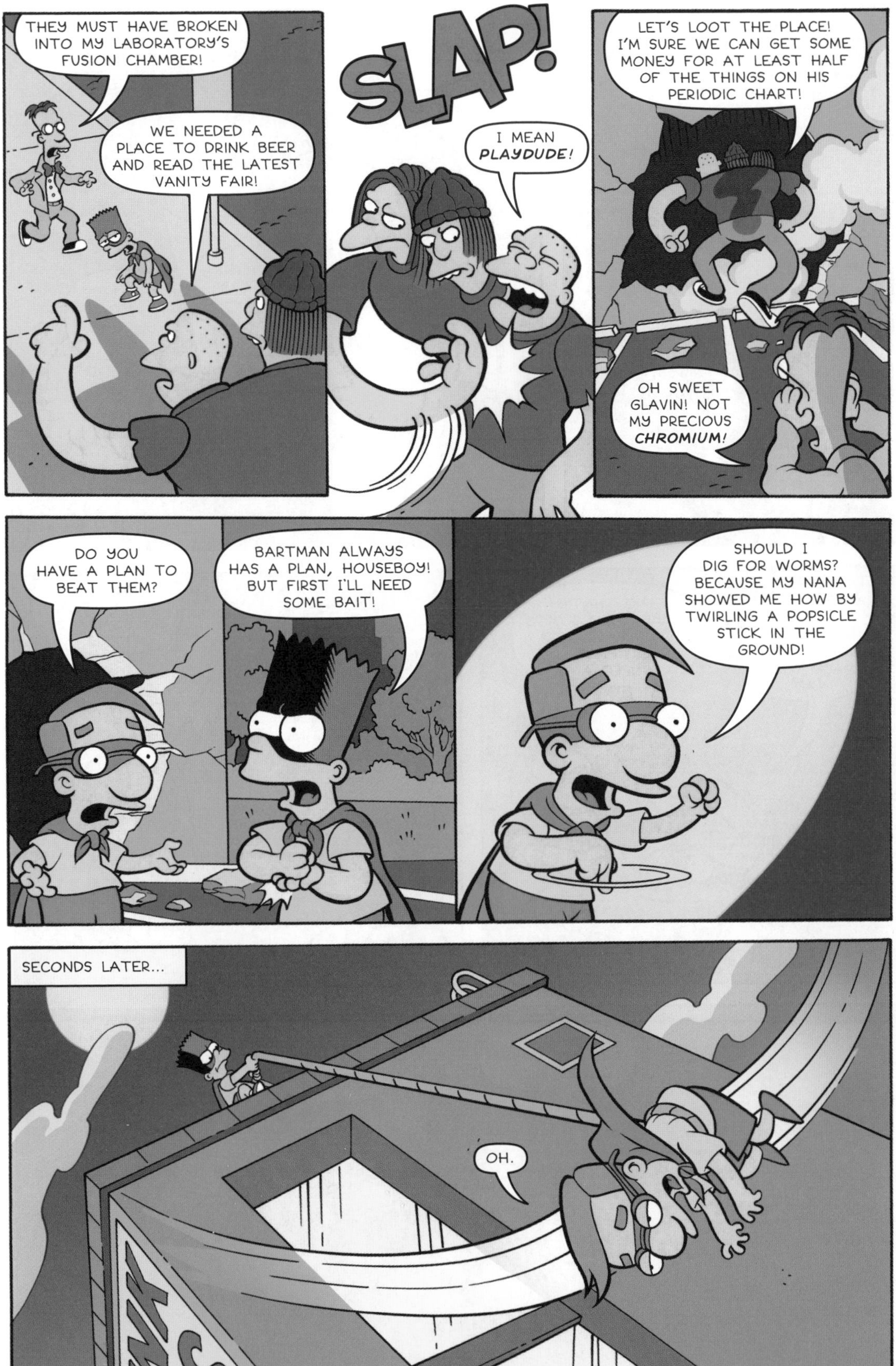

THEY MUST HAVE BROKEN INTO MY LABORATORY'S FUSION CHAMBER!
WE NEEDED A PLACE TO DRINK BEER AND READ THE LATEST VANITY FAIR!
SLAP!
I MEAN PLAYDUDE!
LET'S LOOT THE PLACE! I'M SURE WE CAN GET SOME MONEY FOR AT LEAST HALF OF THE THINGS ON HIS PERIODIC CHART!
OH SWEET GLAVIN! NOT MY PRECIOUS CHROMIUM!
DO YOU HAVE A PLAN TO BEAT THEM?
BARTMAN ALWAYS HAS A PLAN, HOUSEBOY! BUT FIRST I'LL NEED SOME BAIT!
SHOULD I DIG FOR WORMS? BECAUSE MY NANA SHOWED ME HOW BY TWIRLING A POPSICLE STICK IN THE GROUND!
SECONDS LATER...
OH.

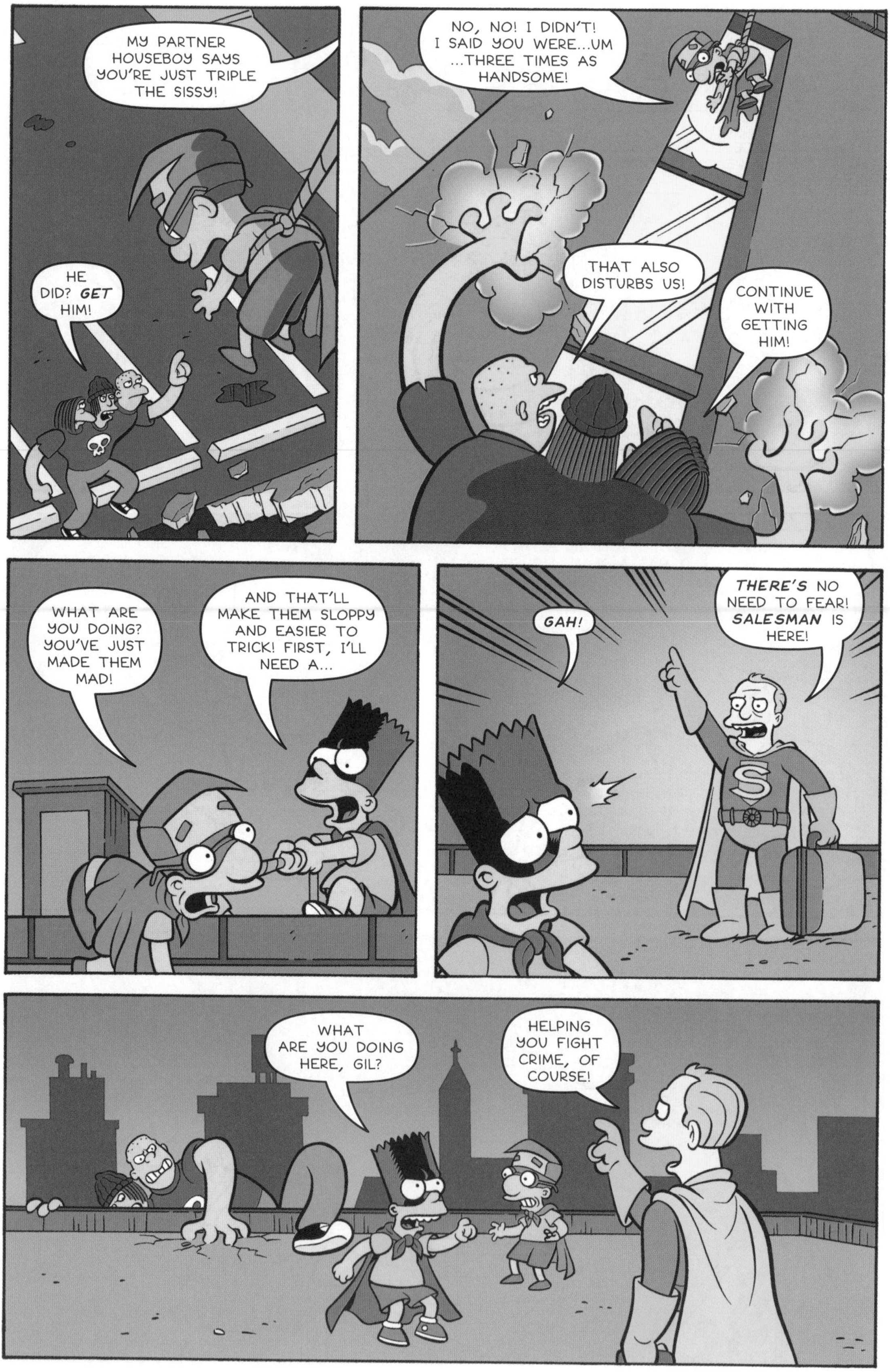
MY PARTNER HOUSEBOY SAYS YOU'RE JUST TRIPLE THE SISSY!
HE DID? GET HIM!
NO, NO! I DIDN'T! I SAID YOU WERE...UM ...THREE TIMES AS HANDSOME!
THAT ALSO DISTURBS US!
CONTINUE WITH GETTING HIM!
WHAT ARE YOU DOING? YOU'VE JUST MADE THEM MAD!
AND THAT'LL MAKE THEM SLOPPY AND EASIER TO TRICK! FIRST, I'LL NEED A...
GAH!
THERE'S NO NEED TO FEAR! SALESMAN IS HERE!
WHAT ARE YOU DOING HERE, GIL?
HELPING YOU FIGHT CRIME, OF COURSE!

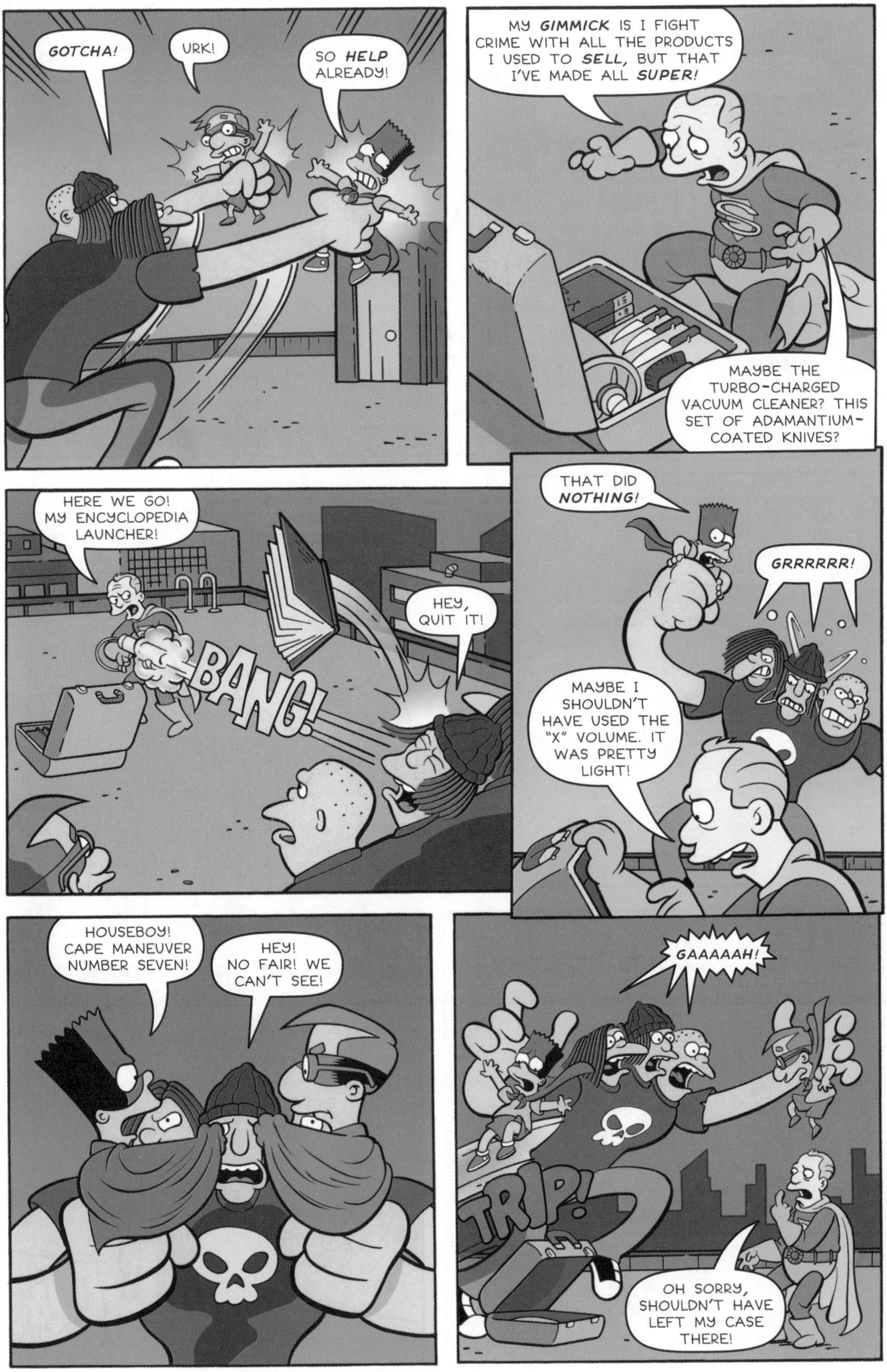
GOTCHA!
URK!
SO HELP ALREADY!
MY GIMMICK IS I FIGHT CRIME WITH ALL THE PRODUCTS I USED TO SELL, BUT THAT I'VE MADE ALL SUPER!
MAYBE THE TURBO-CHARGED VACUUM CLEANER? THIS SET OF ADAMANTIUM-COATED KNIVES?
HERE WE GO! MY ENCYCLOPEDIA LAUNCHER!
BANG!
HEY, QUIT IT!
THAT DID NOTHING!
GRRRRRR!
MAYBE I SHOULDN'T HAVE USED THE "X" VOLUME. IT WAS PRETTY LIGHT!
HOUSEBOY! CAPE MANEUVER NUMBER SEVEN!
HEY! NO FAIR! WE CAN'T SEE!
GAAAAAH!
TRIP!
OH SORRY, SHOULDN'T HAVE LEFT MY CASE THERE!

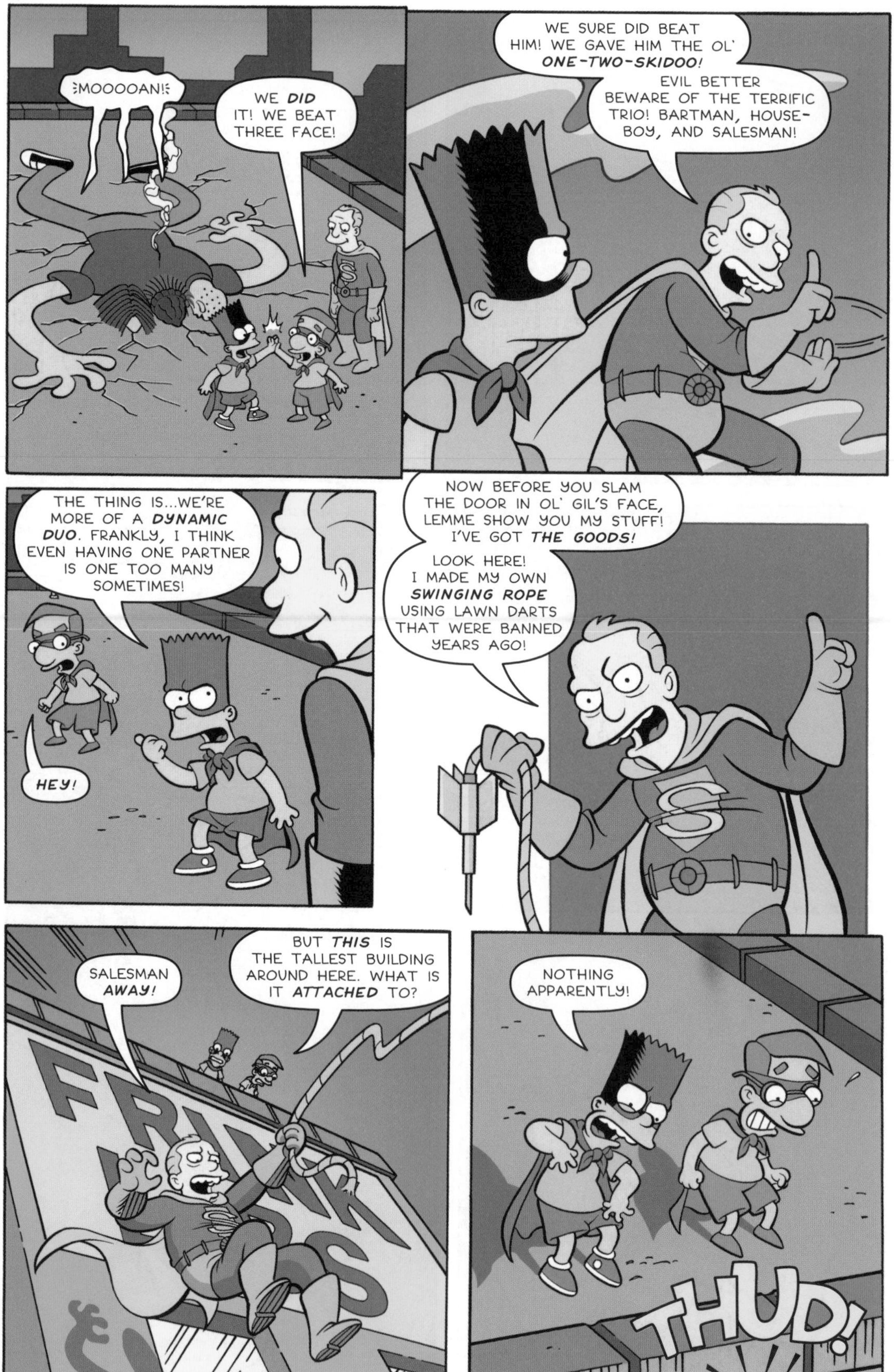
MOOOOAN!
WE DID IT! WE BEAT THREE FACE!
WE SURE DID BEAT HIM! WE GAVE HIM THE OL' ONE-TWO-SKIDOO!
EVIL BETTER BEWARE OF THE TERRIFIC TRIO! BARTMAN, HOUSE-BOY, AND SALESMAN!
THE THING IS...WE'RE MORE OF A DYNAMIC DUO. FRANKLY, I THINK EVEN HAVING ONE PARTNER IS ONE TOO MANY SOMETIMES!
HEY!
NOW BEFORE YOU SLAM THE DOOR IN OL' GIL'S FACE, LEMME SHOW YOU MY STUFF! I'VE GOT THE GOODS!
LOOK HERE! I MADE MY OWN SWINGING ROPE USING LAWN DARTS THAT WERE BANNED YEARS AGO!
SALESMAN AWAY!
BUT THIS IS THE TALLEST BUILDING AROUND HERE. WHAT IS IT ATTACHED TO?
NOTHING APPARENTLY!
THUD!

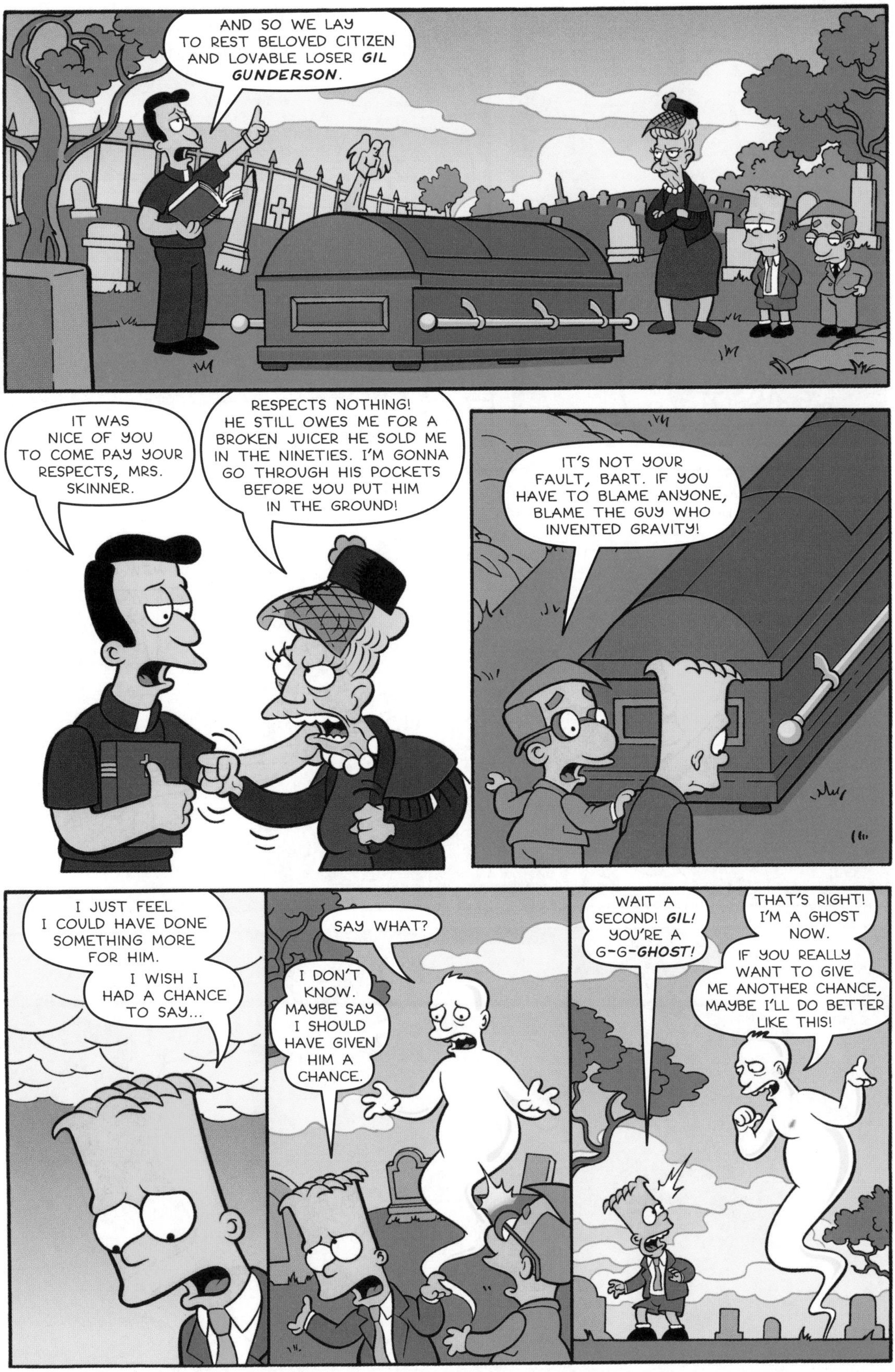
AND SO WE LAY TO REST BELOVED CITIZEN AND LOVABLE LOSER *GIL GUNDERSON*.
IT WAS NICE OF YOU TO COME PAY YOUR RESPECTS, MRS. SKINNER.
RESPECTS NOTHING! HE STILL OWES ME FOR A BROKEN JUICER HE SOLD ME IN THE NINETIES. I'M GONNA GO THROUGH HIS POCKETS BEFORE YOU PUT HIM IN THE GROUND!
IT'S NOT YOUR FAULT, BART. IF YOU HAVE TO BLAME ANYONE, BLAME THE GUY WHO INVENTED GRAVITY!
I JUST FEEL I COULD HAVE DONE SOMETHING MORE FOR HIM.
I WISH I HAD A CHANCE TO SAY...
SAY WHAT?
I DON'T KNOW. MAYBE SAY I SHOULD HAVE GIVEN HIM A CHANCE.
WAIT A SECOND! *GIL!* YOU'RE A G-G-*GHOST*!
THAT'S RIGHT! I'M A GHOST NOW.
IF YOU REALLY WANT TO GIVE ME ANOTHER CHANCE, MAYBE I'LL DO BETTER LIKE THIS!

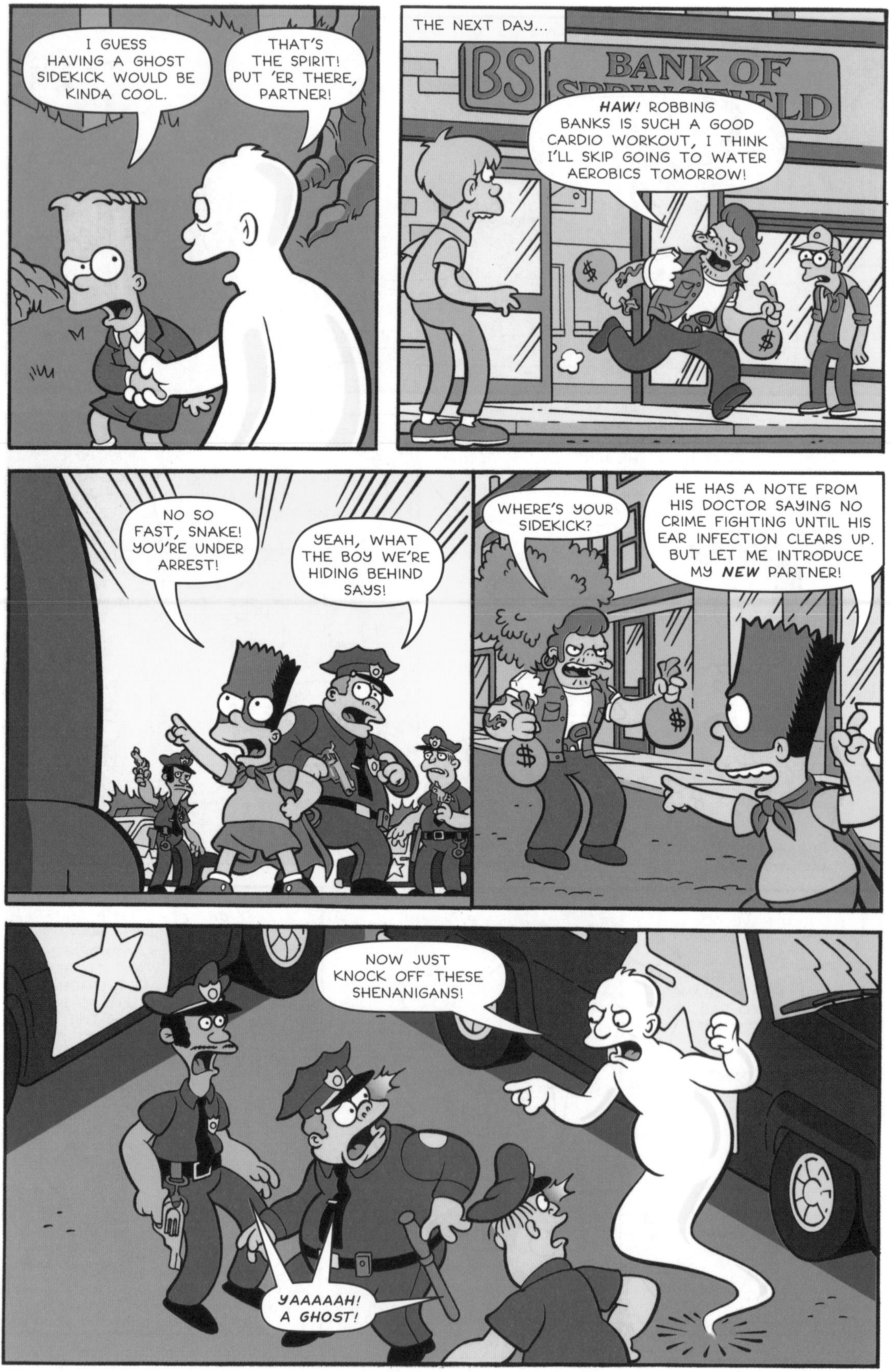
I GUESS HAVING A GHOST SIDEKICK WOULD BE KINDA COOL.
THAT'S THE SPIRIT! PUT 'ER THERE, PARTNER!
THE NEXT DAY...
BS
BANK OF
HAW! ROBBING BANKS IS SUCH A GOOD CARDIO WORKOUT, I THINK I'LL SKIP GOING TO WATER AEROBICS TOMORROW!
NO SO FAST, SNAKE! YOU'RE UNDER ARREST!
YEAH, WHAT THE BOY WE'RE HIDING BEHIND SAYS!
WHERE'S YOUR SIDEKICK?
HE HAS A NOTE FROM HIS DOCTOR SAYING NO CRIME FIGHTING UNTIL HIS EAR INFECTION CLEARS UP. BUT LET ME INTRODUCE MY *NEW* PARTNER!
NOW JUST KNOCK OFF THESE SHENANIGANS!
YAAAAAH! A GHOST!

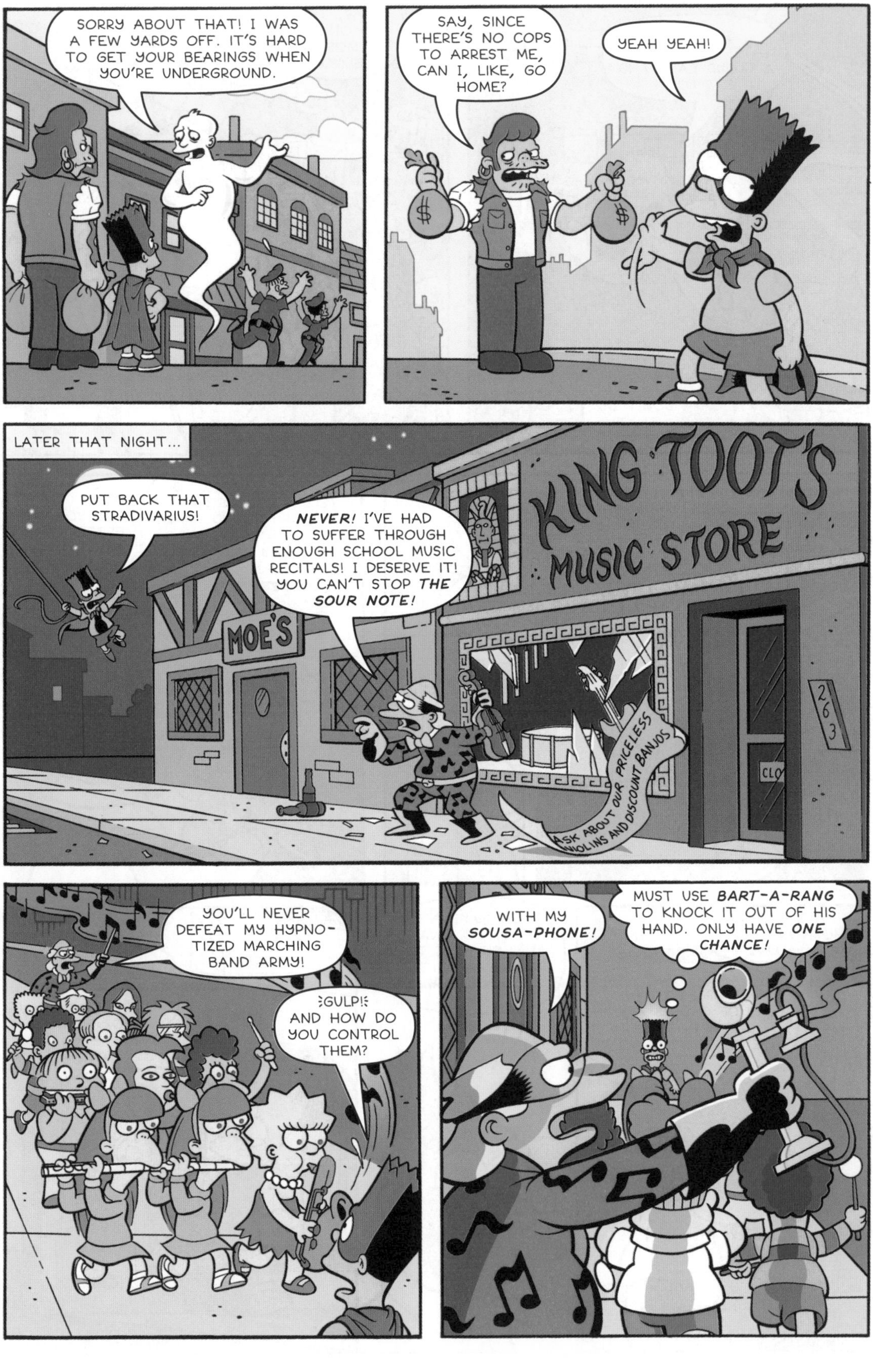
SORRY ABOUT THAT! I WAS A FEW YARDS OFF. IT'S HARD TO GET YOUR BEARINGS WHEN YOU'RE UNDERGROUND.
SAY, SINCE THERE'S NO COPS TO ARREST ME, CAN I, LIKE, GO HOME?
YEAH YEAH!
LATER THAT NIGHT...
PUT BACK THAT STRADIVARIUS!
NEVER! I'VE HAD TO SUFFER THROUGH ENOUGH SCHOOL MUSIC RECITALS! I DESERVE IT! YOU CAN'T STOP THE SOUR NOTE!
KING TOOT'S MUSIC STORE
MOE'S
263
ASK ABOUT OUR PRICELESS VIOLINS AND DISCOUNT BANJOS
YOU'LL NEVER DEFEAT MY HYPNO-TIZED MARCHING BAND ARMY!
GULP! AND HOW DO YOU CONTROL THEM?
WITH MY SOUSA-PHONE!
MUST USE BART-A-RANG TO KNOCK IT OUT OF HIS HAND. ONLY HAVE ONE CHANCE!

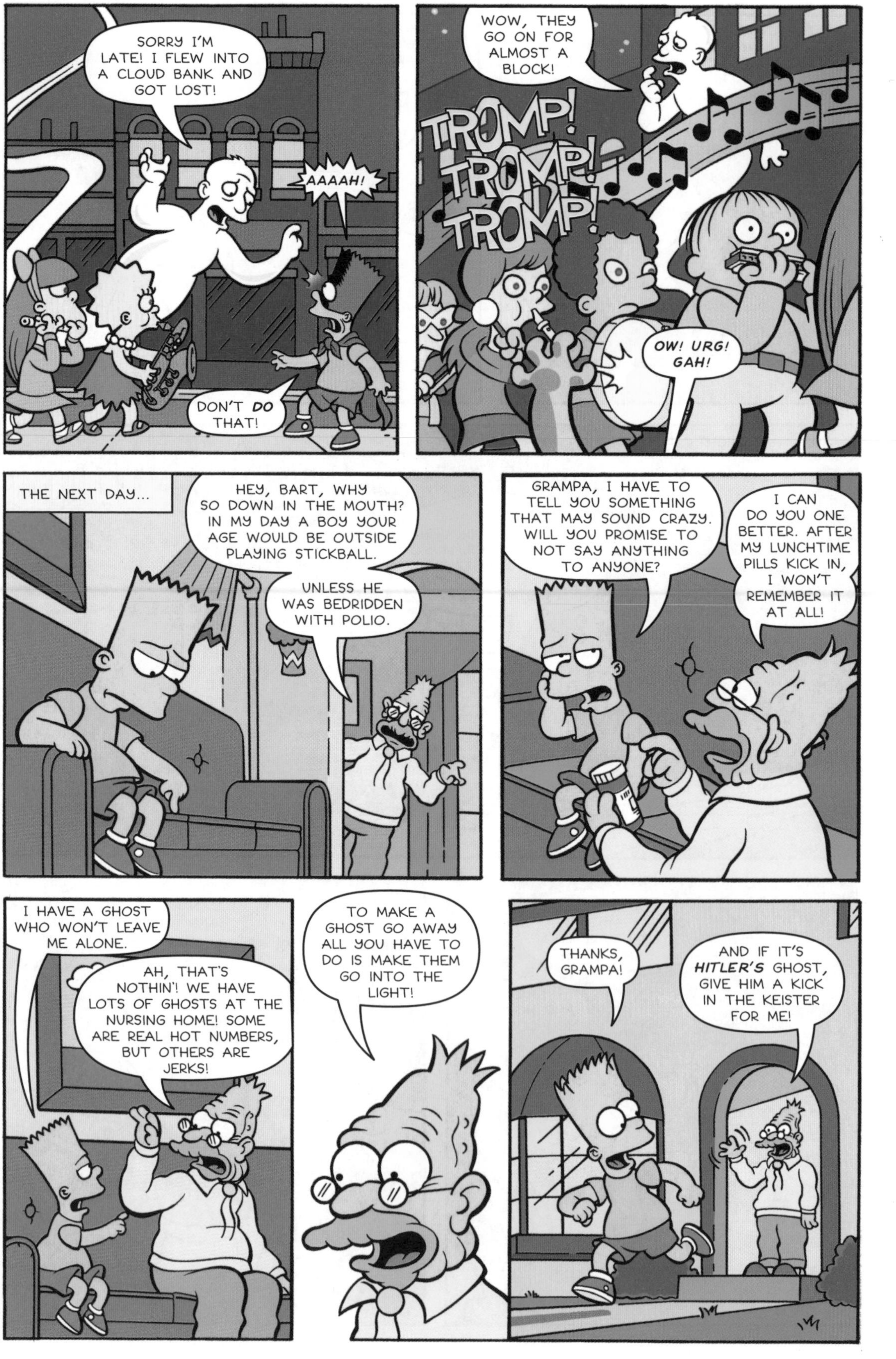

SORRY I'M LATE! I FLEW INTO A CLOUD BANK AND GOT LOST!
AAAAH!
DON'T DO THAT!
WOW, THEY GO ON FOR ALMOST A BLOCK!
TROMP! TROMP! TROMP!
OW! URG! GAH!
THE NEXT DAY...
HEY, BART, WHY SO DOWN IN THE MOUTH? IN MY DAY A BOY YOUR AGE WOULD BE OUTSIDE PLAYING STICKBALL.
UNLESS HE WAS BEDRIDDEN WITH POLIO.
GRAMPA, I HAVE TO TELL YOU SOMETHING THAT MAY SOUND CRAZY. WILL YOU PROMISE TO NOT SAY ANYTHING TO ANYONE?
I CAN DO YOU ONE BETTER. AFTER MY LUNCHTIME PILLS KICK IN, I WON'T REMEMBER IT AT ALL!
I HAVE A GHOST WHO WON'T LEAVE ME ALONE.
AH, THAT'S NOTHIN'! WE HAVE LOTS OF GHOSTS AT THE NURSING HOME! SOME ARE REAL HOT NUMBERS, BUT OTHERS ARE JERKS!
TO MAKE A GHOST GO AWAY ALL YOU HAVE TO DO IS MAKE THEM GO INTO THE LIGHT!
THANKS, GRAMPA!
AND IF IT'S HITLER'S GHOST, GIVE HIM A KICK IN THE KEISTER FOR ME!

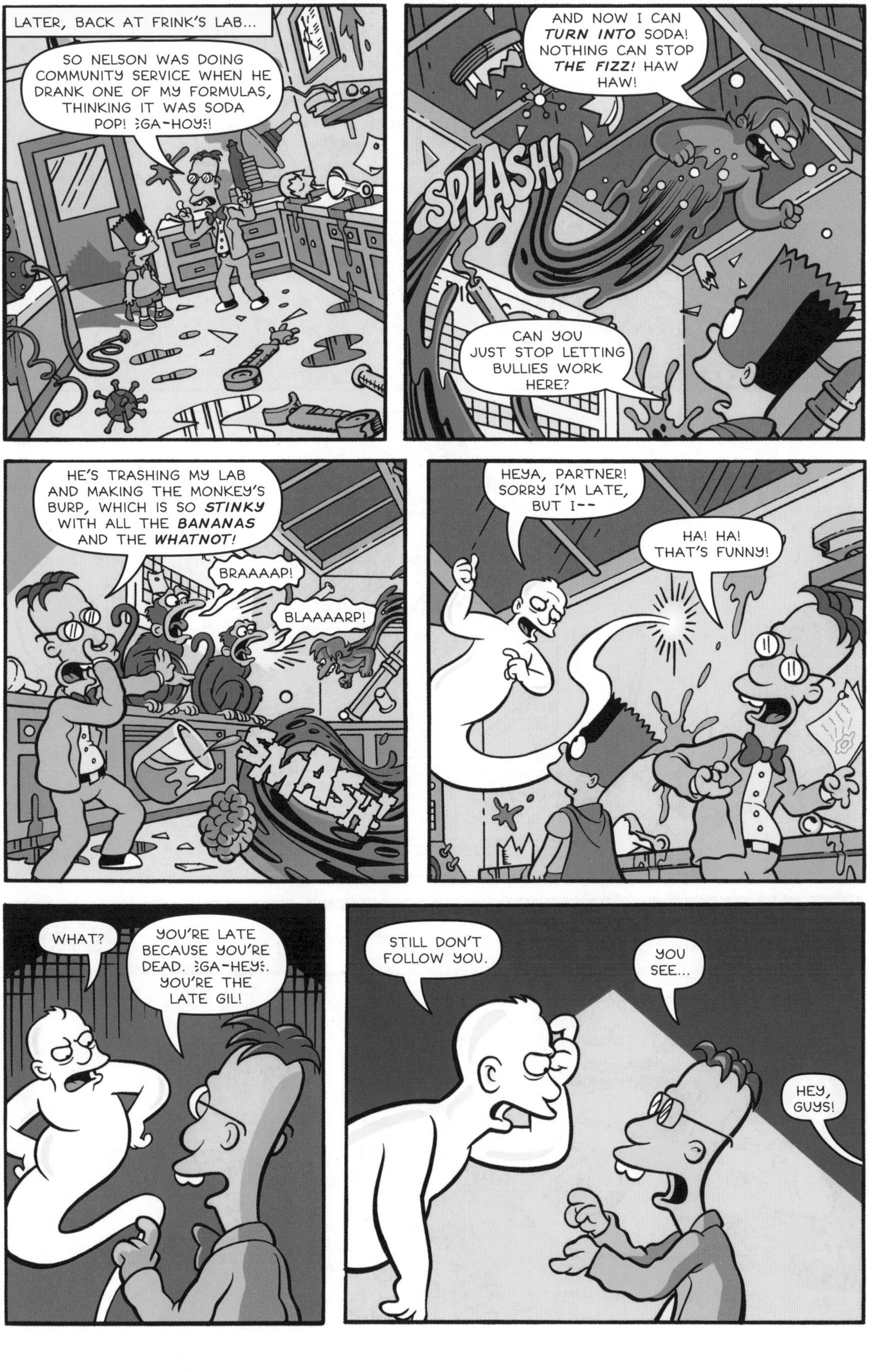
LATER, BACK AT FRINK'S LAB...
SO NELSON WAS DOING COMMUNITY SERVICE WHEN HE DRANK ONE OF MY FORMULAS, THINKING IT WAS SODA POP! GA-HOY!
AND NOW I CAN TURN INTO SODA! NOTHING CAN STOP THE FIZZ! HAW HAW!
SPLASH!
CAN YOU JUST STOP LETTING BULLIES WORK HERE?
HE'S TRASHING MY LAB AND MAKING THE MONKEY'S BURP, WHICH IS SO STINKY WITH ALL THE BANANAS AND THE WHATNOT!
BRAAAAP!
BLAAAARP!
SMASH!
HEYA, PARTNER! SORRY I'M LATE, BUT I--
HA! HA! THAT'S FUNNY!
WHAT?
YOU'RE LATE BECAUSE YOU'RE DEAD. GA-HEY. YOU'RE THE LATE GIL!
STILL DON'T FOLLOW YOU.
YOU SEE...
HEY, GUYS!

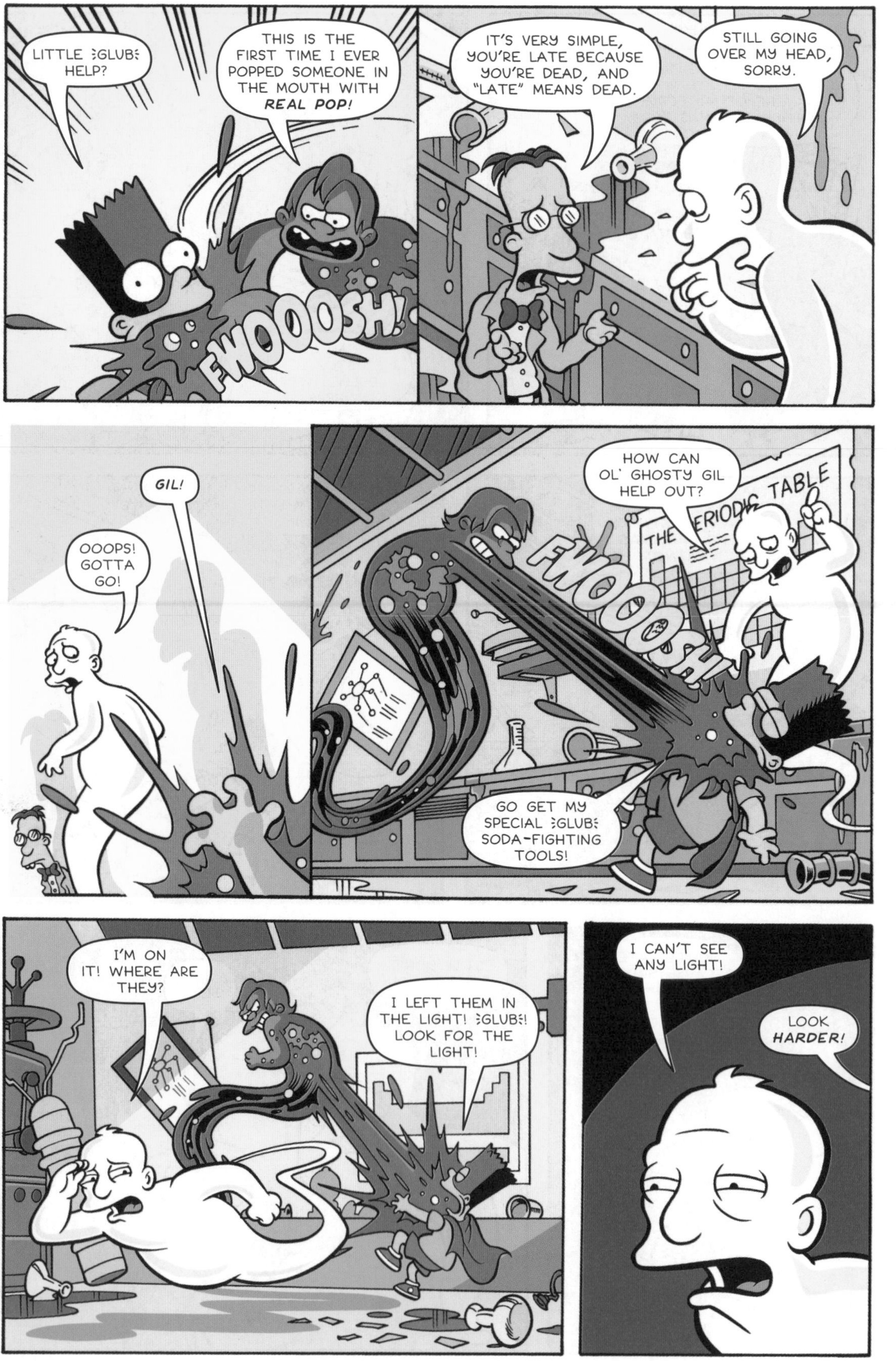

LITTLE GLUB HELP?
THIS IS THE FIRST TIME I EVER POPPED SOMEONE IN THE MOUTH WITH REAL POP!
FWOOOSH!
IT'S VERY SIMPLE, YOU'RE LATE BECAUSE YOU'RE DEAD, AND "LATE" MEANS DEAD.
STILL GOING OVER MY HEAD, SORRY.
GIL!
OOOPS! GOTTA GO!
HOW CAN OL' GHOSTY GIL HELP OUT?
THE PERIODIC TABLE
FWOOOSH!
GO GET MY SPECIAL GLUB SODA-FIGHTING TOOLS!
I'M ON IT! WHERE ARE THEY?
I LEFT THEM IN THE LIGHT! GLUB! LOOK FOR THE LIGHT!
I CAN'T SEE ANY LIGHT!
LOOK HARDER!

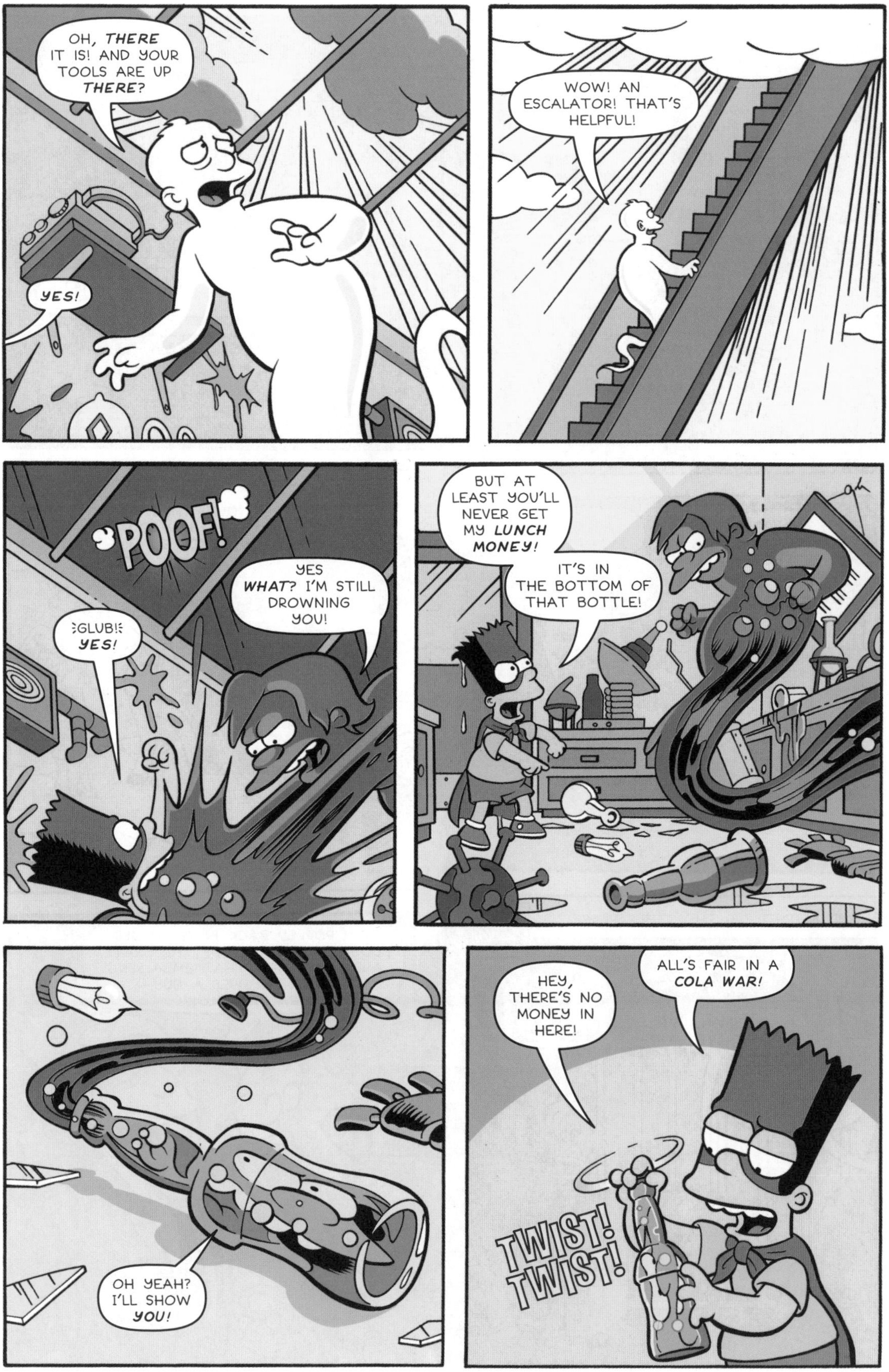
OH, THERE IT IS! AND YOUR TOOLS ARE UP THERE?
YES!
WOW! AN ESCALATOR! THAT'S HELPFUL!
POOF!
YES WHAT? I'M STILL DROWNING YOU!
GLUB! YES!
BUT AT LEAST YOU'LL NEVER GET MY LUNCH MONEY!
IT'S IN THE BOTTOM OF THAT BOTTLE!
OH YEAH? I'LL SHOW YOU!
HEY, THERE'S NO MONEY IN HERE!
ALL'S FAIR IN A COLA WAR!
TWIST! TWIST!

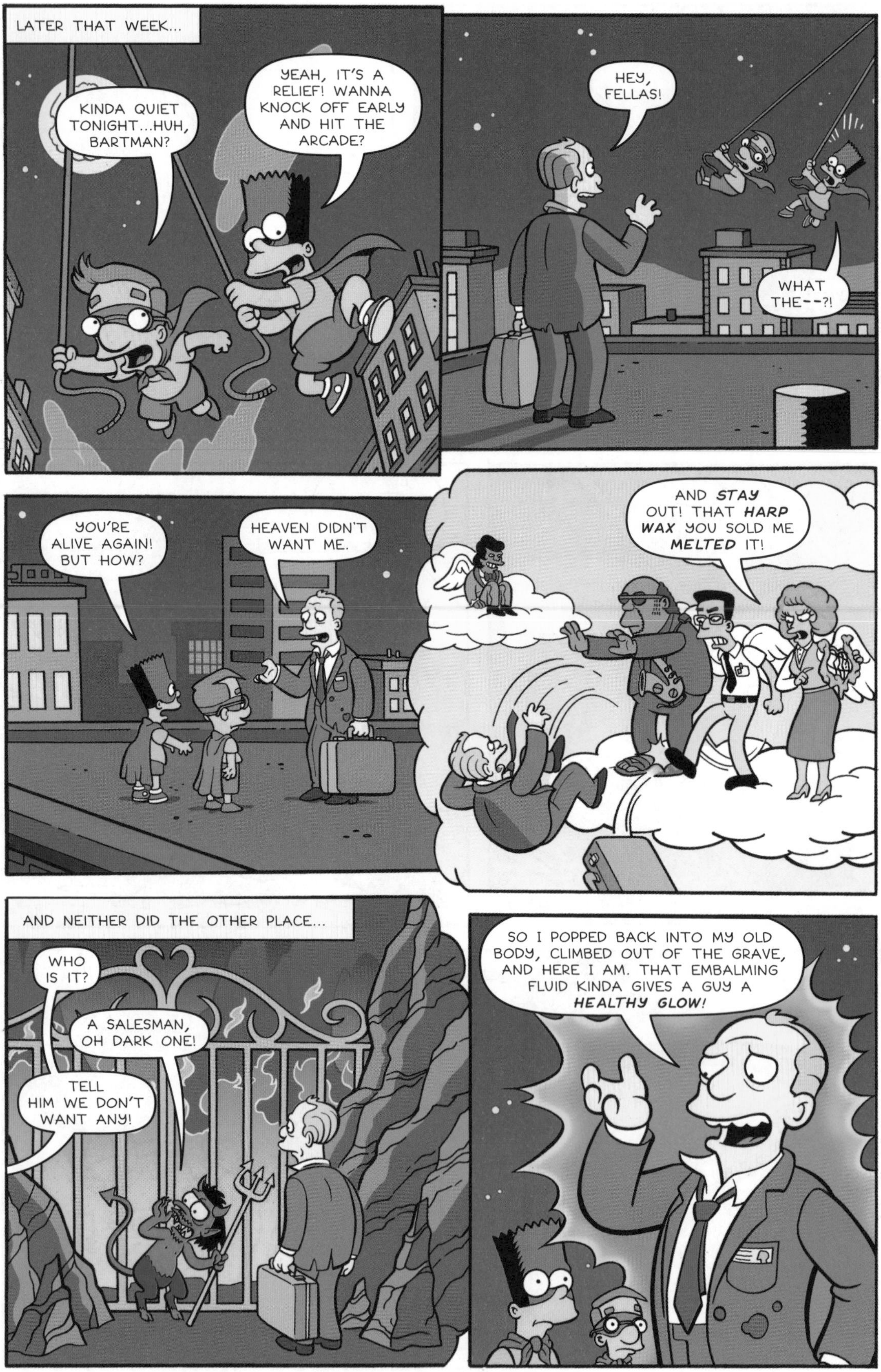
LATER THAT WEEK...
KINDA QUIET TONIGHT...HUH, BARTMAN?
YEAH, IT'S A RELIEF! WANNA KNOCK OFF EARLY AND HIT THE ARCADE?
HEY, FELLAS!
WHAT THE--?!
YOU'RE ALIVE AGAIN! BUT HOW?
HEAVEN DIDN'T WANT ME.
AND STAY OUT! THAT HARP WAX YOU SOLD ME MELTED IT!
AND NEITHER DID THE OTHER PLACE...
WHO IS IT?
A SALESMAN, OH DARK ONE!
TELL HIM WE DON'T WANT ANY!
SO I POPPED BACK INTO MY OLD BODY, CLIMBED OUT OF THE GRAVE, AND HERE I AM. THAT EMBALMING FLUID KINDA GIVES A GUY A HEALTHY GLOW!

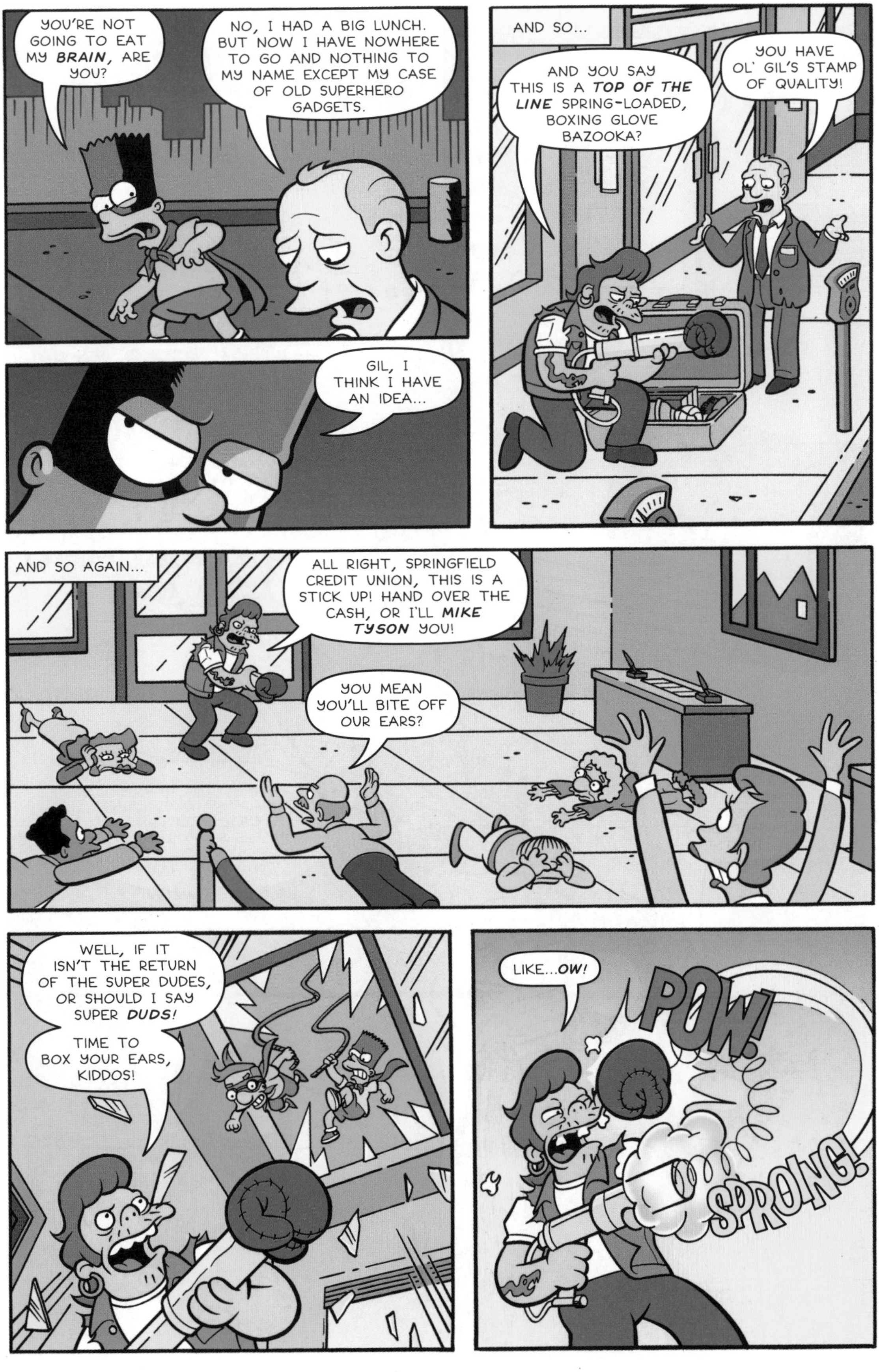
YOU'RE NOT GOING TO EAT MY BRAIN, ARE YOU?
NO, I HAD A BIG LUNCH. BUT NOW I HAVE NOWHERE TO GO AND NOTHING TO MY NAME EXCEPT MY CASE OF OLD SUPERHERO GADGETS.
GIL, I THINK I HAVE AN IDEA...
AND SO...
AND YOU SAY THIS IS A TOP OF THE LINE SPRING-LOADED, BOXING GLOVE BAZOOKA?
YOU HAVE OL' GIL'S STAMP OF QUALITY!
AND SO AGAIN...
ALL RIGHT, SPRINGFIELD CREDIT UNION, THIS IS A STICK UP! HAND OVER THE CASH, OR I'LL MIKE TYSON YOU!
YOU MEAN YOU'LL BITE OFF OUR EARS?
WELL, IF IT ISN'T THE RETURN OF THE SUPER DUDES, OR SHOULD I SAY SUPER DUDS!
TIME TO BOX YOUR EARS, KIDDOS!
LIKE...OW!
POW!
SPRONG!

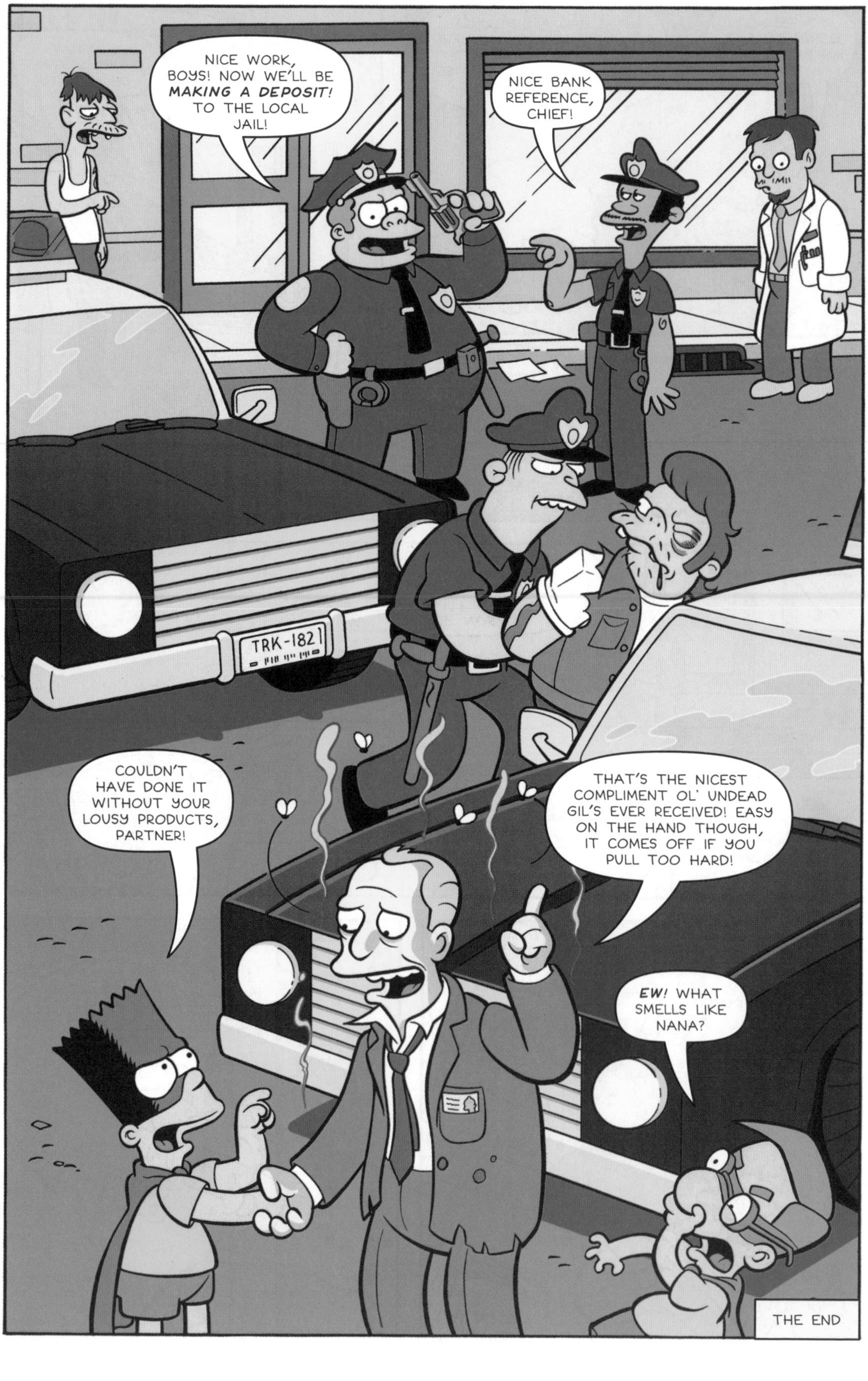
NICE WORK, BOYS! NOW WE'LL BE *MAKING A DEPOSIT*! TO THE LOCAL JAIL!
NICE BANK REFERENCE, CHIEF!
TRK-1821
COULDN'T HAVE DONE IT WITHOUT YOUR LOUSY PRODUCTS, PARTNER!
THAT'S THE NICEST COMPLIMENT OL' UNDEAD GIL'S EVER RECEIVED! EASY ON THE HAND THOUGH, IT COMES OFF IF YOU PULL TOO HARD!
EW! WHAT SMELLS LIKE NANA?
THE END

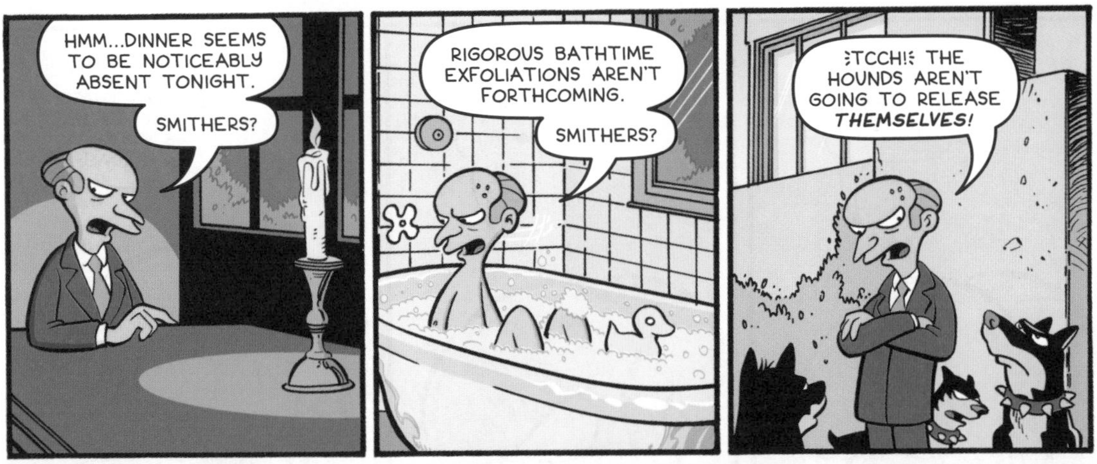
HMM...DINNER SEEMS TO BE NOTICEABLY ABSENT TONIGHT.
SMITHERS?
RIGOROUS BATHTIME EXFOLIATIONS AREN'T FORTHCOMING.
SMITHERS?
TCCH! THE HOUNDS AREN'T GOING TO RELEASE *THEMSELVES!*

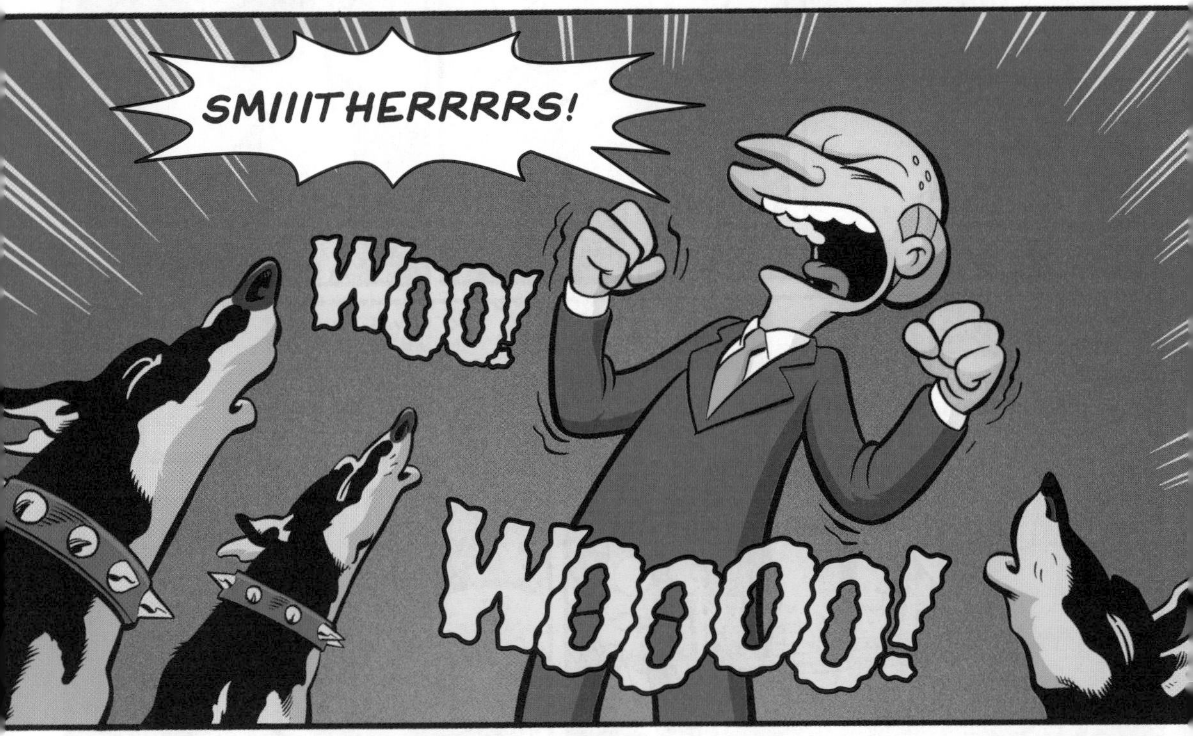
SMIIITHERRRRS!
WOO!
WOOOO!

MR. BURNS TO THE RESCUE

NATHAN KANE SCRIPT · *TONE RODRIGUEZ* PENCILS · *ANDREW PEPOY* INKS · *ART VILLANUEVA* COLORS · *KAREN BATES* LETTERS

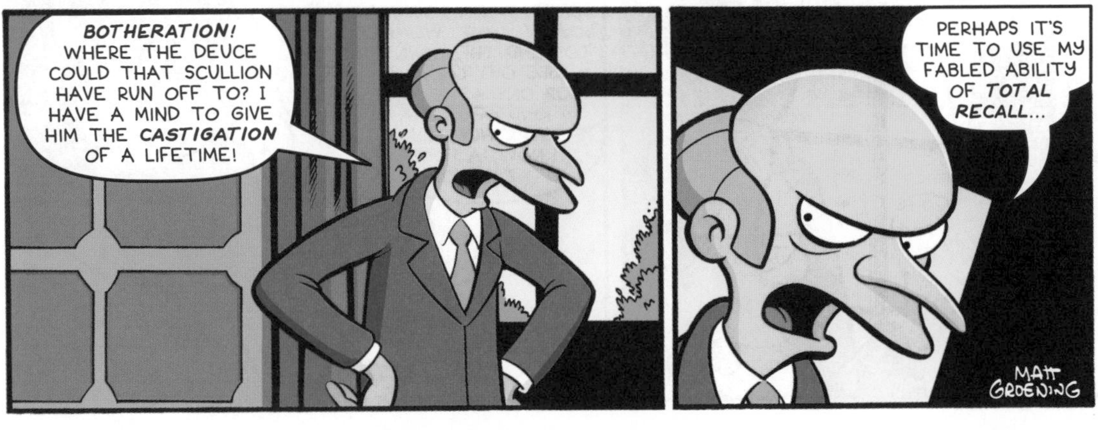
BOTHERATION! WHERE THE DEUCE COULD THAT SCULLION HAVE RUN OFF TO? I HAVE A MIND TO GIVE HIM THE *CASTIGATION* OF A LIFETIME!
PERHAPS IT'S TIME TO USE MY FABLED ABILITY OF *TOTAL RECALL*...
MATT GROENING

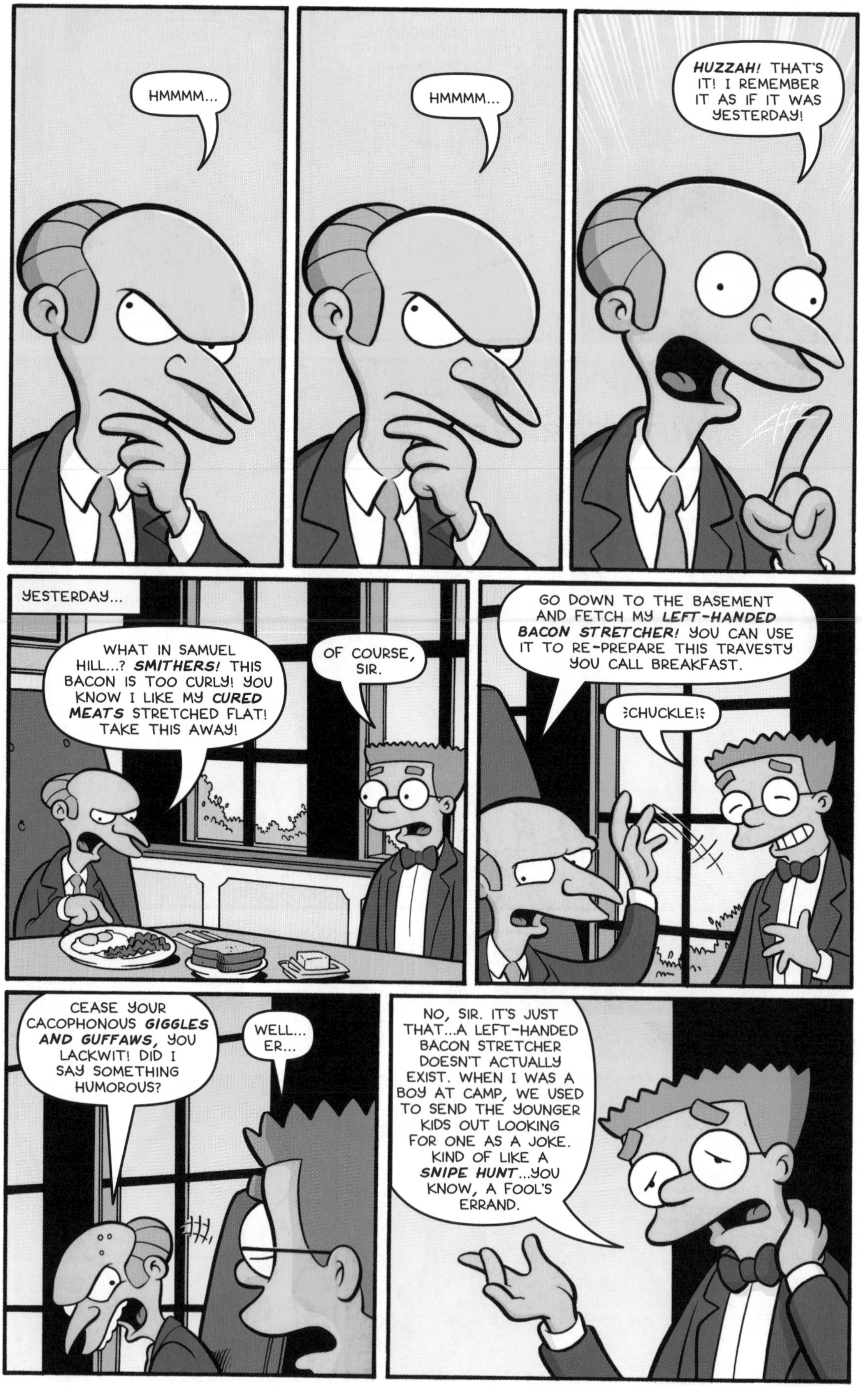
HMMMM...
HMMMM...
HUZZAH! THAT'S IT! I REMEMBER IT AS IF IT WAS YESTERDAY!
YESTERDAY...
WHAT IN SAMUEL HILL...? SMITHERS! THIS BACON IS TOO CURLY! YOU KNOW I LIKE MY CURED MEATS STRETCHED FLAT! TAKE THIS AWAY!
OF COURSE, SIR.
GO DOWN TO THE BASEMENT AND FETCH MY LEFT-HANDED BACON STRETCHER! YOU CAN USE IT TO RE-PREPARE THIS TRAVESTY YOU CALL BREAKFAST.
CHUCKLE!
CEASE YOUR CACOPHONOUS GIGGLES AND GUFFAWS, YOU LACKWIT! DID I SAY SOMETHING HUMOROUS?
WELL... ER...
NO, SIR. IT'S JUST THAT...A LEFT-HANDED BACON STRETCHER DOESN'T ACTUALLY EXIST. WHEN I WAS A BOY AT CAMP, WE USED TO SEND THE YOUNGER KIDS OUT LOOKING FOR ONE AS A JOKE. KIND OF LIKE A SNIPE HUNT...YOU KNOW, A FOOL'S ERRAND.

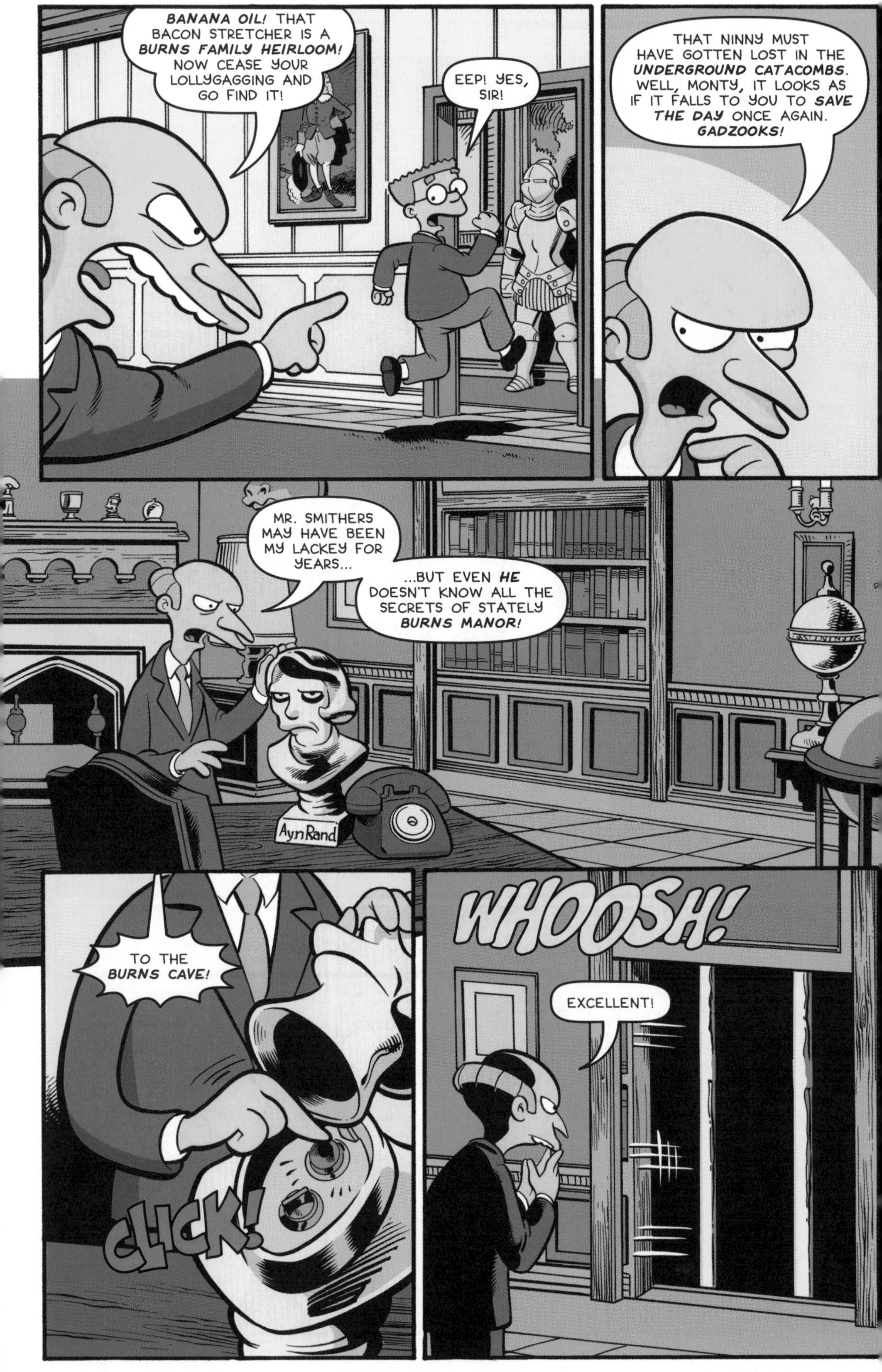
BANANA OIL! THAT BACON STRETCHER IS A BURNS FAMILY HEIRLOOM! NOW CEASE YOUR LOLLYGAGGING AND GO FIND IT!
EEP! YES, SIR!
THAT NINNY MUST HAVE GOTTEN LOST IN THE UNDERGROUND CATACOMBS. WELL, MONTY, IT LOOKS AS IF IT FALLS TO YOU TO SAVE THE DAY ONCE AGAIN. GADZOOKS!
MR. SMITHERS MAY HAVE BEEN MY LACKEY FOR YEARS...
...BUT EVEN HE DOESN'T KNOW ALL THE SECRETS OF STATELY BURNS MANOR!
Ayn Rand
TO THE BURNS CAVE!
CLICK!
WHOOSH!
EXCELLENT!

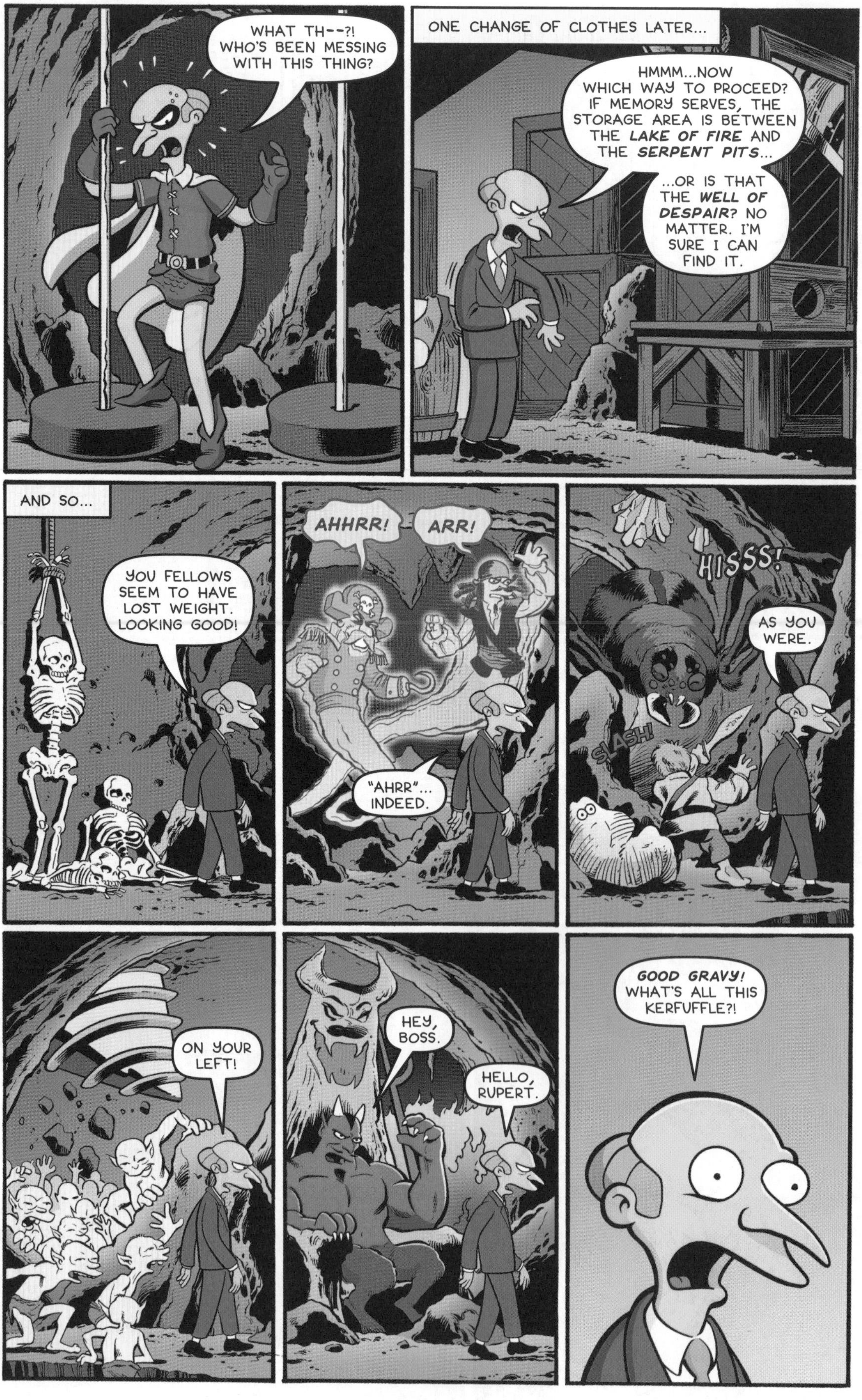
WHAT TH--?!
WHO'S BEEN MESSING
WITH THIS THING?
ONE CHANGE OF CLOTHES LATER...
HMMM...NOW
WHICH WAY TO PROCEED?
IF MEMORY SERVES, THE
STORAGE AREA IS BETWEEN
THE LAKE OF FIRE AND
THE SERPENT PITS...
...OR IS THAT
THE WELL OF
DESPAIR? NO
MATTER. I'M
SURE I CAN
FIND IT.
AND SO...
YOU FELLOWS
SEEM TO HAVE
LOST WEIGHT.
LOOKING GOOD!
AHHRR!
ARR!
"AHRR"...
INDEED.
HISSS!
AS YOU
WERE.
SLASH!
ON YOUR
LEFT!
HEY,
BOSS.
HELLO,
RUPERT.
GOOD GRAVY!
WHAT'S ALL THIS
KERFUFFLE?!

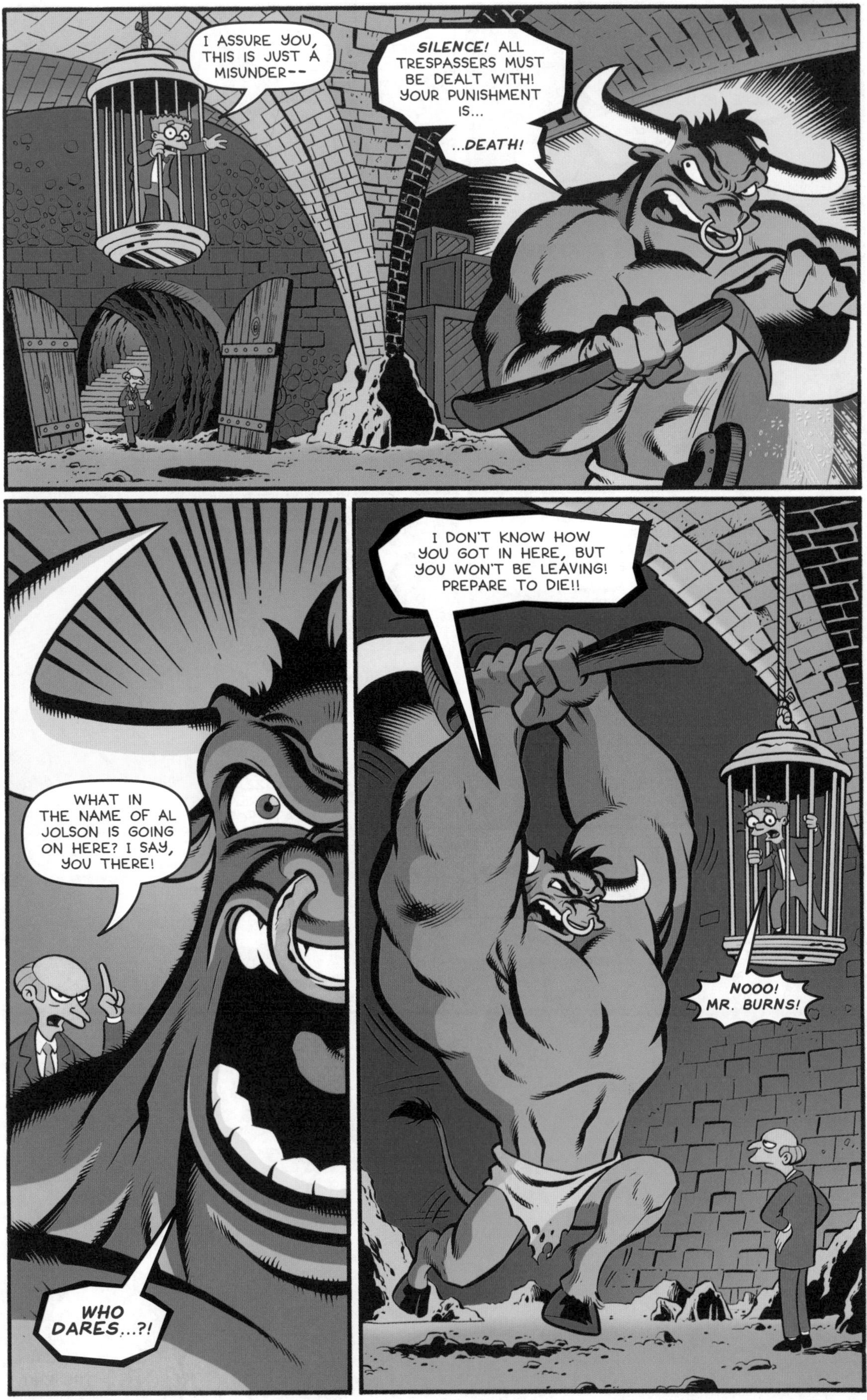

I ASSURE YOU, THIS IS JUST A MISUNDER--
SILENCE! ALL TRESPASSERS MUST BE DEALT WITH! YOUR PUNISHMENT IS...
...*DEATH!*
WHAT IN THE NAME OF AL JOLSON IS GOING ON HERE? I SAY, YOU THERE!
WHO DARES...?!
I DON'T KNOW HOW YOU GOT IN HERE, BUT YOU WON'T BE LEAVING! PREPARE TO DIE!!
NOOO! MR. BURNS!

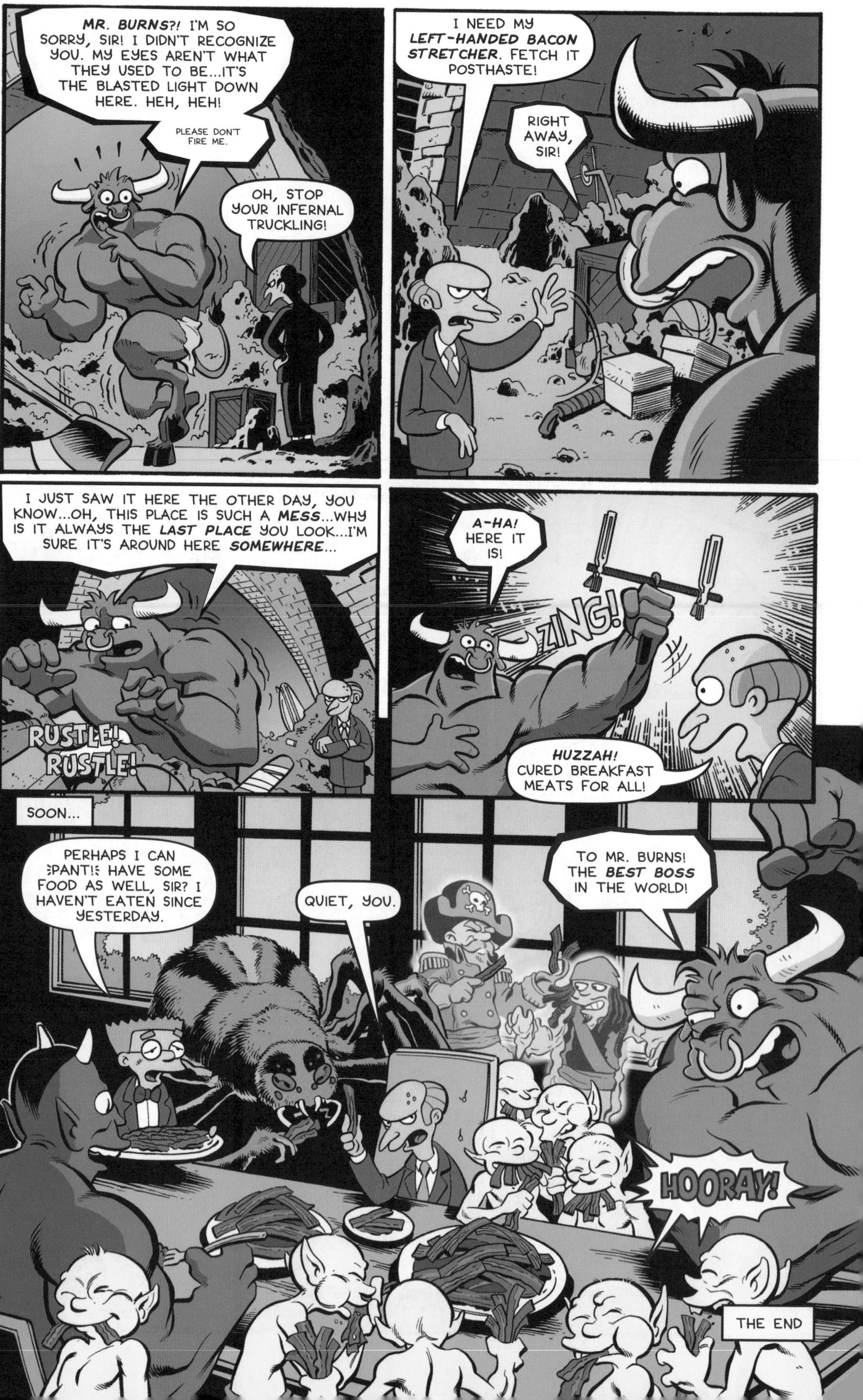
MR. BURNS?! I'M SO SORRY, SIR! I DIDN'T RECOGNIZE YOU. MY EYES AREN'T WHAT THEY USED TO BE...IT'S THE BLASTED LIGHT DOWN HERE. HEH, HEH!
PLEASE DON'T FIRE ME.
OH, STOP YOUR INFERNAL TRUCKLING!
I NEED MY LEFT-HANDED BACON STRETCHER. FETCH IT POSTHASTE!
RIGHT AWAY, SIR!
I JUST SAW IT HERE THE OTHER DAY, YOU KNOW...OH, THIS PLACE IS SUCH A MESS...WHY IS IT ALWAYS THE LAST PLACE YOU LOOK...I'M SURE IT'S AROUND HERE SOMEWHERE...
RUSTLE! RUSTLE!
A-HA! HERE IT IS!
ZING!
HUZZAH! CURED BREAKFAST MEATS FOR ALL!
SOON...
PERHAPS I CAN :PANT!: HAVE SOME FOOD AS WELL, SIR? I HAVEN'T EATEN SINCE YESTERDAY.
QUIET, YOU.
TO MR. BURNS! THE BEST BOSS IN THE WORLD!
HOORAY!
THE END

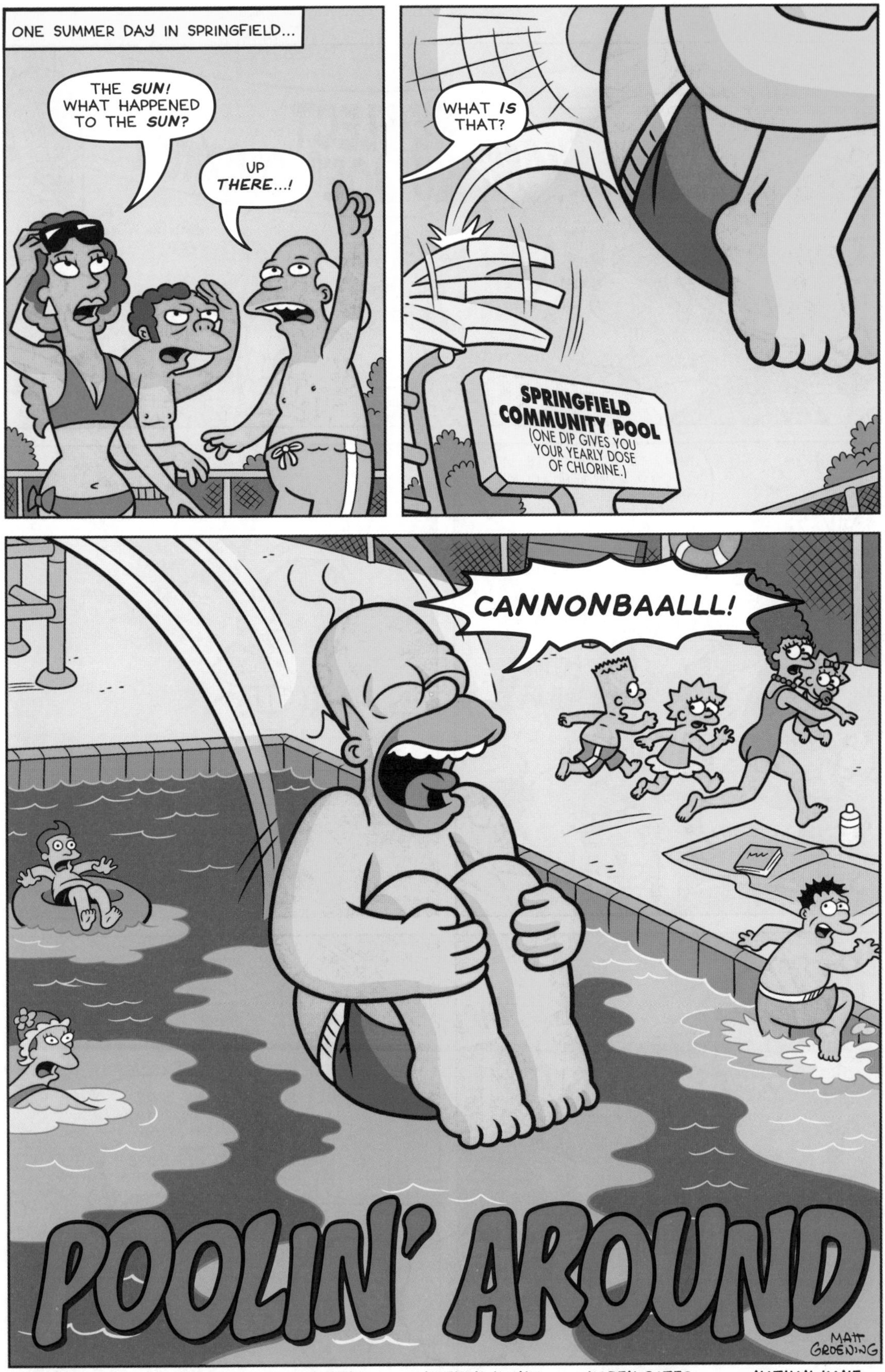
ONE SUMMER DAY IN SPRINGFIELD...
THE *SUN!* WHAT HAPPENED TO THE *SUN?*
UP *THERE...!*
WHAT *IS* THAT?
SPRINGFIELD COMMUNITY POOL
(ONE DIP GIVES YOU YOUR YEARLY DOSE OF CHLORINE.)
CANNONBAALLL!
POOLIN' AROUND
MATT GROENING

MIKE W. BARR SCRIPT | **REX LINDSEY** PENCILS | **DAN DAVIS** INKS | **NATHAN HAMILL** COLORS | **KAREN BATES** LETTERS | **NATHAN KANE** EDITOR

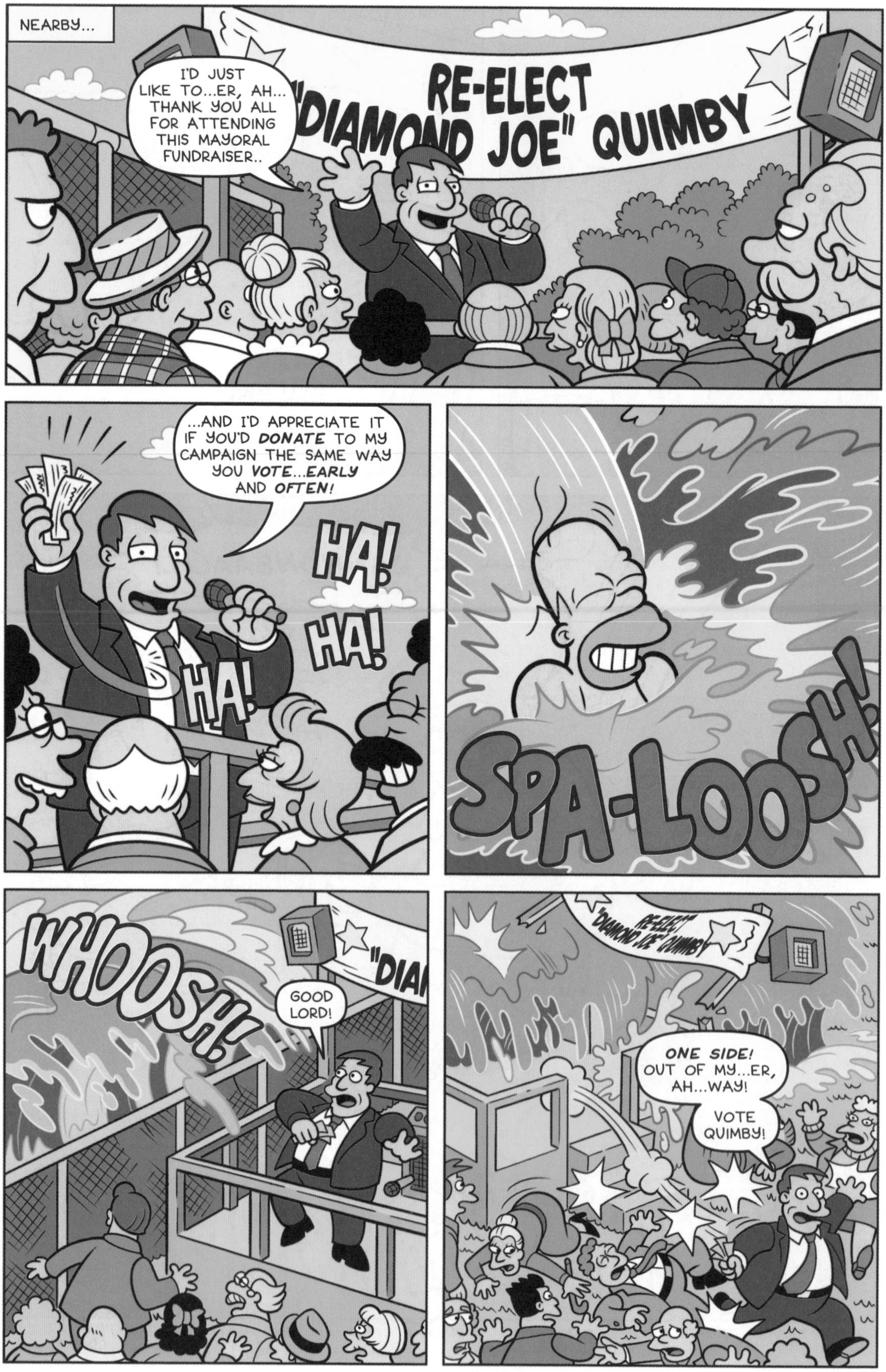
NEARBY...
RE-ELECT "DIAMOND JOE" QUIMBY
I'D JUST LIKE TO...ER, AH... THANK YOU ALL FOR ATTENDING THIS MAYORAL FUNDRAISER..
...AND I'D APPRECIATE IT IF YOU'D DONATE TO MY CAMPAIGN THE SAME WAY YOU VOTE...EARLY AND OFTEN!
HA!
HA!
HA!
SPA-LOOSH!
WHOOSH!
"DIA
GOOD LORD!
RE-ELECT "DIAMOND JOE" QUIMBY
ONE SIDE! OUT OF MY...ER, AH...WAY!
VOTE QUIMBY!

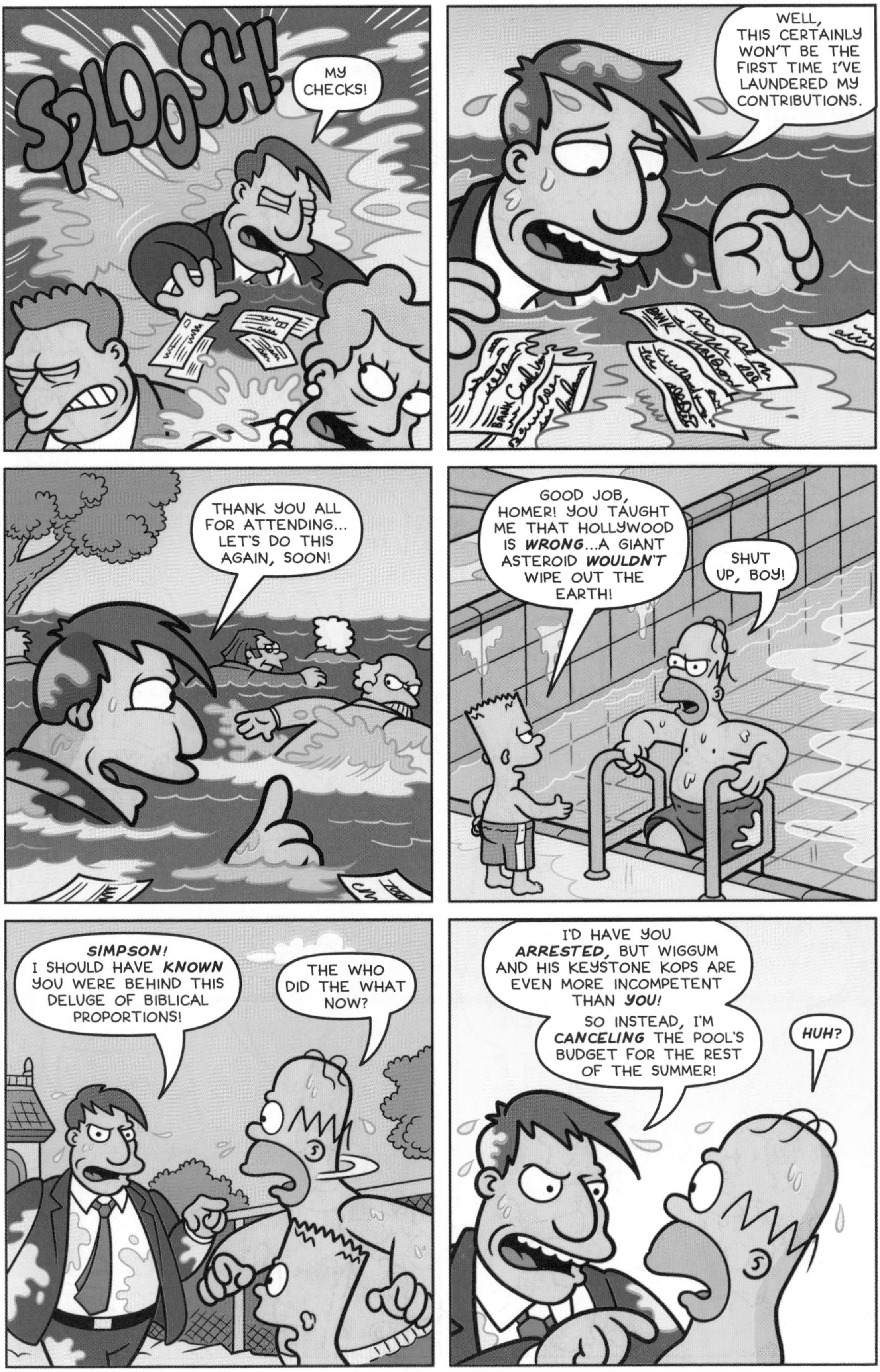
SPLOOSH!
MY CHECKS!
WELL, THIS CERTAINLY WON'T BE THE FIRST TIME I'VE LAUNDERED MY CONTRIBUTIONS.
THANK YOU ALL FOR ATTENDING... LET'S DO THIS AGAIN, SOON!
GOOD JOB, HOMER! YOU TAUGHT ME THAT HOLLYWOOD IS *WRONG*...A GIANT ASTEROID *WOULDN'T* WIPE OUT THE EARTH!
SHUT UP, BOY!
SIMPSON! I SHOULD HAVE *KNOWN* YOU WERE BEHIND THIS DELUGE OF BIBLICAL PROPORTIONS!
THE WHO DID THE WHAT NOW?
I'D HAVE YOU *ARRESTED,* BUT WIGGUM AND HIS KEYSTONE KOPS ARE EVEN MORE INCOMPETENT THAN *YOU!*
SO INSTEAD, I'M *CANCELING* THE POOL'S BUDGET FOR THE REST OF THE SUMMER!
HUH?

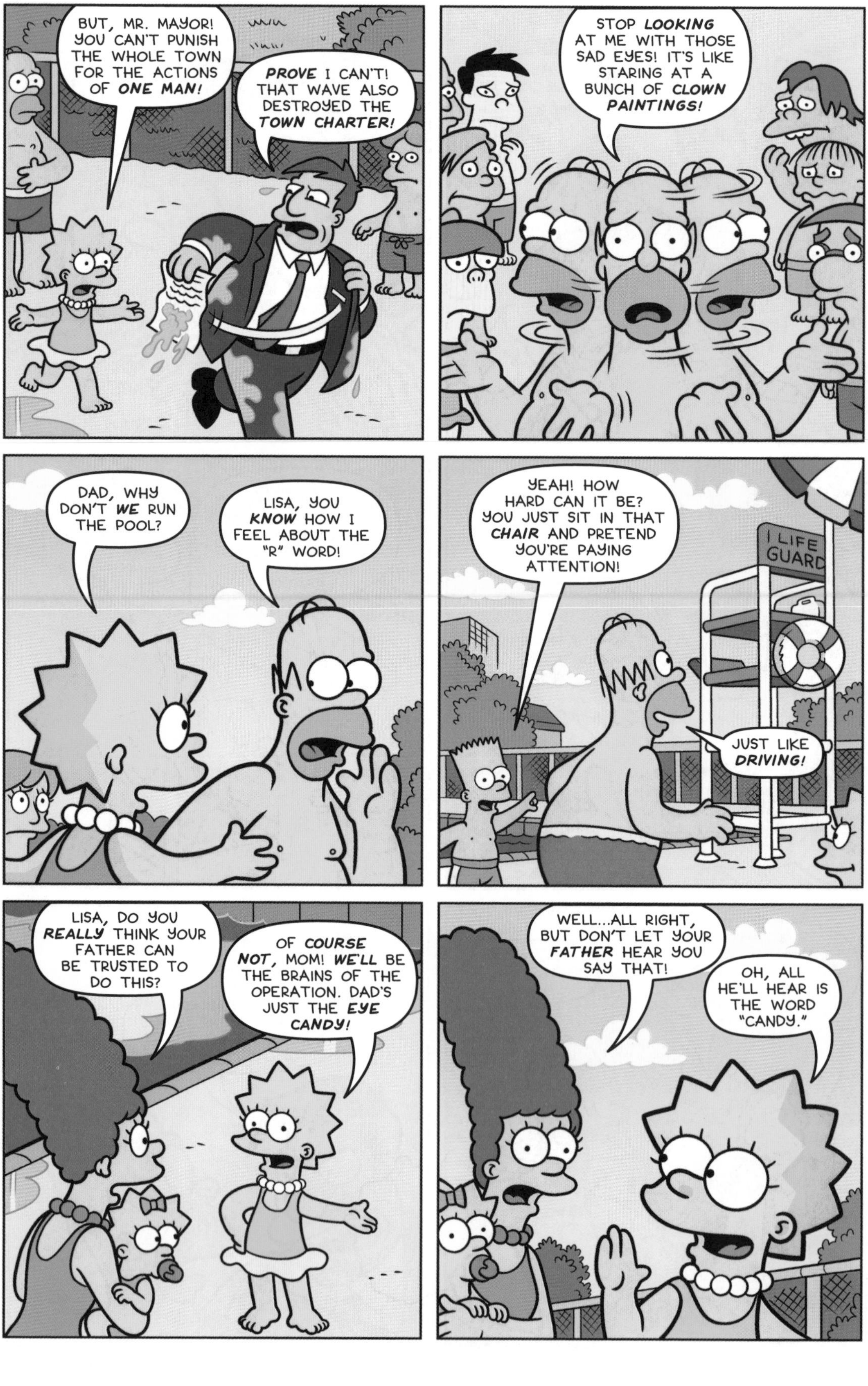
BUT, MR. MAYOR! YOU CAN'T PUNISH THE WHOLE TOWN FOR THE ACTIONS OF ONE MAN!
PROVE I CAN'T! THAT WAVE ALSO DESTROYED THE TOWN CHARTER!
STOP LOOKING AT ME WITH THOSE SAD EYES! IT'S LIKE STARING AT A BUNCH OF CLOWN PAINTINGS!
DAD, WHY DON'T WE RUN THE POOL?
LISA, YOU KNOW HOW I FEEL ABOUT THE "R" WORD!
YEAH! HOW HARD CAN IT BE? YOU JUST SIT IN THAT CHAIR AND PRETEND YOU'RE PAYING ATTENTION!
LIFE GUARD
JUST LIKE DRIVING!
LISA, DO YOU REALLY THINK YOUR FATHER CAN BE TRUSTED TO DO THIS?
OF COURSE NOT, MOM! WE'LL BE THE BRAINS OF THE OPERATION. DAD'S JUST THE EYE CANDY!
WELL...ALL RIGHT, BUT DON'T LET YOUR FATHER HEAR YOU SAY THAT!
OH, ALL HE'LL HEAR IS THE WORD "CANDY."

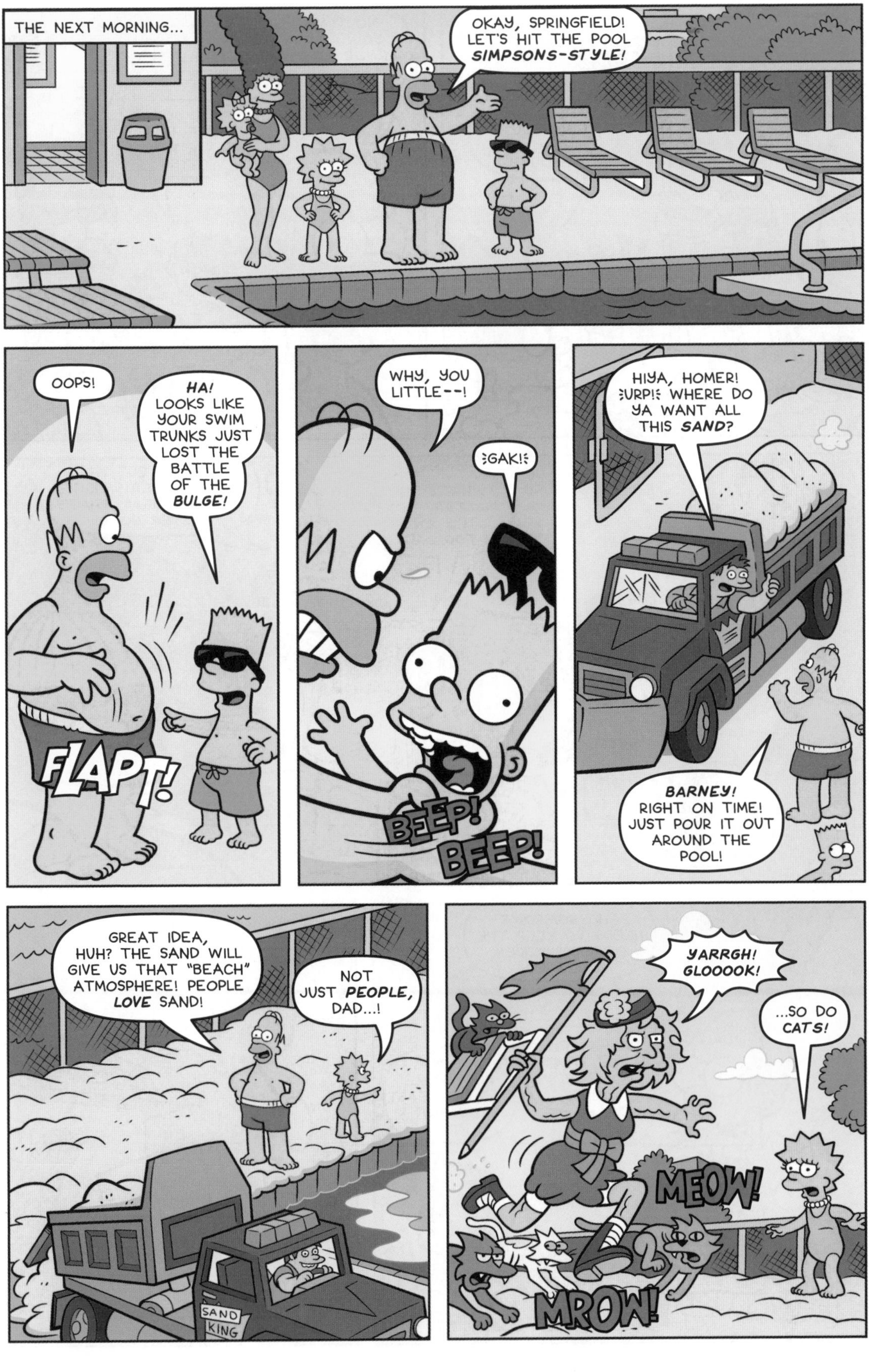
THE NEXT MORNING...
OKAY, SPRINGFIELD! LET'S HIT THE POOL SIMPSONS-STYLE!
OOPS!
HA! LOOKS LIKE YOUR SWIM TRUNKS JUST LOST THE BATTLE OF THE BULGE!
FLAPT!
WHY, YOU LITTLE--!
GAK!
BEEP! BEEP!
HIYA, HOMER! URP! WHERE DO YA WANT ALL THIS SAND?
BARNEY! RIGHT ON TIME! JUST POUR IT OUT AROUND THE POOL!
GREAT IDEA, HUH? THE SAND WILL GIVE US THAT "BEACH" ATMOSPHERE! PEOPLE LOVE SAND!
NOT JUST PEOPLE, DAD...!
SAND KING
YARRGH! GLOOOOK!
...SO DO CATS!
MEOW!
MROW!

WELL, NO WORRIES! PEOPLE *LIKE* CATS!

DAD, I DON'T THINK YOU'RE THINKING THIS THROUGH.

NO TIME, LISA! YOU TALK SOME *SENSE* INTO THOSE CATS! *I'VE* GOT ANOTHER IDEA!

BUT YOU *CAN'T* TALK SENSE INTO CATS!

OH, DEAR...

WHAT'S THE *MATTER,* MOM? THIS ISN'T *TOO* BAD.

NOT YET, BUT WHEN YOUR FATHER SAYS HE HAS "AN IDEA"...THAT'S *NEVER* GOOD!

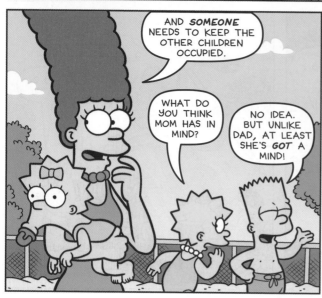

AND *SOMEONE* NEEDS TO KEEP THE OTHER CHILDREN OCCUPIED.

WHAT DO YOU THINK MOM HAS IN MIND?

NO IDEA. BUT UNLIKE DAD, AT LEAST SHE'S *GOT* A MIND!

SOMETIME LATER...

?

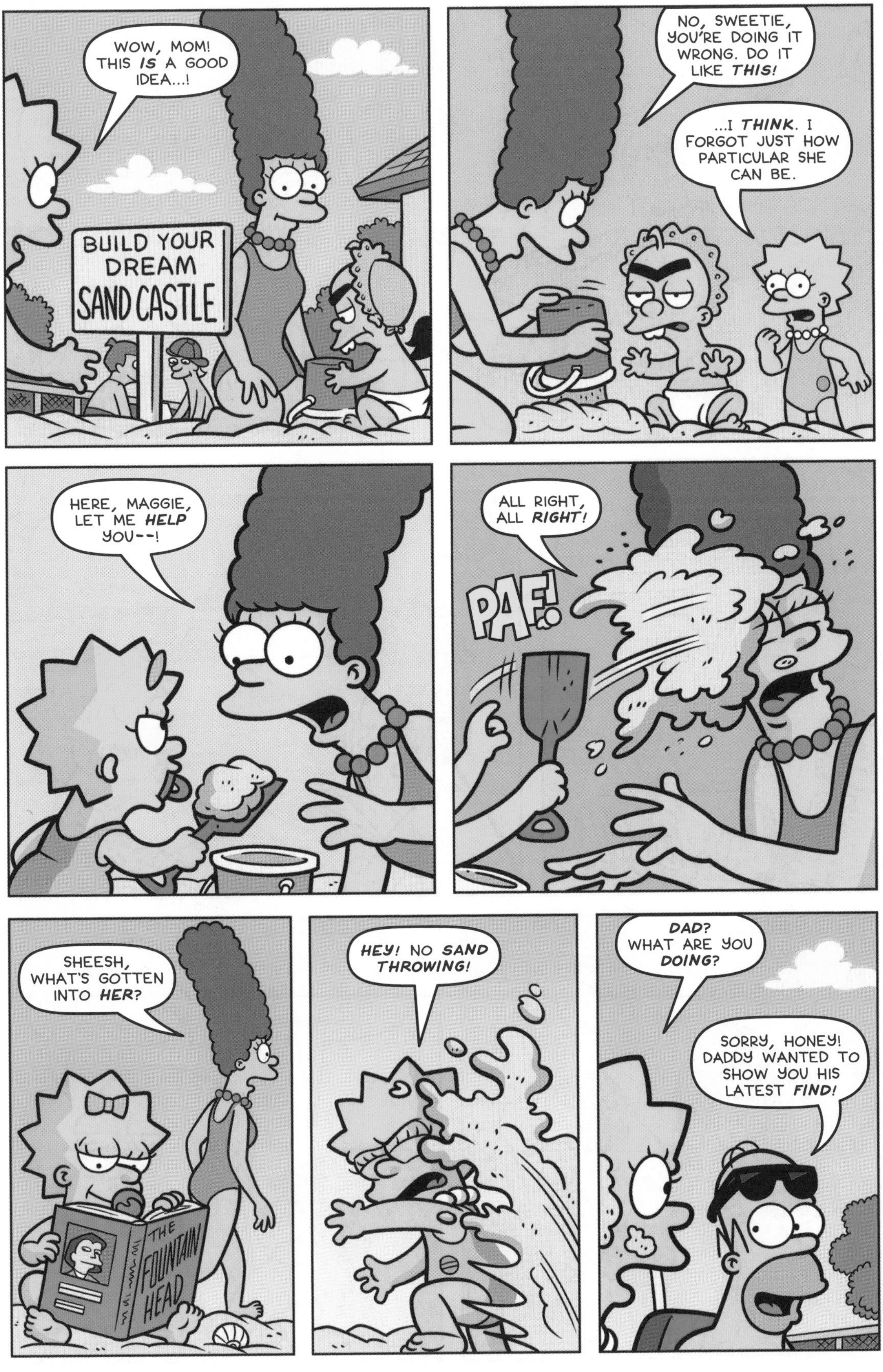
WOW, MOM! THIS IS A GOOD IDEA...!
BUILD YOUR DREAM SAND CASTLE
NO, SWEETIE, YOU'RE DOING IT WRONG. DO IT LIKE THIS!
...I THINK. I FORGOT JUST HOW PARTICULAR SHE CAN BE.
HERE, MAGGIE, LET ME HELP YOU--!
ALL RIGHT, ALL RIGHT!
PAF!
SHEESH, WHAT'S GOTTEN INTO HER?
THE FOUNTAIN HEAD
HEY! NO SAND THROWING!
DAD? WHAT ARE YOU DOING?
SORRY, HONEY! DADDY WANTED TO SHOW YOU HIS LATEST FIND!

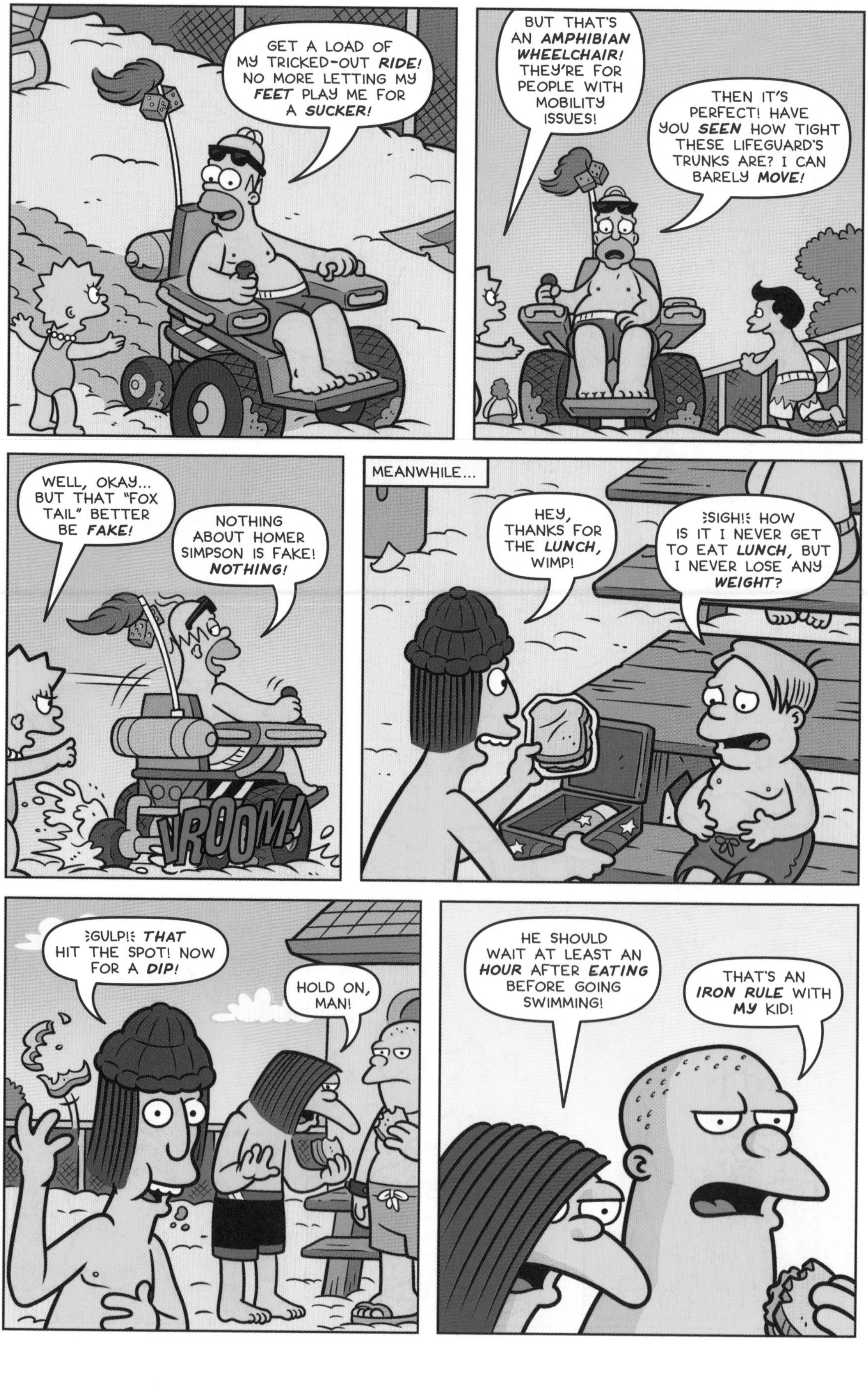
GET A LOAD OF MY TRICKED-OUT RIDE! NO MORE LETTING MY FEET PLAY ME FOR A SUCKER!
BUT THAT'S AN AMPHIBIAN WHEELCHAIR! THEY'RE FOR PEOPLE WITH MOBILITY ISSUES!
THEN IT'S PERFECT! HAVE YOU SEEN HOW TIGHT THESE LIFEGUARD'S TRUNKS ARE? I CAN BARELY MOVE!
WELL, OKAY... BUT THAT "FOX TAIL" BETTER BE FAKE!
NOTHING ABOUT HOMER SIMPSON IS FAKE! NOTHING!
VROOM!
MEANWHILE...
HEY, THANKS FOR THE LUNCH, WIMP!
SIGH! HOW IS IT I NEVER GET TO EAT LUNCH, BUT I NEVER LOSE ANY WEIGHT?
GULP! THAT HIT THE SPOT! NOW FOR A DIP!
HOLD ON, MAN!
HE SHOULD WAIT AT LEAST AN HOUR AFTER EATING BEFORE GOING SWIMMING!
THAT'S AN IRON RULE WITH MY KID!

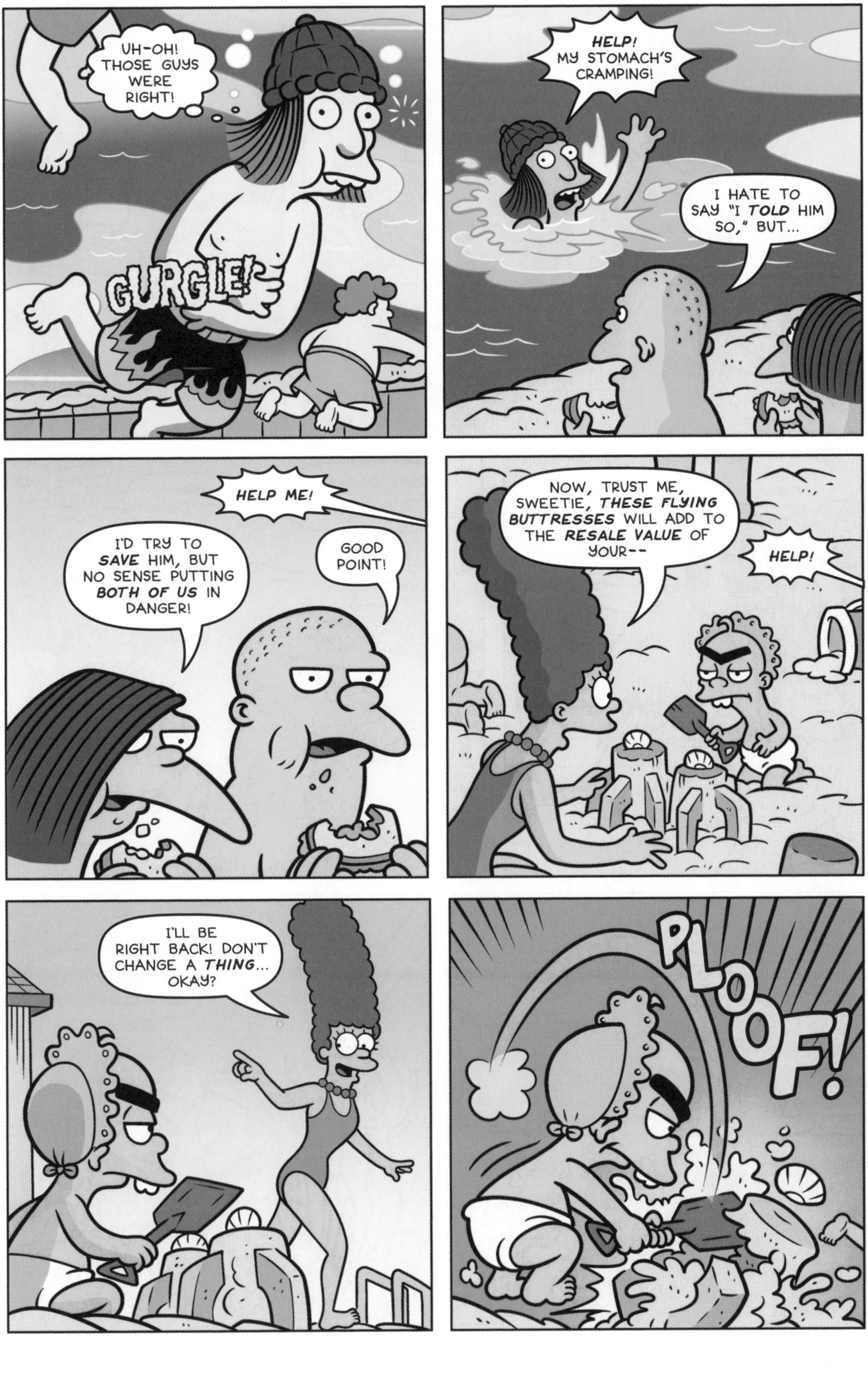
UH-OH! THOSE GUYS WERE RIGHT!
GURGLE!
HELP! MY STOMACH'S CRAMPING!
I HATE TO SAY "I TOLD HIM SO," BUT...
HELP ME!
I'D TRY TO SAVE HIM, BUT NO SENSE PUTTING BOTH OF US IN DANGER!
GOOD POINT!
NOW, TRUST ME, SWEETIE, THESE FLYING BUTTRESSES WILL ADD TO THE RESALE VALUE OF YOUR--
HELP!
I'LL BE RIGHT BACK! DON'T CHANGE A THING... OKAY?
PLOOF!

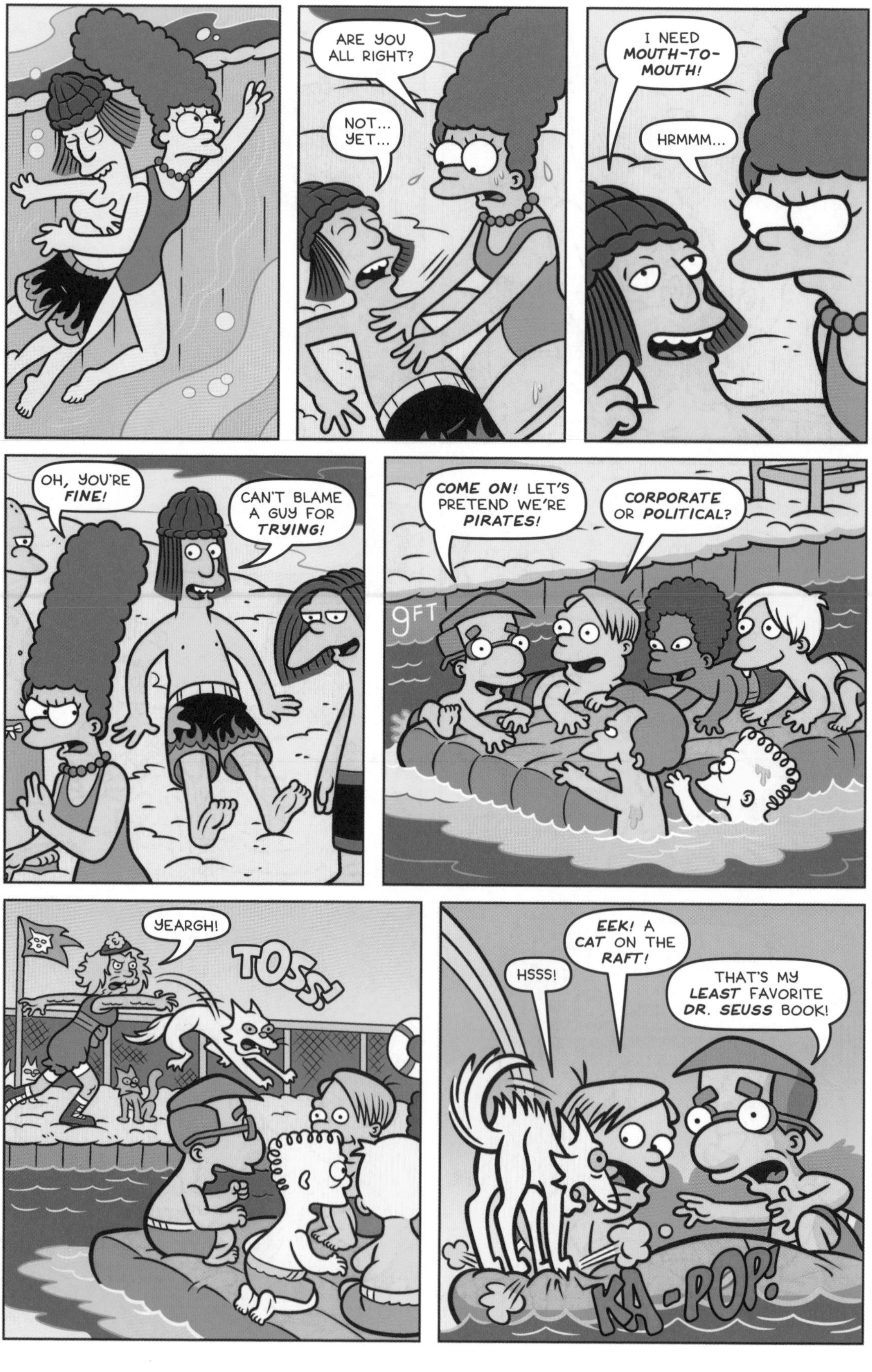
ARE YOU ALL RIGHT?
NOT... YET...
I NEED MOUTH-TO-MOUTH!
HRMMM...
OH, YOU'RE FINE!
CAN'T BLAME A GUY FOR TRYING!
COME ON! LET'S PRETEND WE'RE PIRATES!
CORPORATE OR POLITICAL?
9FT
YEARGH!
TOSS!
HSSS!
EEK! A CAT ON THE RAFT!
THAT'S MY LEAST FAVORITE DR. SEUSS BOOK!
KA-POP!

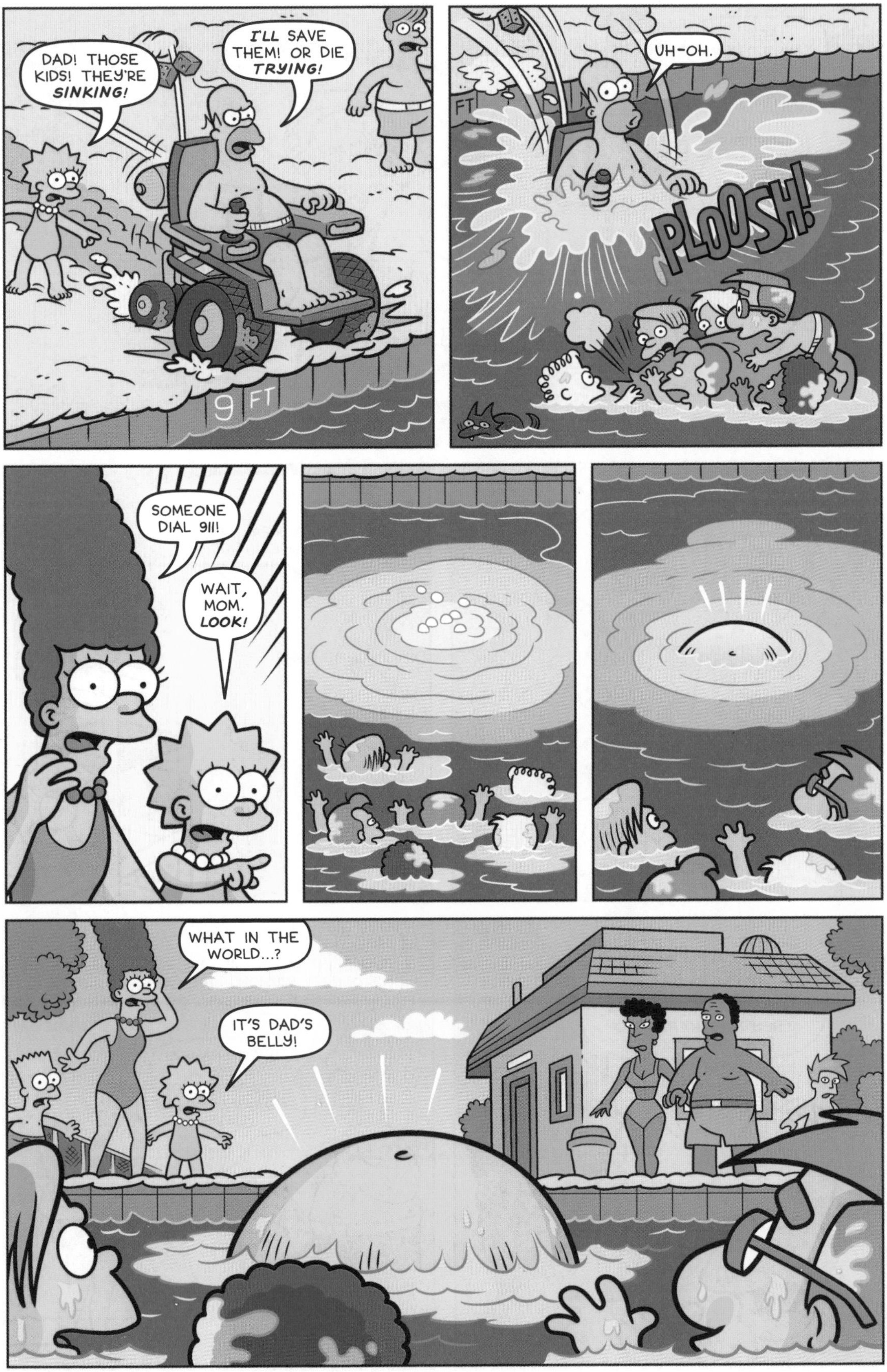
DAD! THOSE KIDS! THEY'RE SINKING!
I'LL SAVE THEM! OR DIE TRYING!
UH-OH.
PLOOSH!
9 FT
SOMEONE DIAL 911!
WAIT, MOM. LOOK!
WHAT IN THE WORLD...?
IT'S DAD'S BELLY!

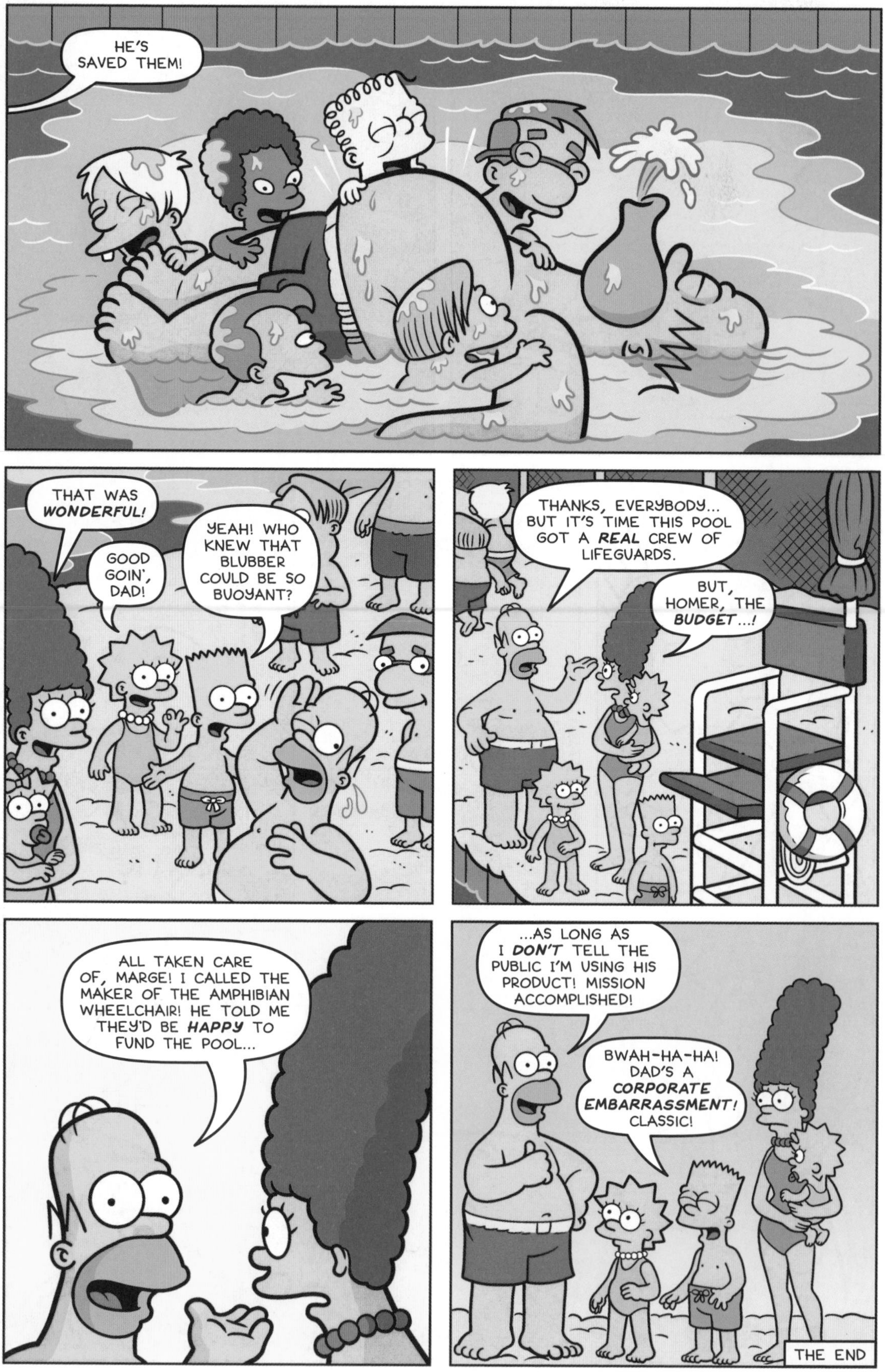
HE'S SAVED THEM!
THAT WAS WONDERFUL!
GOOD GOIN', DAD!
YEAH! WHO KNEW THAT BLUBBER COULD BE SO BUOYANT?
THANKS, EVERYBODY... BUT IT'S TIME THIS POOL GOT A REAL CREW OF LIFEGUARDS.
BUT, HOMER, THE BUDGET...!
ALL TAKEN CARE OF, MARGE! I CALLED THE MAKER OF THE AMPHIBIAN WHEELCHAIR! HE TOLD ME THEY'D BE HAPPY TO FUND THE POOL...
...AS LONG AS I DON'T TELL THE PUBLIC I'M USING HIS PRODUCT! MISSION ACCOMPLISHED!
BWAH-HA-HA! DAD'S A CORPORATE EMBARRASSMENT! CLASSIC!
THE END

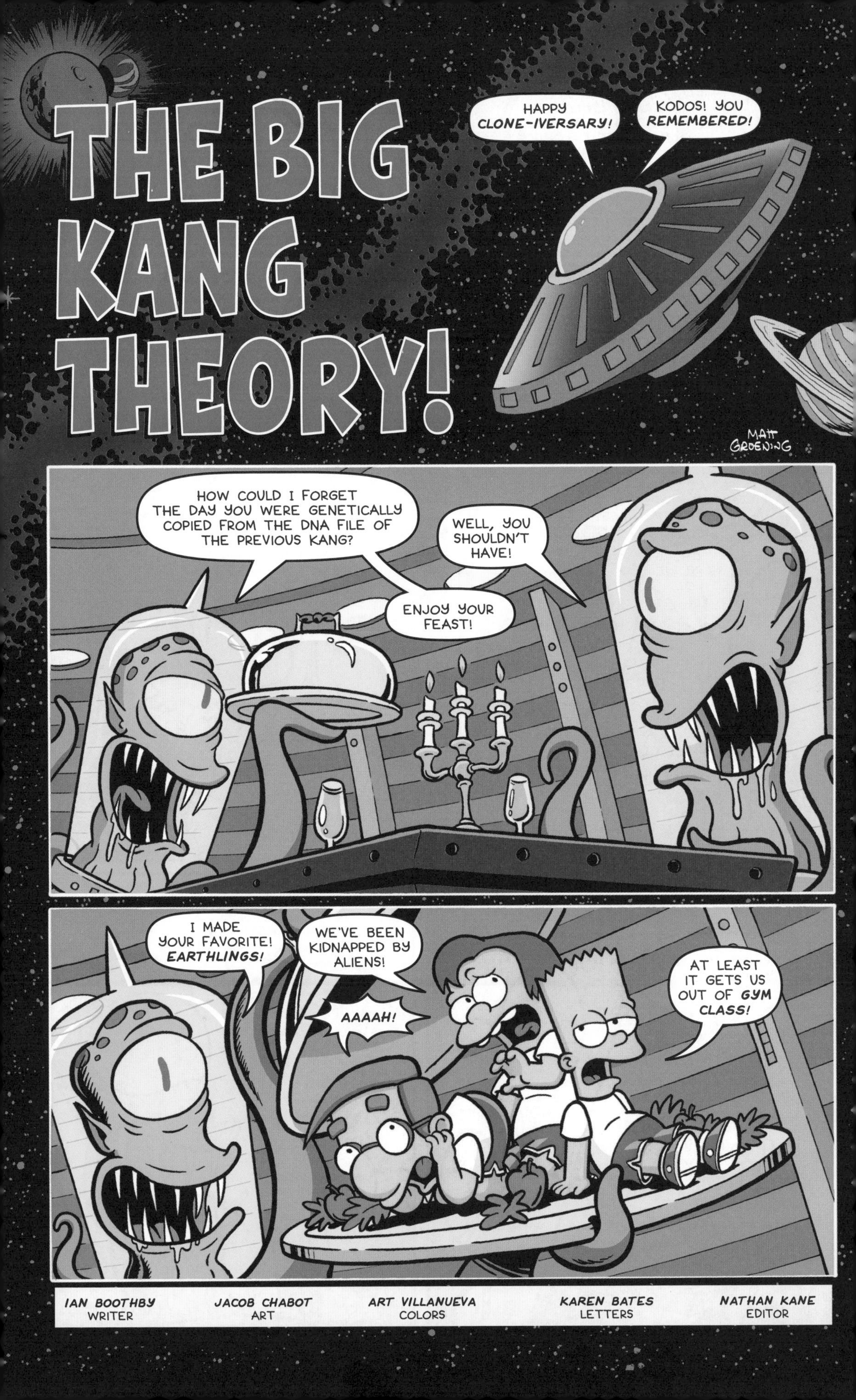
THE BIG KANG THEORY!
HAPPY CLONE-IVERSARY!
KODOS! YOU REMEMBERED!
MATT GROENING
HOW COULD I FORGET THE DAY YOU WERE GENETICALLY COPIED FROM THE DNA FILE OF THE PREVIOUS KANG?
WELL, YOU SHOULDN'T HAVE!
ENJOY YOUR FEAST!
I MADE YOUR FAVORITE! EARTHLINGS!
WE'VE BEEN KIDNAPPED BY ALIENS!
AAAAH!
AT LEAST IT GETS US OUT OF GYM CLASS!
IAN BOOTHBY WRITER
JACOB CHABOT ART
ART VILLANUEVA COLORS
KAREN BATES LETTERS
NATHAN KANE EDITOR

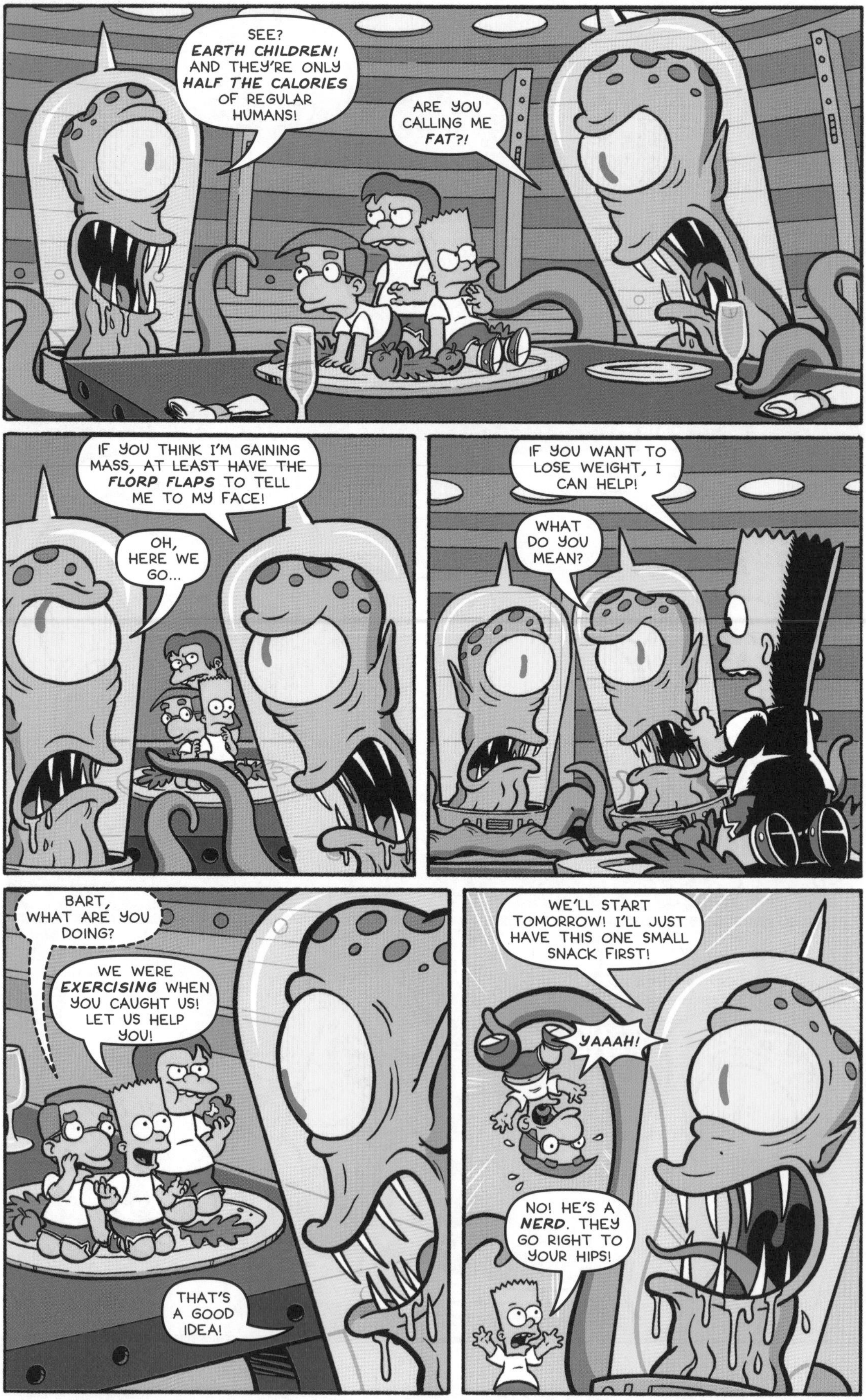
SEE? EARTH CHILDREN! AND THEY'RE ONLY HALF THE CALORIES OF REGULAR HUMANS!
ARE YOU CALLING ME FAT?!
IF YOU THINK I'M GAINING MASS, AT LEAST HAVE THE FLORP FLAPS TO TELL ME TO MY FACE!
OH, HERE WE GO...
IF YOU WANT TO LOSE WEIGHT, I CAN HELP!
WHAT DO YOU MEAN?
BART, WHAT ARE YOU DOING?
WE WERE EXERCISING WHEN YOU CAUGHT US! LET US HELP YOU!
THAT'S A GOOD IDEA!
WE'LL START TOMORROW! I'LL JUST HAVE THIS ONE SMALL SNACK FIRST!
YAAAH!
NO! HE'S A NERD. THEY GO RIGHT TO YOUR HIPS!

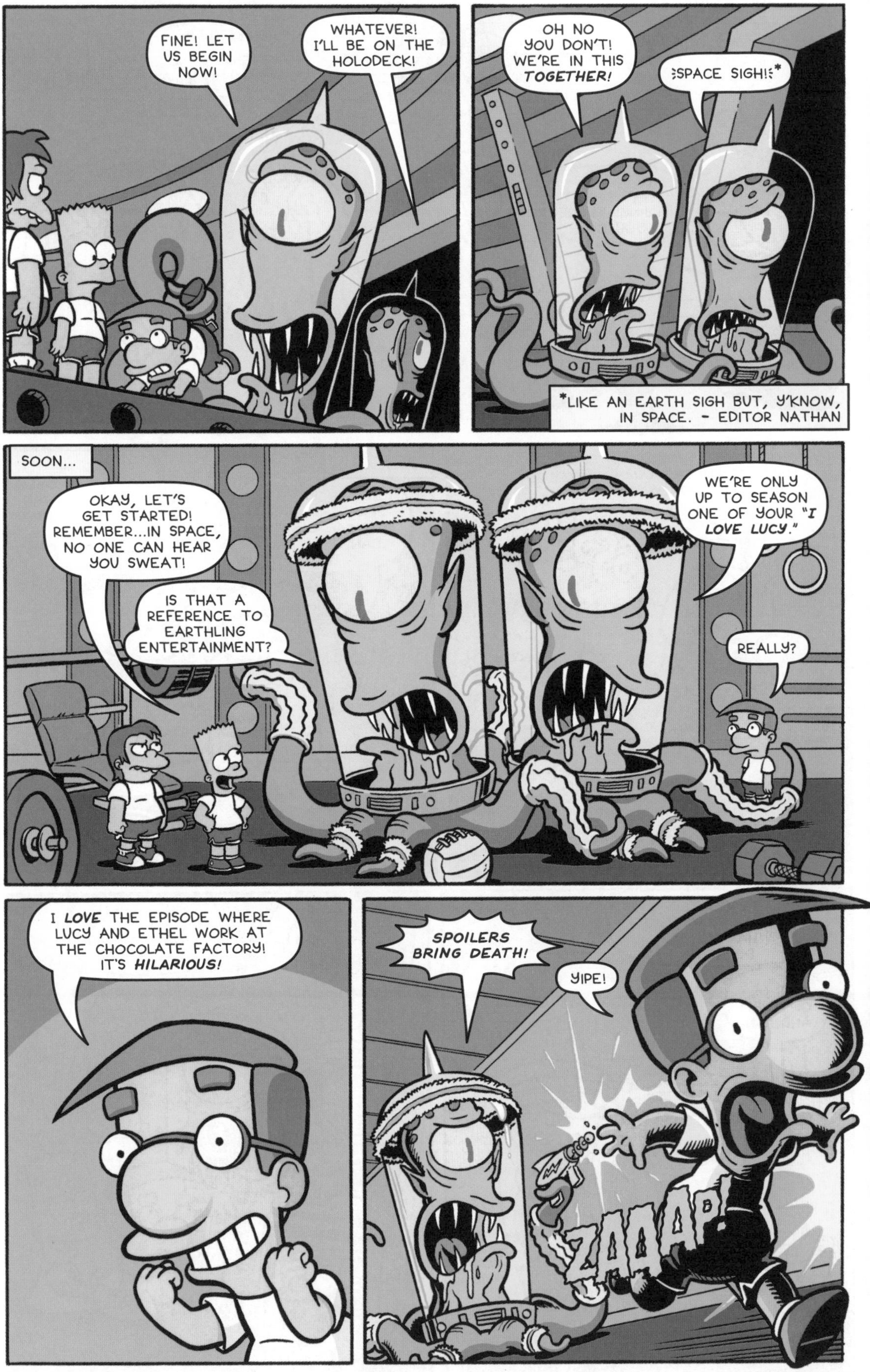
FINE! LET US BEGIN NOW!
WHATEVER! I'LL BE ON THE HOLODECK!
OH NO YOU DON'T! WE'RE IN THIS *TOGETHER*!
SPACE SIGH!*
*LIKE AN EARTH SIGH BUT, Y'KNOW, IN SPACE. - EDITOR NATHAN
SOON...
OKAY, LET'S GET STARTED! REMEMBER...IN SPACE, NO ONE CAN HEAR YOU SWEAT!
IS THAT A REFERENCE TO EARTHLING ENTERTAINMENT?
WE'RE ONLY UP TO SEASON ONE OF YOUR "*I LOVE LUCY*."
REALLY?
I *LOVE* THE EPISODE WHERE LUCY AND ETHEL WORK AT THE CHOCOLATE FACTORY! IT'S *HILARIOUS!*
SPOILERS BRING DEATH!
YIPE!
ZAAAP!

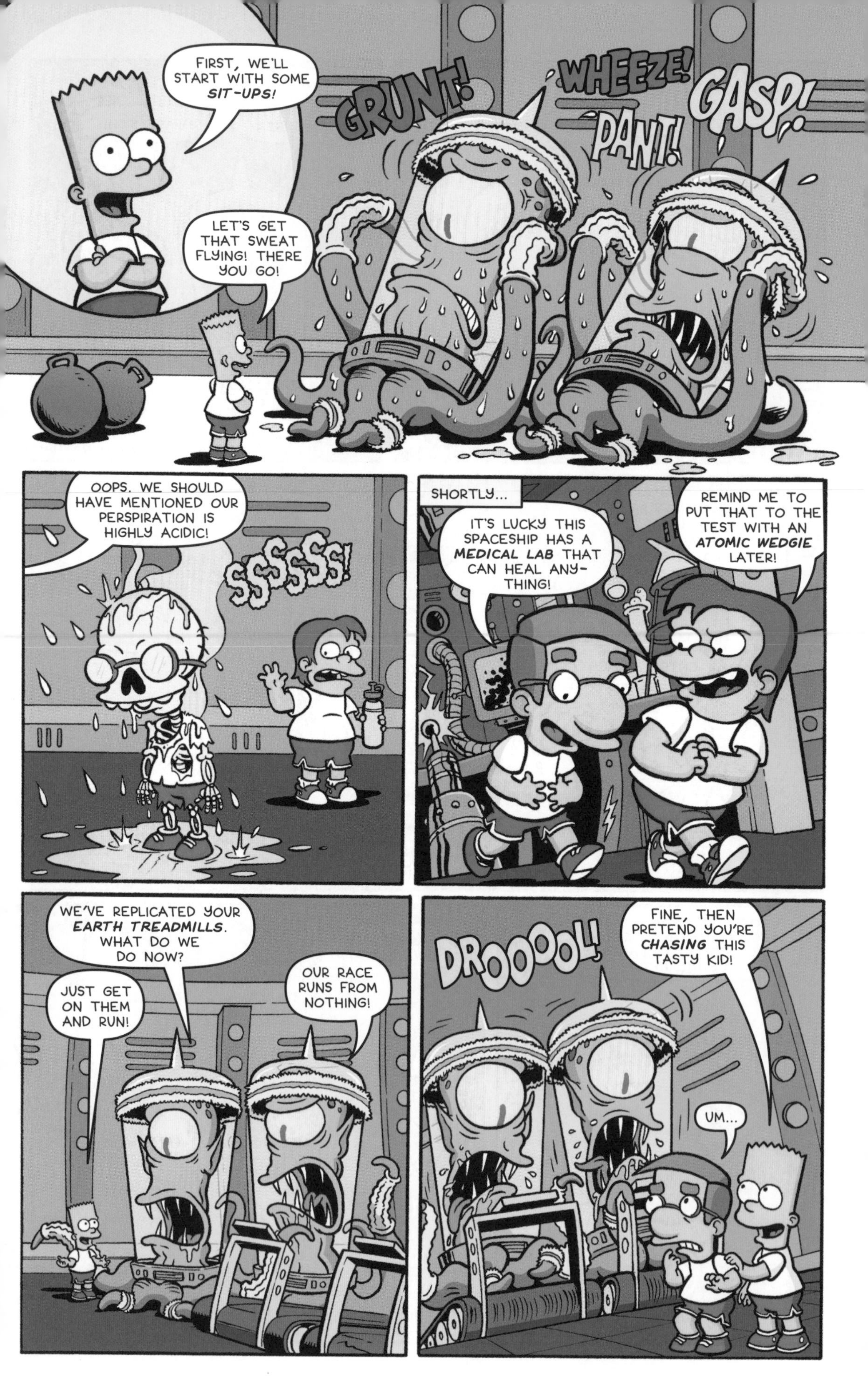

FIRST, WE'LL START WITH SOME SIT-UPS!
GRUNT!
WHEEZE!
PANT!
GASP!
LET'S GET THAT SWEAT FLYING! THERE YOU GO!
OOPS. WE SHOULD HAVE MENTIONED OUR PERSPIRATION IS HIGHLY ACIDIC!
SSSSSS!
SHORTLY...
IT'S LUCKY THIS SPACESHIP HAS A MEDICAL LAB THAT CAN HEAL ANY-THING!
REMIND ME TO PUT THAT TO THE TEST WITH AN ATOMIC WEDGIE LATER!
WE'VE REPLICATED YOUR EARTH TREADMILLS. WHAT DO WE DO NOW?
JUST GET ON THEM AND RUN!
OUR RACE RUNS FROM NOTHING!
DROOOOL!
FINE, THEN PRETEND YOU'RE CHASING THIS TASTY KID!
UM...

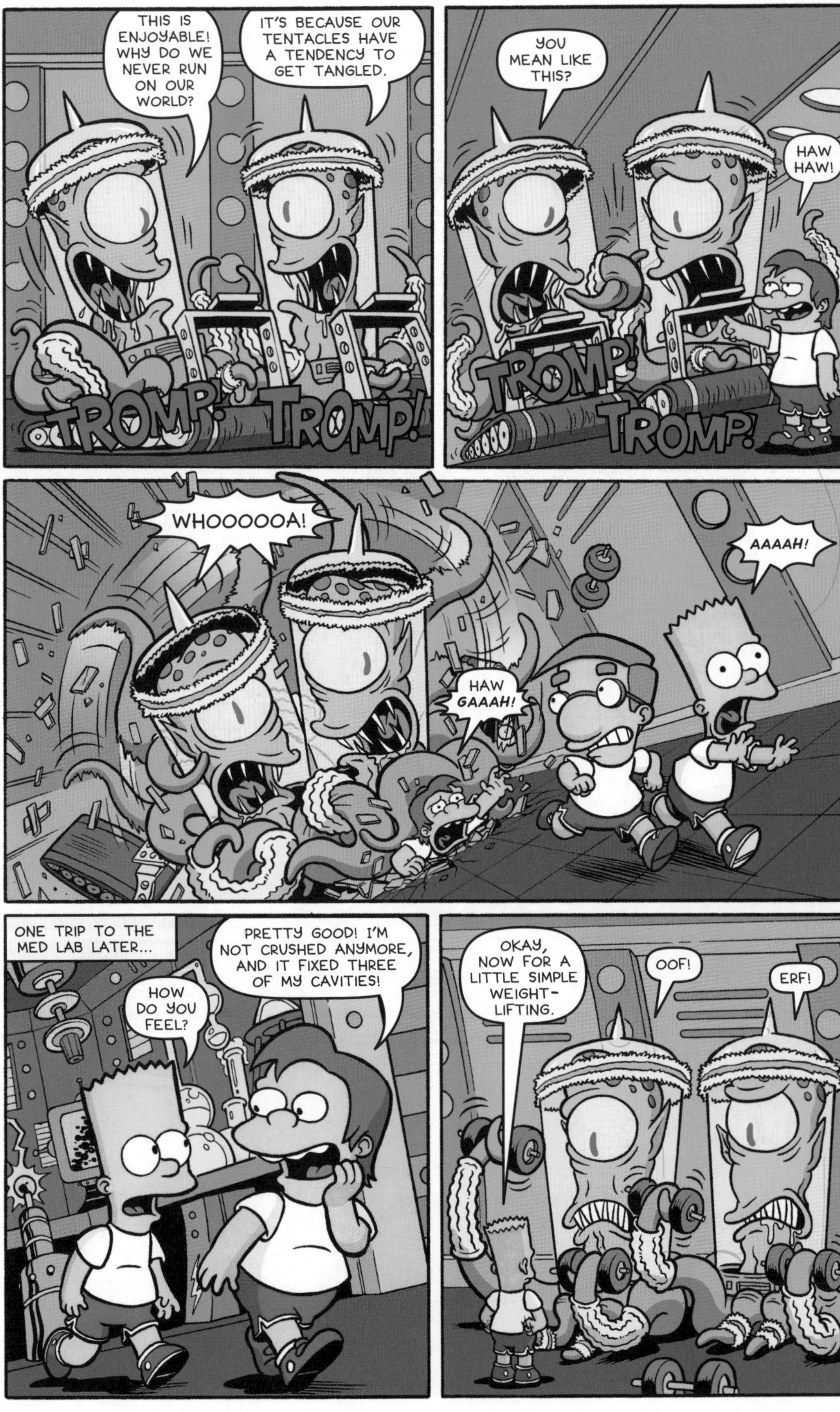
THIS IS ENJOYABLE! WHY DO WE NEVER RUN ON OUR WORLD?
IT'S BECAUSE OUR TENTACLES HAVE A TENDENCY TO GET TANGLED.
TROMP! TROMP!
YOU MEAN LIKE THIS?
HAW HAW!
TROMP! TROMP!
WHOOOOOA!
AAAAH!
HAW GAAAH!
ONE TRIP TO THE MED LAB LATER...
HOW DO YOU FEEL?
PRETTY GOOD! I'M NOT CRUSHED ANYMORE, AND IT FIXED THREE OF MY CAVITIES!
OKAY, NOW FOR A LITTLE SIMPLE WEIGHT-LIFTING.
OOF!
ERF!

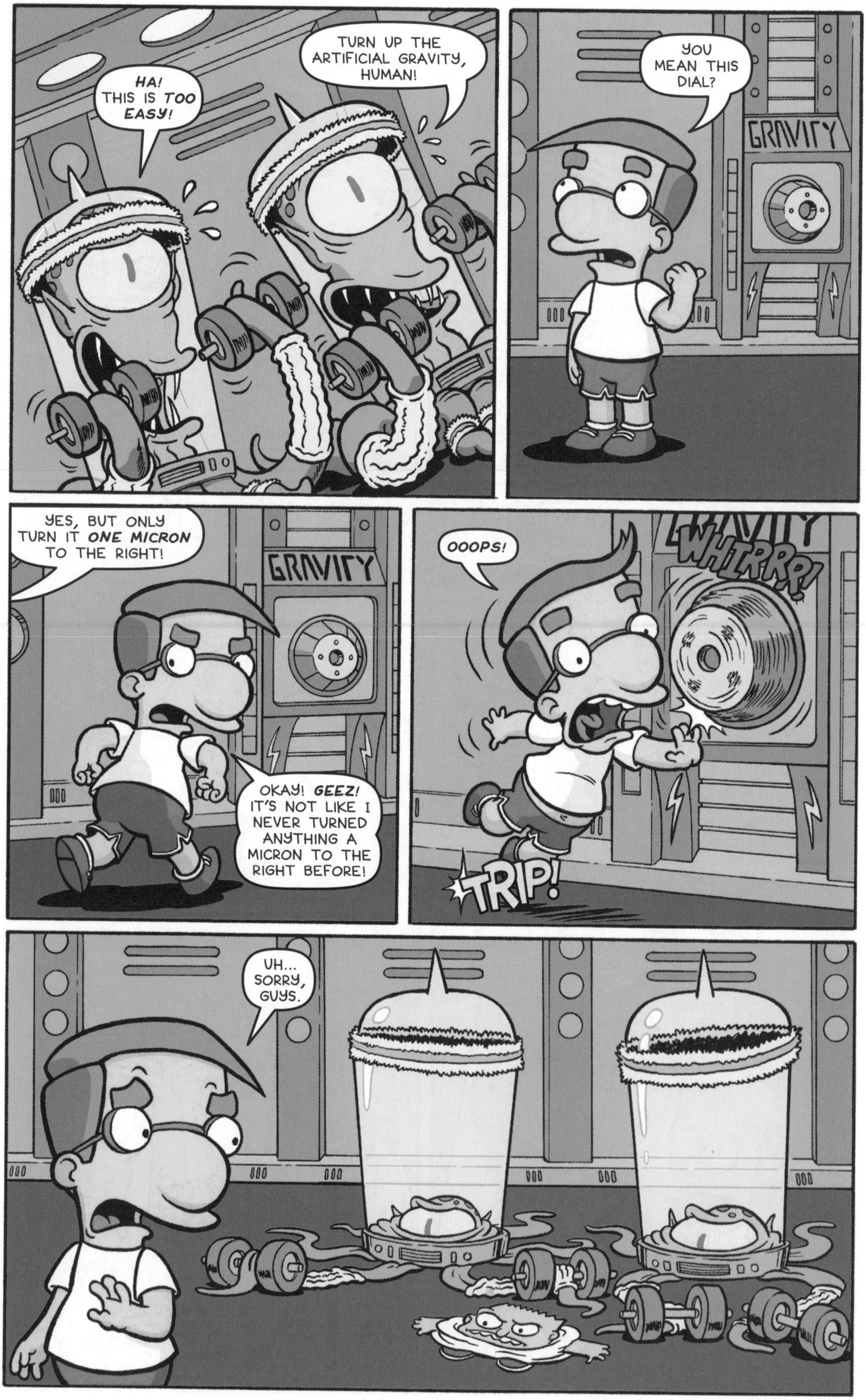

HA! THIS IS TOO EASY!
TURN UP THE ARTIFICIAL GRAVITY, HUMAN!
YOU MEAN THIS DIAL?
GRAVITY
YES, BUT ONLY TURN IT ONE MICRON TO THE RIGHT!
GRAVITY
OKAY! GEEZ! IT'S NOT LIKE I NEVER TURNED ANYTHING A MICRON TO THE RIGHT BEFORE!
OOOPS!
WHIRRR!
TRIP!
UH... SORRY, GUYS.

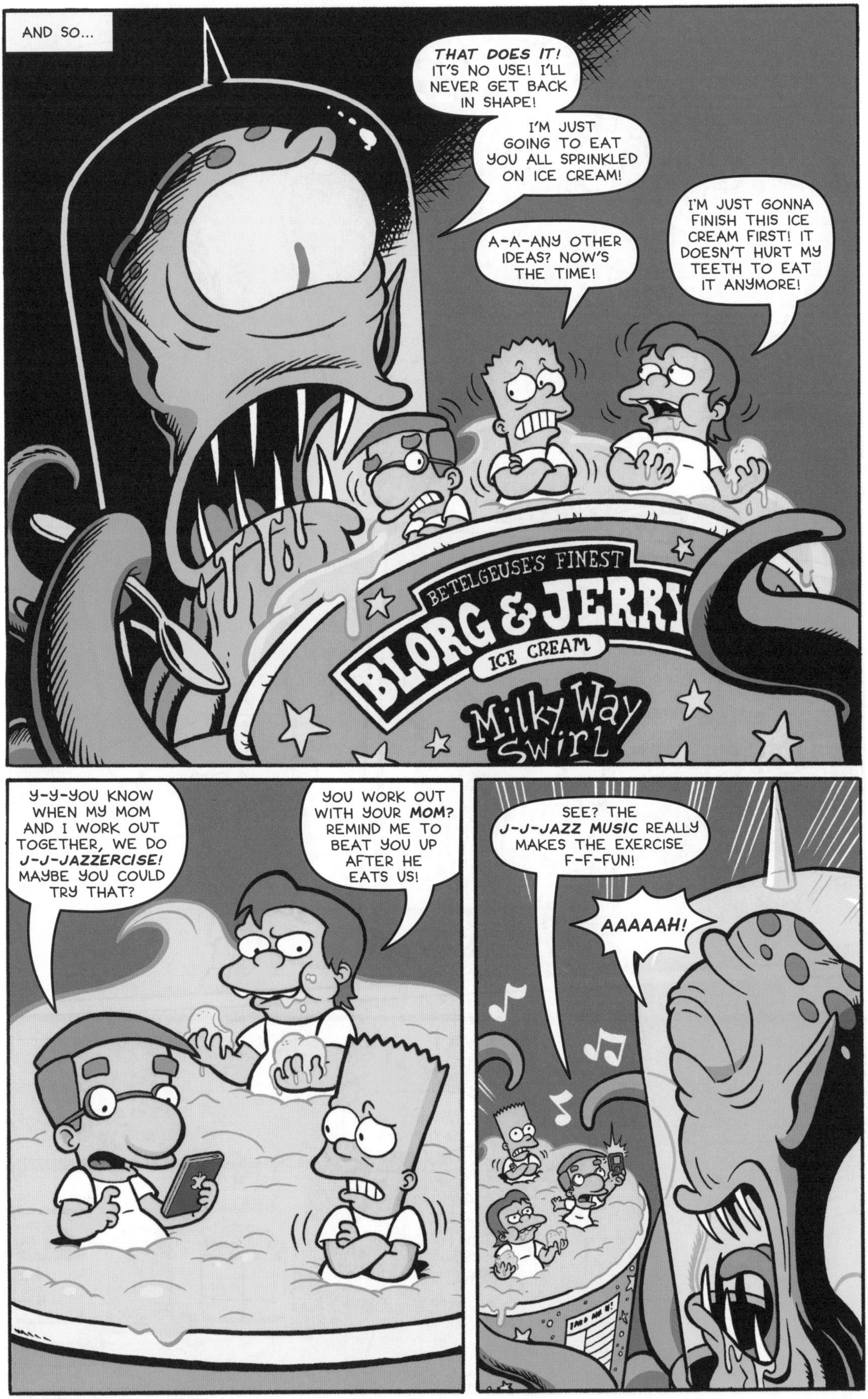
AND SO...
THAT DOES IT! IT'S NO USE! I'LL NEVER GET BACK IN SHAPE!
I'M JUST GOING TO EAT YOU ALL SPRINKLED ON ICE CREAM!
A-A-ANY OTHER IDEAS? NOW'S THE TIME!
I'M JUST GONNA FINISH THIS ICE CREAM FIRST! IT DOESN'T HURT MY TEETH TO EAT IT ANYMORE!
BETELGEUSE'S FINEST
BLORG & JERRY
ICE CREAM
Milky Way Swirl
Y-Y-YOU KNOW WHEN MY MOM AND I WORK OUT TOGETHER, WE DO J-J-JAZZERCISE! MAYBE YOU COULD TRY THAT?
YOU WORK OUT WITH YOUR MOM? REMIND ME TO BEAT YOU UP AFTER HE EATS US!
SEE? THE J-J-JAZZ MUSIC REALLY MAKES THE EXERCISE F-F-FUN!
AAAAAH!

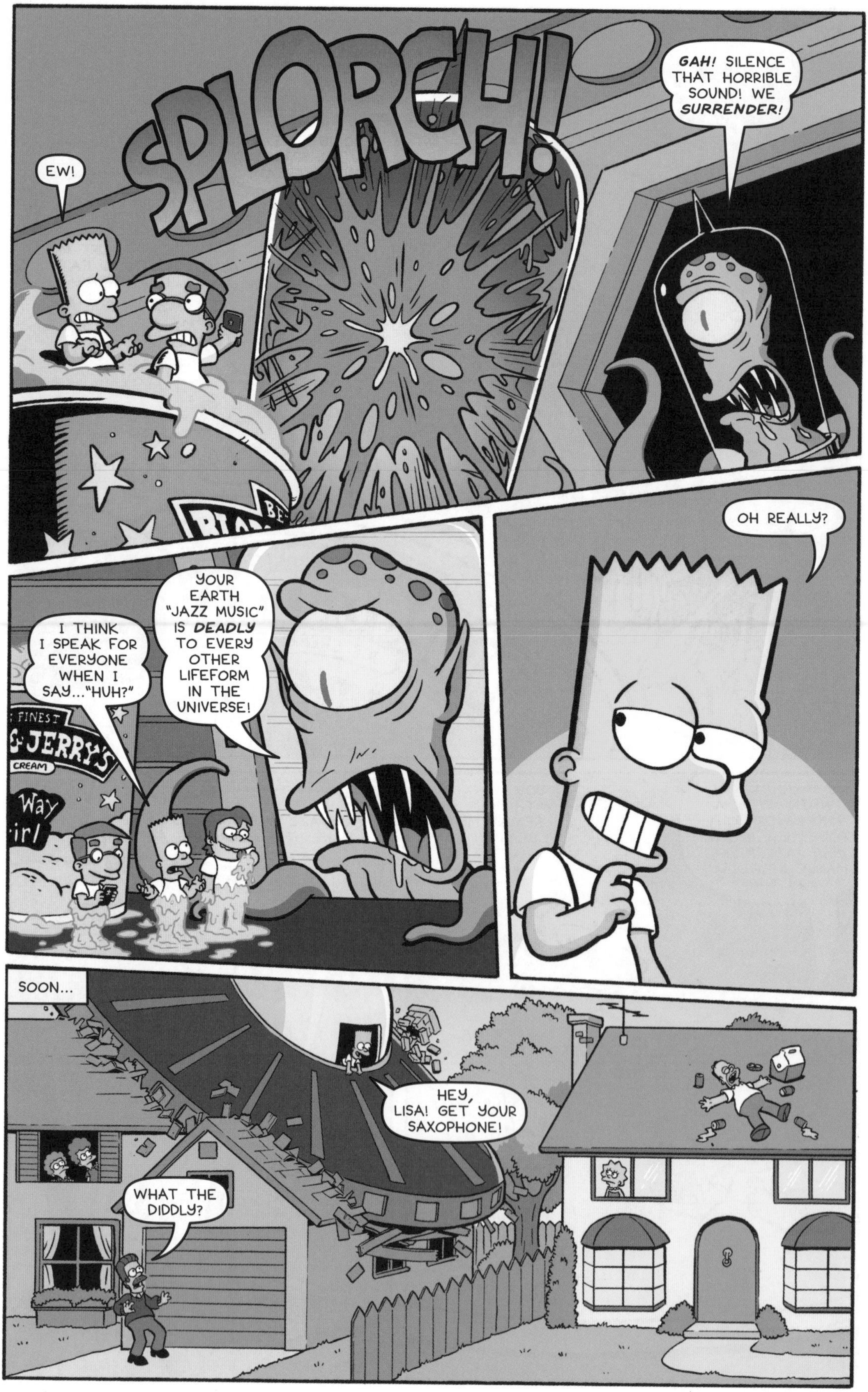
SPLORCH!
EW!
GAH! SILENCE THAT HORRIBLE SOUND! WE SURRENDER!
FINEST
-JERRY'S
CREAM
Way
irl
I THINK I SPEAK FOR EVERYONE WHEN I SAY..."HUH?"
YOUR EARTH "JAZZ MUSIC" IS DEADLY TO EVERY OTHER LIFEFORM IN THE UNIVERSE!
OH REALLY?
SOON...
HEY, LISA! GET YOUR SAXOPHONE!
WHAT THE DIDDLY?

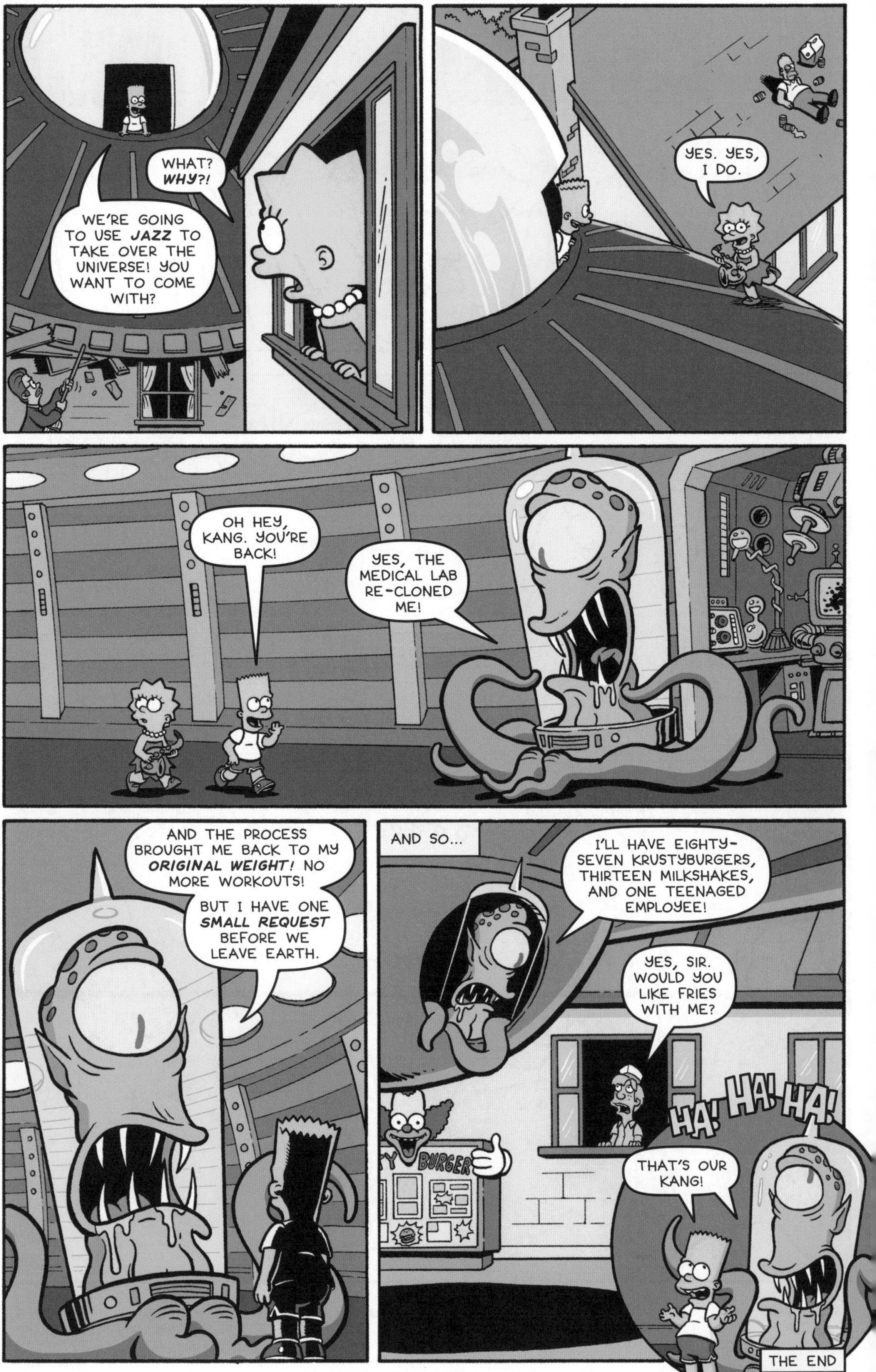

WHAT? **WHY**?!
WE'RE GOING TO USE **JAZZ** TO TAKE OVER THE UNIVERSE! YOU WANT TO COME WITH?
YES. YES, I DO.
OH HEY, KANG. YOU'RE BACK!
YES, THE MEDICAL LAB RE-CLONED ME!
AND THE PROCESS BROUGHT ME BACK TO MY **ORIGINAL WEIGHT**! NO MORE WORKOUTS!
BUT I HAVE ONE **SMALL REQUEST** BEFORE WE LEAVE EARTH.
AND SO...
I'LL HAVE EIGHTY-SEVEN KRUSTYBURGERS, THIRTEEN MILKSHAKES, AND ONE TEENAGED EMPLOYEE!
YES, SIR. WOULD YOU LIKE FRIES WITH ME?
HA! HA! HA!
THAT'S OUR KANG!
THE END

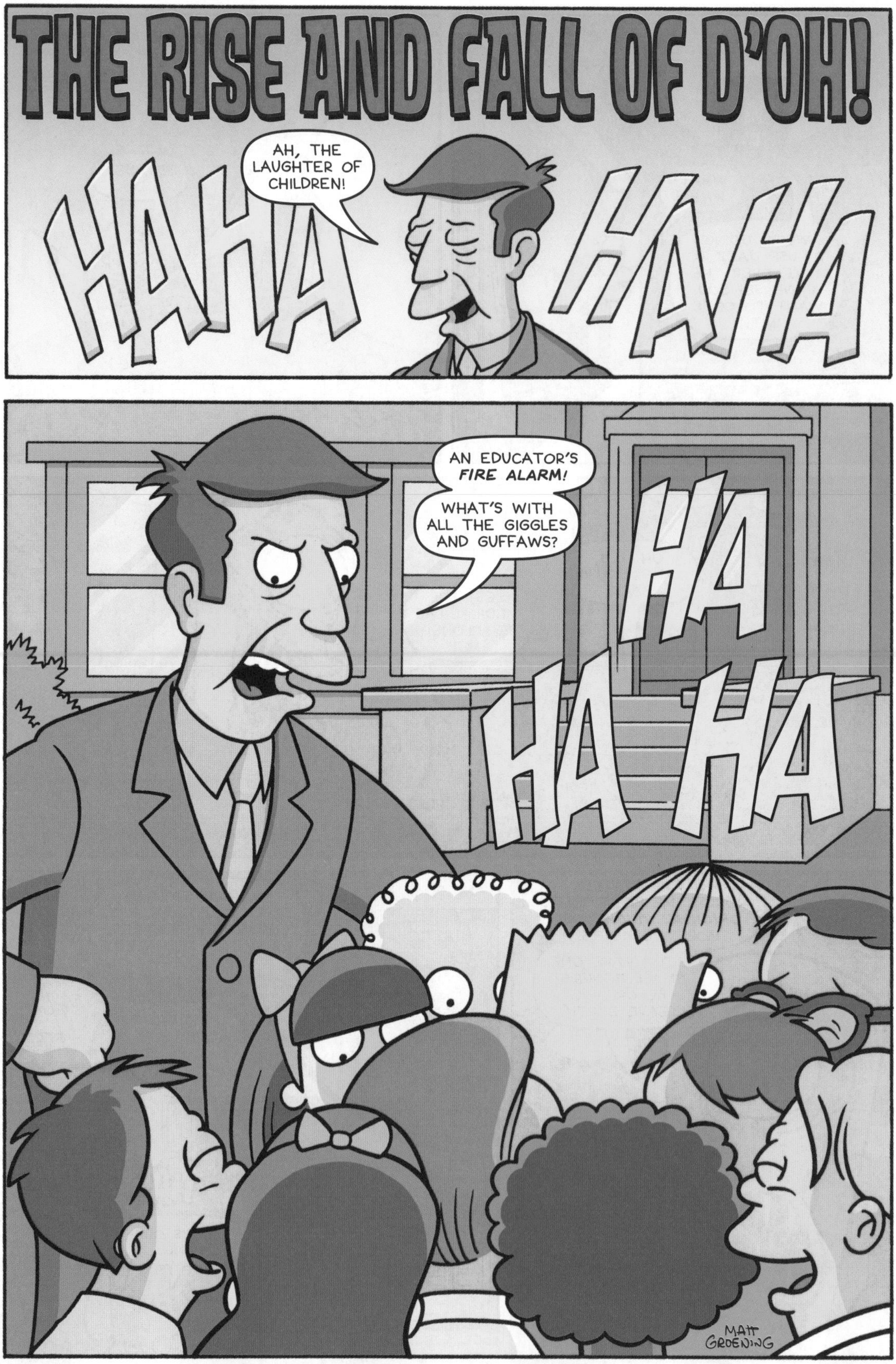
THE RISE AND FALL OF D'OH!
HAHA
AH, THE LAUGHTER OF CHILDREN!
HAHA
AN EDUCATOR'S *FIRE ALARM!*
WHAT'S WITH ALL THE GIGGLES AND GUFFAWS?
HA
HA
HA
MATT GROENING

IAN **BOOTHBY** STORY

JOHN **COSTANZA** PENCILS

PHYLLIS **NOVIN** INKS

ART **VILLANUEVA** COLORS

KAREN **BATES** LETTERS

NATHAN **KANE** EDITOR

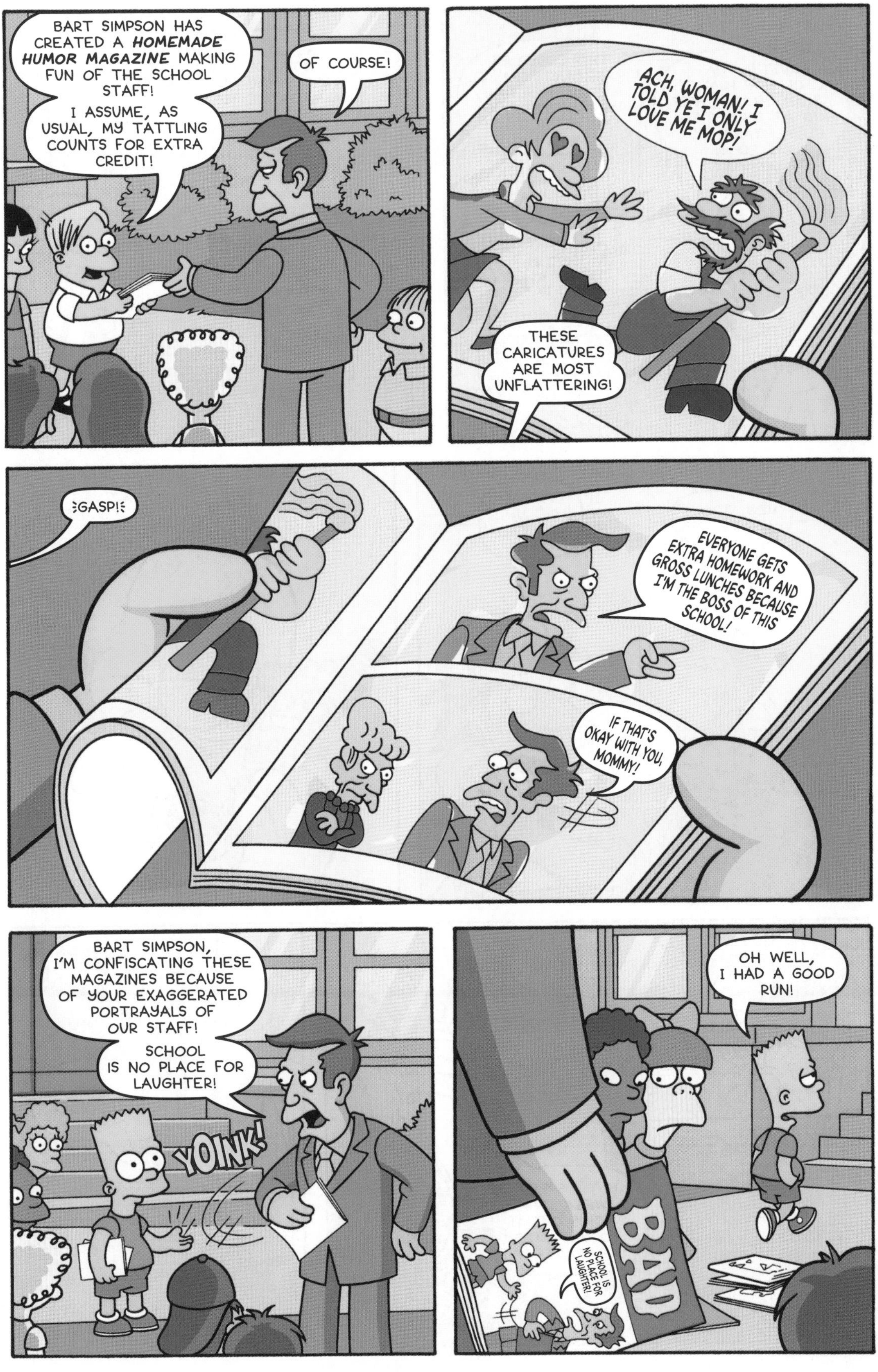
BART SIMPSON HAS CREATED A **HOMEMADE HUMOR MAGAZINE** MAKING FUN OF THE SCHOOL STAFF!
I ASSUME, AS USUAL, MY TATTLING COUNTS FOR EXTRA CREDIT!
OF COURSE!
ACH, WOMAN! I TOLD YE I ONLY LOVE ME MOP!
THESE CARICATURES ARE MOST UNFLATTERING!
GASP!
EVERYONE GETS EXTRA HOMEWORK AND GROSS LUNCHES BECAUSE I'M THE BOSS OF THIS SCHOOL!
IF THAT'S OKAY WITH YOU, MOMMY!
BART SIMPSON, I'M CONFISCATING THESE MAGAZINES BECAUSE OF YOUR EXAGGERATED PORTRAYALS OF OUR STAFF!
SCHOOL IS NO PLACE FOR LAUGHTER!
YOINK!
OH WELL, I HAD A GOOD RUN!
BAD
SCHOOL IS NO PLACE FOR LAUGHTER!

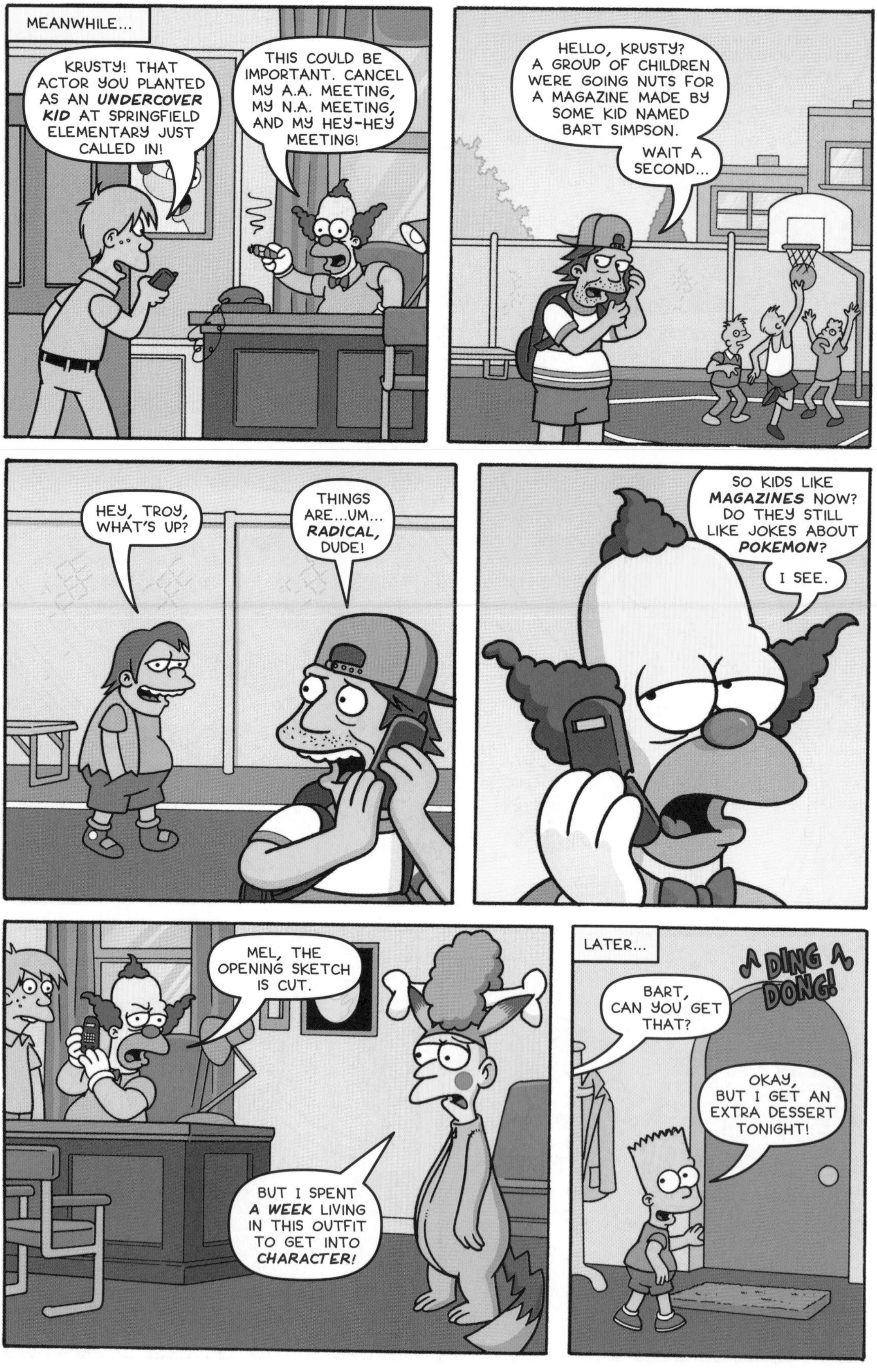
MEANWHILE...
KRUSTY! THAT ACTOR YOU PLANTED AS AN **UNDERCOVER KID** AT SPRINGFIELD ELEMENTARY JUST CALLED IN!
THIS COULD BE IMPORTANT. CANCEL MY A.A. MEETING, MY N.A. MEETING, AND MY HEY-HEY MEETING!
HELLO, KRUSTY? A GROUP OF CHILDREN WERE GOING NUTS FOR A MAGAZINE MADE BY SOME KID NAMED BART SIMPSON.
WAIT A SECOND...
HEY, TROY, WHAT'S UP?
THINGS ARE...UM... **RADICAL,** DUDE!
SO KIDS LIKE **MAGAZINES** NOW? DO THEY STILL LIKE JOKES ABOUT **POKEMON**?
I SEE.
MEL, THE OPENING SKETCH IS CUT.
BUT I SPENT **A WEEK** LIVING IN THIS OUTFIT TO GET INTO **CHARACTER**!
LATER...
DING DONG!
BART, CAN YOU GET THAT?
OKAY, BUT I GET AN EXTRA DESSERT TONIGHT!

KRUSTY!

I KNOW... WHAT AN *AMAZING HONOR* THAT I'M HERE...YOU'RE A HUGE FAN...BLAH, BLAH, BLAH.

LONG STORY SHORT, I'M STEALING YOUR MAGAZINE IDEA, AND I WANT YOU TO WRITE IT!

COOL! BUT WHY DO YOU NEED TO STEAL MY IDEAS? YOU'RE *HILARIOUS!*

I STEAL *EVERY-THING* NOW! I LOST MY CREATIVITY YEARS AGO IN A POKER GAME WITH *BUDDY HACKETT!*

THE ONLY THING WE NEED TO CHANGE IS THE NAME. *BAD MAGAZINE* IS TOO CLOSE TO...

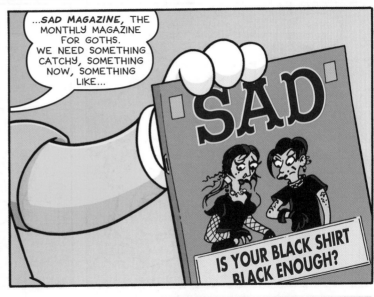

...*SAD MAGAZINE*, THE MONTHLY MAGAZINE FOR GOTHS. WE NEED SOMETHING CATCHY, SOMETHING NOW, SOMETHING LIKE...

SAD

IS YOUR BLACK SHIRT BLACK ENOUGH?

D'OH!

THAT'S IT! *D'OH MAGAZINE!* YOU'RE A *GENIUS!*

I THINK A *REAL* GENIUS WOULD READ THE INSTRUCTIONS FIRST!

NEVER!

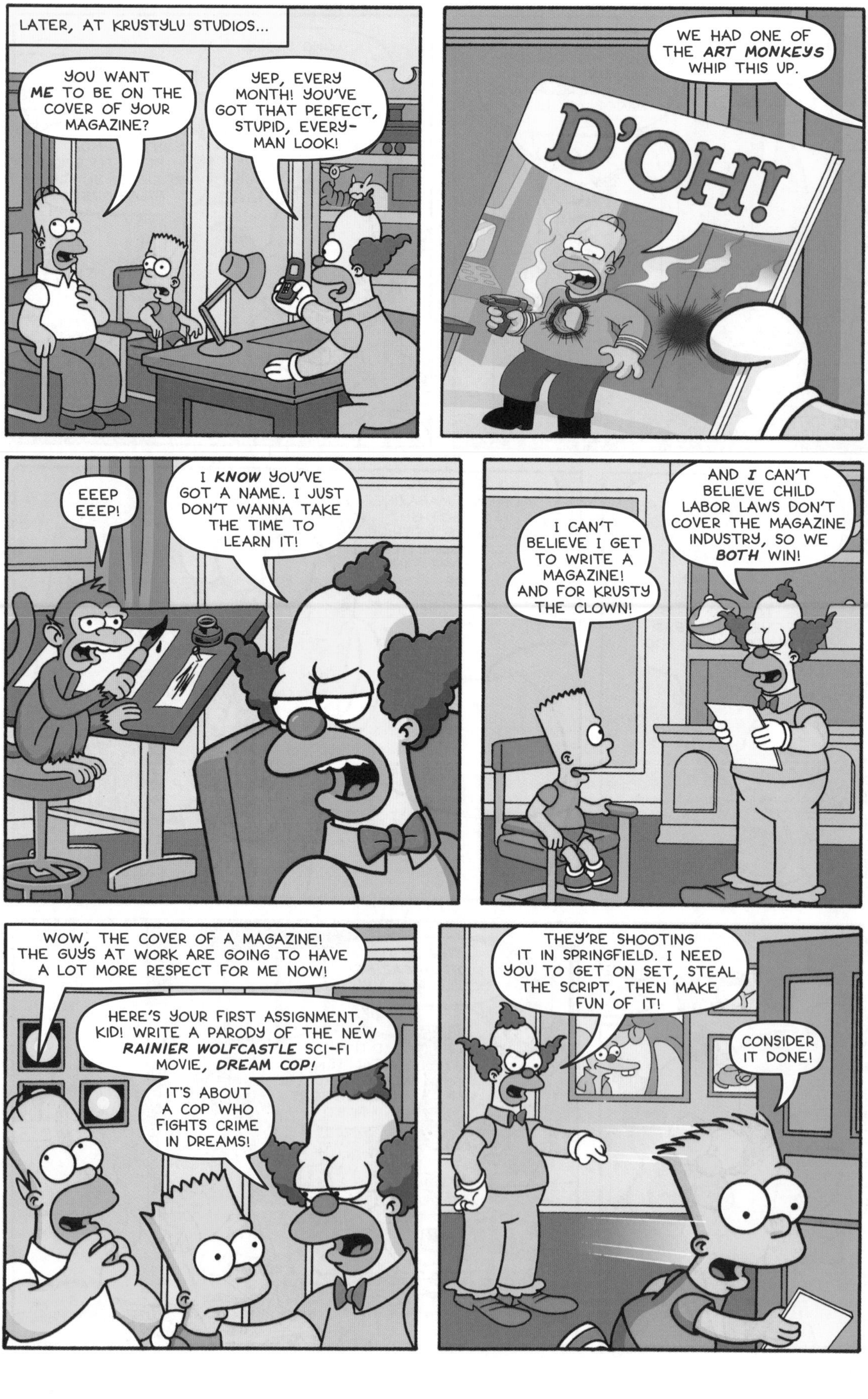
LATER, AT KRUSTYLU STUDIOS...
YOU WANT **ME** TO BE ON THE COVER OF YOUR MAGAZINE?
YEP, EVERY MONTH! YOU'VE GOT THAT PERFECT, STUPID, EVERY-MAN LOOK!
WE HAD ONE OF THE **ART MONKEYS** WHIP THIS UP.
D'OH!
EEEP EEEP!
I **KNOW** YOU'VE GOT A NAME. I JUST DON'T WANNA TAKE THE TIME TO LEARN IT!
I CAN'T BELIEVE I GET TO WRITE A MAGAZINE! AND FOR KRUSTY THE CLOWN!
AND **I** CAN'T BELIEVE CHILD LABOR LAWS DON'T COVER THE MAGAZINE INDUSTRY, SO WE **BOTH** WIN!
WOW, THE COVER OF A MAGAZINE! THE GUYS AT WORK ARE GOING TO HAVE A LOT MORE RESPECT FOR ME NOW!
HERE'S YOUR FIRST ASSIGNMENT, KID! WRITE A PARODY OF THE NEW **RAINIER WOLFCASTLE** SCI-FI MOVIE, **DREAM COP!**
IT'S ABOUT A COP WHO FIGHTS CRIME IN DREAMS!
THEY'RE SHOOTING IT IN SPRINGFIELD. I NEED YOU TO GET ON SET, STEAL THE SCRIPT, THEN MAKE FUN OF IT!
CONSIDER IT DONE!

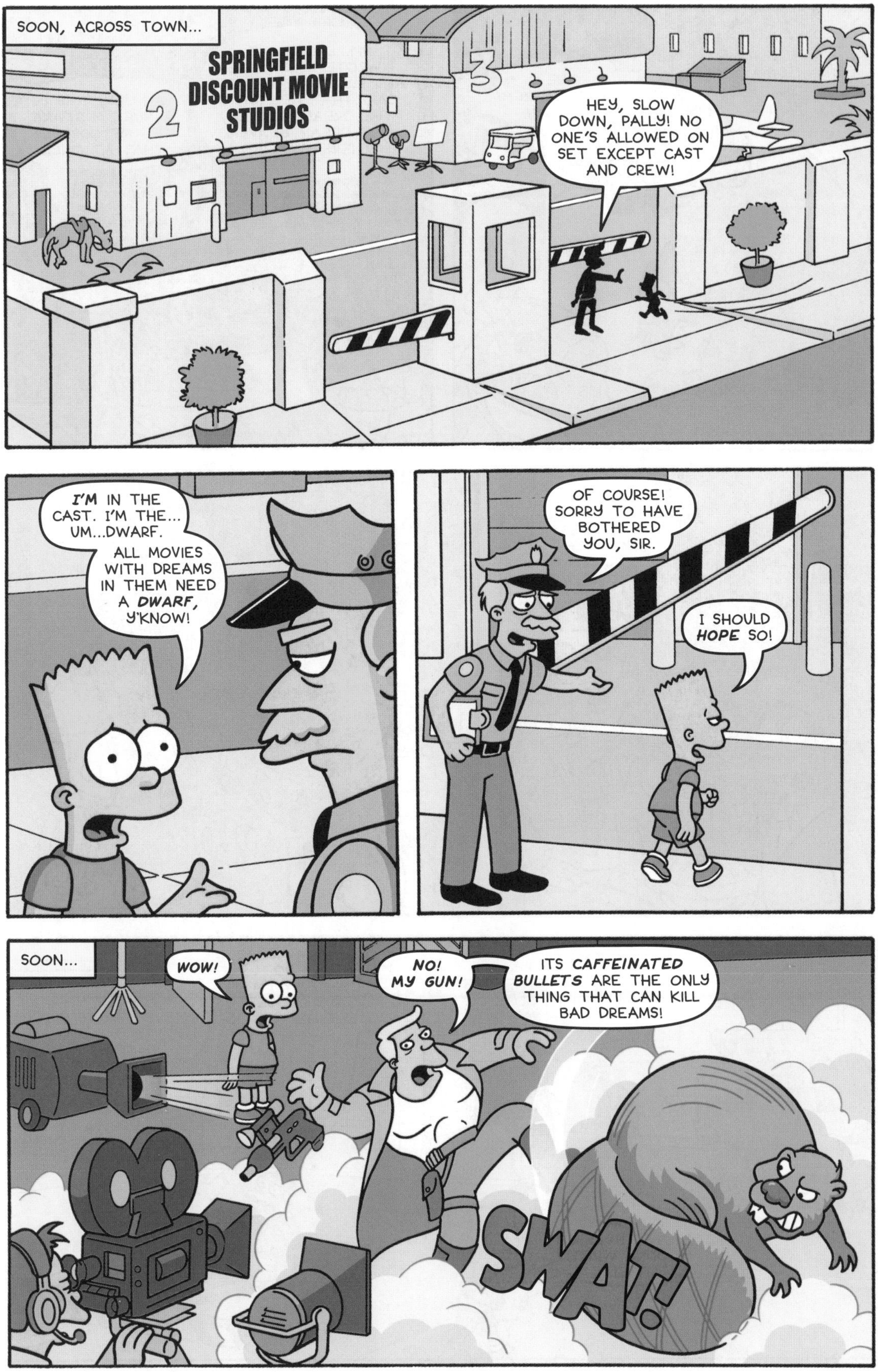
SOON, ACROSS TOWN...
SPRINGFIELD DISCOUNT MOVIE STUDIOS
HEY, SLOW DOWN, PALLY! NO ONE'S ALLOWED ON SET EXCEPT CAST AND CREW!
I'M IN THE CAST. I'M THE... UM...DWARF.
ALL MOVIES WITH DREAMS IN THEM NEED A DWARF, Y'KNOW!
OF COURSE! SORRY TO HAVE BOTHERED YOU, SIR.
I SHOULD HOPE SO!
SOON...
WOW!
NO! MY GUN!
ITS CAFFEINATED BULLETS ARE THE ONLY THING THAT CAN KILL BAD DREAMS!
SWAT!

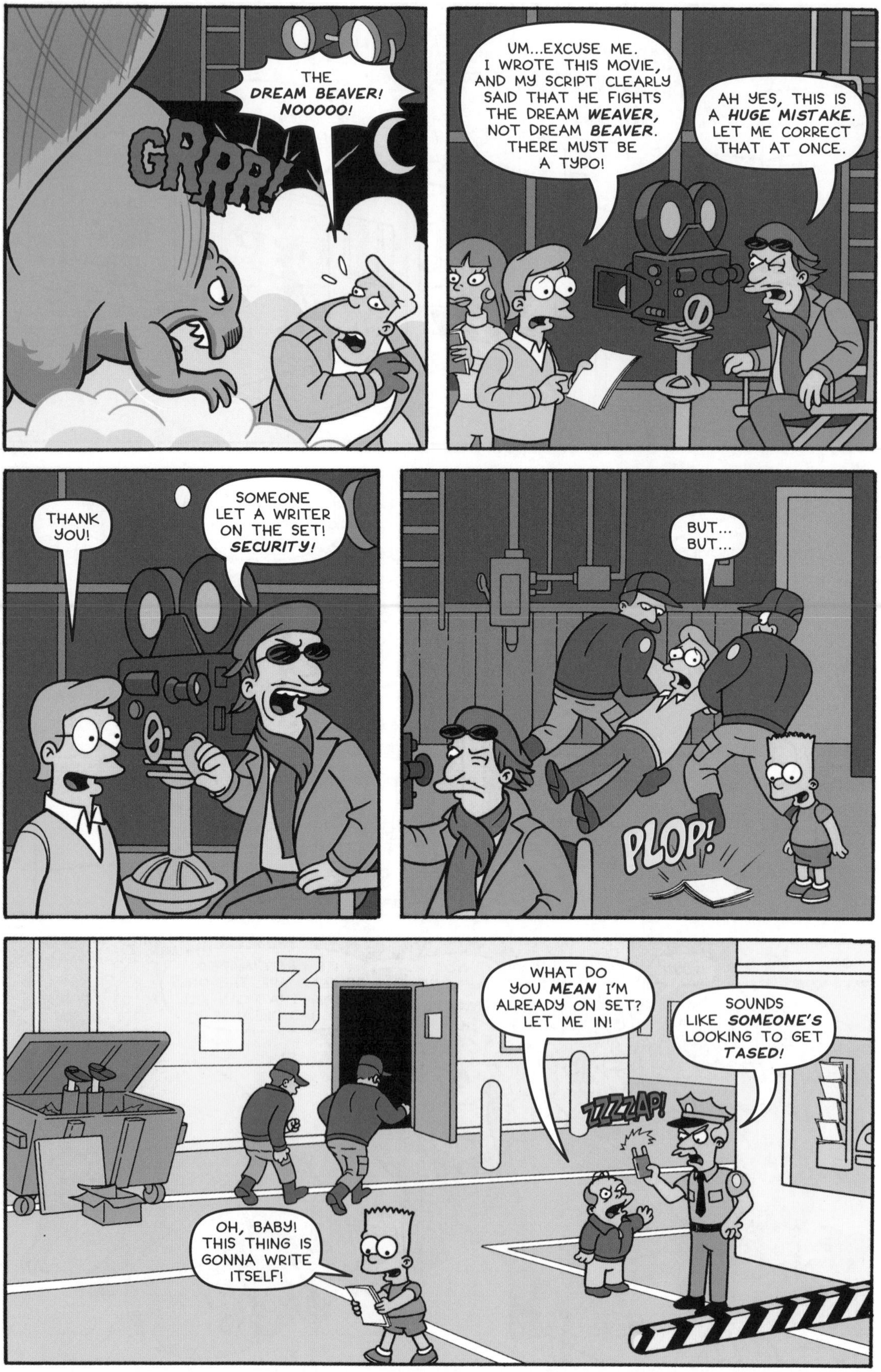

THE DREAM BEAVER! NOOOOO!
GRRR!
UM...EXCUSE ME. I WROTE THIS MOVIE, AND MY SCRIPT CLEARLY SAID THAT HE FIGHTS THE DREAM WEAVER, NOT DREAM BEAVER. THERE MUST BE A TYPO!
AH YES, THIS IS A HUGE MISTAKE. LET ME CORRECT THAT AT ONCE.
THANK YOU!
SOMEONE LET A WRITER ON THE SET! SECURITY!
BUT... BUT...
PLOP!
3
WHAT DO YOU MEAN I'M ALREADY ON SET? LET ME IN!
SOUNDS LIKE SOMEONE'S LOOKING TO GET TASED!
ZZZZAP!
OH, BABY! THIS THING IS GONNA WRITE ITSELF!

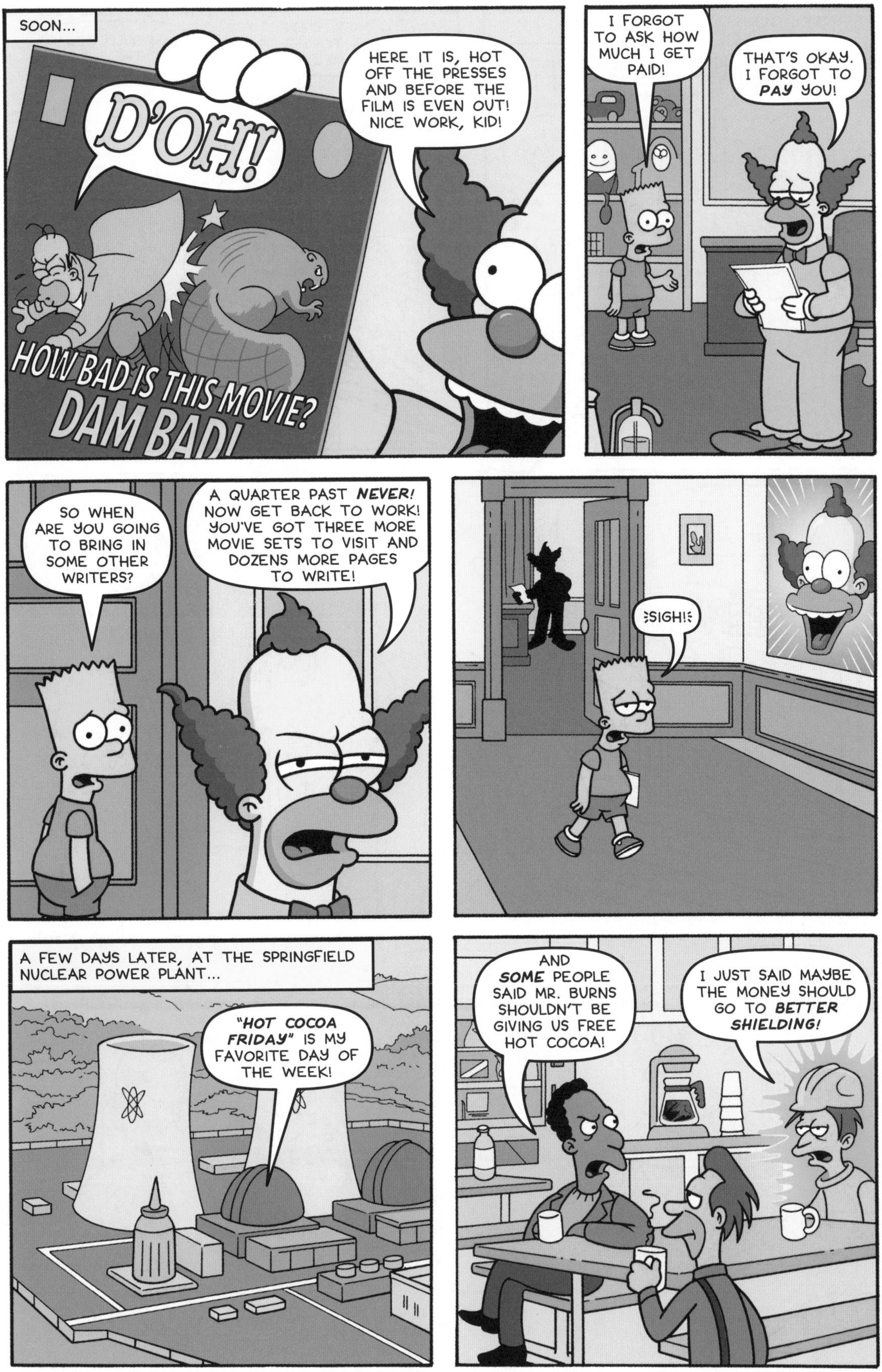
SOON...
D'OH!
HOW BAD IS THIS MOVIE? DAM BAD!
HERE IT IS, HOT OFF THE PRESSES AND BEFORE THE FILM IS EVEN OUT! NICE WORK, KID!
I FORGOT TO ASK HOW MUCH I GET PAID!
THAT'S OKAY. I FORGOT TO PAY YOU!
SO WHEN ARE YOU GOING TO BRING IN SOME OTHER WRITERS?
A QUARTER PAST NEVER! NOW GET BACK TO WORK! YOU'VE GOT THREE MORE MOVIE SETS TO VISIT AND DOZENS MORE PAGES TO WRITE!
SIGH!
A FEW DAYS LATER, AT THE SPRINGFIELD NUCLEAR POWER PLANT...
"HOT COCOA FRIDAY" IS MY FAVORITE DAY OF THE WEEK!
AND SOME PEOPLE SAID MR. BURNS SHOULDN'T BE GIVING US FREE HOT COCOA!
I JUST SAID MAYBE THE MONEY SHOULD GO TO BETTER SHIELDING!

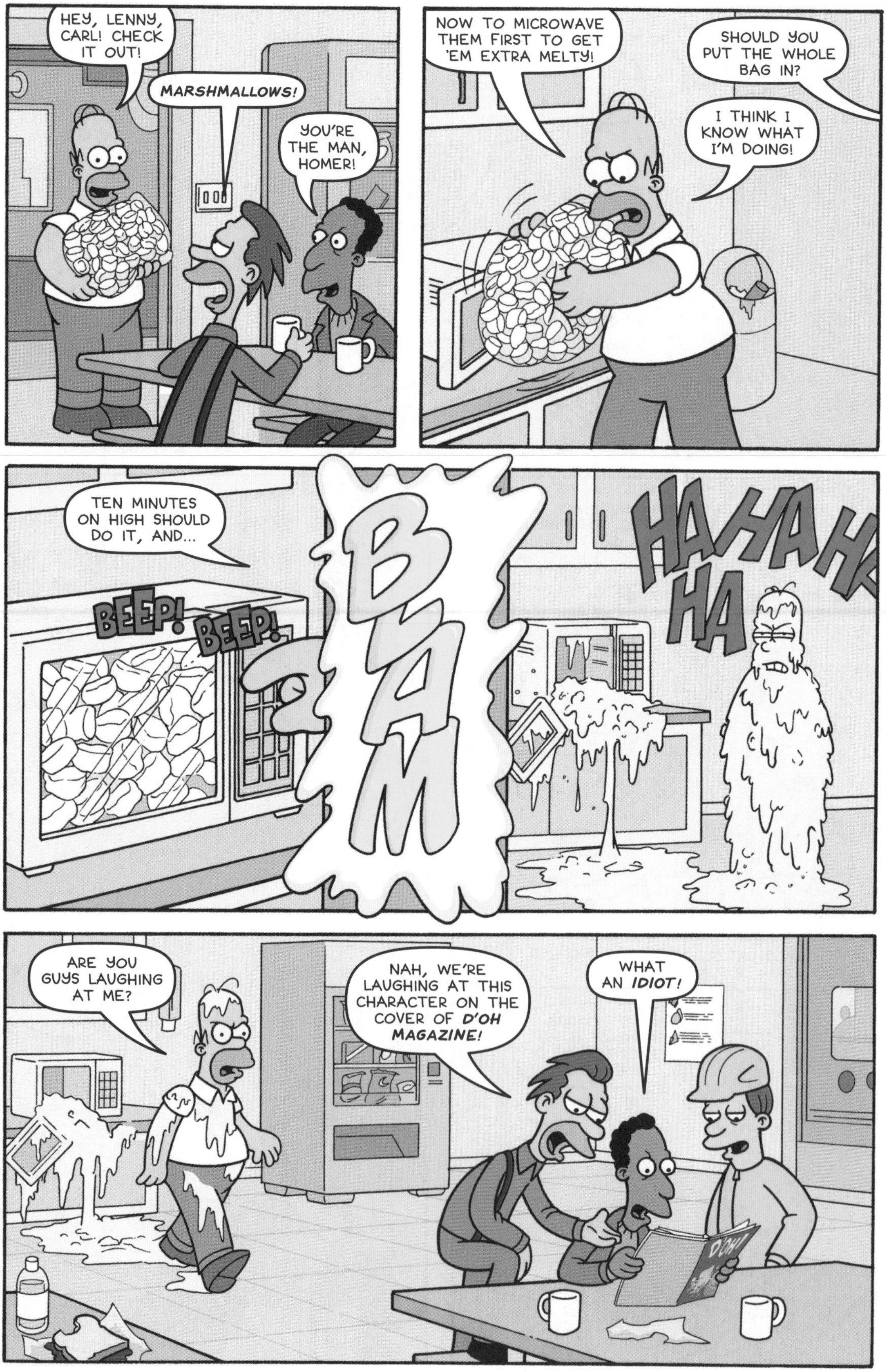
HEY, LENNY, CARL! CHECK IT OUT!
MARSHMALLOWS!
YOU'RE THE MAN, HOMER!
NOW TO MICROWAVE THEM FIRST TO GET 'EM EXTRA MELTY!
SHOULD YOU PUT THE WHOLE BAG IN?
I THINK I KNOW WHAT I'M DOING!
TEN MINUTES ON HIGH SHOULD DO IT, AND...
BEEP! BEEP!
BLAM
HAHAHA HA
ARE YOU GUYS LAUGHING AT ME?
NAH, WE'RE LAUGHING AT THIS CHARACTER ON THE COVER OF D'OH MAGAZINE!
WHAT AN IDIOT!
D'OH!

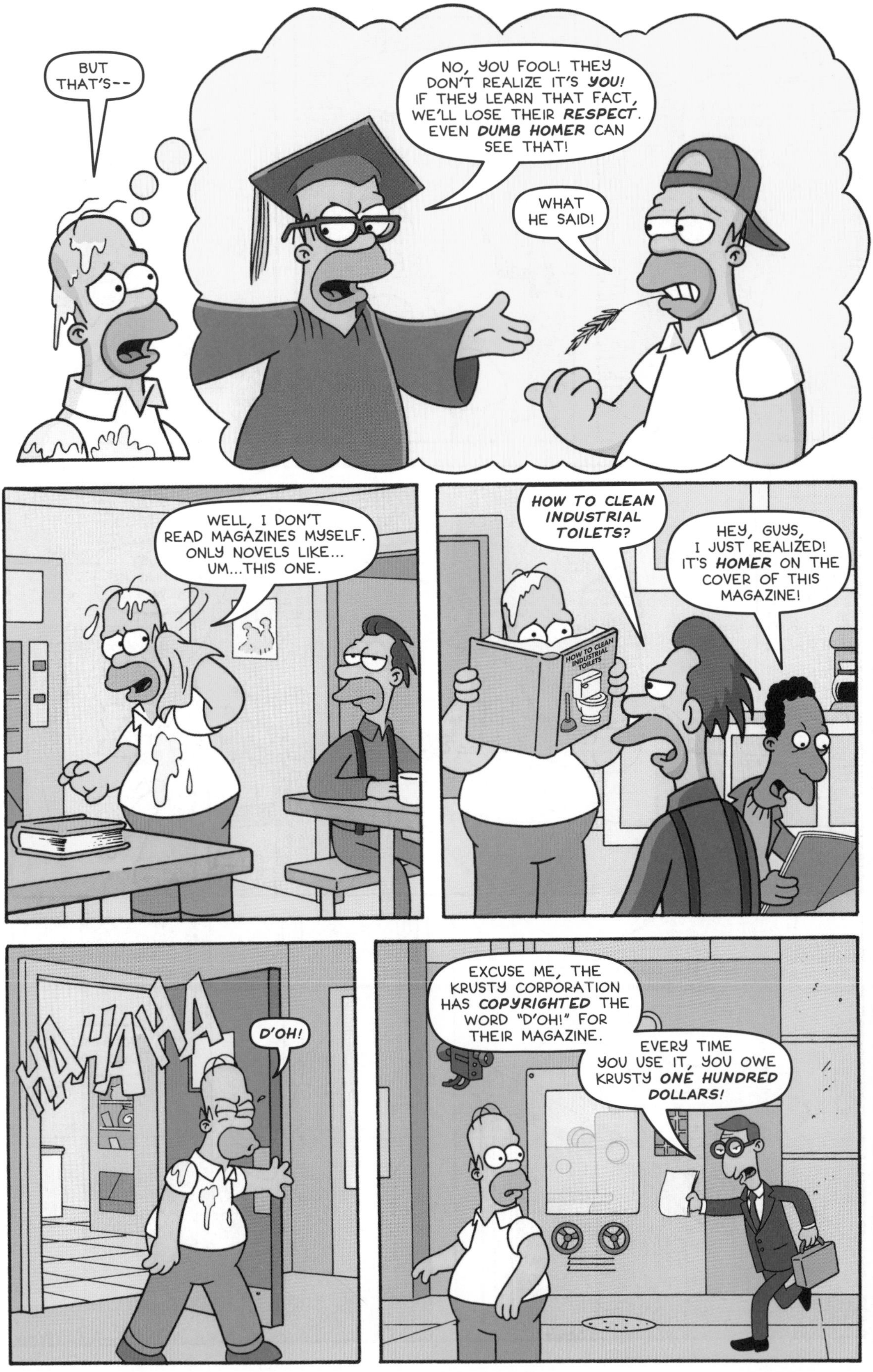
BUT THAT'S--
NO, YOU FOOL! THEY DON'T REALIZE IT'S YOU! IF THEY LEARN THAT FACT, WE'LL LOSE THEIR RESPECT. EVEN DUMB HOMER CAN SEE THAT!
WHAT HE SAID!
WELL, I DON'T READ MAGAZINES MYSELF. ONLY NOVELS LIKE... UM...THIS ONE.
HOW TO CLEAN INDUSTRIAL TOILETS?
HOW TO CLEAN INDUSTRIAL TOILETS
HEY, GUYS, I JUST REALIZED! IT'S HOMER ON THE COVER OF THIS MAGAZINE!
HAHAHA
D'OH!
EXCUSE ME, THE KRUSTY CORPORATION HAS COPYRIGHTED THE WORD "D'OH!" FOR THEIR MAGAZINE.
EVERY TIME YOU USE IT, YOU OWE KRUSTY ONE HUNDRED DOLLARS!

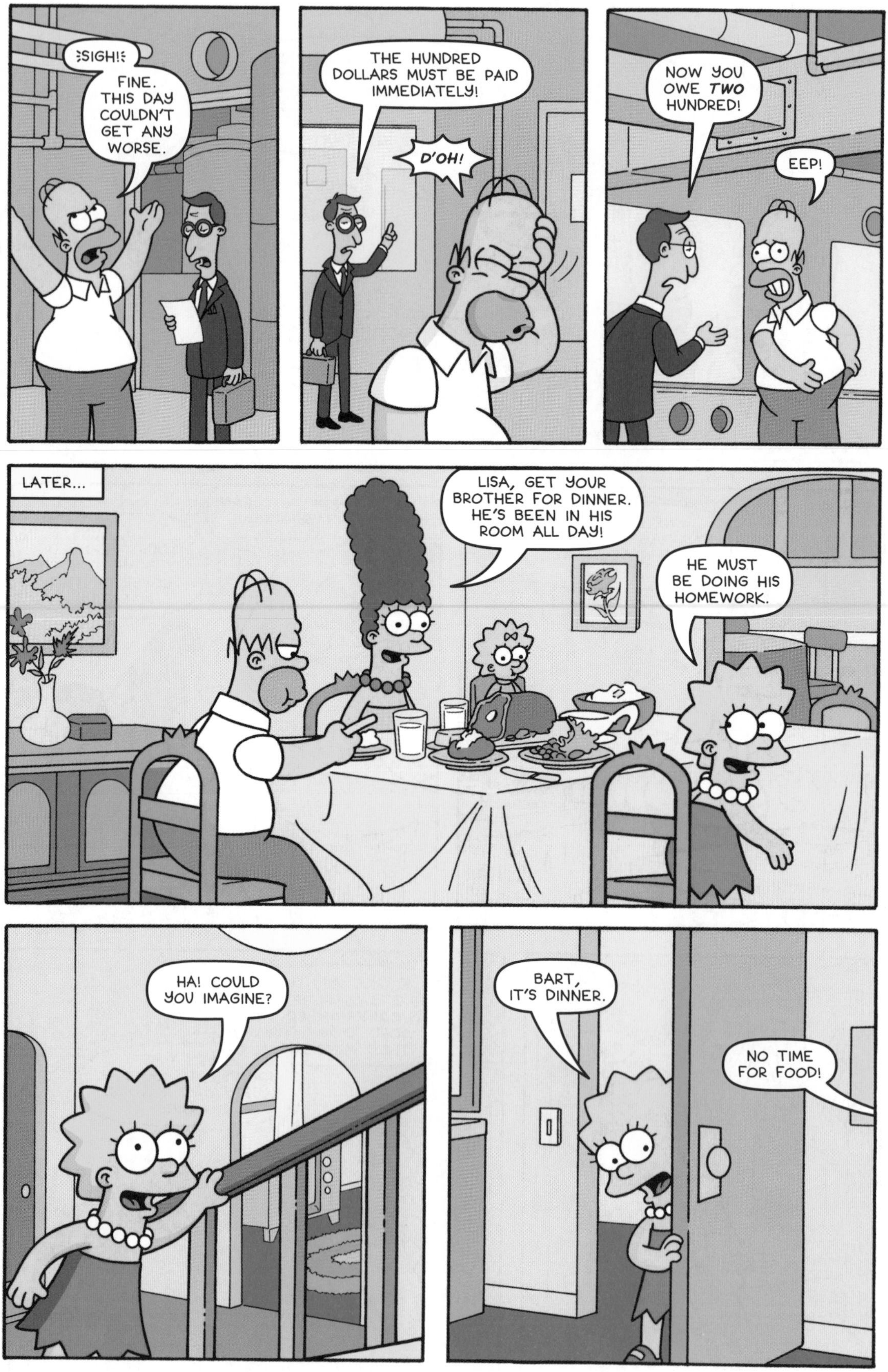

SIGH!
FINE. THIS DAY COULDN'T GET ANY WORSE.
THE HUNDRED DOLLARS MUST BE PAID IMMEDIATELY!
D'OH!
NOW YOU OWE *TWO* HUNDRED!
EEP!
LATER...
LISA, GET YOUR BROTHER FOR DINNER. HE'S BEEN IN HIS ROOM ALL DAY!
HE MUST BE DOING HIS HOMEWORK.
HA! COULD YOU IMAGINE?
BART, IT'S DINNER.
NO TIME FOR FOOD!

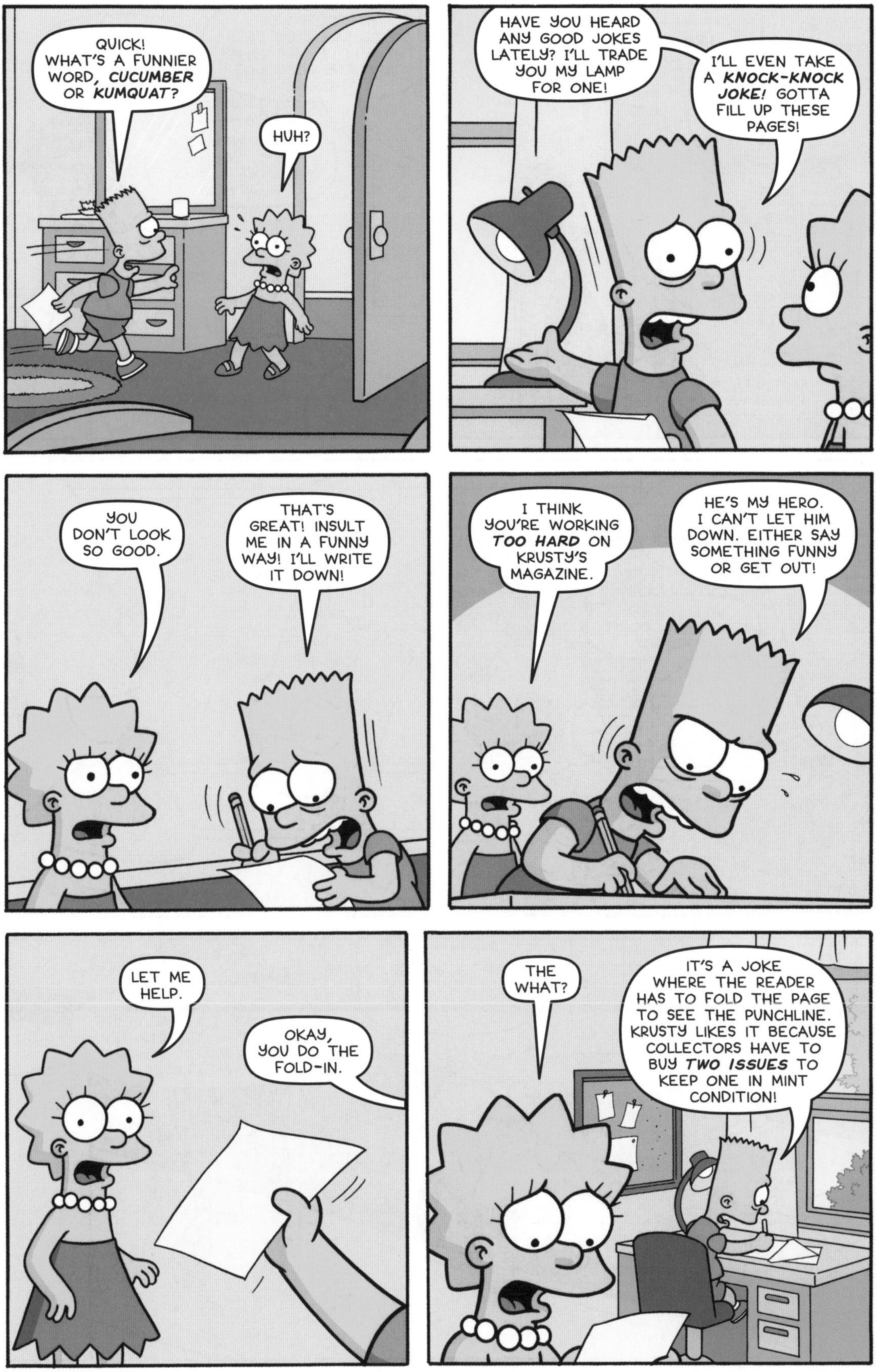

QUICK! WHAT'S A FUNNIER WORD, **CUCUMBER** OR **KUMQUAT**?
HUH?
HAVE YOU HEARD ANY GOOD JOKES LATELY? I'LL TRADE YOU MY LAMP FOR ONE!
I'LL EVEN TAKE A **KNOCK-KNOCK JOKE!** GOTTA FILL UP THESE PAGES!
YOU DON'T LOOK SO GOOD.
THAT'S GREAT! INSULT ME IN A FUNNY WAY! I'LL WRITE IT DOWN!
I THINK YOU'RE WORKING **TOO HARD** ON KRUSTY'S MAGAZINE.
HE'S MY HERO. I CAN'T LET HIM DOWN. EITHER SAY SOMETHING FUNNY OR GET OUT!
LET ME HELP.
OKAY, YOU DO THE FOLD-IN.
THE WHAT?
IT'S A JOKE WHERE THE READER HAS TO FOLD THE PAGE TO SEE THE PUNCHLINE. KRUSTY LIKES IT BECAUSE COLLECTORS HAVE TO BUY **TWO ISSUES** TO KEEP ONE IN MINT CONDITION!

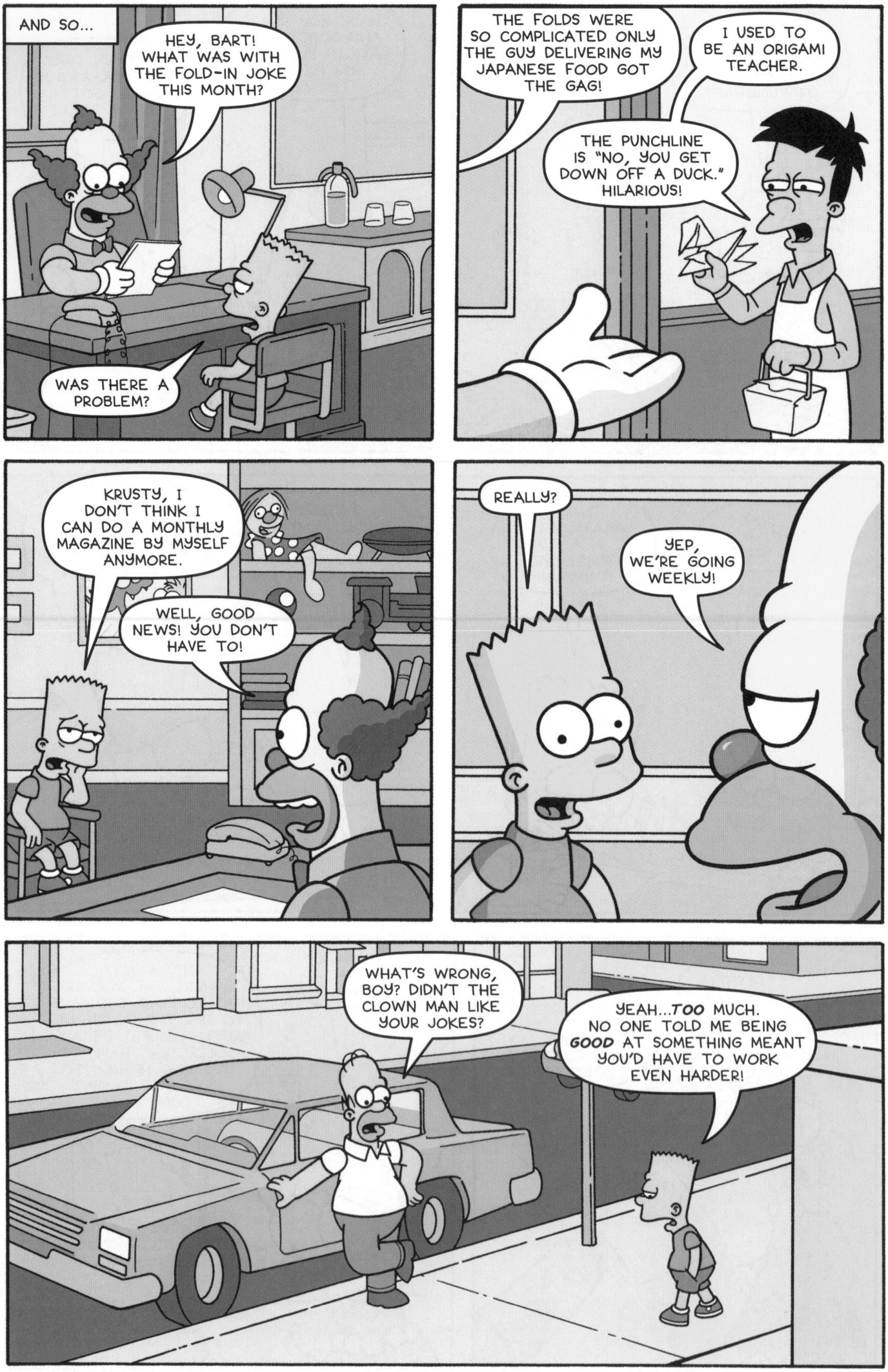
AND SO...
HEY, BART! WHAT WAS WITH THE FOLD-IN JOKE THIS MONTH?
WAS THERE A PROBLEM?
THE FOLDS WERE SO COMPLICATED ONLY THE GUY DELIVERING MY JAPANESE FOOD GOT THE GAG!
I USED TO BE AN ORIGAMI TEACHER.
THE PUNCHLINE IS "NO, YOU GET DOWN OFF A DUCK." HILARIOUS!
KRUSTY, I DON'T THINK I CAN DO A MONTHLY MAGAZINE BY MYSELF ANYMORE.
WELL, GOOD NEWS! YOU DON'T HAVE TO!
REALLY?
YEP, WE'RE GOING WEEKLY!
WHAT'S WRONG, BOY? DIDN'T THE CLOWN MAN LIKE YOUR JOKES?
YEAH...*TOO* MUCH. NO ONE TOLD ME BEING ***GOOD*** AT SOMETHING MEANT YOU'D HAVE TO WORK EVEN HARDER!

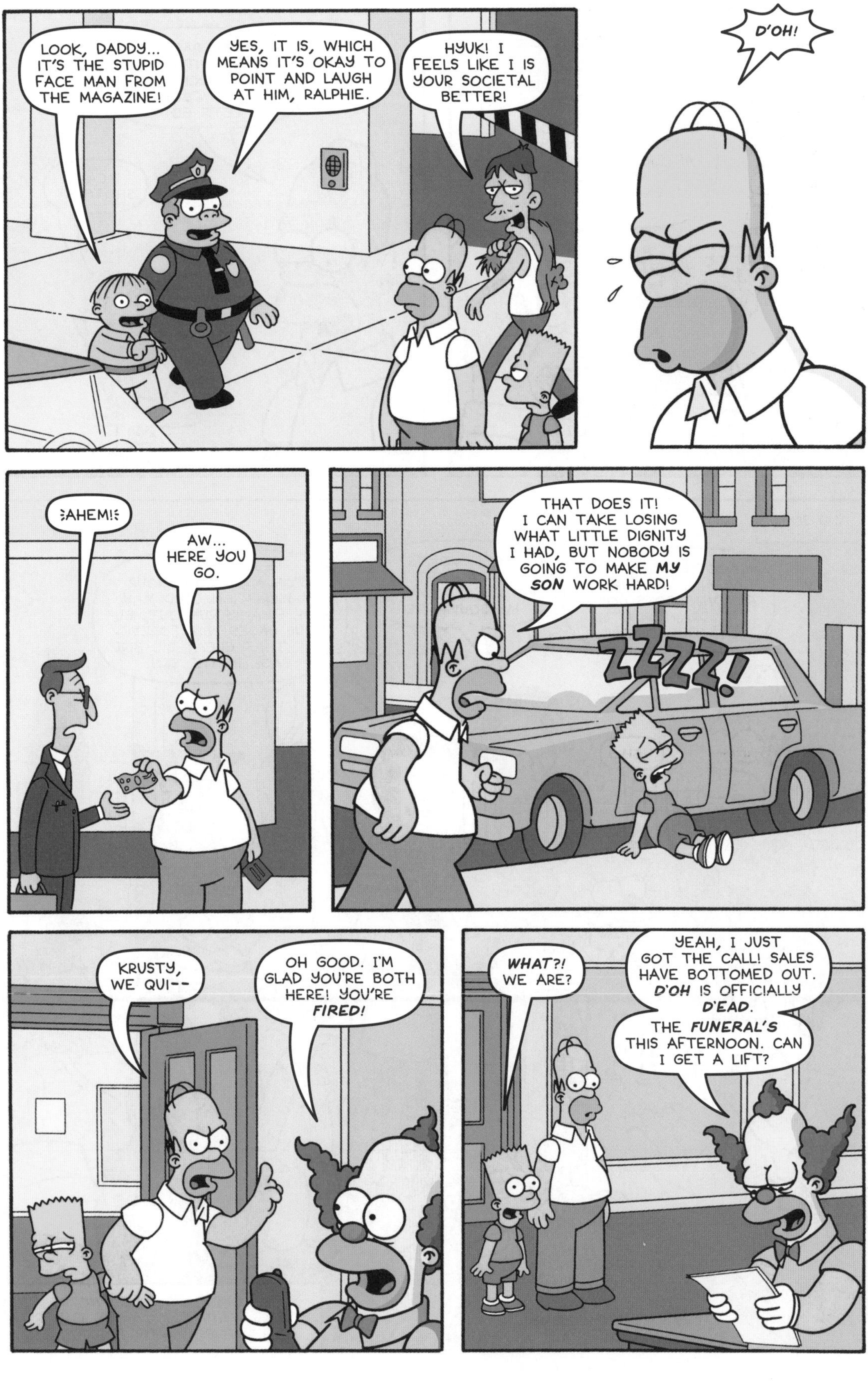
LOOK, DADDY... IT'S THE STUPID FACE MAN FROM THE MAGAZINE!
YES, IT IS, WHICH MEANS IT'S OKAY TO POINT AND LAUGH AT HIM, RALPHIE.
HYUK! I FEELS LIKE I IS YOUR SOCIETAL BETTER!
D'OH!
AHEM!
AW... HERE YOU GO.
THAT DOES IT! I CAN TAKE LOSING WHAT LITTLE DIGNITY I HAD, BUT NOBODY IS GOING TO MAKE **MY SON** WORK HARD!
ZZZZZ!
KRUSTY, WE QUI--
OH GOOD. I'M GLAD YOU'RE BOTH HERE! YOU'RE **FIRED!**
WHAT?! WE ARE?
YEAH, I JUST GOT THE CALL! SALES HAVE BOTTOMED OUT. **D'OH** IS OFFICIALLY **D'EAD**.
THE **FUNERAL'S** THIS AFTERNOON. CAN I GET A LIFT?

A FUNERAL? FOR A *MAGAZINE*?

OF COURSE! THAT WAY I GET TO THROW A BIG PARTY AFTER AND WRITE IT OFF AS A BUSINESS EXPENSE. I DO IT ALL THE TIME.

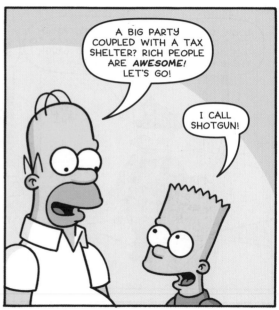

A BIG PARTY COUPLED WITH A TAX SHELTER? RICH PEOPLE ARE *AWESOME!* LET'S GO!

I CALL SHOTGUN!

AND SO...

ANOTHER SHINING BEACON OF *BATHROOM READING* GOES DOWN THE DRAIN. PRINT IS TRULY DEAD, LISA.

UGH...

THEIR *JOKES* WERE ALMOST AS *WATERED DOWN* AS MY SQUISHEES!

REST IN PEACE, *D'OH MAGAZINE.* YOUR SUBSCRIPTION CARD MAY HAVE FINALLY RUN OUT, BUT YOUR PAGES WILL FOREVER LINE THAT GREAT BIG BIRD CAGE IN THE SKY.

ZZZZZ!

R.I.P. *D'OH*

THE END! BUT DON'T WORRY FOLKS, *THIS* COMIC BOOK IS HERE TO STAY! RIGHT? *RIGHT*?!

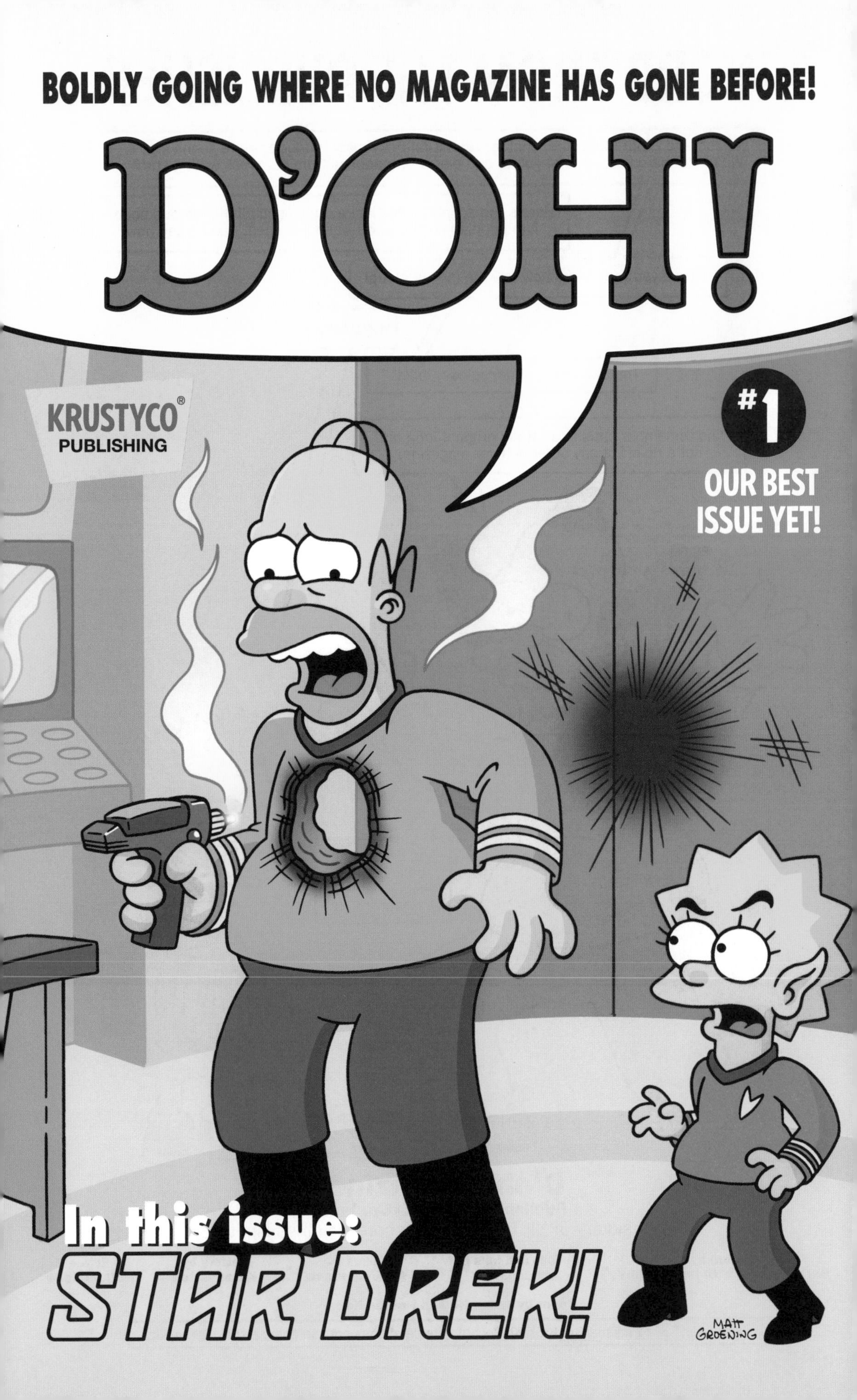
BOLDLY GOING WHERE NO MAGAZINE HAS GONE BEFORE!
D'OH!
KRUSTYCO®
PUBLISHING
#1
OUR BEST
ISSUE YET!
In this issue:
STAR DREK!
MATT
GROENING

A WORD FROM THE PUBLISHER...

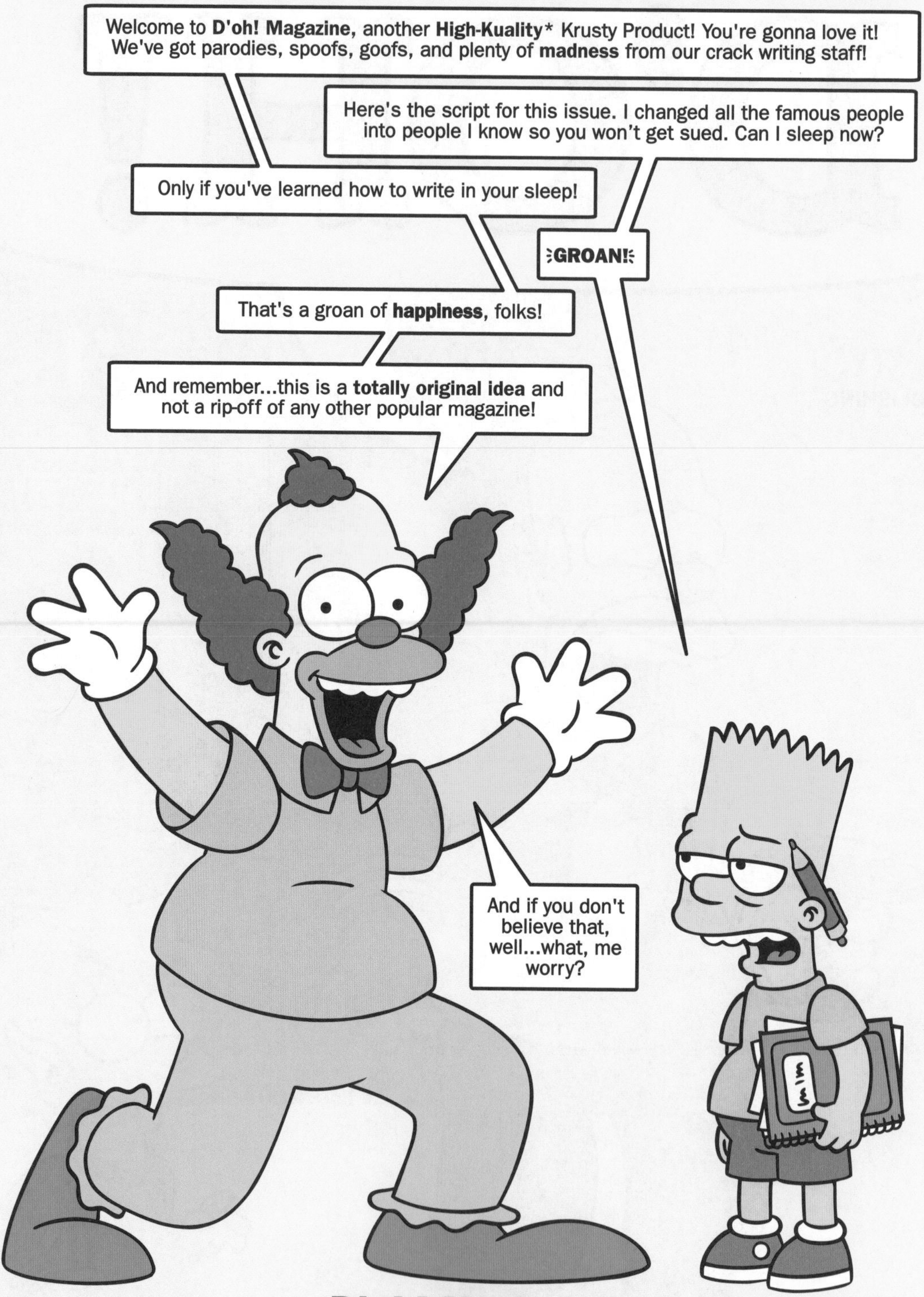

Welcome to **D'oh! Magazine,** another **High-Kuality*** Krusty Product! You're gonna love it! We've got parodies, spoofs, goofs, and plenty of **madness** from our crack writing staff!
Here's the script for this issue. I changed all the famous people into people I know so you won't get sued. Can I sleep now?
Only if you've learned how to write in your sleep!
GROAN!
That's a groan of **happiness**, folks!
And remember...this is a **totally original idea** and not a rip-off of any other popular magazine!
And if you don't believe that, well...what, me worry?

D'oh! Magazine

Published By KrustyCo, Inc.

A Subsidiary of HK Rustofski Offshore Holdings Limited

Written by
Bart Simpson with Ian Boothby

Pencils and Inks by
James Lloyd

Colors by
Art Villanueva

Letters by
Karen Bates

Editor
Nathan Kane

Cover by Jason Ho and Nathan Kane

* "High-Kuality" is a trademark of KrustyCo Incorporated and does not guarantee actual high quality.

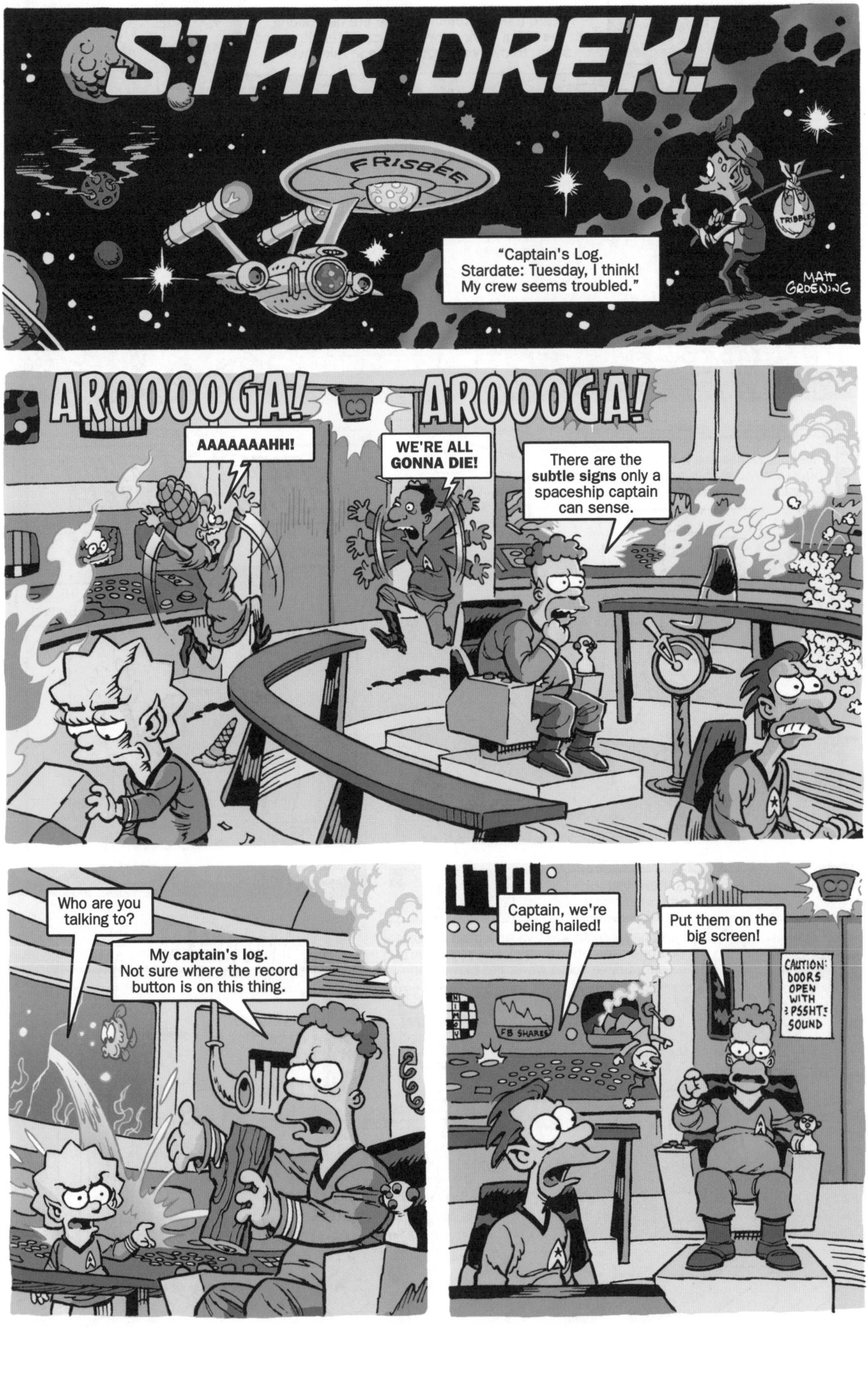
STAR DREK!
FRISBEE
TRIBBLES
"Captain's Log. Stardate: Tuesday, I think! My crew seems troubled."
MATT GROENING
AROOOOOGA!
AROOOGA!
AAAAAAAHH!
WE'RE ALL GONNA DIE!
There are the subtle signs only a spaceship captain can sense.
Who are you talking to?
My captain's log. Not sure where the record button is on this thing.
Captain, we're being hailed!
Put them on the big screen!
NIMOY
FB SHARES
CAUTION: DOORS OPEN WITH PSSHT SOUND

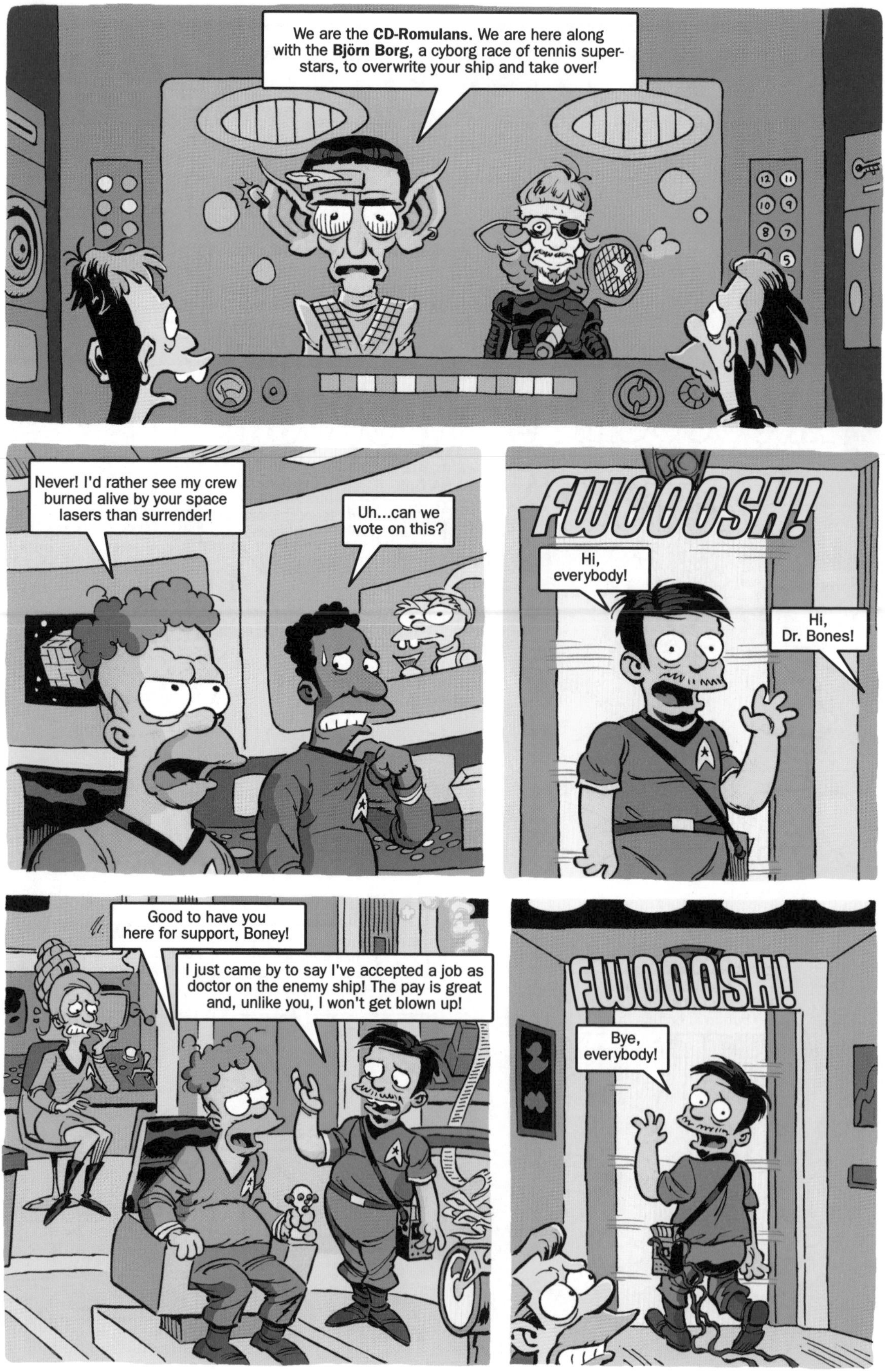
We are the **CD-Romulans.** We are here along with the **Björn Borg**, a cyborg race of tennis superstars, to overwrite your ship and take over!
Never! I'd rather see my crew burned alive by your space lasers than surrender!
Uh...can we vote on this?
FWOOOSH!
Hi, everybody!
Hi, Dr. Bones!
Good to have you here for support, Boney!
I just came by to say I've accepted a job as doctor on the enemy ship! The pay is great and, unlike you, I won't get blown up!
FWOOOSH!
Bye, everybody!

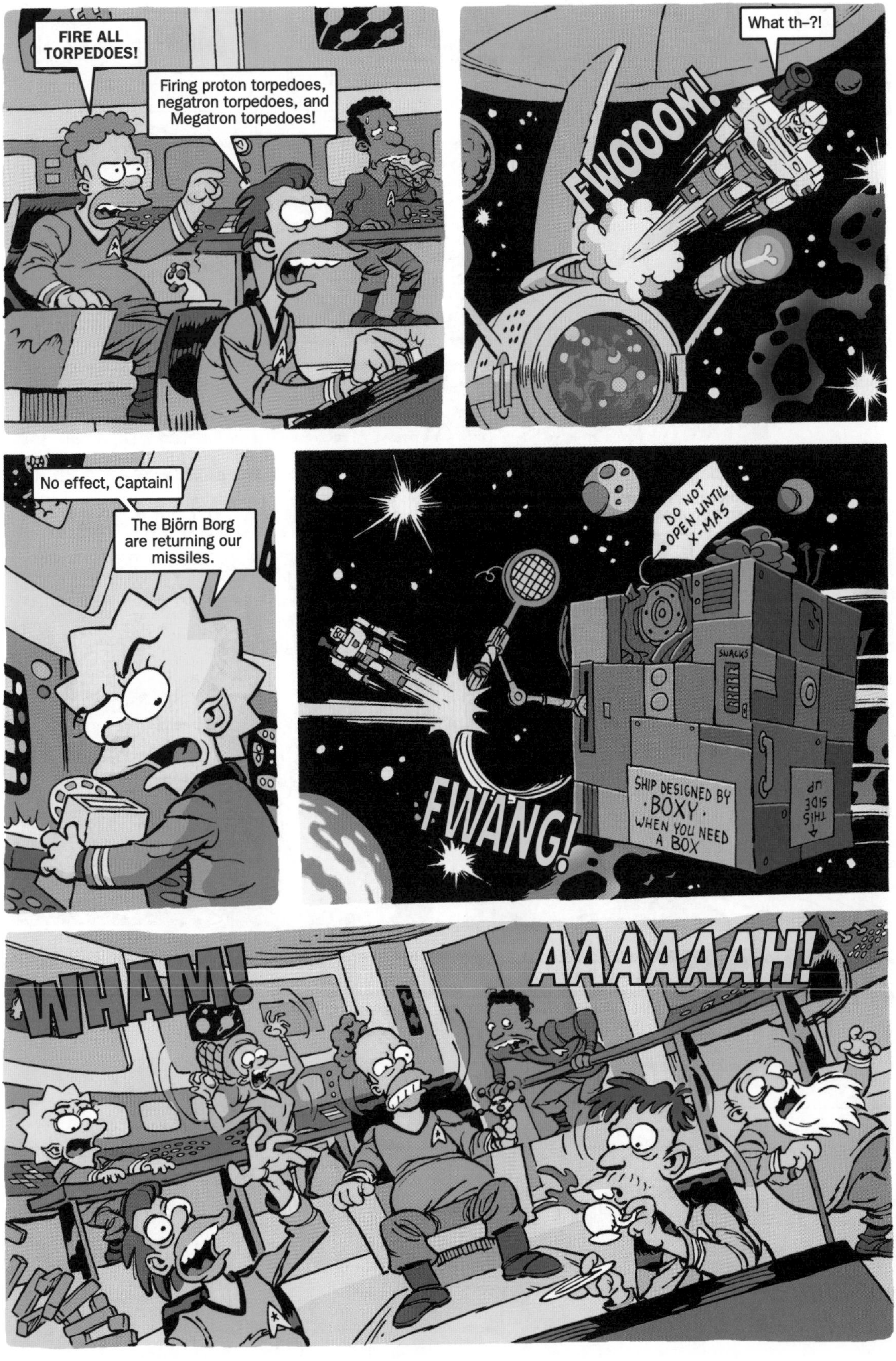
FIRE ALL TORPEDOES!
Firing proton torpedoes, negatron torpedoes, and Megatron torpedoes!
What th–?!
FWOOOM!
No effect, Captain!
The Björn Borg are returning our missiles.
DO NOT OPEN UNTIL X-MAS
SNACKS
SHIP DESIGNED BY ·BOXY· WHEN YOU NEED A BOX
THIS SIDE UP
FWANG!
WHAM!
AAAAAAH!

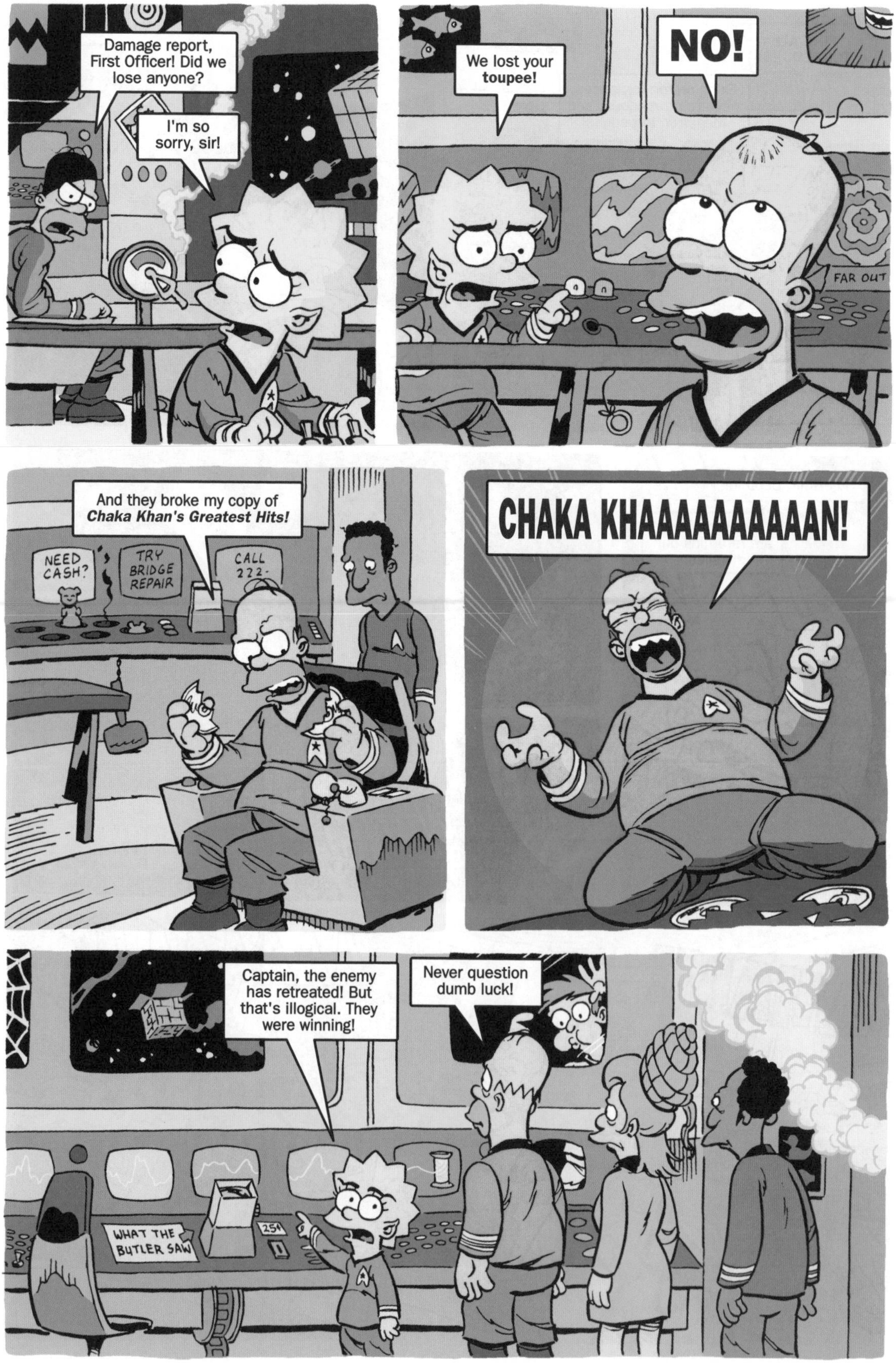
Damage report, First Officer! Did we lose anyone?
I'm so sorry, sir!
We lost your **toupee!**
NO!
FAR OUT
And they broke my copy of ***Chaka Khan's Greatest Hits!***
NEED CASH?
TRY BRIDGE REPAIR
CALL 222-
CHAKA KHAAAAAAAAAAN!
Captain, the enemy has retreated! But that's illogical. They were winning!
Never question dumb luck!
WHAT THE BUTLER SAW
25¢

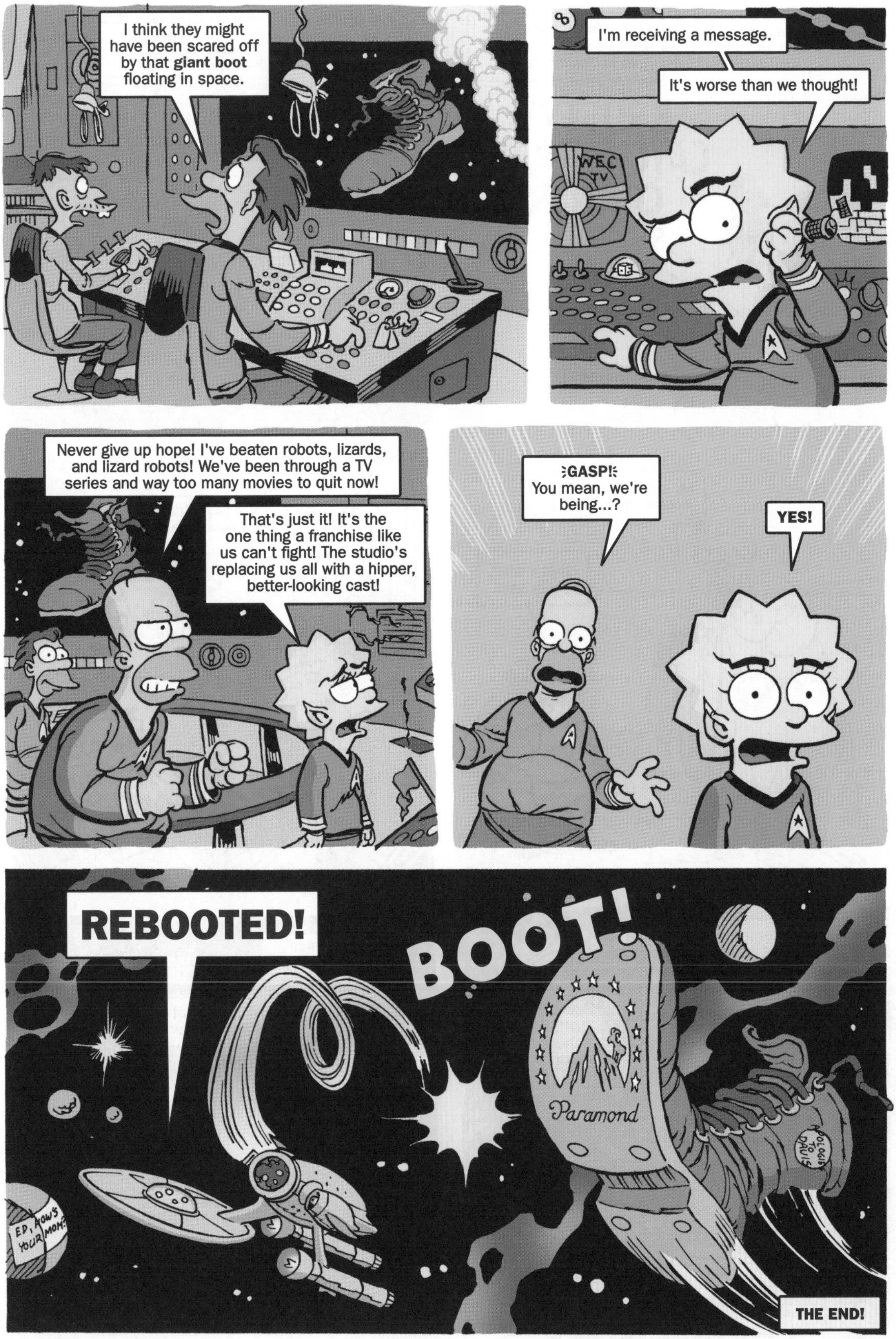
I think they might have been scared off by that **giant boot** floating in space.
I'm receiving a message.
It's worse than we thought!
WEC TV
Never give up hope! I've beaten robots, lizards, and lizard robots! We've been through a TV series and way too many movies to quit now!
That's just it! It's the one thing a franchise like us can't fight! The studio's replacing us all with a hipper, better-looking cast!
GASP!
You mean, we're being...?
YES!
REBOOTED!
BOOT!
Paramond
ED, HOW'S YOUR MOM?
THE END!

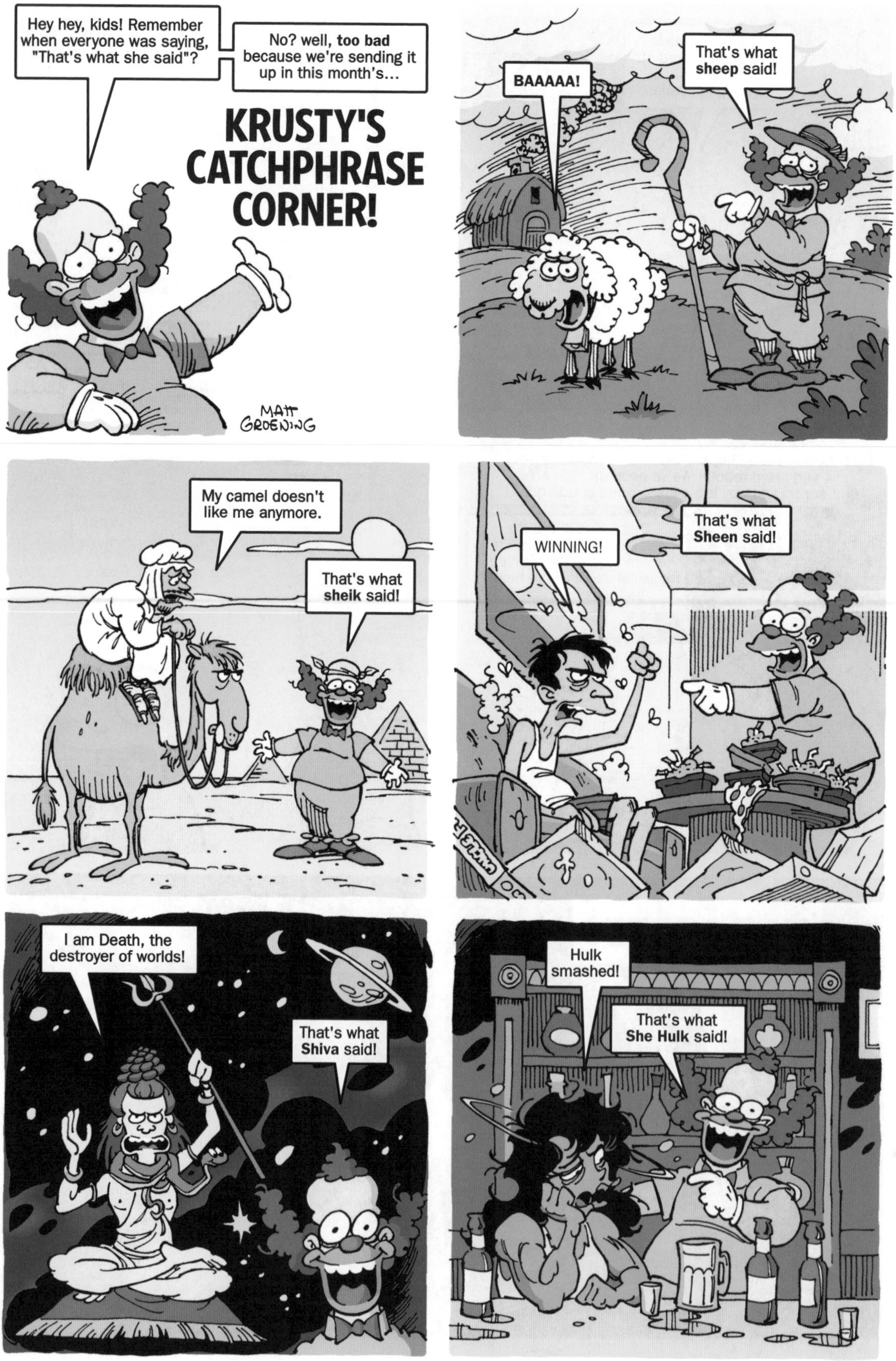
Hey hey, kids! Remember when everyone was saying, "That's what she said"?
No? well, too bad because we're sending it up in this month's...
KRUSTY'S CATCHPHRASE CORNER!
MATT GROENING
BAAAAA!
That's what sheep said!
My camel doesn't like me anymore.
That's what sheik said!
WINNING!
That's what Sheen said!
I am Death, the destroyer of worlds!
That's what Shiva said!
Hulk smashed!
That's what She Hulk said!

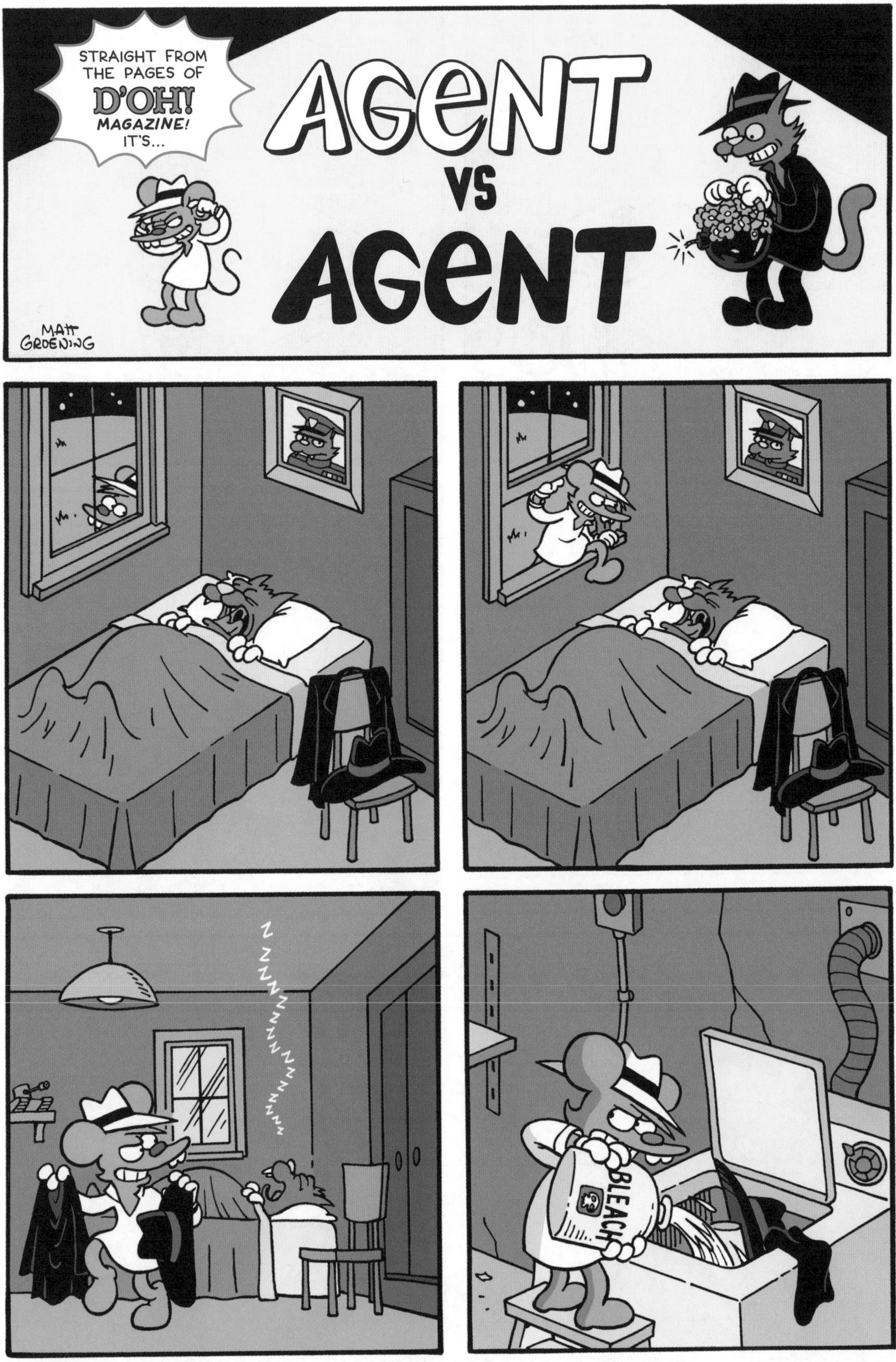
STRAIGHT FROM THE PAGES OF D'OH! MAGAZINE! IT'S...
AGENT VS AGENT
MATT GROENING
BLEACH

IAN BOOTHBY STORY

JAMES LLOYD ART

NATHAN HAMILL COLORS

KAREN BATES LETTERS

NATHAN KANE EDITOR

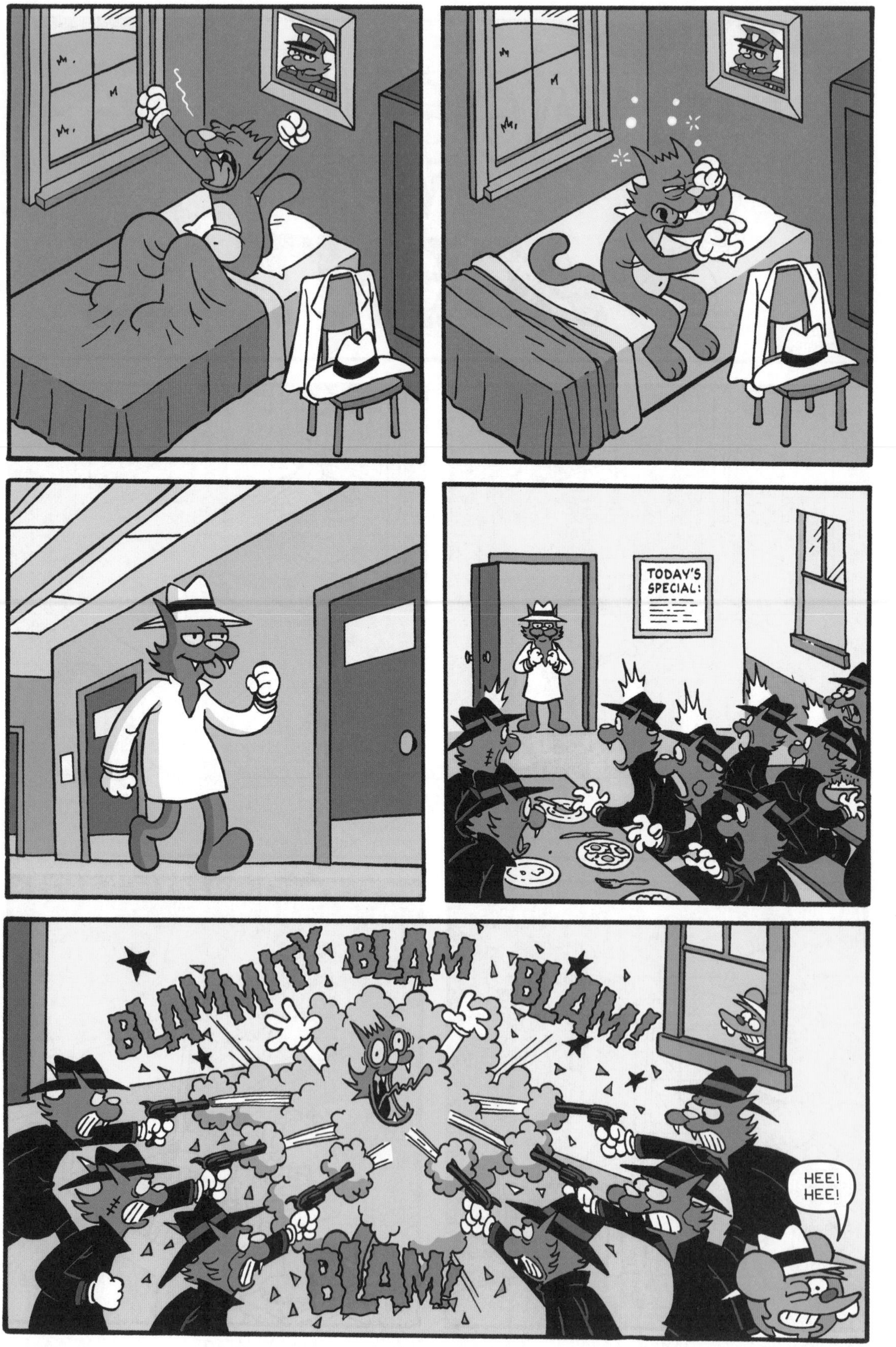
TODAY'S SPECIAL:
BLAMMITY BLAM BLAM!
HEE! HEE!
BLAM!

THE SOUND AND THE FUNNY

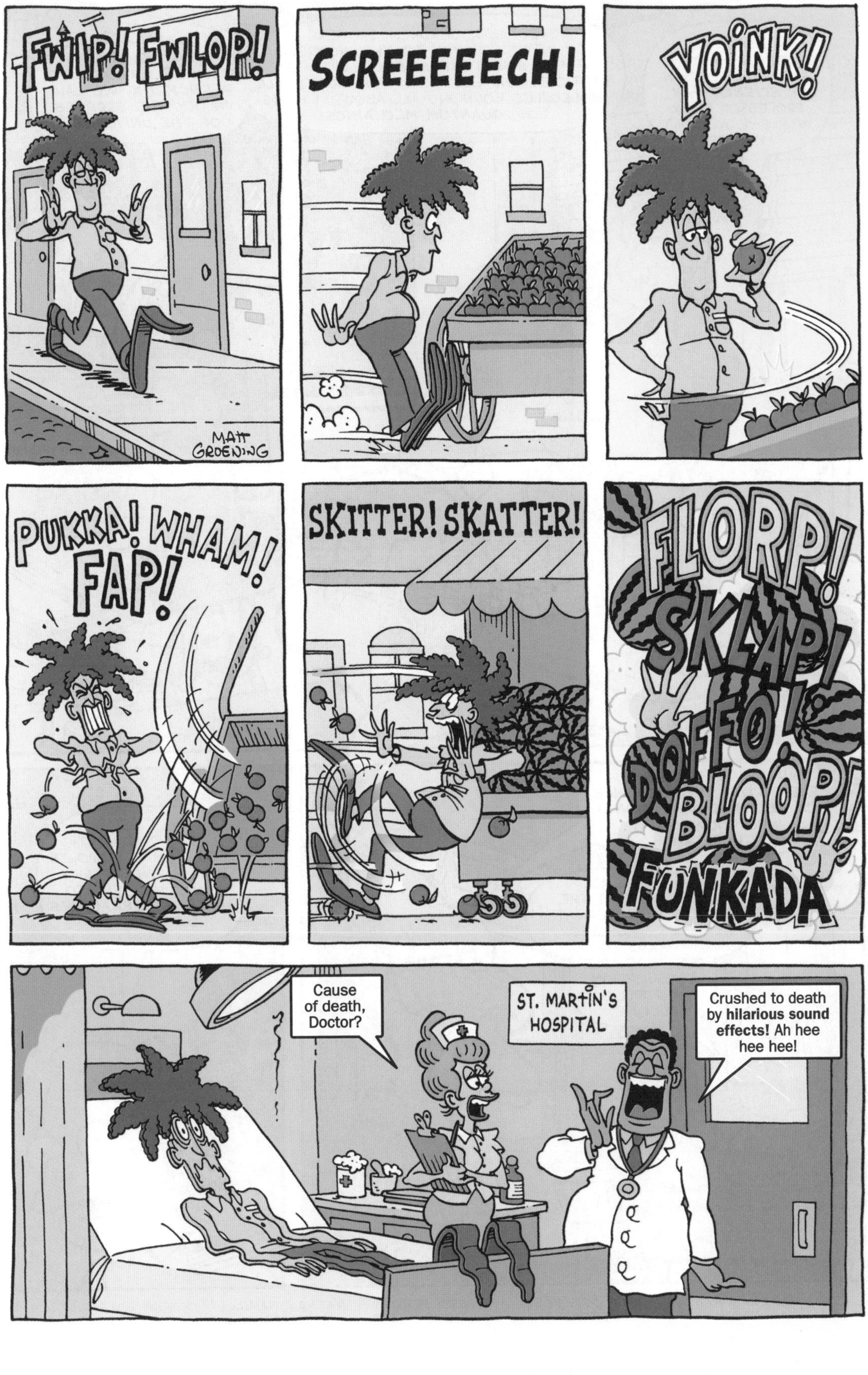
FWIP! FWLOP!
MATT GROENING
SCREEEEEECH!
YOINK!
PUKKA! WHAM!
FAP!
SKITTER! SKATTER!
FLORP!
SKLAP!
DOFFO!
BLOOP!
FUNKADA
Cause of death, Doctor?
ST. MARTIN'S HOSPITAL
Crushed to death by **hilarious sound effects!** Ah hee hee hee!

SYNCHRONICITY FOR TWO

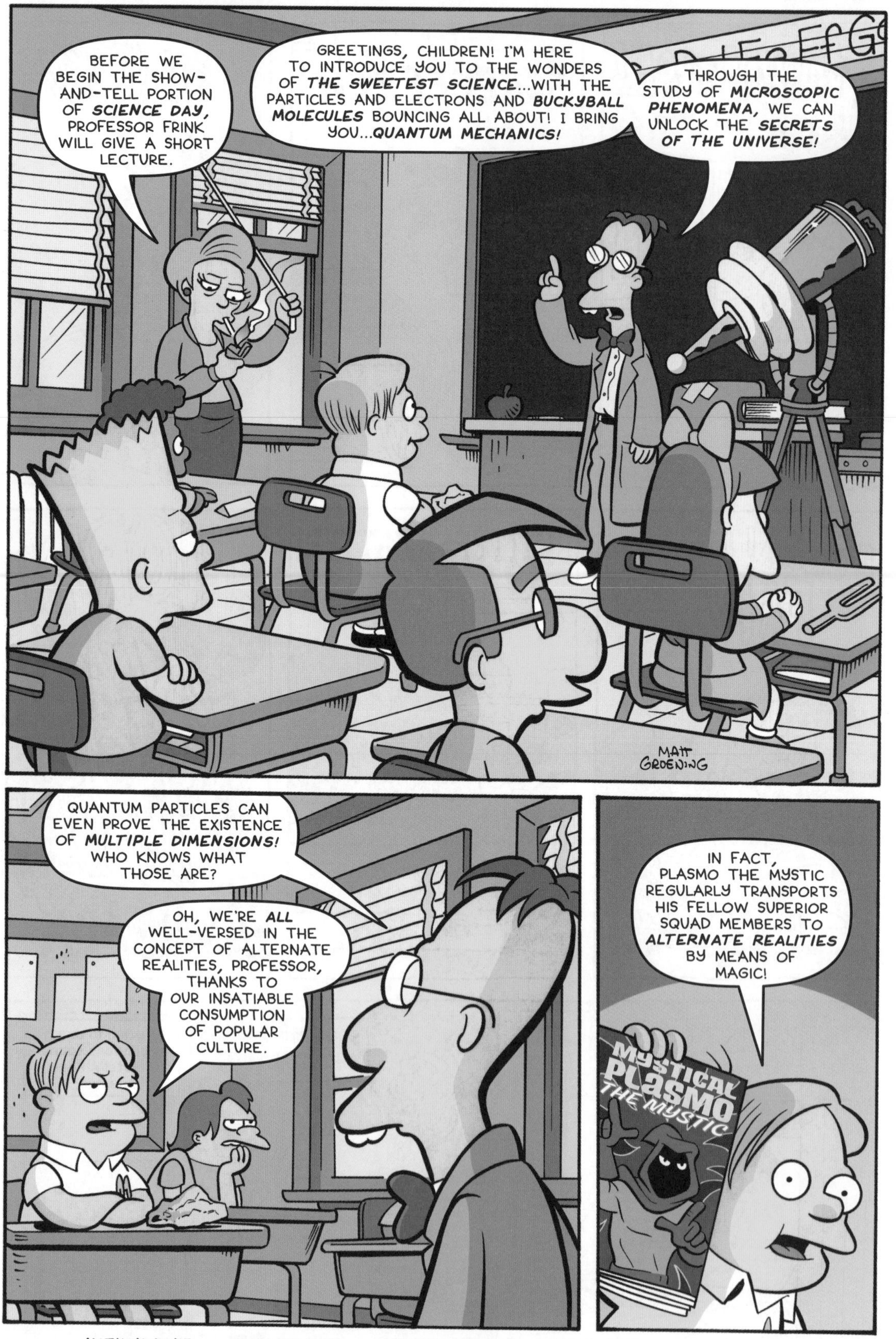
BEFORE WE BEGIN THE SHOW-AND-TELL PORTION OF SCIENCE DAY, PROFESSOR FRINK WILL GIVE A SHORT LECTURE.
GREETINGS, CHILDREN! I'M HERE TO INTRODUCE YOU TO THE WONDERS OF THE SWEETEST SCIENCE...WITH THE PARTICLES AND ELECTRONS AND BUCKYBALL MOLECULES BOUNCING ALL ABOUT! I BRING YOU...QUANTUM MECHANICS!
THROUGH THE STUDY OF MICROSCOPIC PHENOMENA, WE CAN UNLOCK THE SECRETS OF THE UNIVERSE!
MATT GROENING
QUANTUM PARTICLES CAN EVEN PROVE THE EXISTENCE OF MULTIPLE DIMENSIONS! WHO KNOWS WHAT THOSE ARE?
OH, WE'RE ALL WELL-VERSED IN THE CONCEPT OF ALTERNATE REALITIES, PROFESSOR, THANKS TO OUR INSATIABLE CONSUMPTION OF POPULAR CULTURE.
IN FACT, PLASMO THE MYSTIC REGULARLY TRANSPORTS HIS FELLOW SUPERIOR SQUAD MEMBERS TO ALTERNATE REALITIES BY MEANS OF MAGIC!
MYSTICAL PLASMO THE MYSTIC

NATHAN KANE STORY **JOHN DELANEY** PENCILS **ANDREW PEPOY** INKS **NATHAN HAMILL** COLORS **KAREN BATES** LETTERS

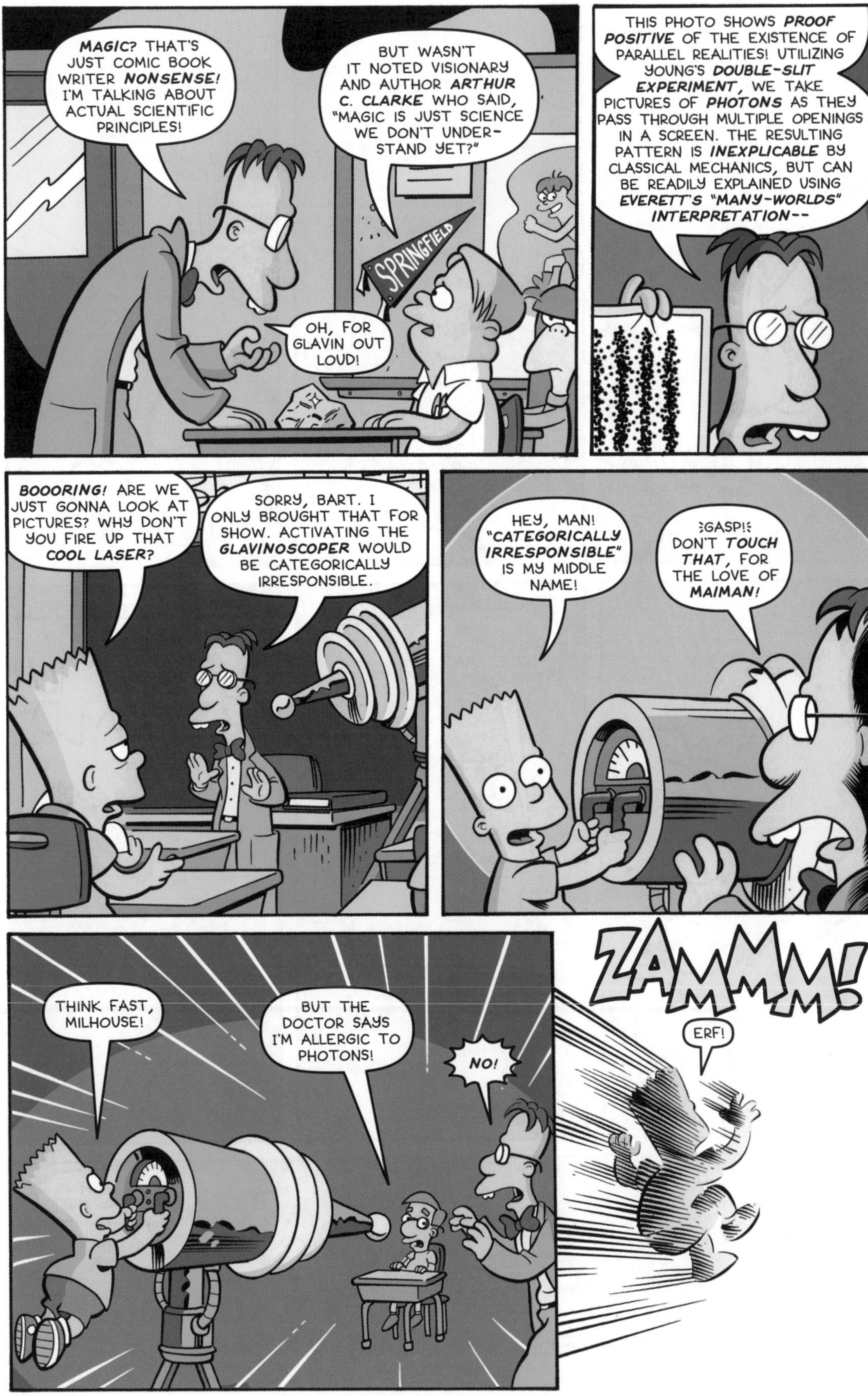
MAGIC? THAT'S JUST COMIC BOOK WRITER NONSENSE! I'M TALKING ABOUT ACTUAL SCIENTIFIC PRINCIPLES!
BUT WASN'T IT NOTED VISIONARY AND AUTHOR ARTHUR C. CLARKE WHO SAID, "MAGIC IS JUST SCIENCE WE DON'T UNDER-STAND YET?"
SPRINGFIELD
OH, FOR GLAVIN OUT LOUD!
THIS PHOTO SHOWS PROOF POSITIVE OF THE EXISTENCE OF PARALLEL REALITIES! UTILIZING YOUNG'S DOUBLE-SLIT EXPERIMENT, WE TAKE PICTURES OF PHOTONS AS THEY PASS THROUGH MULTIPLE OPENINGS IN A SCREEN. THE RESULTING PATTERN IS INEXPLICABLE BY CLASSICAL MECHANICS, BUT CAN BE READILY EXPLAINED USING EVERETT'S "MANY-WORLDS" INTERPRETATION--
BOOORING! ARE WE JUST GONNA LOOK AT PICTURES? WHY DON'T YOU FIRE UP THAT COOL LASER?
SORRY, BART. I ONLY BROUGHT THAT FOR SHOW. ACTIVATING THE GLAVINOSCOPER WOULD BE CATEGORICALLY IRRESPONSIBLE.
HEY, MAN! "CATEGORICALLY IRRESPONSIBLE" IS MY MIDDLE NAME!
GASP! DON'T TOUCH THAT, FOR THE LOVE OF MAIMAN!
THINK FAST, MILHOUSE!
BUT THE DOCTOR SAYS I'M ALLERGIC TO PHOTONS!
NO!
ZAMMM!
ERF!

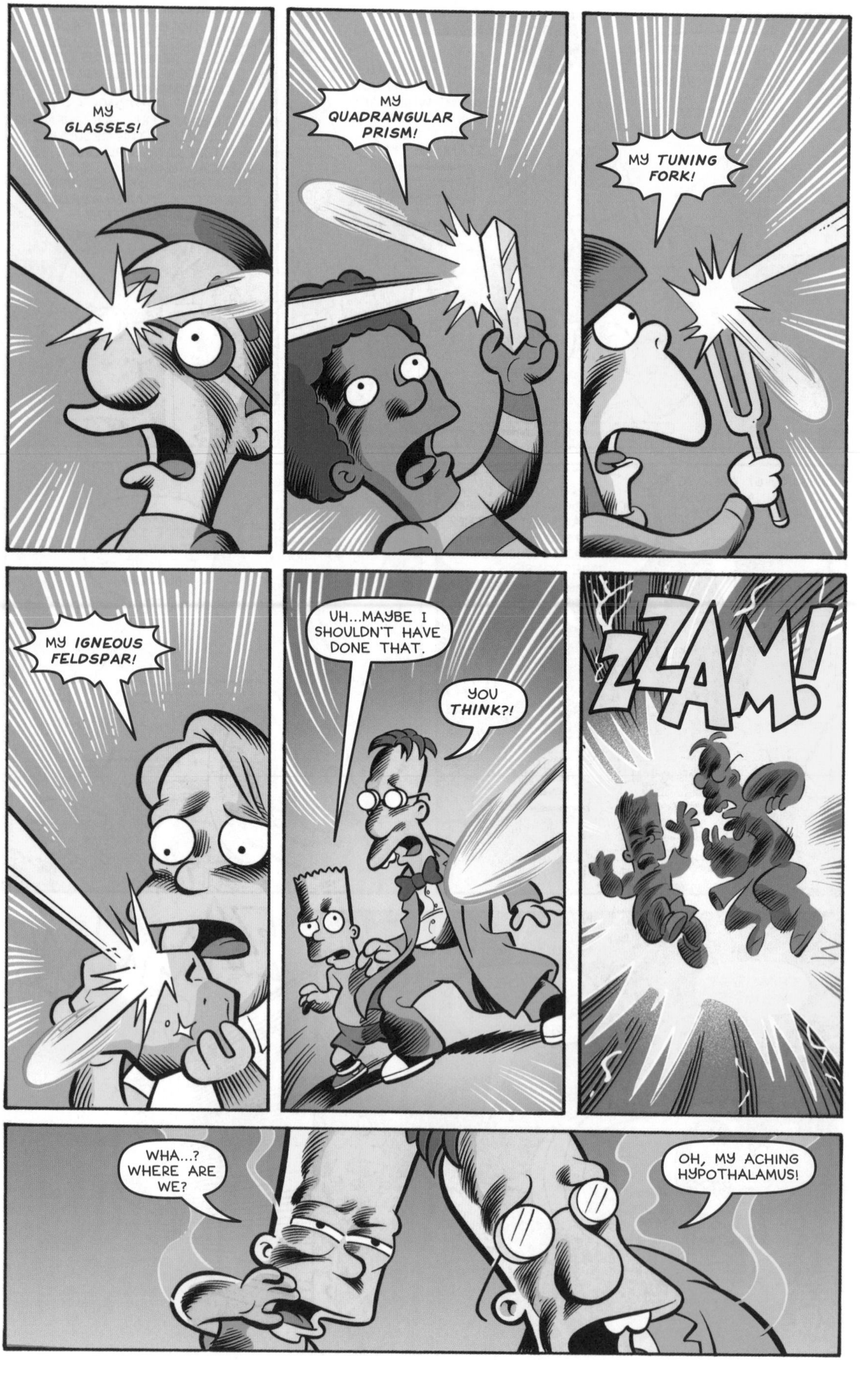
MY GLASSES!
MY QUADRANGULAR PRISM!
MY TUNING FORK!
MY IGNEOUS FELDSPAR!
UH...MAYBE I SHOULDN'T HAVE DONE THAT.
YOU THINK?!
ZZAM!
WHA...? WHERE ARE WE?
OH, MY ACHING HYPOTHALAMUS!

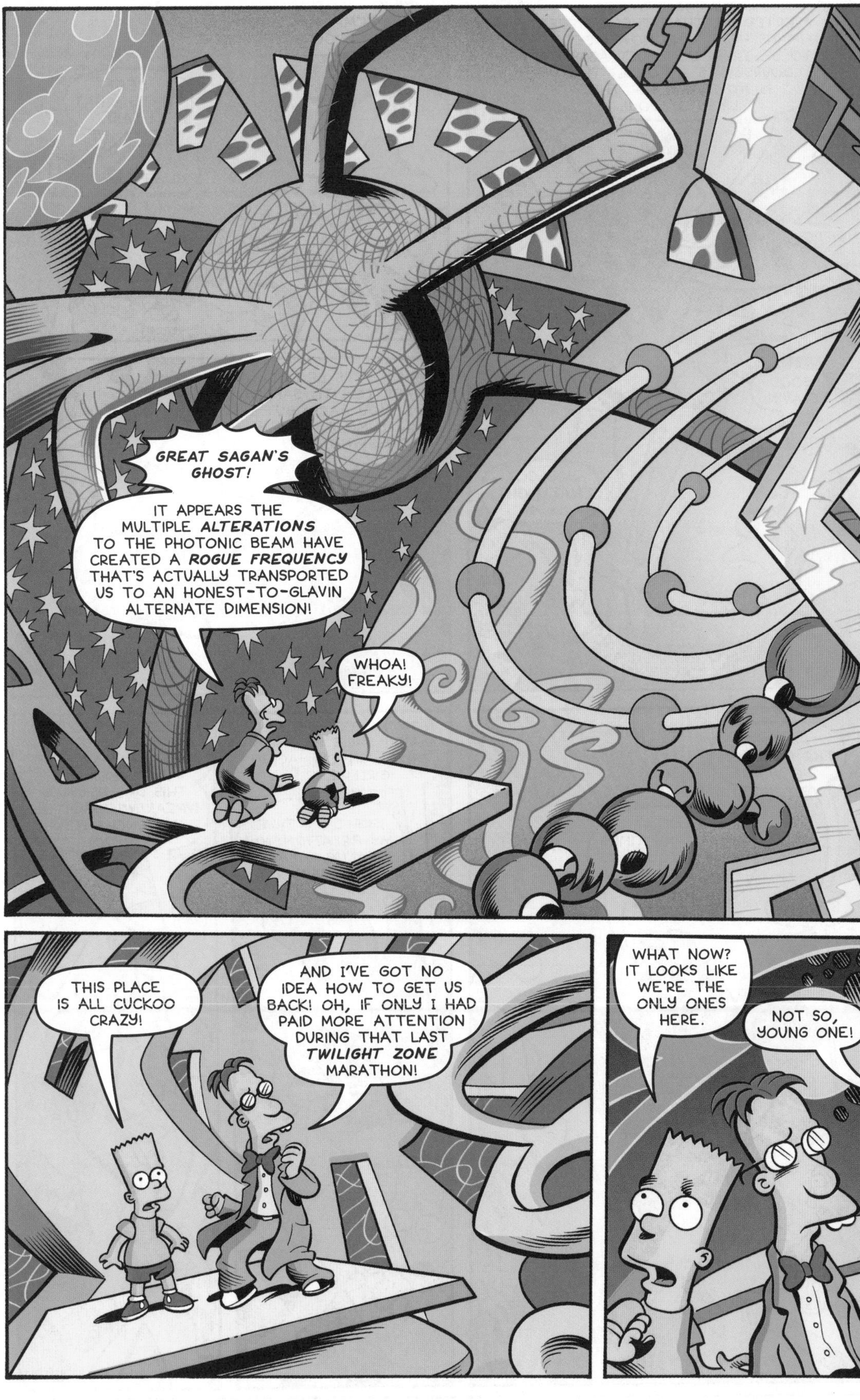
GREAT SAGAN'S GHOST!
IT APPEARS THE MULTIPLE ALTERATIONS TO THE PHOTONIC BEAM HAVE CREATED A ROGUE FREQUENCY THAT'S ACTUALLY TRANSPORTED US TO AN HONEST-TO-GLAVIN ALTERNATE DIMENSION!
WHOA! FREAKY!
THIS PLACE IS ALL CUCKOO CRAZY!
AND I'VE GOT NO IDEA HOW TO GET US BACK! OH, IF ONLY I HAD PAID MORE ATTENTION DURING THAT LAST TWILIGHT ZONE MARATHON!
WHAT NOW? IT LOOKS LIKE WE'RE THE ONLY ONES HERE.
NOT SO, YOUNG ONE!

MY *MYSTIC ORACLES* ALERTED ME THAT THERE WERE HUMANS HERE, AND NOW I SEE IT TO BE TRUE! YOU MUST ABSENT YOURSELVES AT ONCE! THIS IS *NO PLACE* FOR THE LIKES OF YOU!

GOOD GLAVIN!

YOU GOT *THAT* RIGHT, LADY!

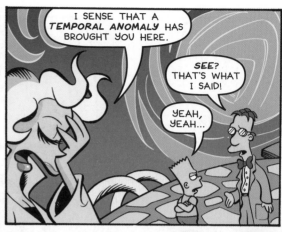

I SENSE THAT A *TEMPORAL ANOMALY* HAS BROUGHT YOU HERE.

SEE? THAT'S WHAT I SAID!

YEAH, YEAH...

ALAS, IT IS BEYOND MY ABILITIES TO SAFELY SEND YOU BACK! BUT I WILL SUMMON SOMEONE WHO *CAN!*

PLASMO THE MYSTIC?! NO WAY!

STARLA?

STARLA! HOW MANY TIMES HAVE I TOLD YOU NOT TO *DO* THAT?!

NOW I RECOGNIZE THIS LADY! SHE'S PLASMO'S ON-AGAIN-OFF-AGAIN GIRLFRIEND! *

∶SIGH!∶ IT'S TRUE. MY *RELATIONSHIP STATUS* IS FATED TO REMAIN "IT'S COMPLICATED."

I'M SORRY, BELOVED... BUT TIME IS OF THE ESSENCE! PLUS, THE ATMOSPHERE OF THIS DIMENSION IS *WREAKING HAVOC* ON MY ENCHANTED UP-DO!

PAF!

*DON'T TAKE BART'S WORD FOR IT! CHECK OUT PLASMO'S ADVENTURES IN THE PAGES OF SIMPSONS SUPER SPECTACULAR! —ED.

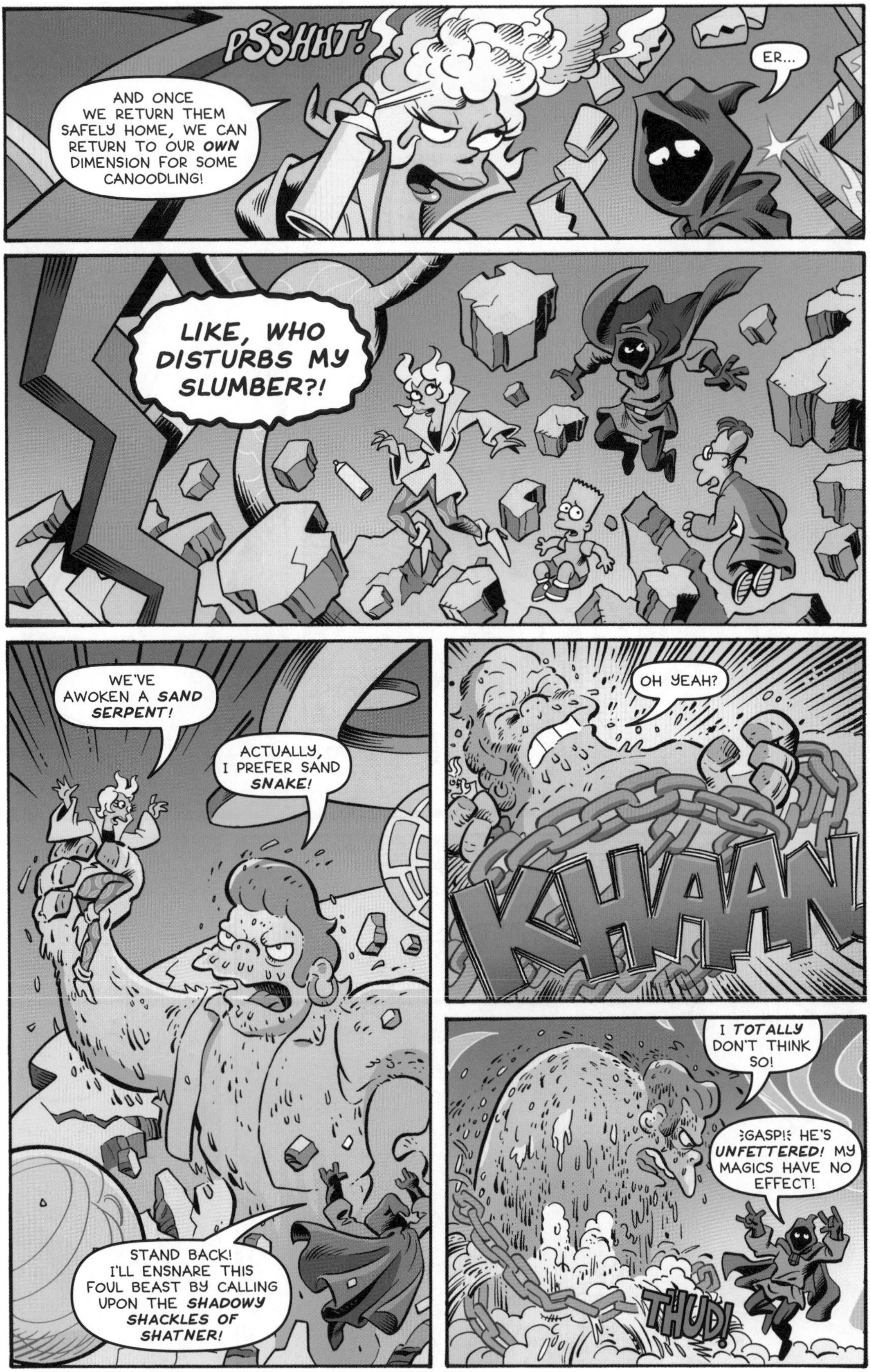
PSSHHT!
AND ONCE WE RETURN THEM SAFELY HOME, WE CAN RETURN TO OUR OWN DIMENSION FOR SOME CANOODLING!
ER...
LIKE, WHO DISTURBS MY SLUMBER?!
WE'VE AWOKEN A SAND SERPENT!
ACTUALLY, I PREFER SAND SNAKE!
STAND BACK! I'LL ENSNARE THIS FOUL BEAST BY CALLING UPON THE SHADOWY SHACKLES OF SHATNER!
OH YEAH?
KHAAN
I TOTALLY DON'T THINK SO!
GASP! HE'S UNFETTERED! MY MAGICS HAVE NO EFFECT!
THUD!

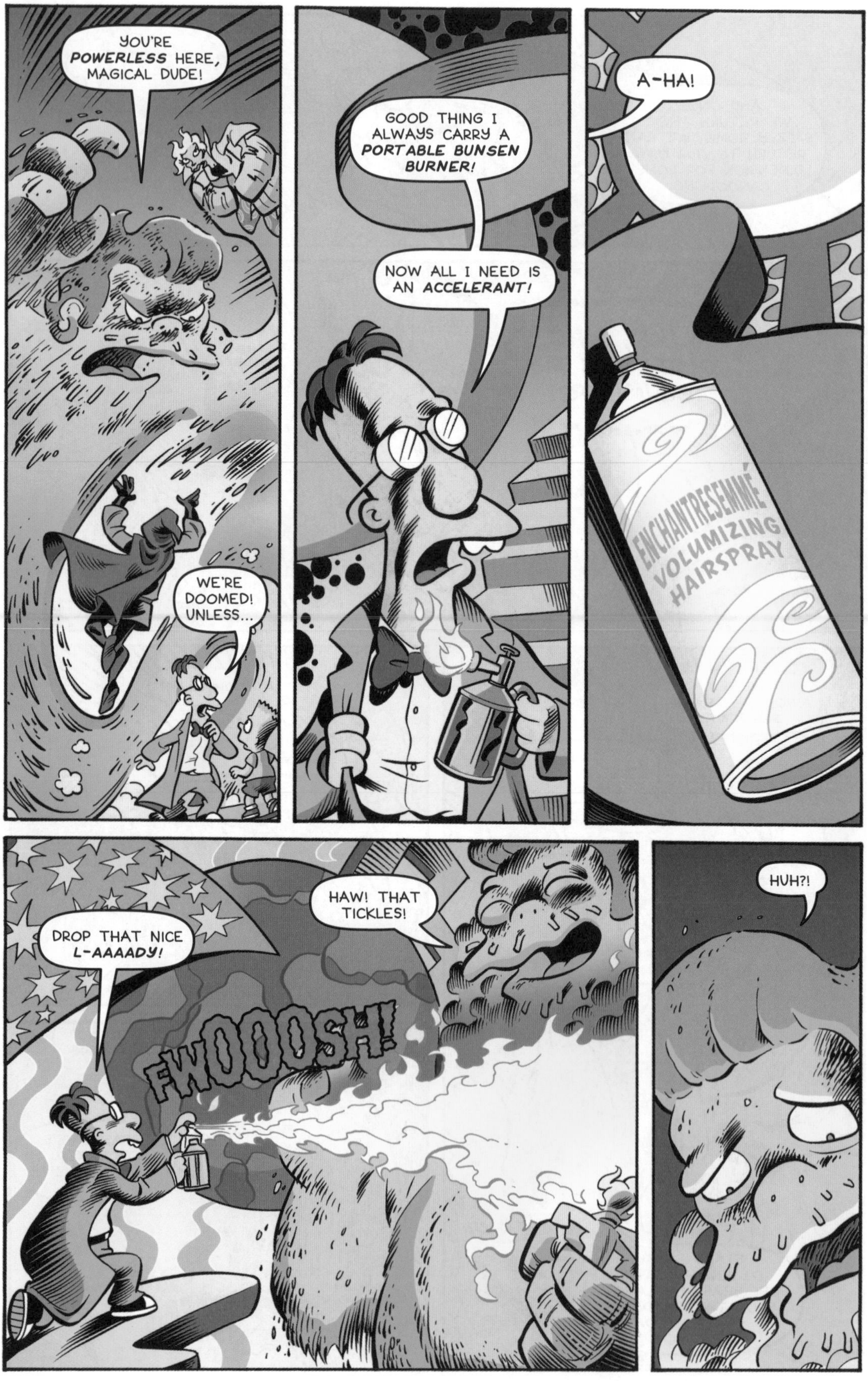
YOU'RE POWERLESS HERE, MAGICAL DUDE!
WE'RE DOOMED! UNLESS...
GOOD THING I ALWAYS CARRY A PORTABLE BUNSEN BURNER!
NOW ALL I NEED IS AN ACCELERANT!
A-HA!
ENCHANTRESEMMÉ VOLUMIZING HAIRSPRAY
DROP THAT NICE L-AAAADY!
HAW! THAT TICKLES!
FWOOOSH!
HUH?!

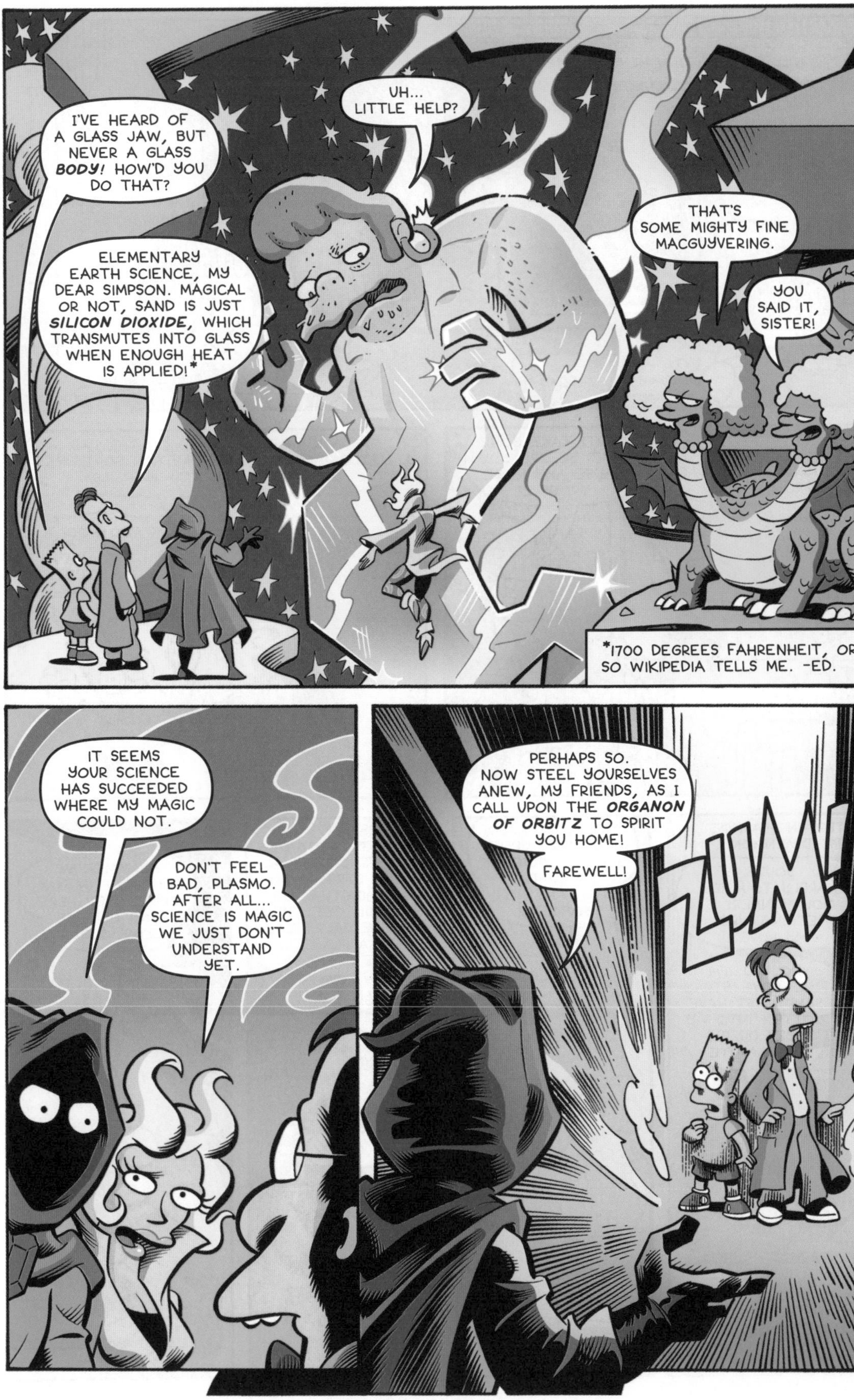
I'VE HEARD OF A GLASS JAW, BUT NEVER A GLASS BODY! HOW'D YOU DO THAT?
ELEMENTARY EARTH SCIENCE, MY DEAR SIMPSON. MAGICAL OR NOT, SAND IS JUST SILICON DIOXIDE, WHICH TRANSMUTES INTO GLASS WHEN ENOUGH HEAT IS APPLIED!*
UH... LITTLE HELP?
THAT'S SOME MIGHTY FINE MACGUYVERING.
YOU SAID IT, SISTER!
*1700 DEGREES FAHRENHEIT, OR SO WIKIPEDIA TELLS ME. -ED.
IT SEEMS YOUR SCIENCE HAS SUCCEEDED WHERE MY MAGIC COULD NOT.
DON'T FEEL BAD, PLASMO. AFTER ALL... SCIENCE IS MAGIC WE JUST DON'T UNDERSTAND YET.
PERHAPS SO. NOW STEEL YOURSELVES ANEW, MY FRIENDS, AS I CALL UPON THE ORGANON OF ORBITZ TO SPIRIT YOU HOME!
FAREWELL!
ZUM!

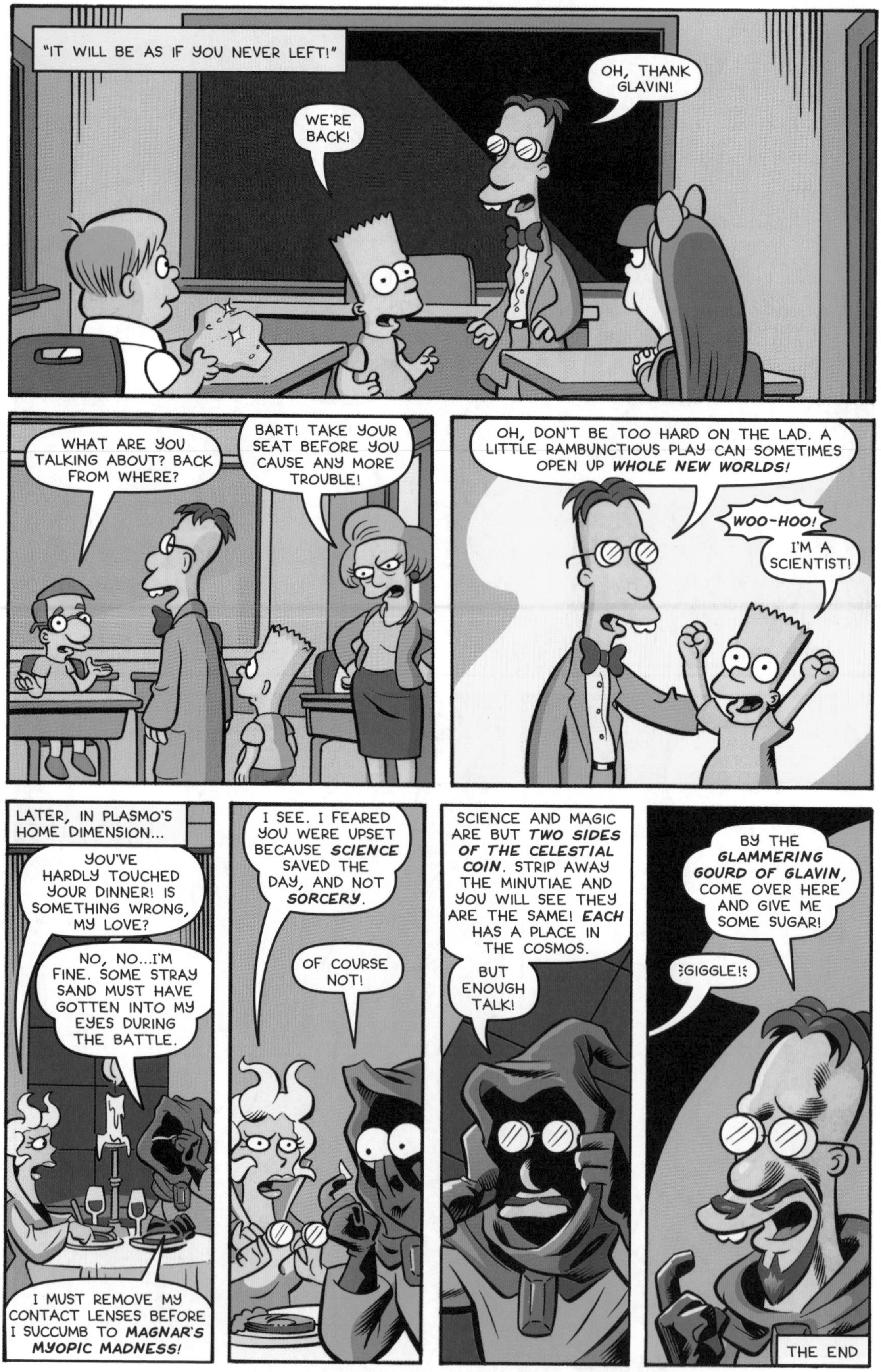
"IT WILL BE AS IF YOU NEVER LEFT!"
WE'RE BACK!
OH, THANK GLAVIN!
WHAT ARE YOU TALKING ABOUT? BACK FROM WHERE?
BART! TAKE YOUR SEAT BEFORE YOU CAUSE ANY MORE TROUBLE!
OH, DON'T BE TOO HARD ON THE LAD. A LITTLE RAMBUNCTIOUS PLAY CAN SOMETIMES OPEN UP WHOLE NEW WORLDS!
WOO-HOO!
I'M A SCIENTIST!
LATER, IN PLASMO'S HOME DIMENSION...
YOU'VE HARDLY TOUCHED YOUR DINNER! IS SOMETHING WRONG, MY LOVE?
NO, NO...I'M FINE. SOME STRAY SAND MUST HAVE GOTTEN INTO MY EYES DURING THE BATTLE.
I MUST REMOVE MY CONTACT LENSES BEFORE I SUCCUMB TO MAGNAR'S MYOPIC MADNESS!
I SEE. I FEARED YOU WERE UPSET BECAUSE SCIENCE SAVED THE DAY, AND NOT SORCERY.
OF COURSE NOT!
SCIENCE AND MAGIC ARE BUT TWO SIDES OF THE CELESTIAL COIN. STRIP AWAY THE MINUTIAE AND YOU WILL SEE THEY ARE THE SAME! EACH HAS A PLACE IN THE COSMOS.
BUT ENOUGH TALK!
BY THE GLAMMERING GOURD OF GLAVIN, COME OVER HERE AND GIVE ME SOME SUGAR!
GIGGLE!
THE END

WHAT THE HOLE?!

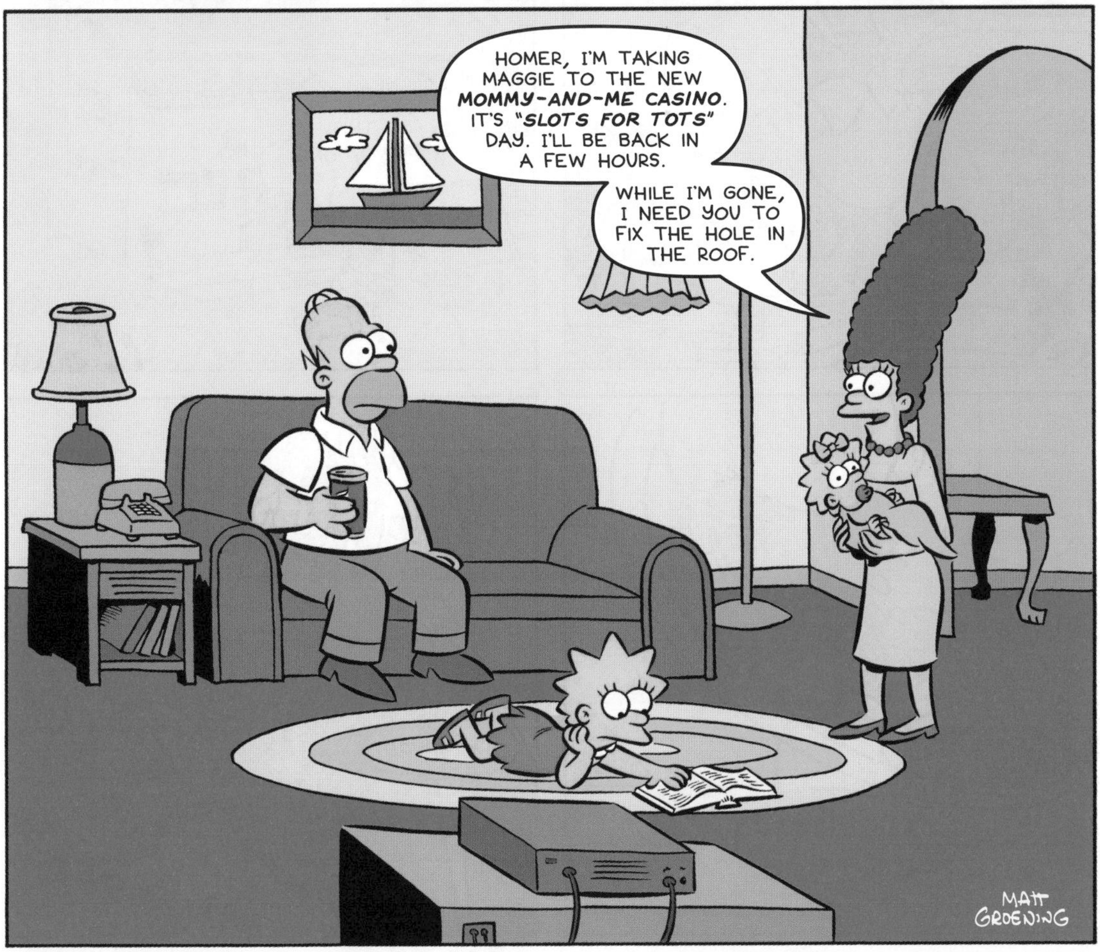
HOMER, I'M TAKING MAGGIE TO THE NEW **MOMMY-AND-ME CASINO**. IT'S "***SLOTS FOR TOTS***" DAY. I'LL BE BACK IN A FEW HOURS.
WHILE I'M GONE, I NEED YOU TO FIX THE HOLE IN THE ROOF.
MATT GROENING

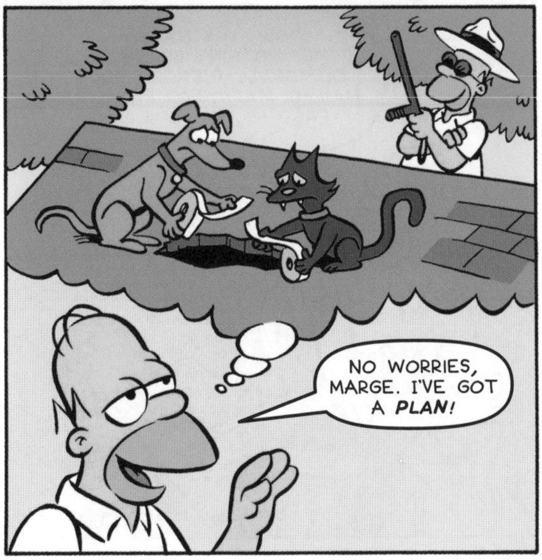
NO WORRIES, MARGE. I'VE GOT A ***PLAN***!

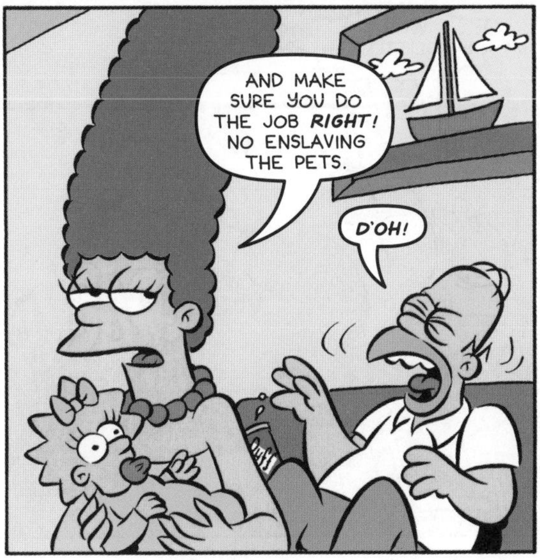
AND MAKE SURE YOU DO THE JOB ***RIGHT***! NO ENSLAVING THE PETS.
D'OH!

DAVID SEIDMAN SCRIPT · ***MIKE KAZALEH*** PENCILS & INKS · ***NATHAN HAMILL*** COLORS · ***KAREN BATES*** LETTERS · ***NATHAN KANE*** EDITOR

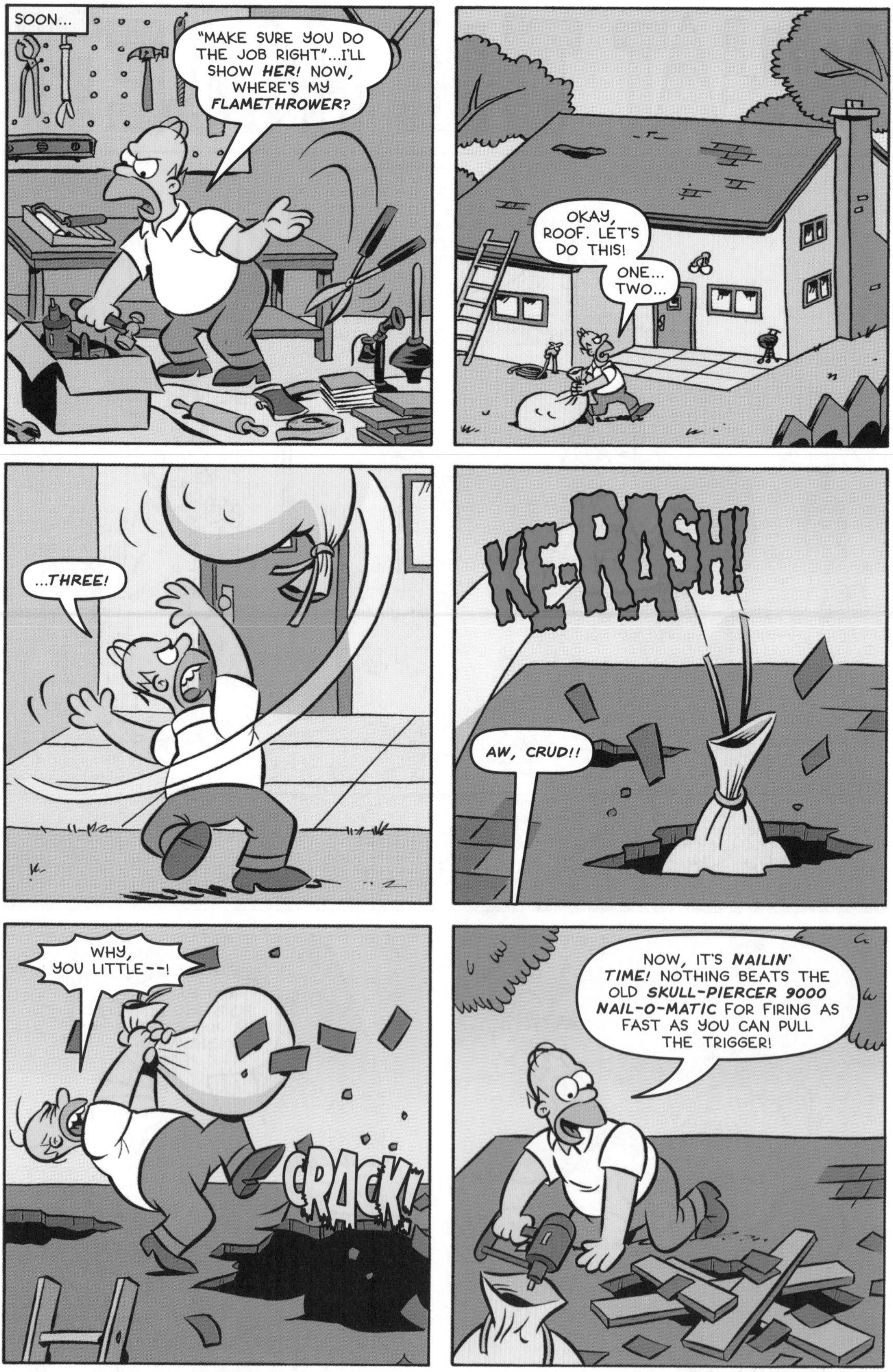
SOON...
"MAKE SURE YOU DO THE JOB RIGHT"...I'LL SHOW HER! NOW, WHERE'S MY FLAMETHROWER?
OKAY, ROOF. LET'S DO THIS!
ONE... TWO...
...THREE!
KE-RASH!
AW, CRUD!!
WHY, YOU LITTLE--!
CRACK!
NOW, IT'S NAILIN' TIME! NOTHING BEATS THE OLD SKULL-PIERCER 9000 NAIL-O-MATIC FOR FIRING AS FAST AS YOU CAN PULL THE TRIGGER!

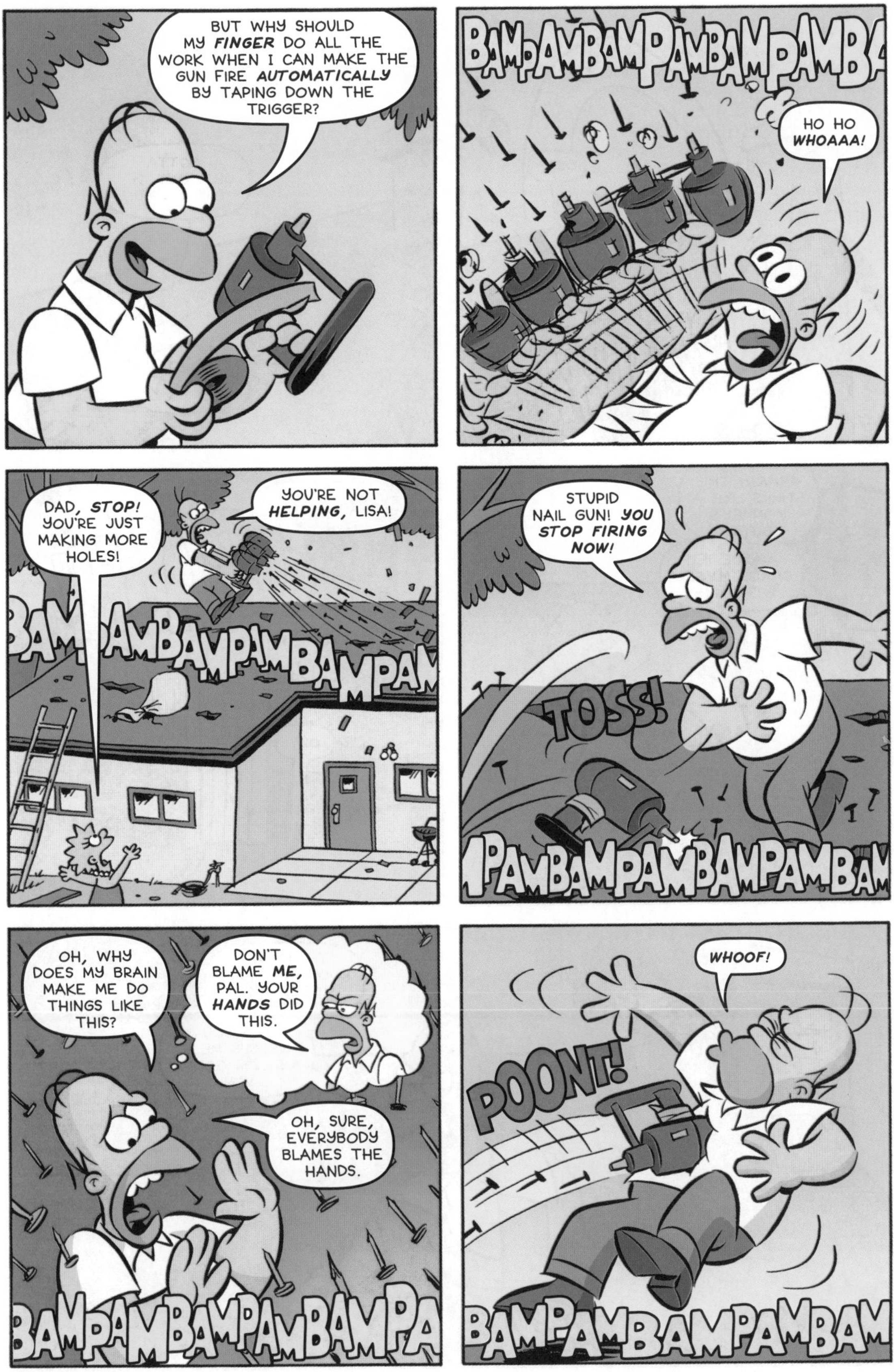
BUT WHY SHOULD MY **FINGER** DO ALL THE WORK WHEN I CAN MAKE THE GUN FIRE **AUTOMATICALLY** BY TAPING DOWN THE TRIGGER?
BAMPAMBAMPAMBAMPAMBA
HO HO **WHOAAA!**
DAD, **STOP!** YOU'RE JUST MAKING MORE HOLES!
YOU'RE NOT **HELPING,** LISA!
BAMPAMBAMPAMBAMPAM
STUPID NAIL GUN! **YOU STOP FIRING NOW!**
TOSS!
PAMBAMPAMBAMPAMBAM
OH, WHY DOES MY BRAIN MAKE ME DO THINGS LIKE THIS?
DON'T BLAME **ME,** PAL. YOUR **HANDS** DID THIS.
OH, SURE, EVERYBODY BLAMES THE HANDS.
BAMPAMBAMPAMBAMPA
WHOOF!
POONT!
BAMPAMBAMPAMBAM

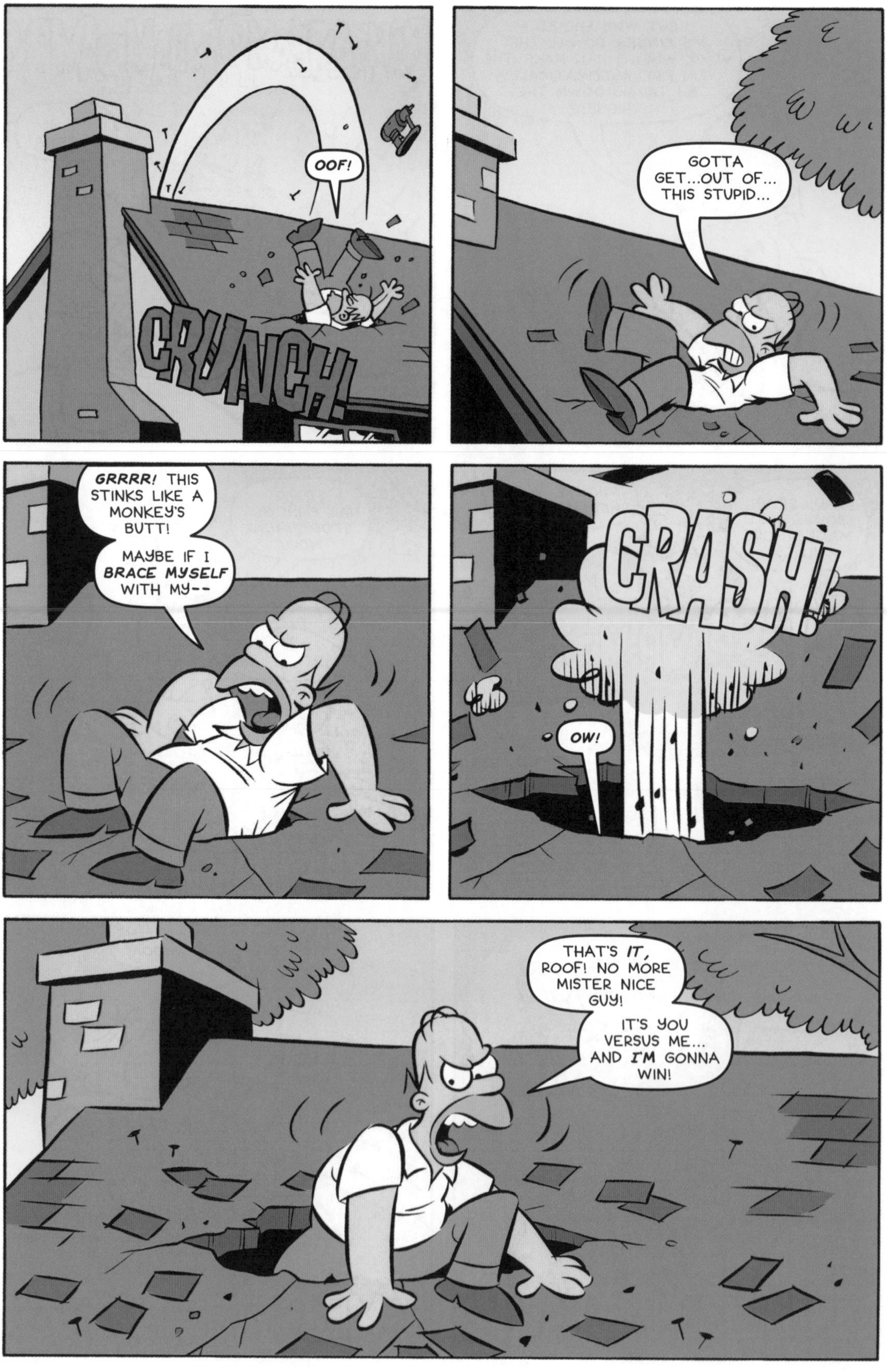
OOF!
CRUNCH!
GOTTA GET...OUT OF... THIS STUPID...
GRRRR! THIS STINKS LIKE A MONKEY'S BUTT!
MAYBE IF I BRACE MYSELF WITH MY--
CRASH!
OW!
THAT'S IT, ROOF! NO MORE MISTER NICE GUY!
IT'S YOU VERSUS ME... AND I'M GONNA WIN!

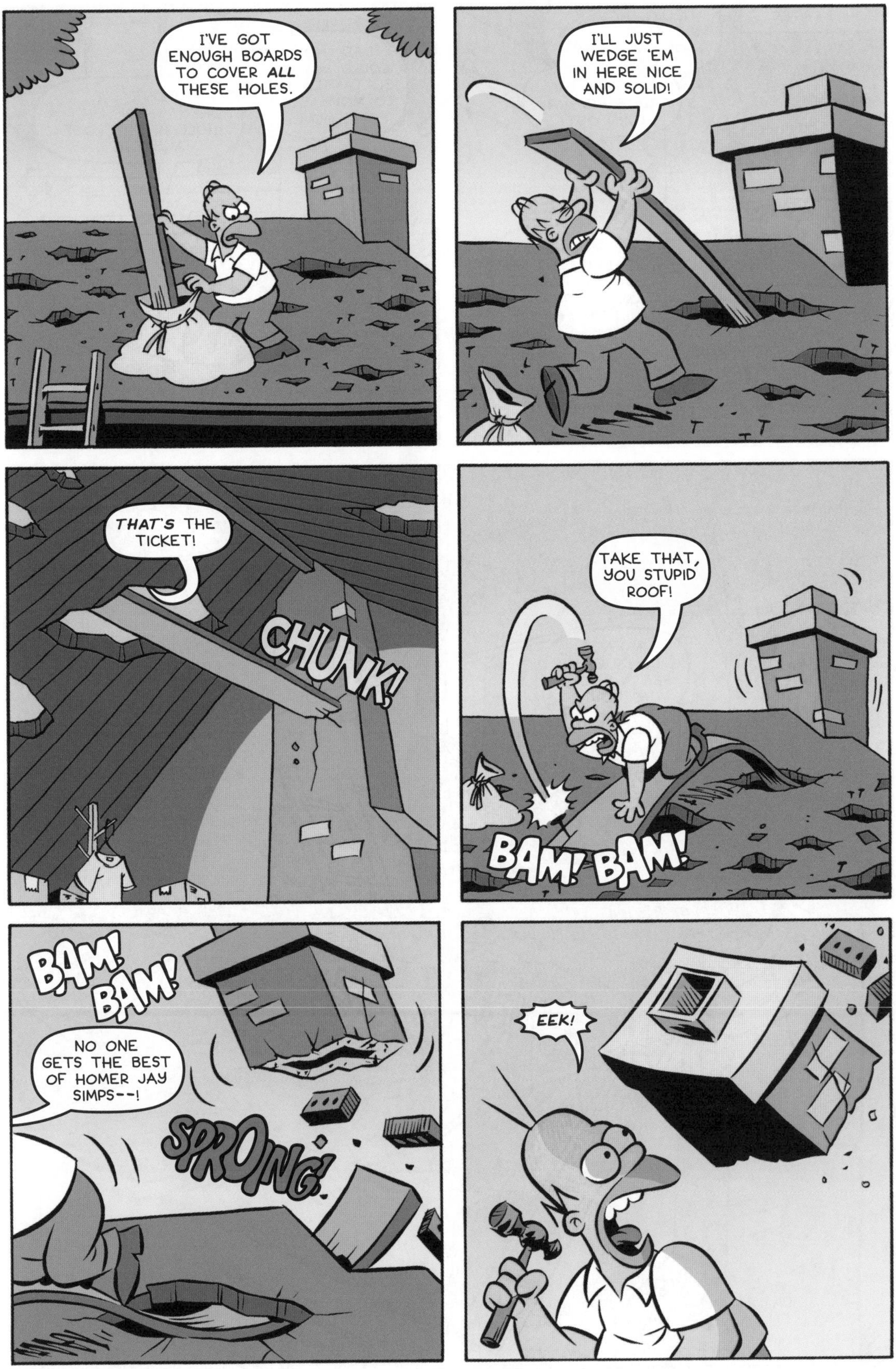
I'VE GOT ENOUGH BOARDS TO COVER ALL THESE HOLES.
I'LL JUST WEDGE 'EM IN HERE NICE AND SOLID!
THAT'S THE TICKET!
CHUNK!
TAKE THAT, YOU STUPID ROOF!
BAM! BAM!
BAM! BAM!
NO ONE GETS THE BEST OF HOMER JAY SIMPS--!
SPROING!
EEK!

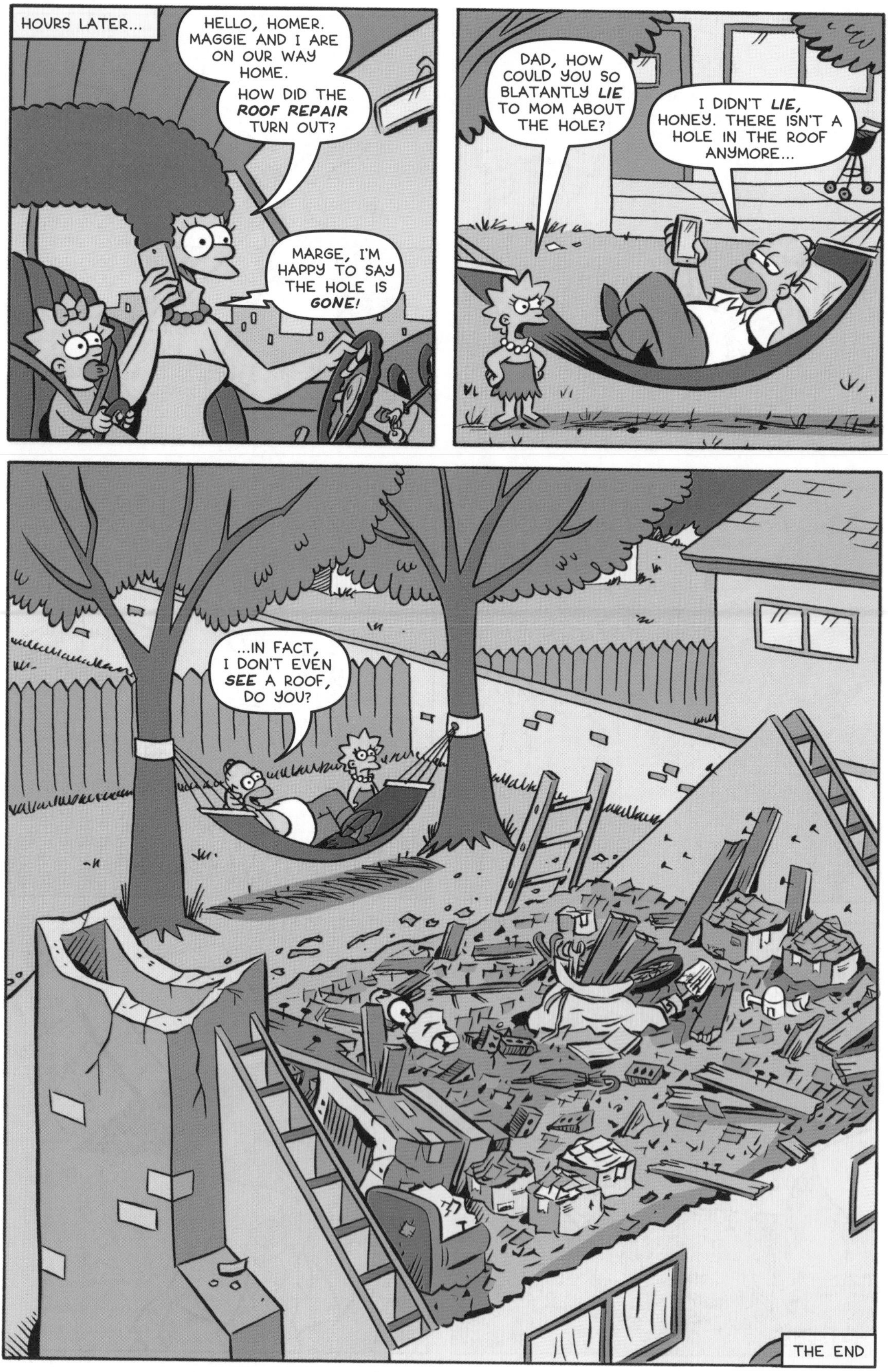
HOURS LATER...
HELLO, HOMER. MAGGIE AND I ARE ON OUR WAY HOME.
HOW DID THE ROOF REPAIR TURN OUT?
MARGE, I'M HAPPY TO SAY THE HOLE IS GONE!
DAD, HOW COULD YOU SO BLATANTLY LIE TO MOM ABOUT THE HOLE?
I DIDN'T LIE, HONEY. THERE ISN'T A HOLE IN THE ROOF ANYMORE...
...IN FACT, I DON'T EVEN SEE A ROOF, DO YOU?
THE END

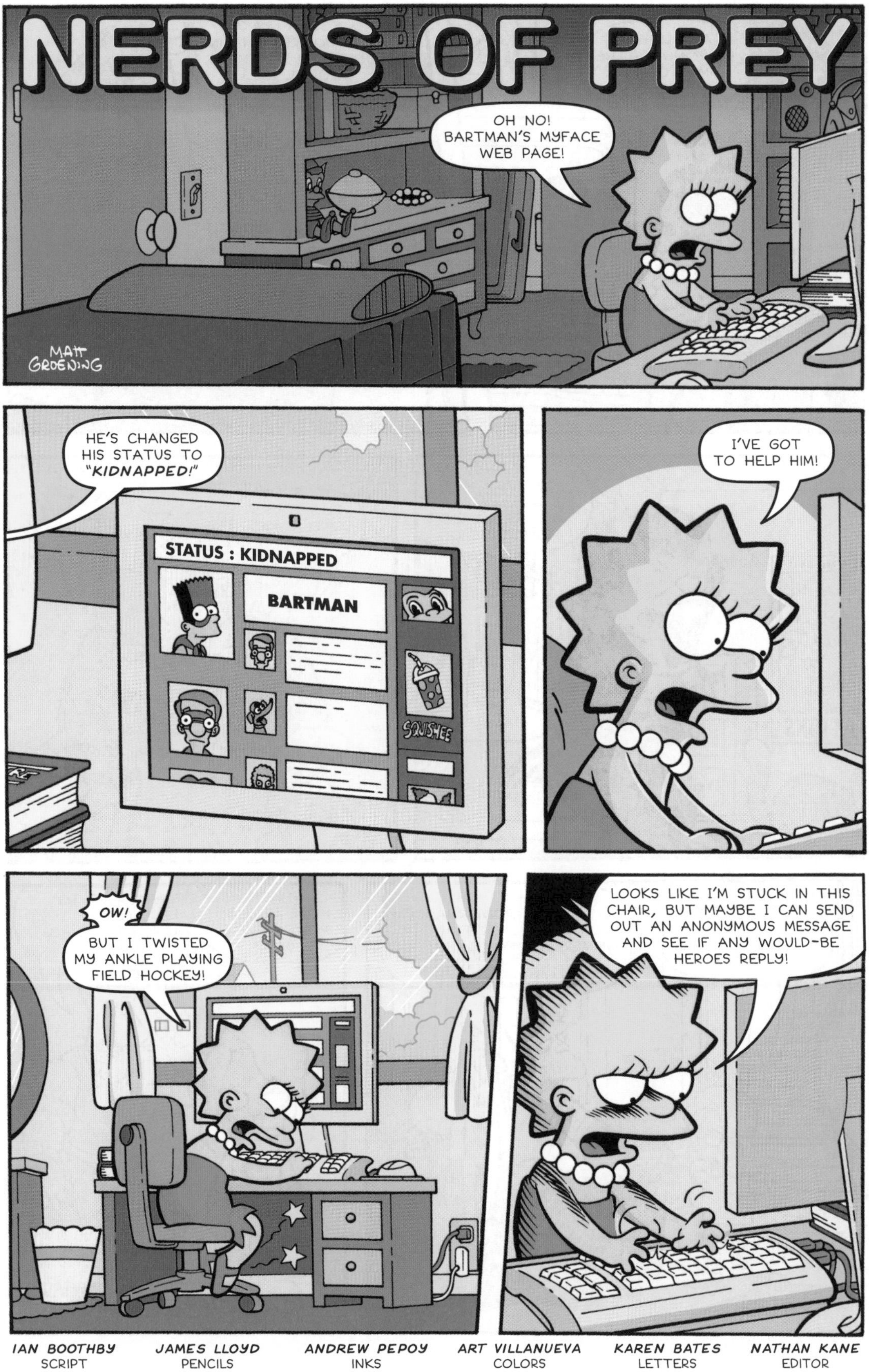
NERDS OF PREY
OH NO! BARTMAN'S MYFACE WEB PAGE!
MATT GROENING
HE'S CHANGED HIS STATUS TO "KIDNAPPED!"
STATUS : KIDNAPPED
BARTMAN
SQUISHEE
I'VE GOT TO HELP HIM!
OW!
BUT I TWISTED MY ANKLE PLAYING FIELD HOCKEY!
LOOKS LIKE I'M STUCK IN THIS CHAIR, BUT MAYBE I CAN SEND OUT AN ANONYMOUS MESSAGE AND SEE IF ANY WOULD-BE HEROES REPLY!

IAN BOOTHBY SCRIPT | *JAMES LLOYD* PENCILS | *ANDREW PEPOY* INKS | *ART VILLANUEVA* COLORS | *KAREN BATES* LETTERS | *NATHAN KANE* EDITOR

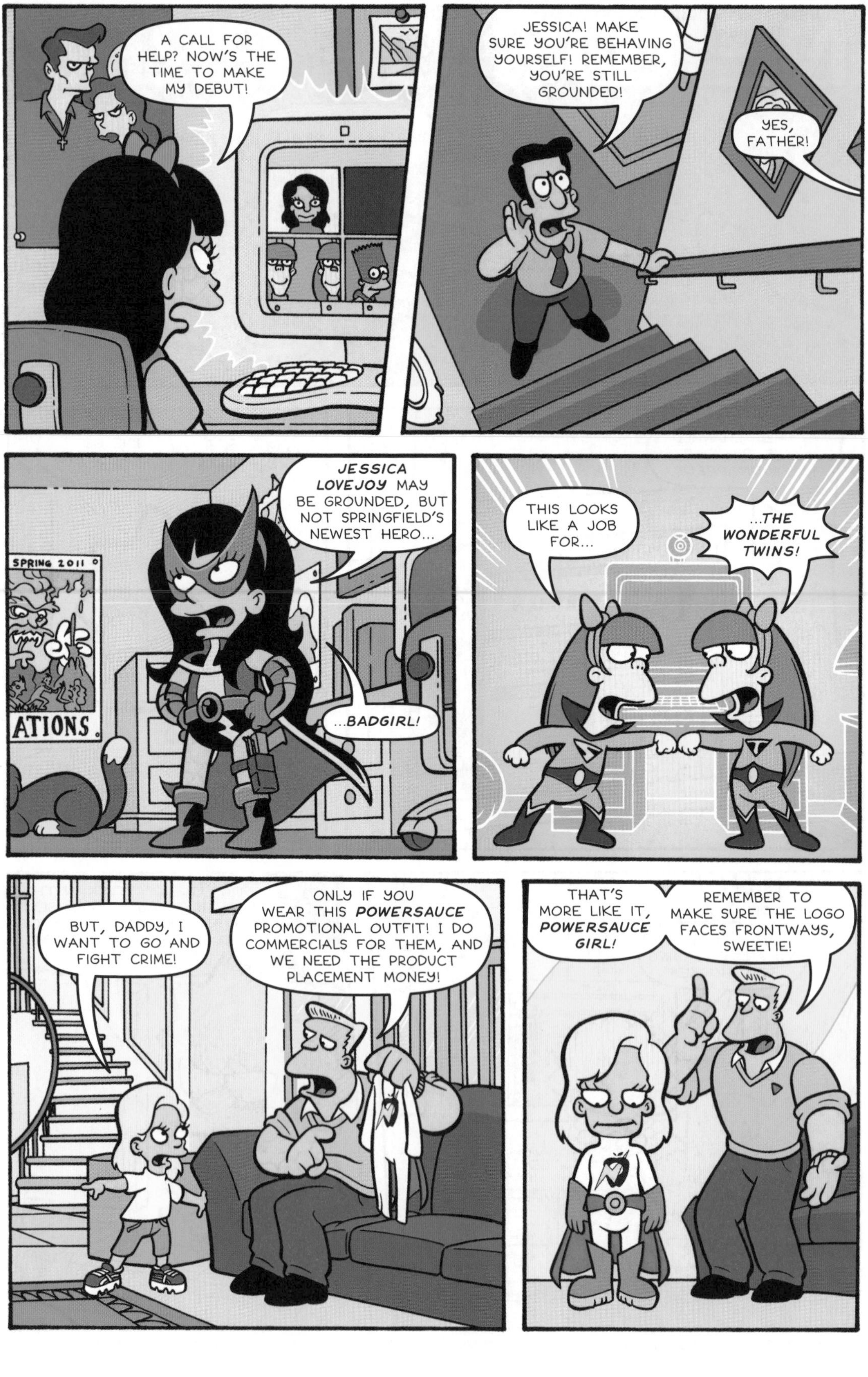
A CALL FOR HELP? NOW'S THE TIME TO MAKE MY DEBUT!
JESSICA! MAKE SURE YOU'RE BEHAVING YOURSELF! REMEMBER, YOU'RE STILL GROUNDED!
YES, FATHER!
JESSICA LOVEJOY MAY BE GROUNDED, BUT NOT SPRINGFIELD'S NEWEST HERO...
...*BADGIRL!*
SPRING 2011
ATIONS
THIS LOOKS LIKE A JOB FOR...
...*THE WONDERFUL TWINS!*
BUT, DADDY, I WANT TO GO AND FIGHT CRIME!
ONLY IF YOU WEAR THIS *POWERSAUCE* PROMOTIONAL OUTFIT! I DO COMMERCIALS FOR THEM, AND WE NEED THE PRODUCT PLACEMENT MONEY!
THAT'S MORE LIKE IT, *POWERSAUCE GIRL!*
REMEMBER TO MAKE SURE THE LOGO FACES FRONTWAYS, SWEETIE!

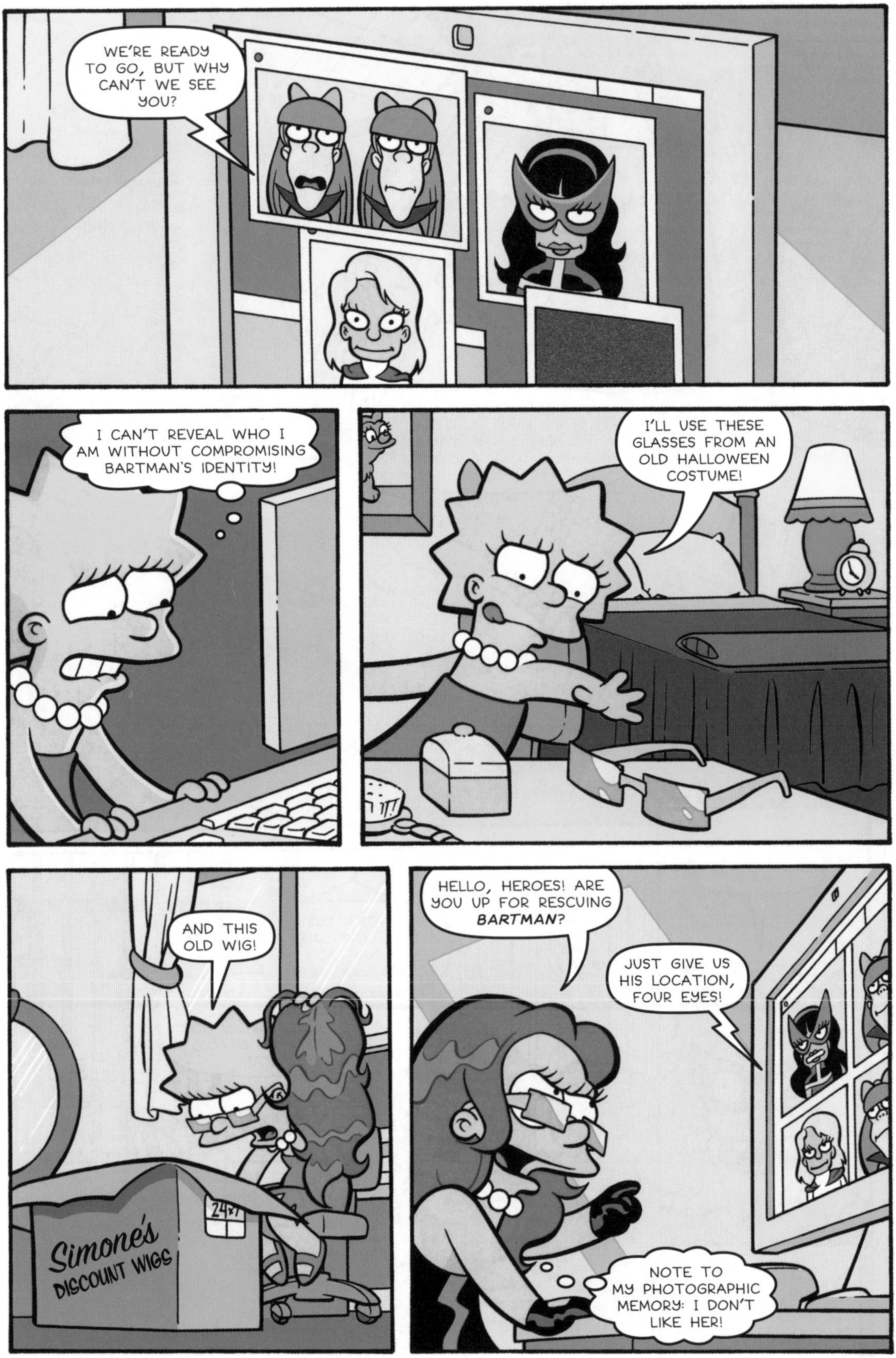
WE'RE READY TO GO, BUT WHY CAN'T WE SEE YOU?
I CAN'T REVEAL WHO I AM WITHOUT COMPROMISING BARTMAN'S IDENTITY!
I'LL USE THESE GLASSES FROM AN OLD HALLOWEEN COSTUME!
AND THIS OLD WIG!
Simone's DISCOUNT WIGS
24x7
HELLO, HEROES! ARE YOU UP FOR RESCUING ***BARTMAN***?
JUST GIVE US HIS LOCATION, FOUR EYES!
NOTE TO MY PHOTOGRAPHIC MEMORY: I DON'T LIKE HER!

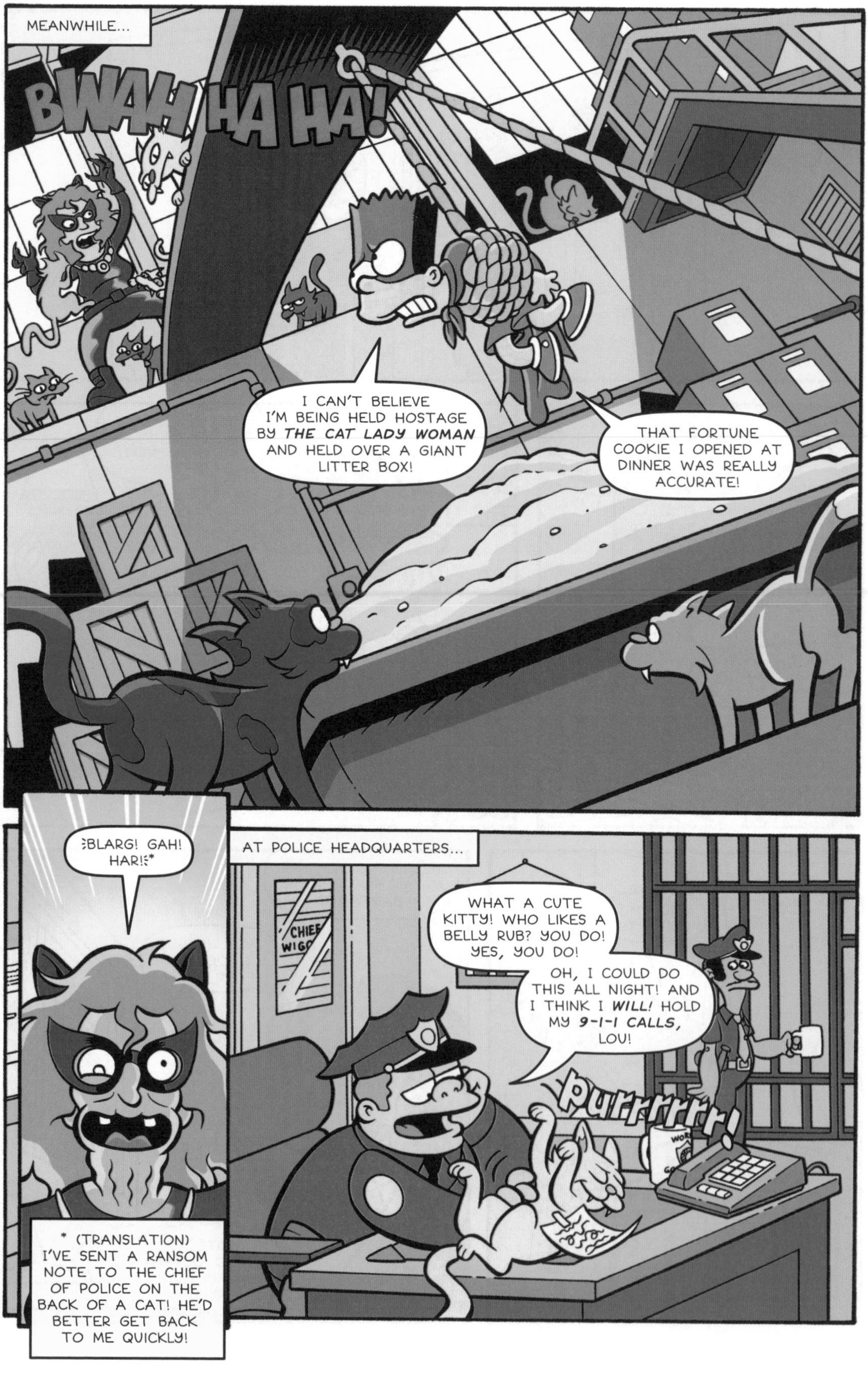
MEANWHILE...
BWAH HA HA!
I CAN'T BELIEVE I'M BEING HELD HOSTAGE BY *THE CAT LADY WOMAN* AND HELD OVER A GIANT LITTER BOX!
THAT FORTUNE COOKIE I OPENED AT DINNER WAS REALLY ACCURATE!
BLARG! GAH! HAR!*
* (TRANSLATION) I'VE SENT A RANSOM NOTE TO THE CHIEF OF POLICE ON THE BACK OF A CAT! HE'D BETTER GET BACK TO ME QUICKLY!
AT POLICE HEADQUARTERS...
CHIEF WIGG
WHAT A CUTE KITTY! WHO LIKES A BELLY RUB? YOU DO! YES, YOU DO!
OH, I COULD DO THIS ALL NIGHT! AND I THINK I *WILL!* HOLD MY *9-1-1 CALLS,* LOU!
PURRRRRR!

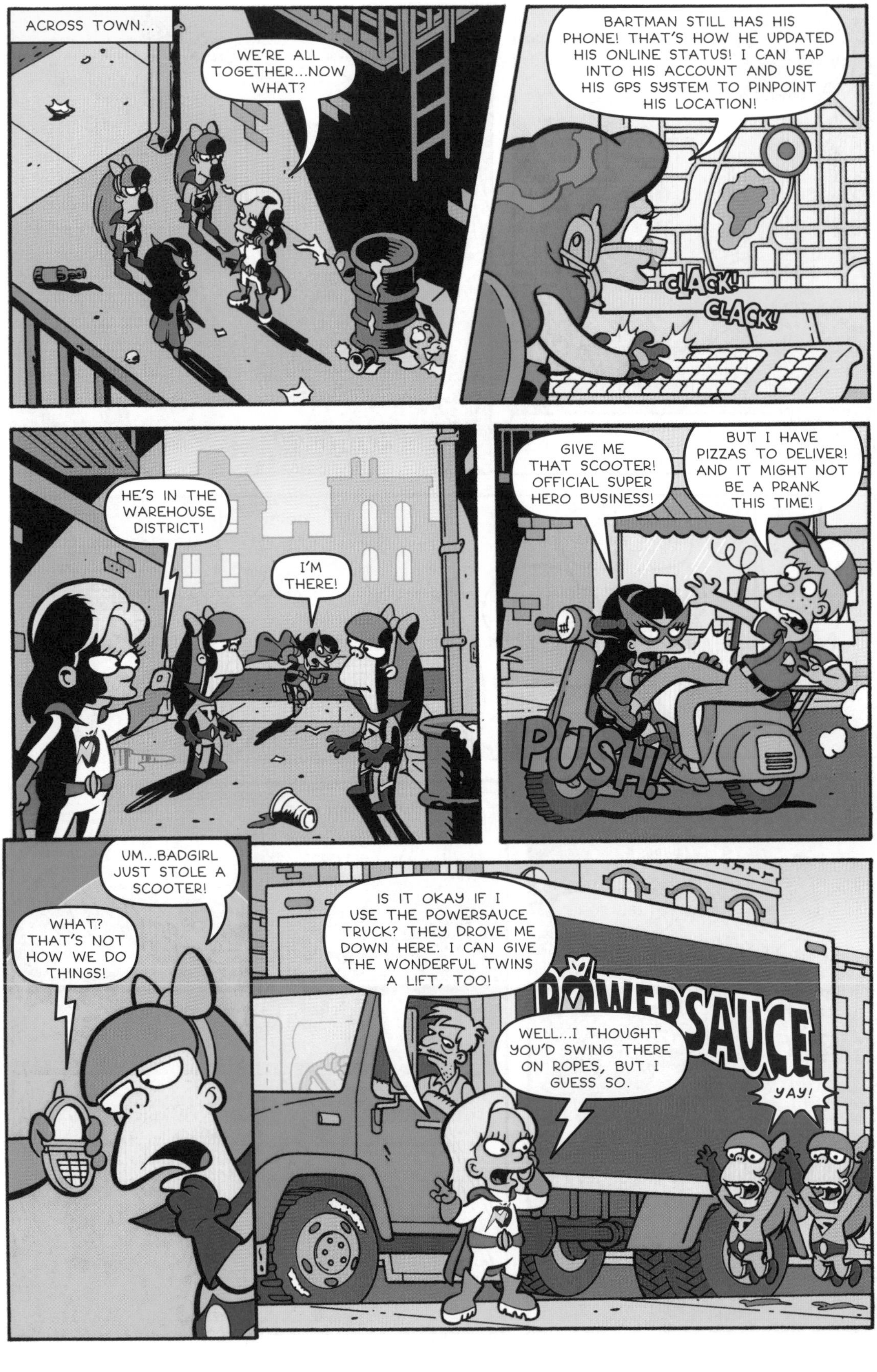
ACROSS TOWN...
WE'RE ALL TOGETHER...NOW WHAT?
BARTMAN STILL HAS HIS PHONE! THAT'S HOW HE UPDATED HIS ONLINE STATUS! I CAN TAP INTO HIS ACCOUNT AND USE HIS GPS SYSTEM TO PINPOINT HIS LOCATION!
CLACK!
CLACK!
HE'S IN THE WAREHOUSE DISTRICT!
I'M THERE!
GIVE ME THAT SCOOTER! OFFICIAL SUPER HERO BUSINESS!
BUT I HAVE PIZZAS TO DELIVER! AND IT MIGHT NOT BE A PRANK THIS TIME!
PUSH!
UM...BADGIRL JUST STOLE A SCOOTER!
WHAT? THAT'S NOT HOW WE DO THINGS!
IS IT OKAY IF I USE THE POWERSAUCE TRUCK? THEY DROVE ME DOWN HERE. I CAN GIVE THE WONDERFUL TWINS A LIFT, TOO!
POWERSAUCE
WELL...I THOUGHT YOU'D SWING THERE ON ROPES, BUT I GUESS SO.
YAY!

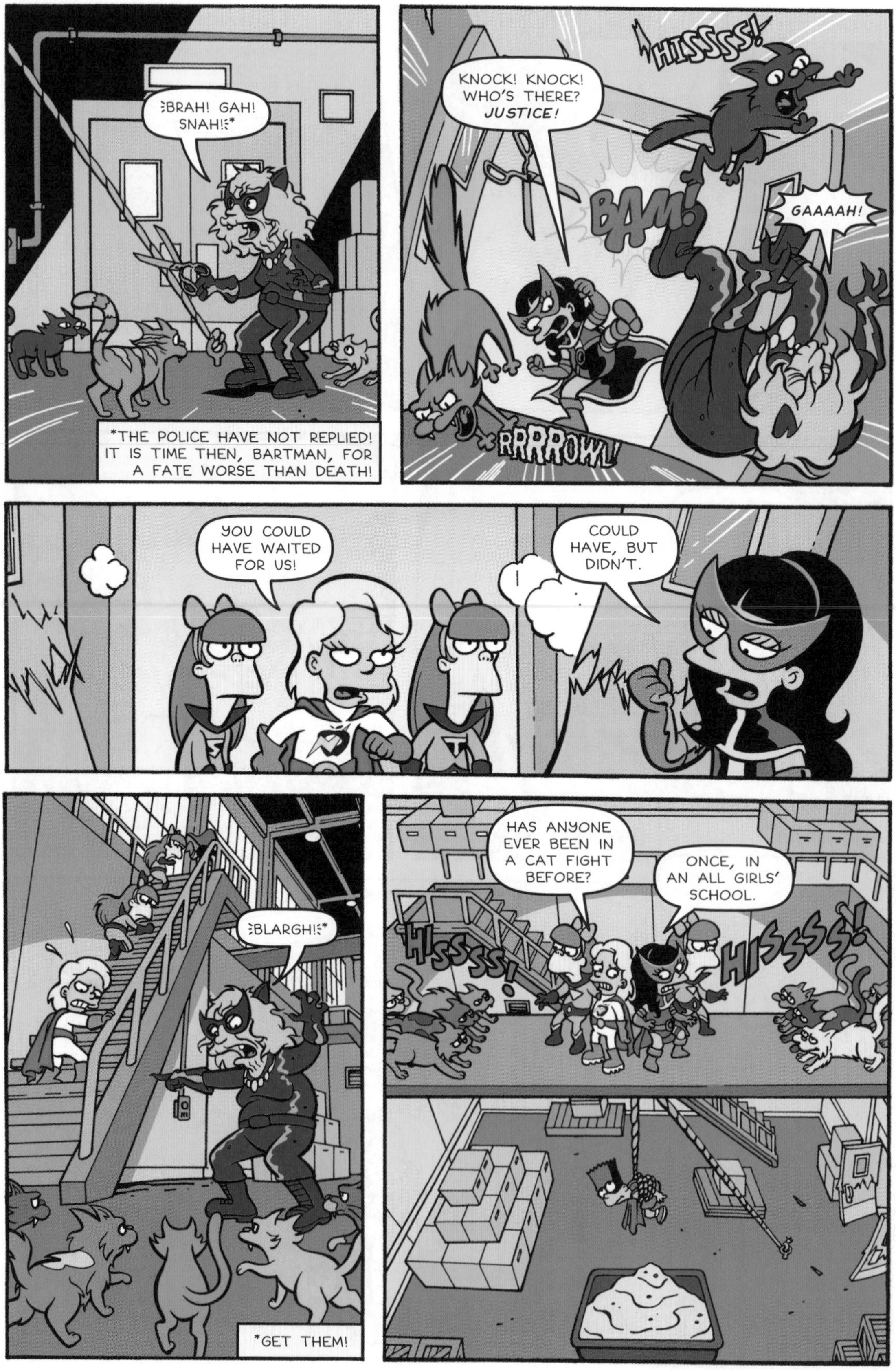

BRAH! GAH! SNAH!*
*THE POLICE HAVE NOT REPLIED! IT IS TIME THEN, BARTMAN, FOR A FATE WORSE THAN DEATH!
HISSSSS!
KNOCK! KNOCK! WHO'S THERE? *JUSTICE!*
BAM!
GAAAAH!
RRRROWL!
YOU COULD HAVE WAITED FOR US!
COULD HAVE, BUT DIDN'T.
BLARGH!*
*GET THEM!
HAS ANYONE EVER BEEN IN A CAT FIGHT BEFORE?
ONCE, IN AN ALL GIRLS' SCHOOL.
HISSSS!
HISSSS!

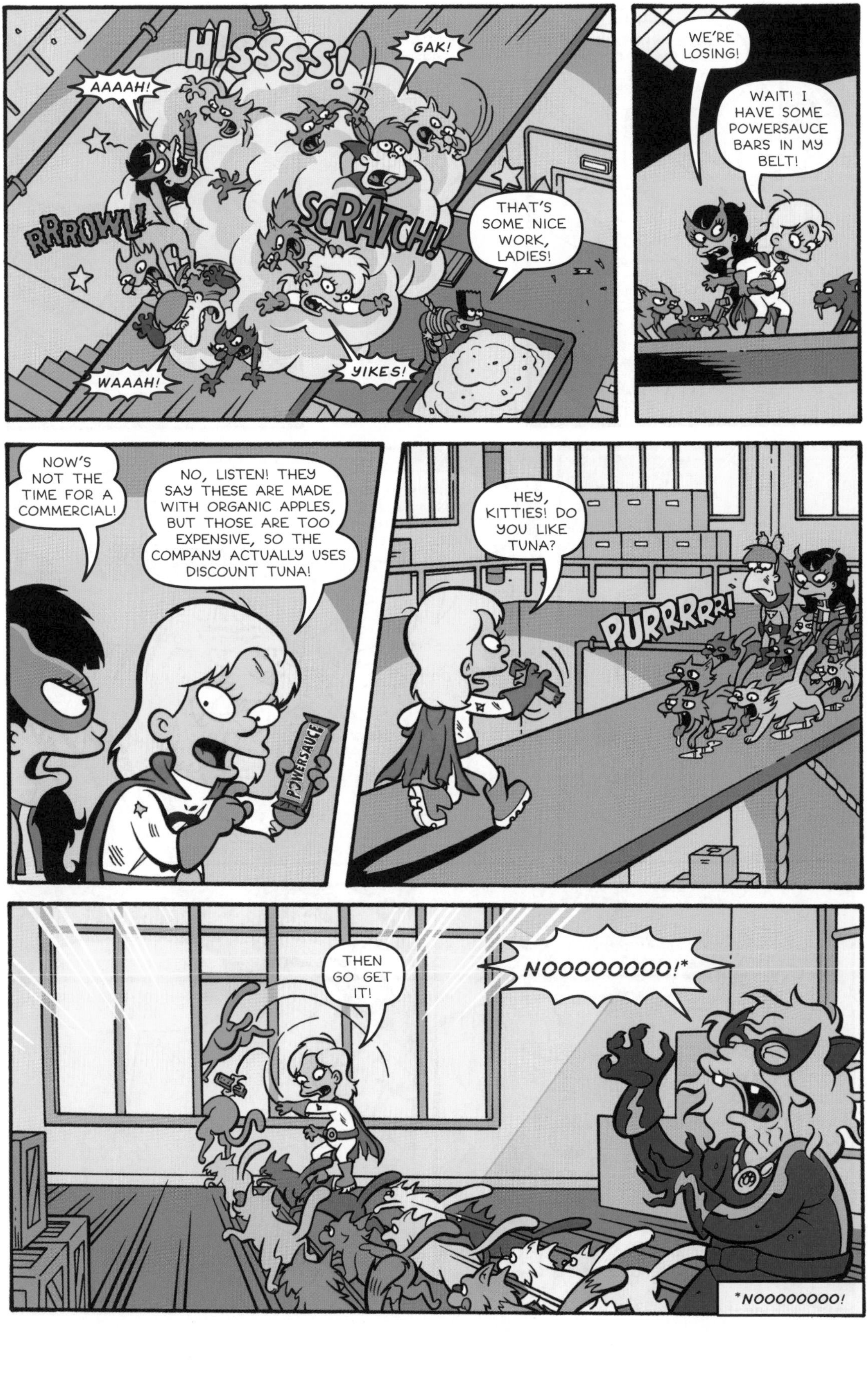
HISSSS!
AAAAH!
GAK!
RRROWL!
SCRATCH!
THAT'S SOME NICE WORK, LADIES!
WAAAH!
YIKES!
WE'RE LOSING!
WAIT! I HAVE SOME POWERSAUCE BARS IN MY BELT!
NOW'S NOT THE TIME FOR A COMMERCIAL!
NO, LISTEN! THEY SAY THESE ARE MADE WITH ORGANIC APPLES, BUT THOSE ARE TOO EXPENSIVE, SO THE COMPANY ACTUALLY USES DISCOUNT TUNA!
POWERSAUCE
HEY, KITTIES! DO YOU LIKE TUNA?
PURRRRR!
THEN GO GET IT!
NOOOOOOOO!*
*NOOOOOOOO!

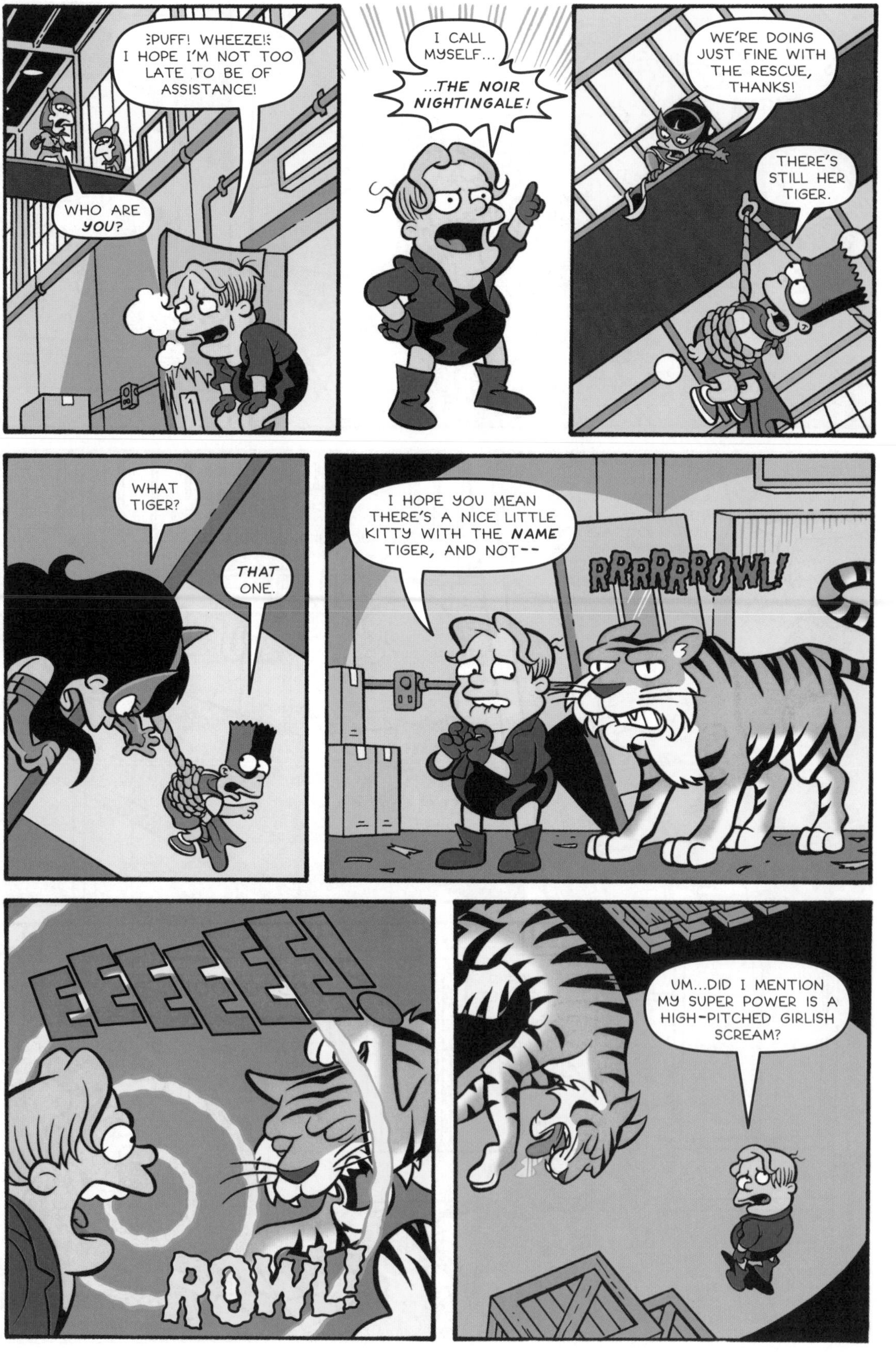

PUFF! WHEEZE! I HOPE I'M NOT TOO LATE TO BE OF ASSISTANCE!
WHO ARE *YOU*?
I CALL MYSELF...
...*THE NOIR NIGHTINGALE!*
WE'RE DOING JUST FINE WITH THE RESCUE, THANKS!
THERE'S STILL HER TIGER.
WHAT TIGER?
THAT ONE.
I HOPE YOU MEAN THERE'S A NICE LITTLE KITTY WITH THE *NAME* TIGER, AND NOT--
RRRRRROWL!
EEEEEE!
ROWL!
UM...DID I MENTION MY SUPER POWER IS A HIGH-PITCHED GIRLISH SCREAM?

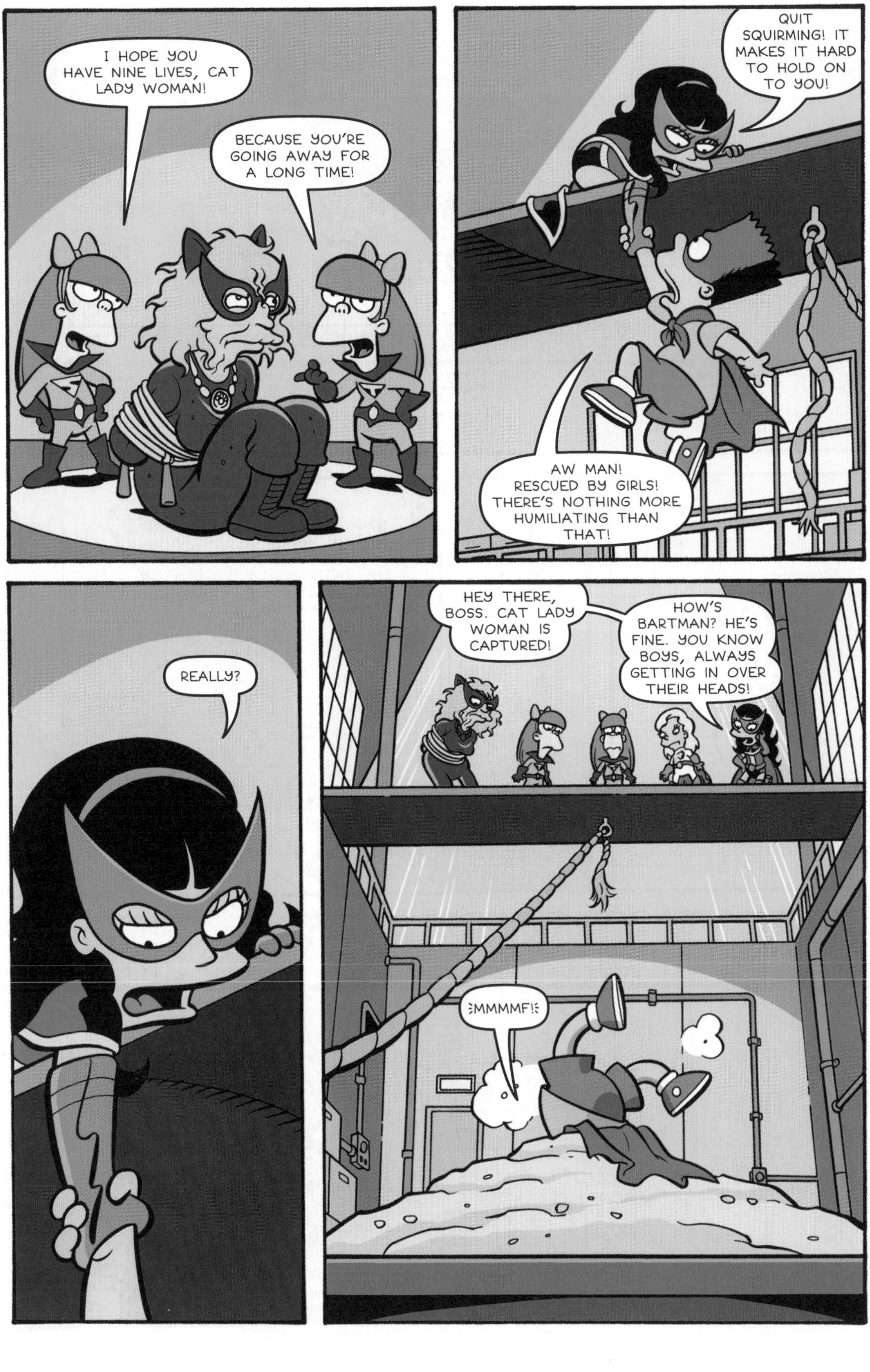
I HOPE YOU HAVE NINE LIVES, CAT LADY WOMAN!
BECAUSE YOU'RE GOING AWAY FOR A LONG TIME!
QUIT SQUIRMING! IT MAKES IT HARD TO HOLD ON TO YOU!
AW MAN! RESCUED BY GIRLS! THERE'S NOTHING MORE HUMILIATING THAN THAT!
REALLY?
HEY THERE, BOSS. CAT LADY WOMAN IS CAPTURED!
HOW'S BARTMAN? HE'S FINE. YOU KNOW BOYS, ALWAYS GETTING IN OVER THEIR HEADS!
MMMMF!

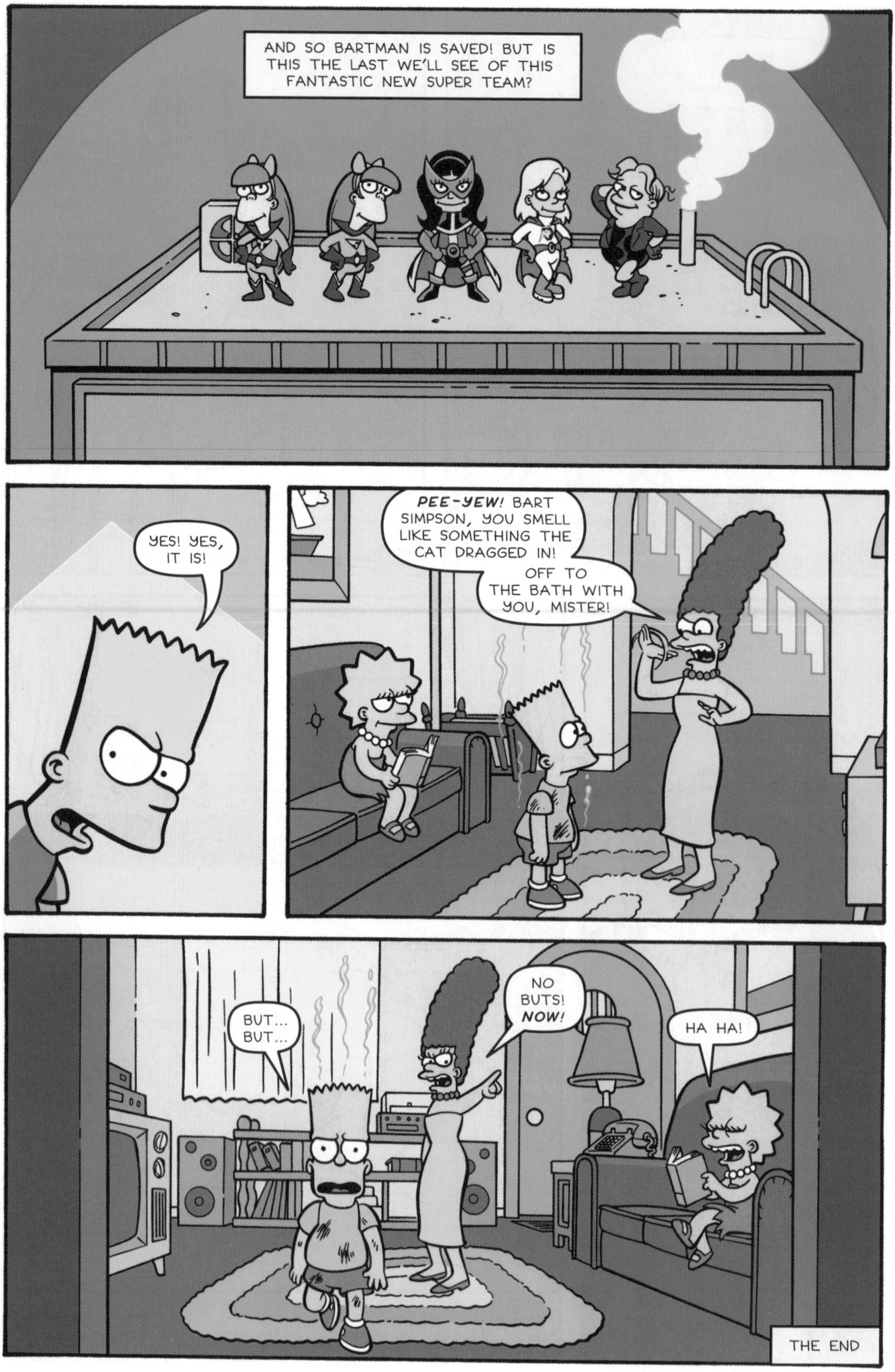

AND SO BARTMAN IS SAVED! BUT IS THIS THE LAST WE'LL SEE OF THIS FANTASTIC NEW SUPER TEAM?
YES! YES, IT IS!
PEE-YEW! BART SIMPSON, YOU SMELL LIKE SOMETHING THE CAT DRAGGED IN!
OFF TO THE BATH WITH YOU, MISTER!
BUT... BUT...
NO BUTS! NOW!
HA HA!
THE END

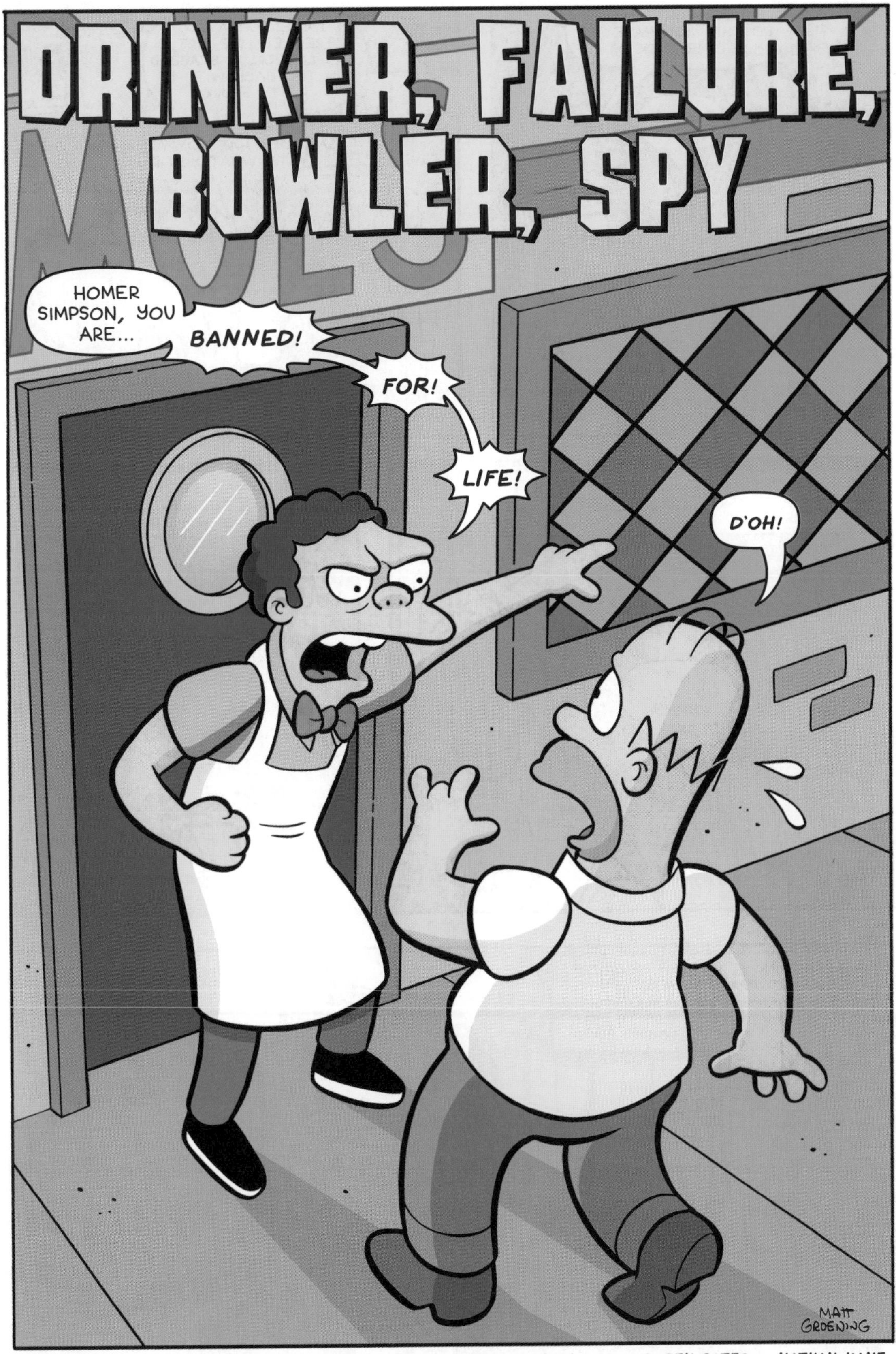
DRINKER, FAILURE, BOWLER, SPY
HOMER SIMPSON, YOU ARE...
BANNED!
FOR!
LIFE!
D'OH!
MATT GROENING

MAX DAVISON WRITER | *NINA MATSUMOTO* PENCILS | *ANDREW PEPOY* INKS | *ART VILLANUEVA* COLORS | *KAREN BATES* LETTERS | *NATHAN KANE* EDITOR

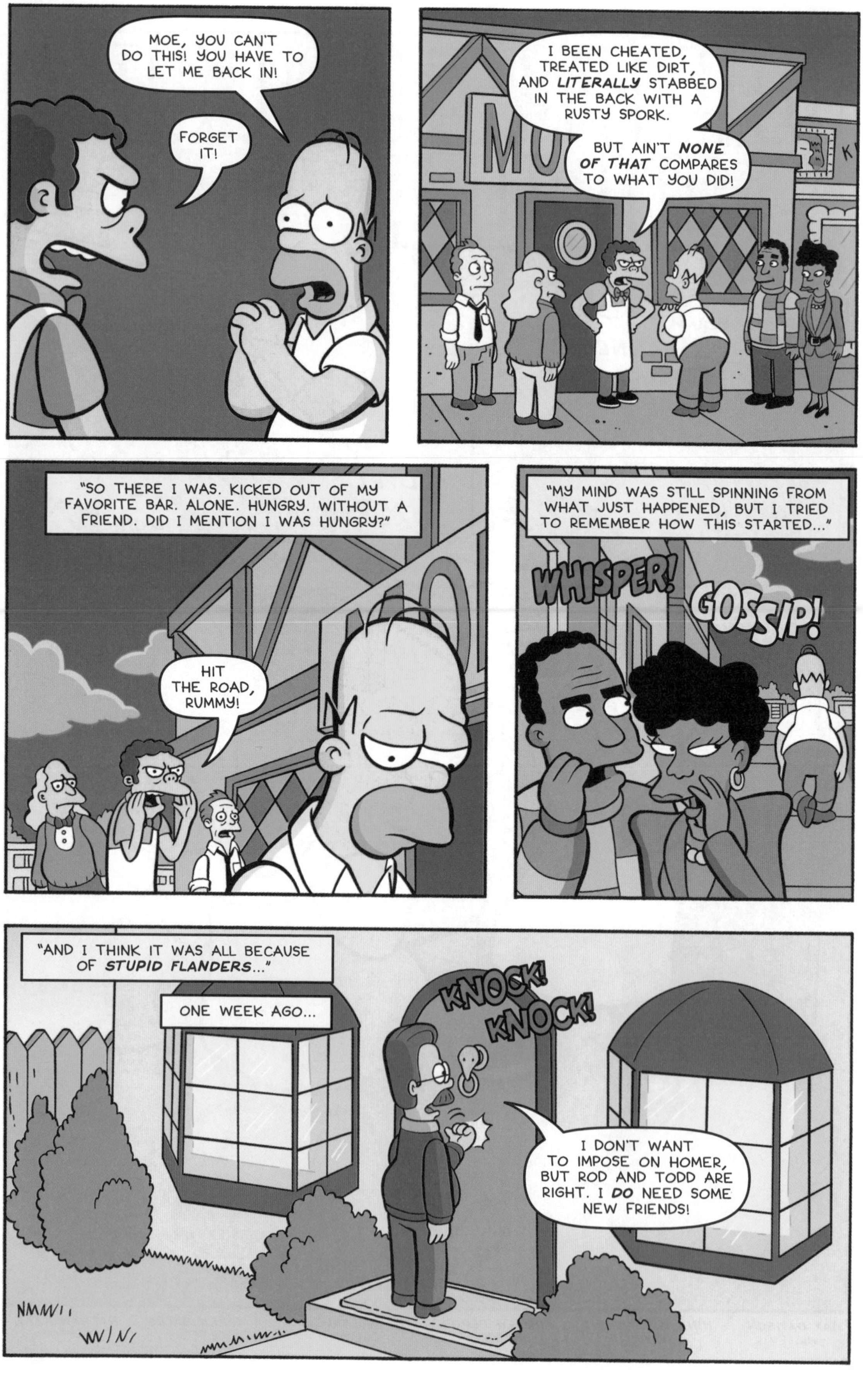
MOE, YOU CAN'T DO THIS! YOU HAVE TO LET ME BACK IN!
FORGET IT!
I BEEN CHEATED, TREATED LIKE DIRT, AND *LITERALLY* STABBED IN THE BACK WITH A RUSTY SPORK.
BUT AIN'T **NONE OF THAT** COMPARES TO WHAT YOU DID!
"SO THERE I WAS. KICKED OUT OF MY FAVORITE BAR. ALONE. HUNGRY. WITHOUT A FRIEND. DID I MENTION I WAS HUNGRY?"
HIT THE ROAD, RUMMY!
"MY MIND WAS STILL SPINNING FROM WHAT JUST HAPPENED, BUT I TRIED TO REMEMBER HOW THIS STARTED..."
WHISPER!
GOSSIP!
"AND I THINK IT WAS ALL BECAUSE OF ***STUPID FLANDERS***..."
ONE WEEK AGO...
KNOCK! KNOCK!
I DON'T WANT TO IMPOSE ON HOMER, BUT ROD AND TODD ARE RIGHT. I ***DO*** NEED SOME NEW FRIENDS!

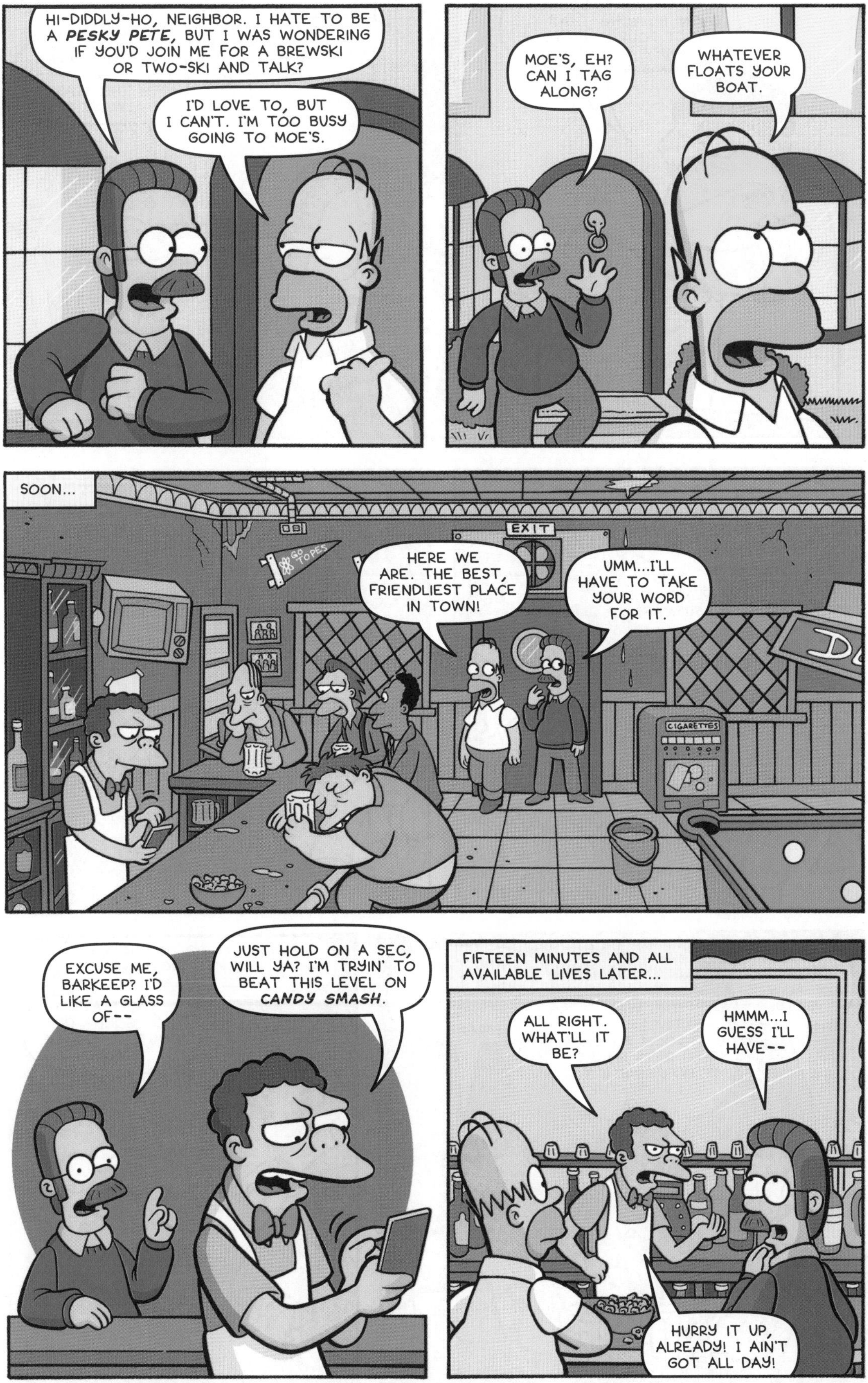
HI-DIDDLY-HO, NEIGHBOR. I HATE TO BE A *PESKY PETE*, BUT I WAS WONDERING IF YOU'D JOIN ME FOR A BREWSKI OR TWO-SKI AND TALK?
I'D LOVE TO, BUT I CAN'T. I'M TOO BUSY GOING TO MOE'S.
MOE'S, EH? CAN I TAG ALONG?
WHATEVER FLOATS YOUR BOAT.
SOON...
EXIT
GO TOPES
HERE WE ARE. THE BEST, FRIENDLIEST PLACE IN TOWN!
UMM...I'LL HAVE TO TAKE YOUR WORD FOR IT.
CIGARETTES
EXCUSE ME, BARKEEP? I'D LIKE A GLASS OF--
JUST HOLD ON A SEC, WILL YA? I'M TRYIN' TO BEAT THIS LEVEL ON *CANDY SMASH*.
FIFTEEN MINUTES AND ALL AVAILABLE LIVES LATER...
ALL RIGHT. WHAT'LL IT BE?
HMMM...I GUESS I'LL HAVE--
HURRY IT UP, ALREADY! I AIN'T GOT ALL DAY!

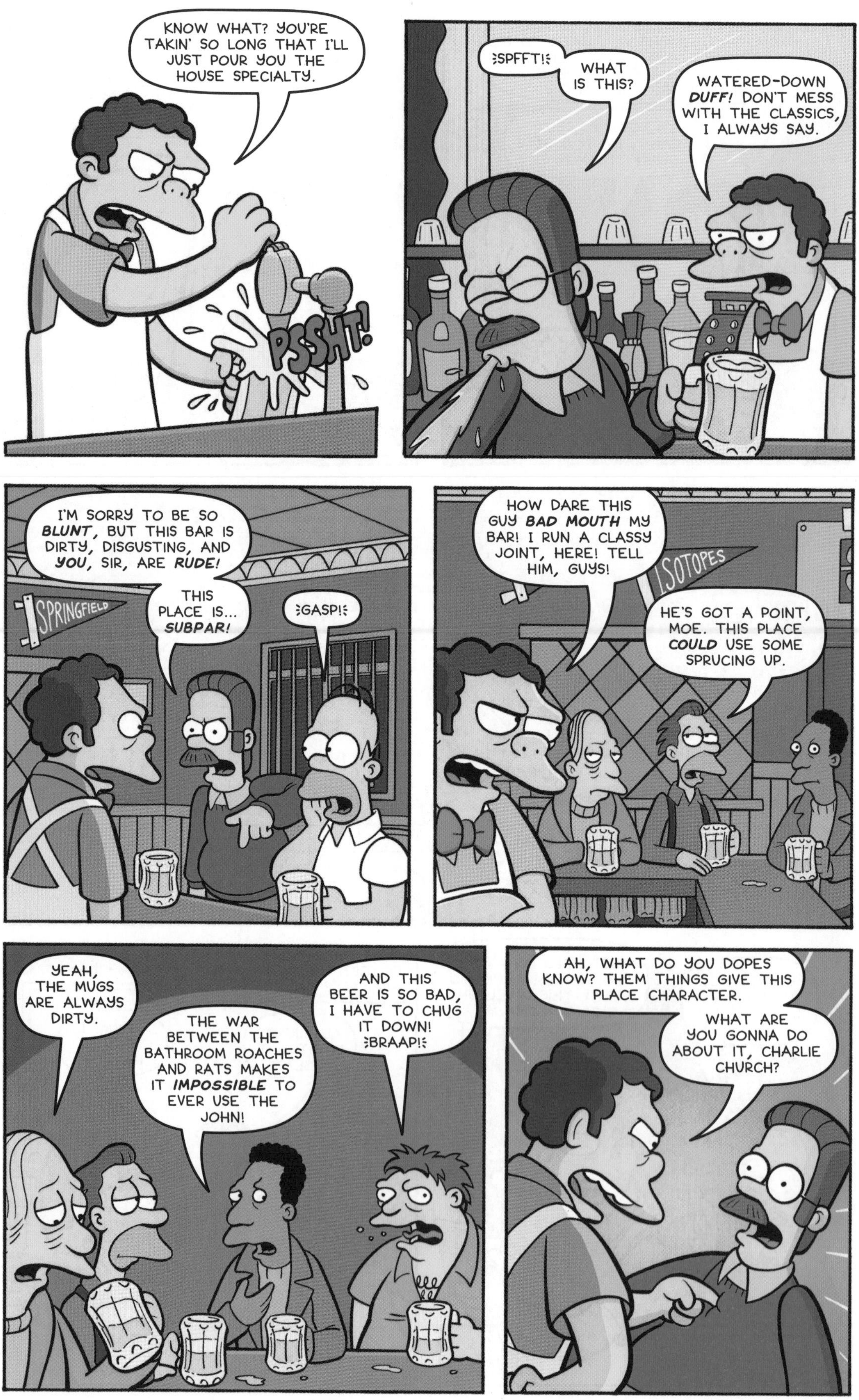
KNOW WHAT? YOU'RE TAKIN' SO LONG THAT I'LL JUST POUR YOU THE HOUSE SPECIALTY.
PSSHT!
SPFFT!
WHAT IS THIS?
WATERED-DOWN DUFF! DON'T MESS WITH THE CLASSICS, I ALWAYS SAY.
SPRINGFIELD
I'M SORRY TO BE SO BLUNT, BUT THIS BAR IS DIRTY, DISGUSTING, AND YOU, SIR, ARE RUDE!
THIS PLACE IS... SUBPAR!
GASP!
HOW DARE THIS GUY BAD MOUTH MY BAR! I RUN A CLASSY JOINT, HERE! TELL HIM, GUYS!
ISOTOPES
HE'S GOT A POINT, MOE. THIS PLACE COULD USE SOME SPRUCING UP.
YEAH, THE MUGS ARE ALWAYS DIRTY.
THE WAR BETWEEN THE BATHROOM ROACHES AND RATS MAKES IT IMPOSSIBLE TO EVER USE THE JOHN!
AND THIS BEER IS SO BAD, I HAVE TO CHUG IT DOWN!
BRAAP!
AH, WHAT DO YOU DOPES KNOW? THEM THINGS GIVE THIS PLACE CHARACTER.
WHAT ARE YOU GONNA DO ABOUT IT, CHARLIE CHURCH?

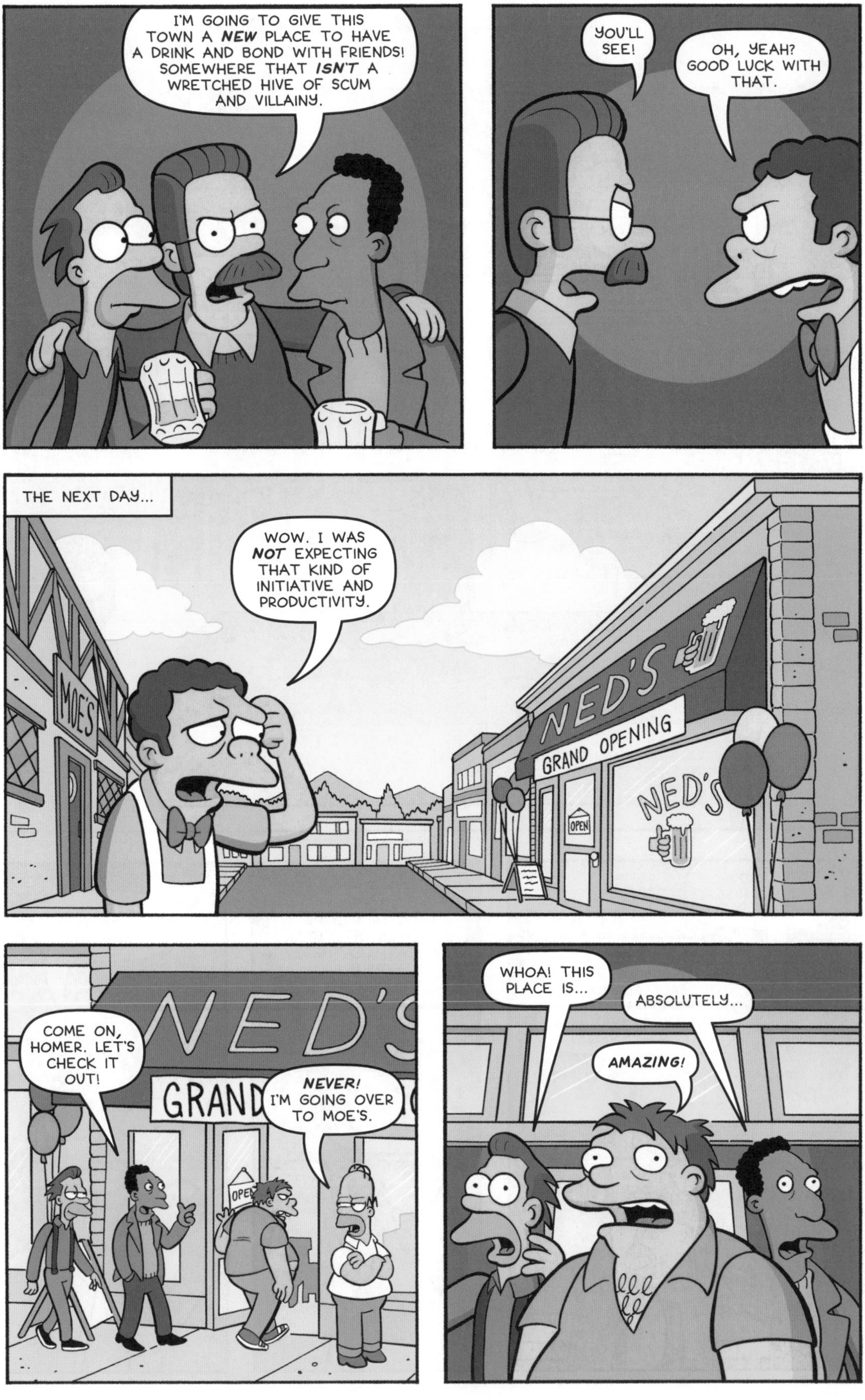
I'M GOING TO GIVE THIS TOWN A ***NEW*** PLACE TO HAVE A DRINK AND BOND WITH FRIENDS! SOMEWHERE THAT ***ISN'T*** A WRETCHED HIVE OF SCUM AND VILLAINY.
YOU'LL SEE!
OH, YEAH? GOOD LUCK WITH THAT.
THE NEXT DAY...
WOW. I WAS ***NOT*** EXPECTING THAT KIND OF INITIATIVE AND PRODUCTIVITY.
MOE'S
NED'S
GRAND OPENING
OPEN
NED'S
COME ON, HOMER. LET'S CHECK IT OUT!
NEVER! I'M GOING OVER TO MOE'S.
WHOA! THIS PLACE IS...
ABSOLUTELY...
AMAZING!

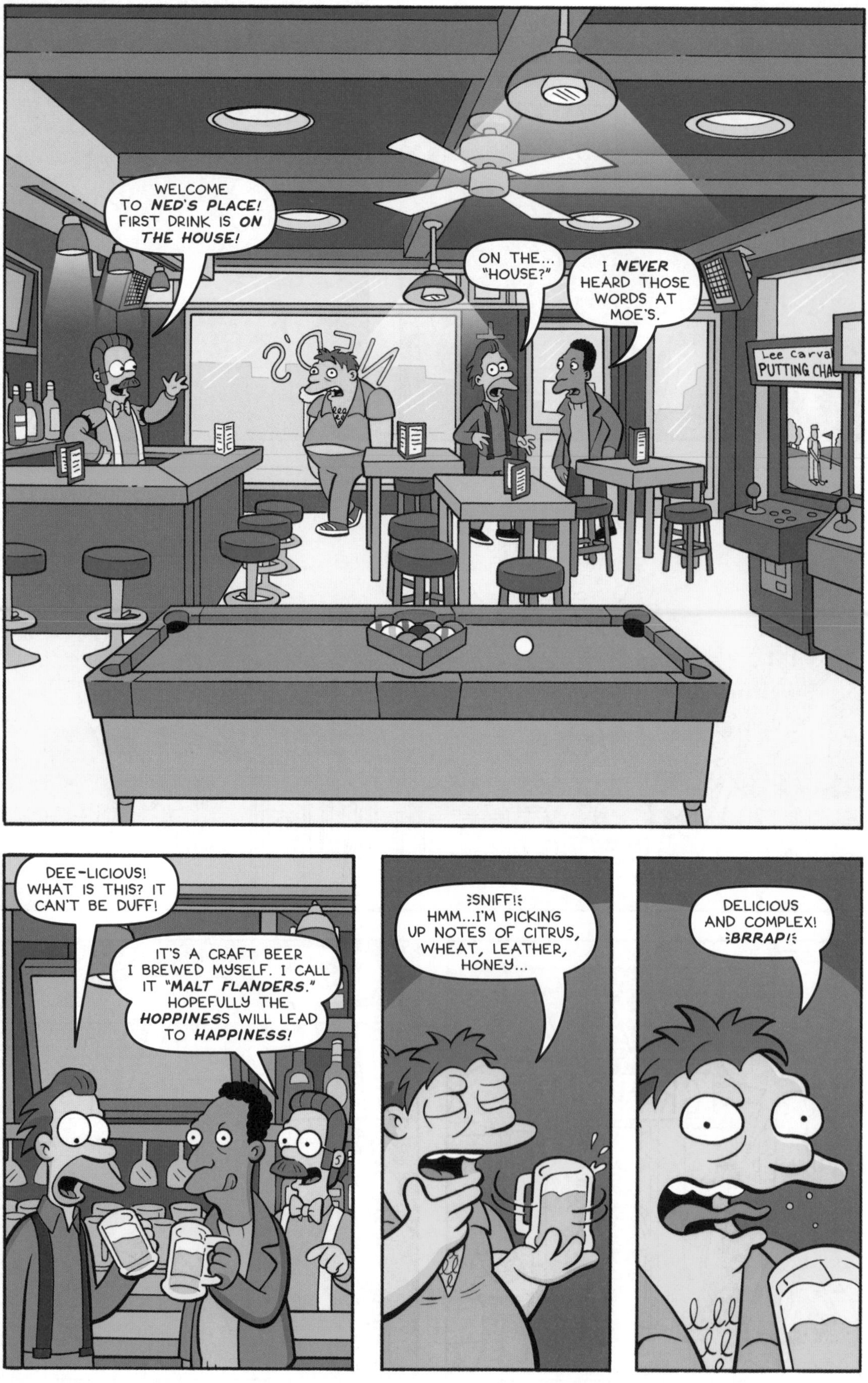
WELCOME TO **NED'S PLACE!** FIRST DRINK IS **ON THE HOUSE!**
ON THE... "HOUSE?"
I **NEVER** HEARD THOSE WORDS AT MOE'S.
DEE-LICIOUS! WHAT IS THIS? IT CAN'T BE DUFF!
IT'S A CRAFT BEER I BREWED MYSELF. I CALL IT "**MALT FLANDERS.**" HOPEFULLY THE **HOPPINES**S WILL LEAD TO **HAPPINESS!**
SNIFF! HMM...I'M PICKING UP NOTES OF CITRUS, WHEAT, LEATHER, HONEY...
DELICIOUS AND COMPLEX! **BRRAP!**

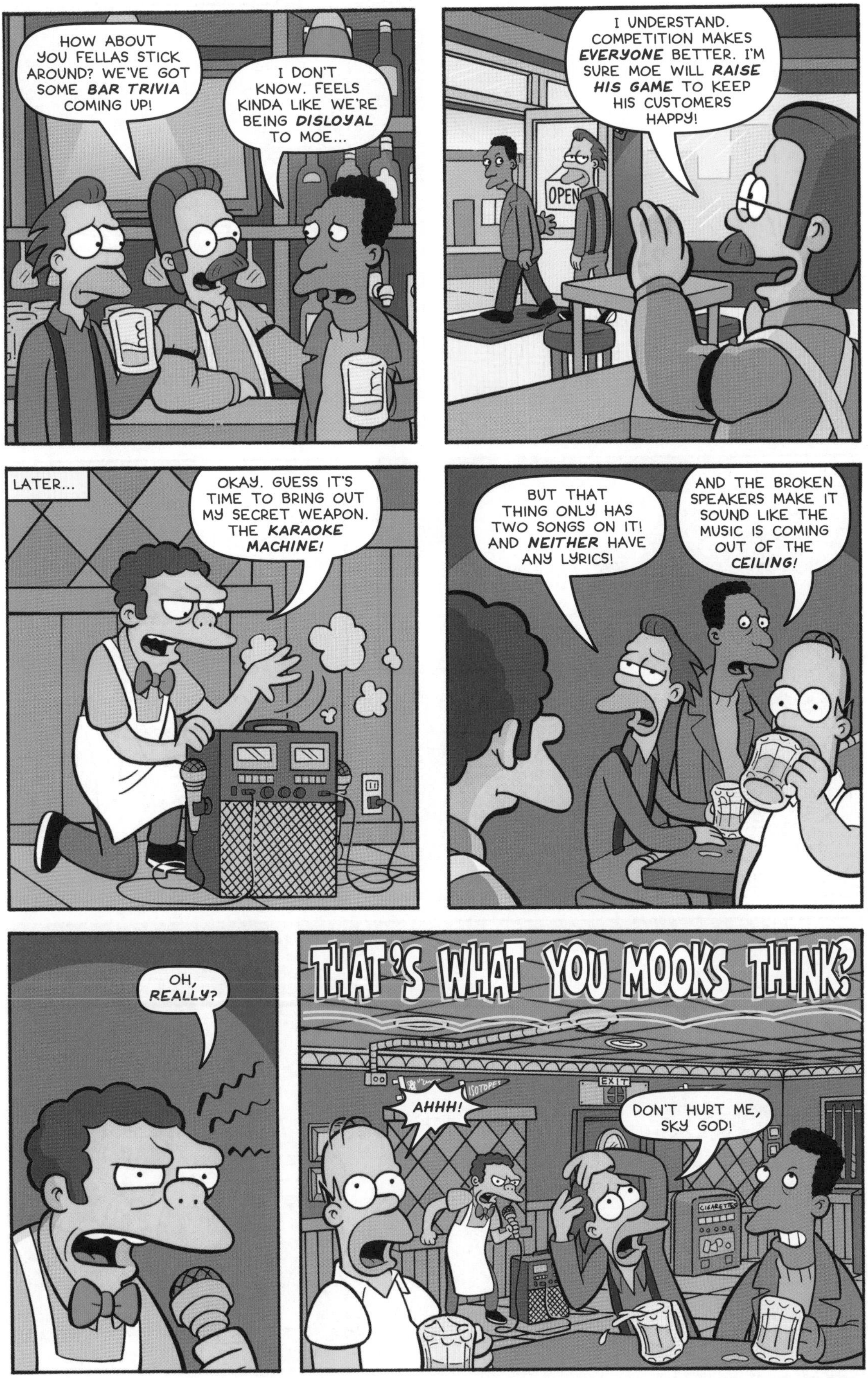
HOW ABOUT YOU FELLAS STICK AROUND? WE'VE GOT SOME BAR TRIVIA COMING UP!
I DON'T KNOW. FEELS KINDA LIKE WE'RE BEING DISLOYAL TO MOE...
I UNDERSTAND. COMPETITION MAKES EVERYONE BETTER. I'M SURE MOE WILL RAISE HIS GAME TO KEEP HIS CUSTOMERS HAPPY!
OPEN
LATER...
OKAY. GUESS IT'S TIME TO BRING OUT MY SECRET WEAPON. THE KARAOKE MACHINE!
BUT THAT THING ONLY HAS TWO SONGS ON IT! AND NEITHER HAVE ANY LYRICS!
AND THE BROKEN SPEAKERS MAKE IT SOUND LIKE THE MUSIC IS COMING OUT OF THE CEILING!
OH, REALLY?
THAT'S WHAT YOU MOOKS THINK?
EXIT
ISOTOPES
AHHH!
DON'T HURT ME, SKY GOD!

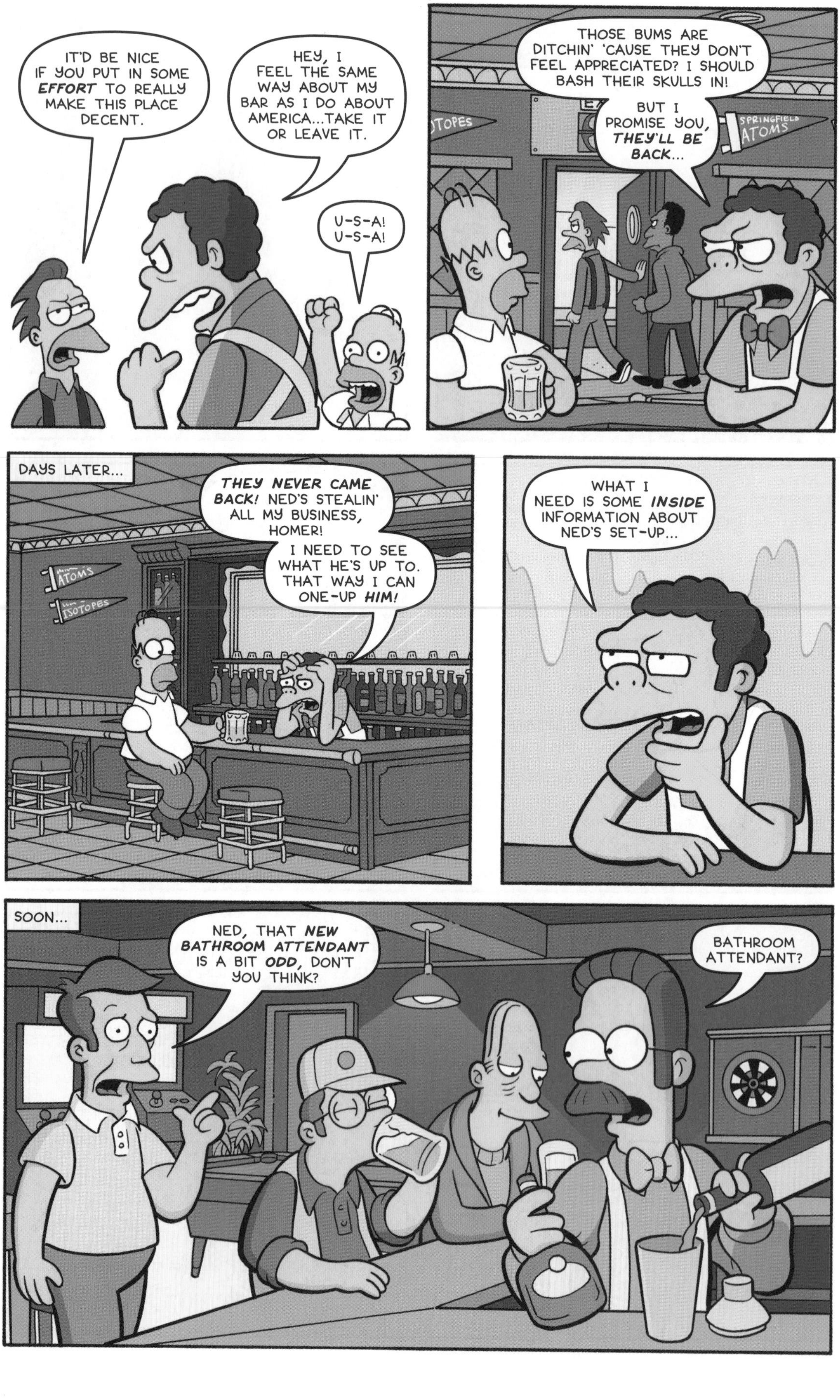
IT'D BE NICE IF YOU PUT IN SOME EFFORT TO REALLY MAKE THIS PLACE DECENT.
HEY, I FEEL THE SAME WAY ABOUT MY BAR AS I DO ABOUT AMERICA...TAKE IT OR LEAVE IT.
U-S-A! U-S-A!
THOSE BUMS ARE DITCHIN' 'CAUSE THEY DON'T FEEL APPRECIATED? I SHOULD BASH THEIR SKULLS IN!
BUT I PROMISE YOU, THEY'LL BE BACK...
DAYS LATER...
THEY NEVER CAME BACK! NED'S STEALIN' ALL MY BUSINESS, HOMER!
I NEED TO SEE WHAT HE'S UP TO. THAT WAY I CAN ONE-UP HIM!
WHAT I NEED IS SOME INSIDE INFORMATION ABOUT NED'S SET-UP...
SOON...
NED, THAT NEW BATHROOM ATTENDANT IS A BIT ODD, DON'T YOU THINK?
BATHROOM ATTENDANT?

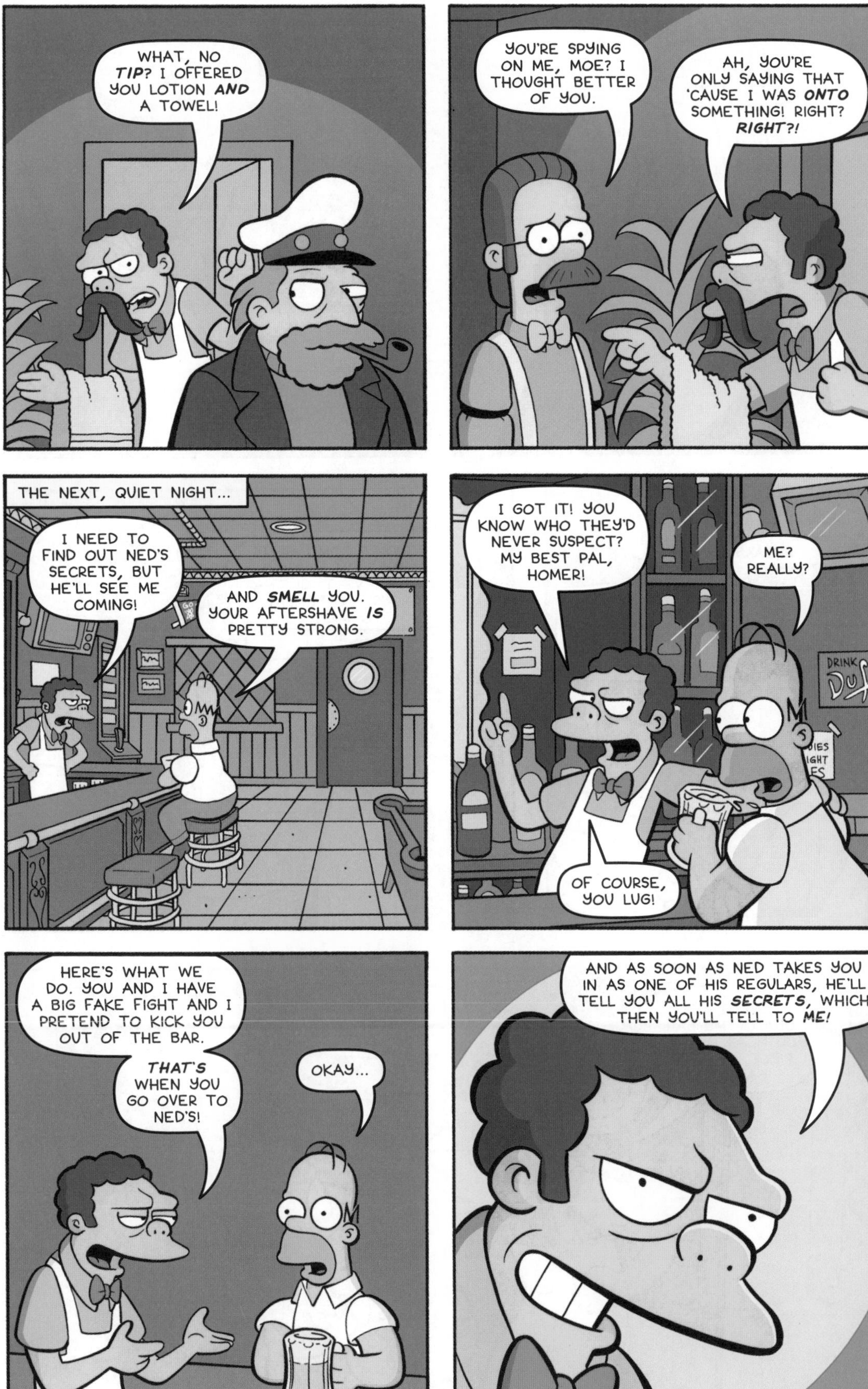

WHAT, NO TIP? I OFFERED YOU LOTION AND A TOWEL!
YOU'RE SPYING ON ME, MOE? I THOUGHT BETTER OF YOU.
AH, YOU'RE ONLY SAYING THAT 'CAUSE I WAS ONTO SOMETHING! RIGHT? RIGHT?!
THE NEXT, QUIET NIGHT...
I NEED TO FIND OUT NED'S SECRETS, BUT HE'LL SEE ME COMING!
AND SMELL YOU. YOUR AFTERSHAVE IS PRETTY STRONG.
I GOT IT! YOU KNOW WHO THEY'D NEVER SUSPECT? MY BEST PAL, HOMER!
ME? REALLY?
OF COURSE, YOU LUG!
DRINK
HERE'S WHAT WE DO. YOU AND I HAVE A BIG FAKE FIGHT AND I PRETEND TO KICK YOU OUT OF THE BAR.
THAT'S WHEN YOU GO OVER TO NED'S!
OKAY...
AND AS SOON AS NED TAKES YOU IN AS ONE OF HIS REGULARS, HE'LL TELL YOU ALL HIS SECRETS, WHICH THEN YOU'LL TELL TO ME!

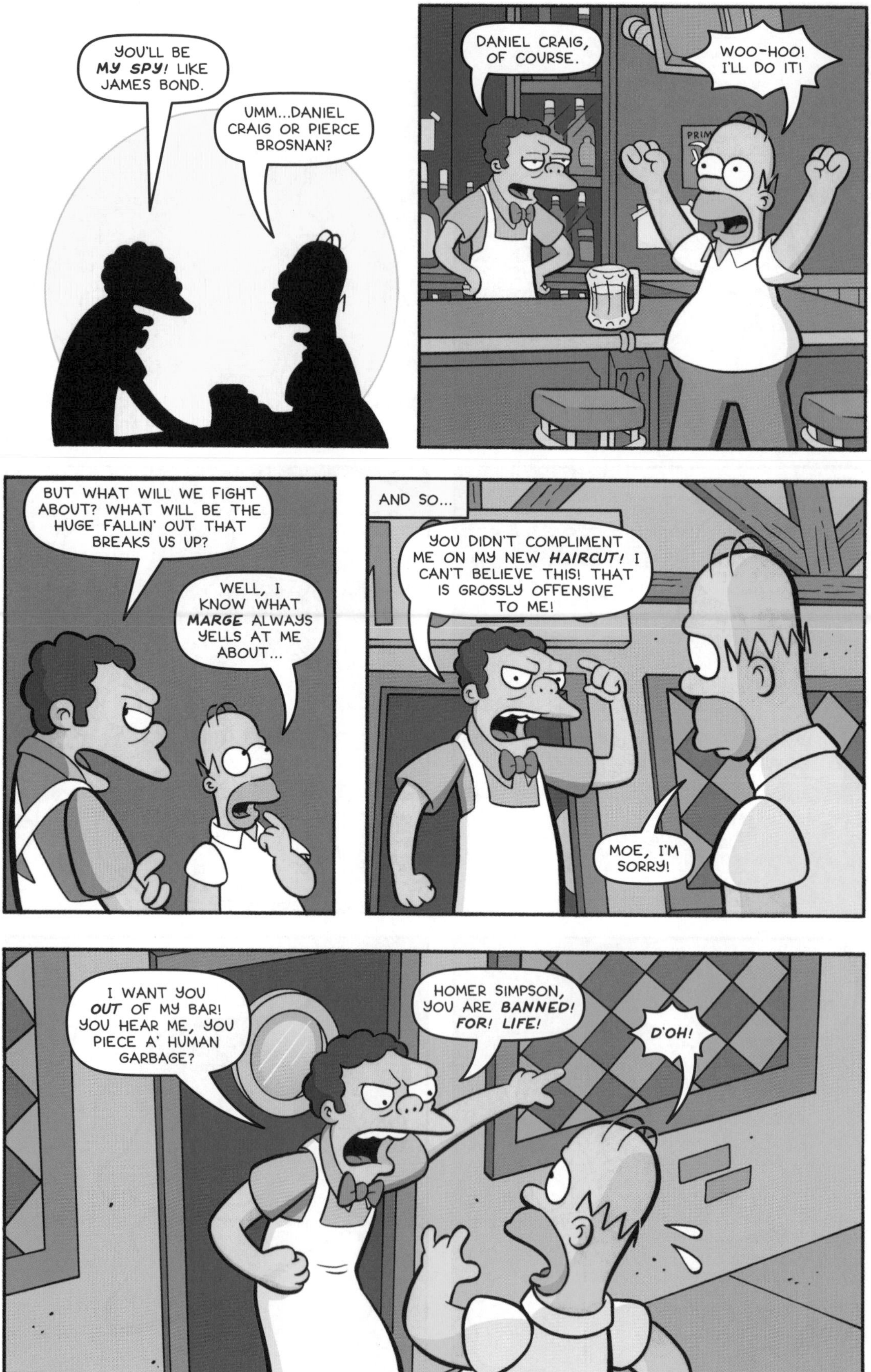
YOU'LL BE MY SPY! LIKE JAMES BOND.
UMM...DANIEL CRAIG OR PIERCE BROSNAN?
DANIEL CRAIG, OF COURSE.
WOO-HOO! I'LL DO IT!
BUT WHAT WILL WE FIGHT ABOUT? WHAT WILL BE THE HUGE FALLIN' OUT THAT BREAKS US UP?
WELL, I KNOW WHAT MARGE ALWAYS YELLS AT ME ABOUT...
AND SO...
YOU DIDN'T COMPLIMENT ME ON MY NEW HAIRCUT! I CAN'T BELIEVE THIS! THAT IS GROSSLY OFFENSIVE TO ME!
MOE, I'M SORRY!
I WANT YOU OUT OF MY BAR! YOU HEAR ME, YOU PIECE A' HUMAN GARBAGE?
HOMER SIMPSON, YOU ARE BANNED! FOR! LIFE!
D'OH!

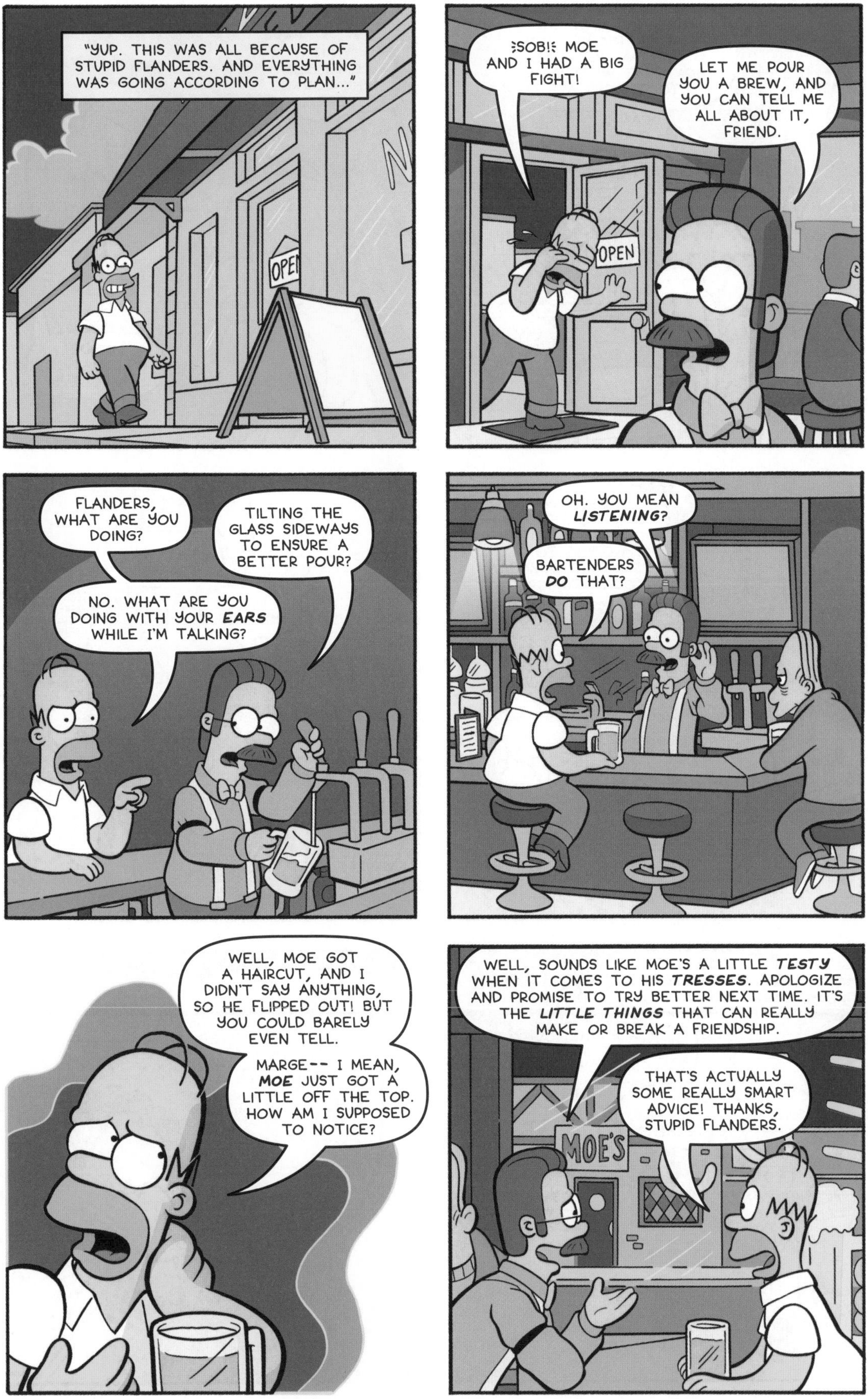
"YUP. THIS WAS ALL BECAUSE OF STUPID FLANDERS. AND EVERYTHING WAS GOING ACCORDING TO PLAN..."
SOB! MOE AND I HAD A BIG FIGHT!
OPEN
LET ME POUR YOU A BREW, AND YOU CAN TELL ME ALL ABOUT IT, FRIEND.
FLANDERS, WHAT ARE YOU DOING?
TILTING THE GLASS SIDEWAYS TO ENSURE A BETTER POUR?
NO. WHAT ARE YOU DOING WITH YOUR **EARS** WHILE I'M TALKING?
OH. YOU MEAN ***LISTENING***?
BARTENDERS ***DO*** THAT?
WELL, MOE GOT A HAIRCUT, AND I DIDN'T SAY ANYTHING, SO HE FLIPPED OUT! BUT YOU COULD BARELY EVEN TELL.
MARGE-- I MEAN, ***MOE*** JUST GOT A LITTLE OFF THE TOP. HOW AM I SUPPOSED TO NOTICE?
WELL, SOUNDS LIKE MOE'S A LITTLE ***TESTY*** WHEN IT COMES TO HIS ***TRESSES***. APOLOGIZE AND PROMISE TO TRY BETTER NEXT TIME. IT'S THE ***LITTLE THINGS*** THAT CAN REALLY MAKE OR BREAK A FRIENDSHIP.
MOE'S
THAT'S ACTUALLY SOME REALLY SMART ADVICE! THANKS, STUPID FLANDERS.

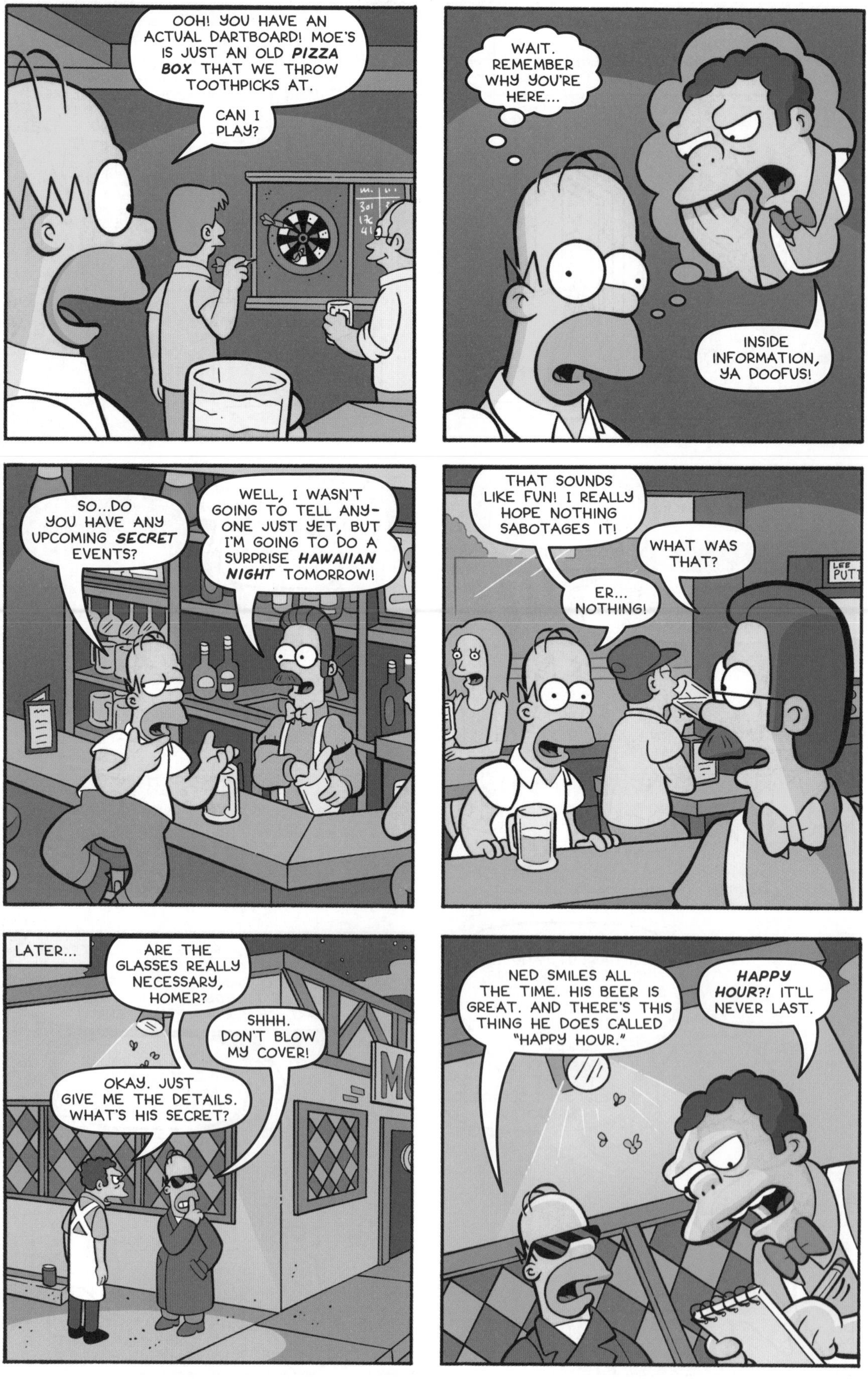
OOH! YOU HAVE AN ACTUAL DARTBOARD! MOE'S IS JUST AN OLD **PIZZA BOX** THAT WE THROW TOOTHPICKS AT.
CAN I PLAY?
WAIT. REMEMBER WHY YOU'RE HERE...
INSIDE INFORMATION, YA DOOFUS!
SO...DO YOU HAVE ANY UPCOMING **SECRET** EVENTS?
WELL, I WASN'T GOING TO TELL ANYONE JUST YET, BUT I'M GOING TO DO A SURPRISE **HAWAIIAN NIGHT** TOMORROW!
THAT SOUNDS LIKE FUN! I REALLY HOPE NOTHING SABOTAGES IT!
WHAT WAS THAT?
ER... NOTHING!
LATER...
ARE THE GLASSES REALLY NECESSARY, HOMER?
SHHH. DON'T BLOW MY COVER!
OKAY. JUST GIVE ME THE DETAILS. WHAT'S HIS SECRET?
NED SMILES ALL THE TIME. HIS BEER IS GREAT. AND THERE'S THIS THING HE DOES CALLED "HAPPY HOUR."
HAPPY HOUR?! IT'LL NEVER LAST.

THERE'S A *THEME NIGHT* COMING UP TOMORROW! HAWAIIAN LUAU!

INTERESTING...

SO...AREN'T YOU GOING TO THANK ME FOR THIS? I'M KINDA GOING OUT ON A LIMB FOR YOU.

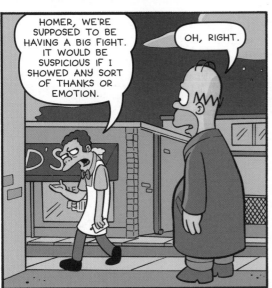

HOMER, WE'RE SUPPOSED TO BE HAVING A BIG FIGHT. IT WOULD BE SUSPICIOUS IF I SHOWED ANY SORT OF THANKS OR EMOTION.

OH, RIGHT.

OKAY. I JUST GOTTA COUNTER NED'S THEME SO'S PEOPLE COME TO MY PLACE INSTEAD.

MAYBE SOMETHING WITH FLAIR...

EXIT

THE NEXT NIGHT...

ARUBA...JAMAICA...OOH, I WANNA TAKE YA...

KOKO-MOE'S

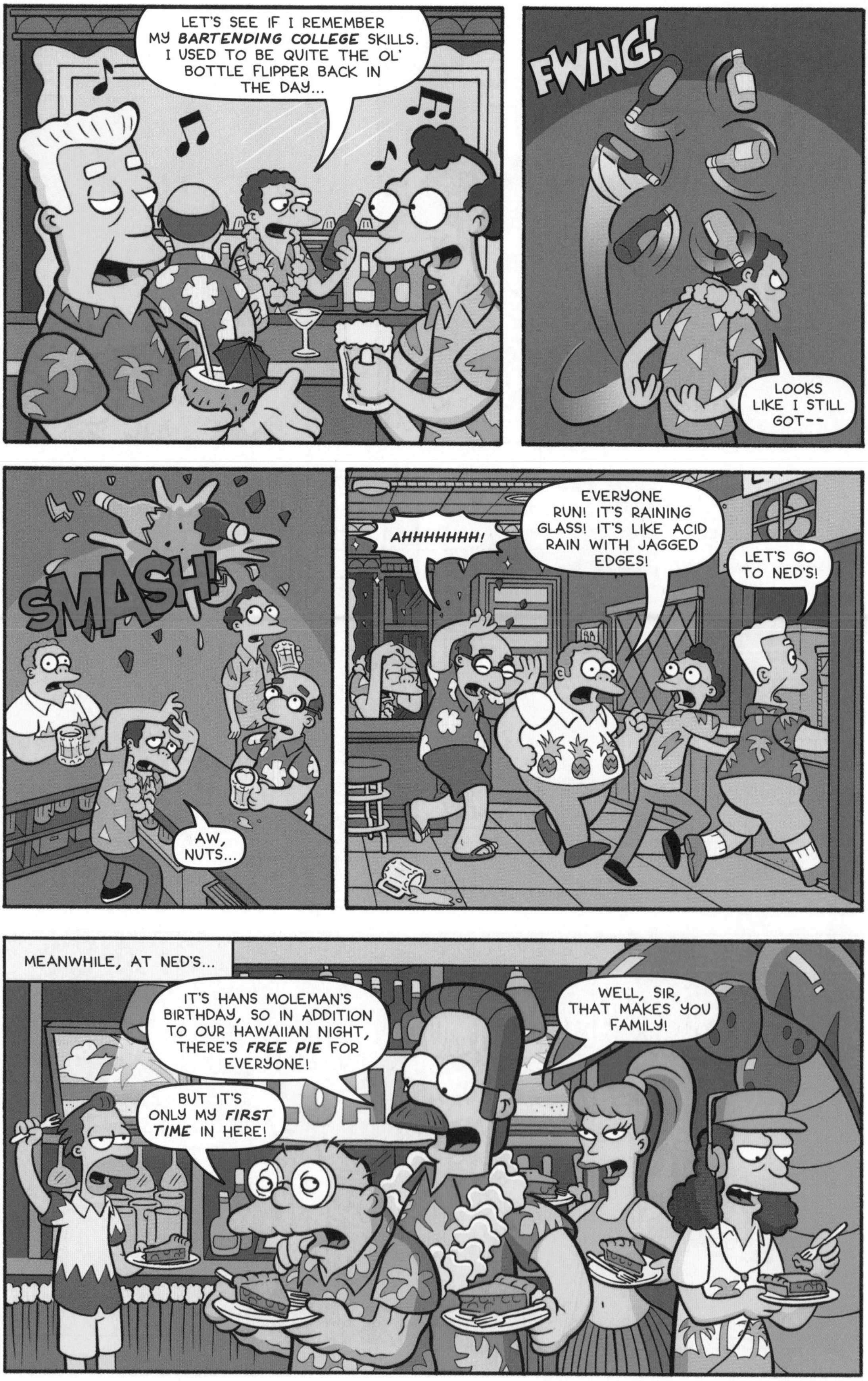
LET'S SEE IF I REMEMBER MY **BARTENDING COLLEGE** SKILLS. I USED TO BE QUITE THE OL' BOTTLE FLIPPER BACK IN THE DAY...
FWING!
LOOKS LIKE I STILL GOT--
SMASH!
AW, NUTS...
AHHHHHHH!
EVERYONE RUN! IT'S RAINING GLASS! IT'S LIKE ACID RAIN WITH JAGGED EDGES!
LET'S GO TO NED'S!
MEANWHILE, AT NED'S...
IT'S HANS MOLEMAN'S BIRTHDAY, SO IN ADDITION TO OUR HAWAIIAN NIGHT, THERE'S **FREE PIE** FOR EVERYONE!
BUT IT'S ONLY MY **FIRST TIME** IN HERE!
WELL, SIR, THAT MAKES YOU FAMILY!

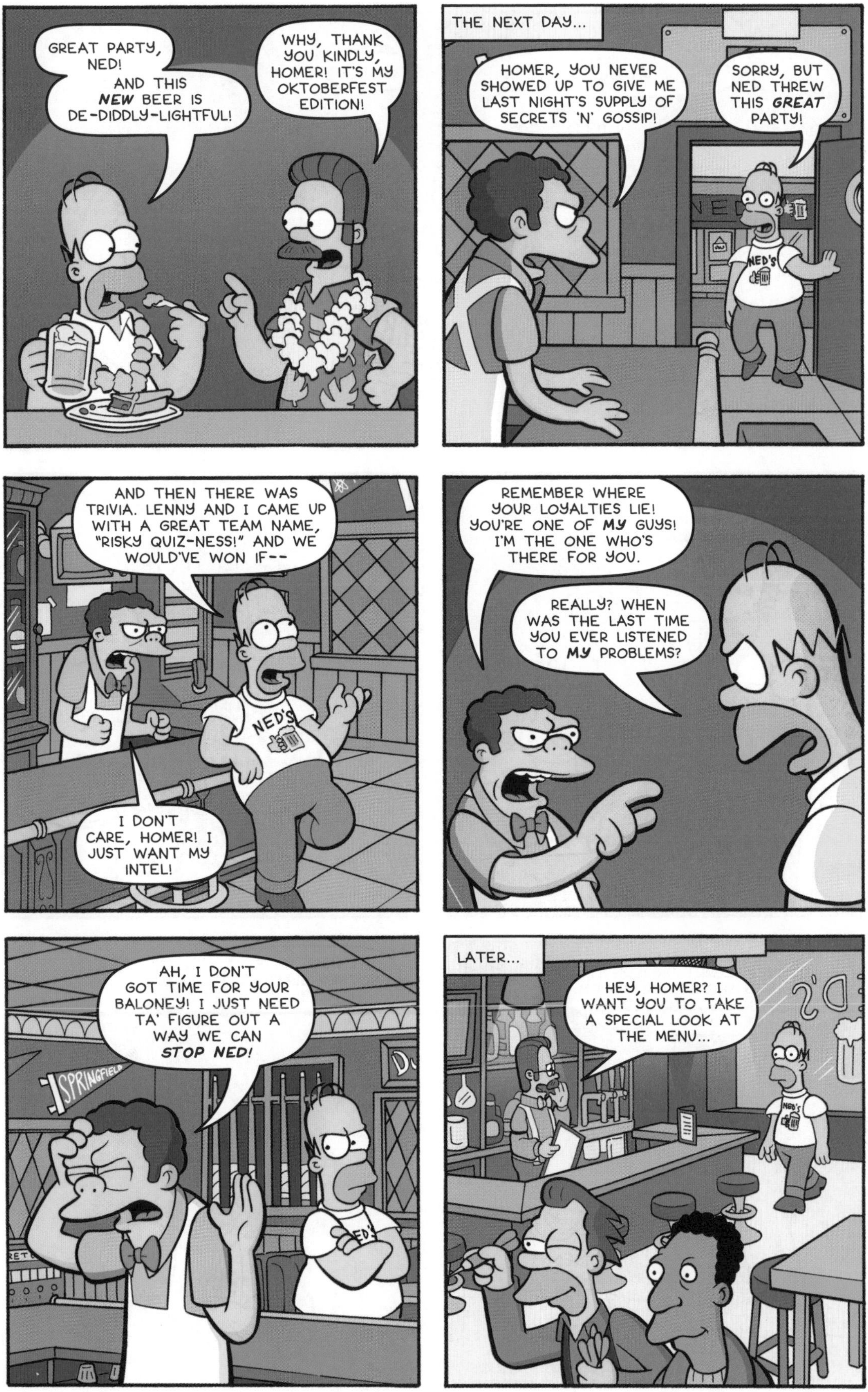
GREAT PARTY, NED! AND THIS NEW BEER IS DE-DIDDLY-LIGHTFUL!
WHY, THANK YOU KINDLY, HOMER! IT'S MY OKTOBERFEST EDITION!
THE NEXT DAY...
HOMER, YOU NEVER SHOWED UP TO GIVE ME LAST NIGHT'S SUPPLY OF SECRETS 'N' GOSSIP!
SORRY, BUT NED THREW THIS GREAT PARTY!
NED'S
AND THEN THERE WAS TRIVIA. LENNY AND I CAME UP WITH A GREAT TEAM NAME, "RISKY QUIZ-NESS!" AND WE WOULD'VE WON IF--
I DON'T CARE, HOMER! I JUST WANT MY INTEL!
REMEMBER WHERE YOUR LOYALTIES LIE! YOU'RE ONE OF MY GUYS! I'M THE ONE WHO'S THERE FOR YOU.
REALLY? WHEN WAS THE LAST TIME YOU EVER LISTENED TO MY PROBLEMS?
AH, I DON'T GOT TIME FOR YOUR BALONEY! I JUST NEED TA' FIGURE OUT A WAY WE CAN STOP NED!
SPRINGFIELD
LATER...
HEY, HOMER? I WANT YOU TO TAKE A SPECIAL LOOK AT THE MENU...

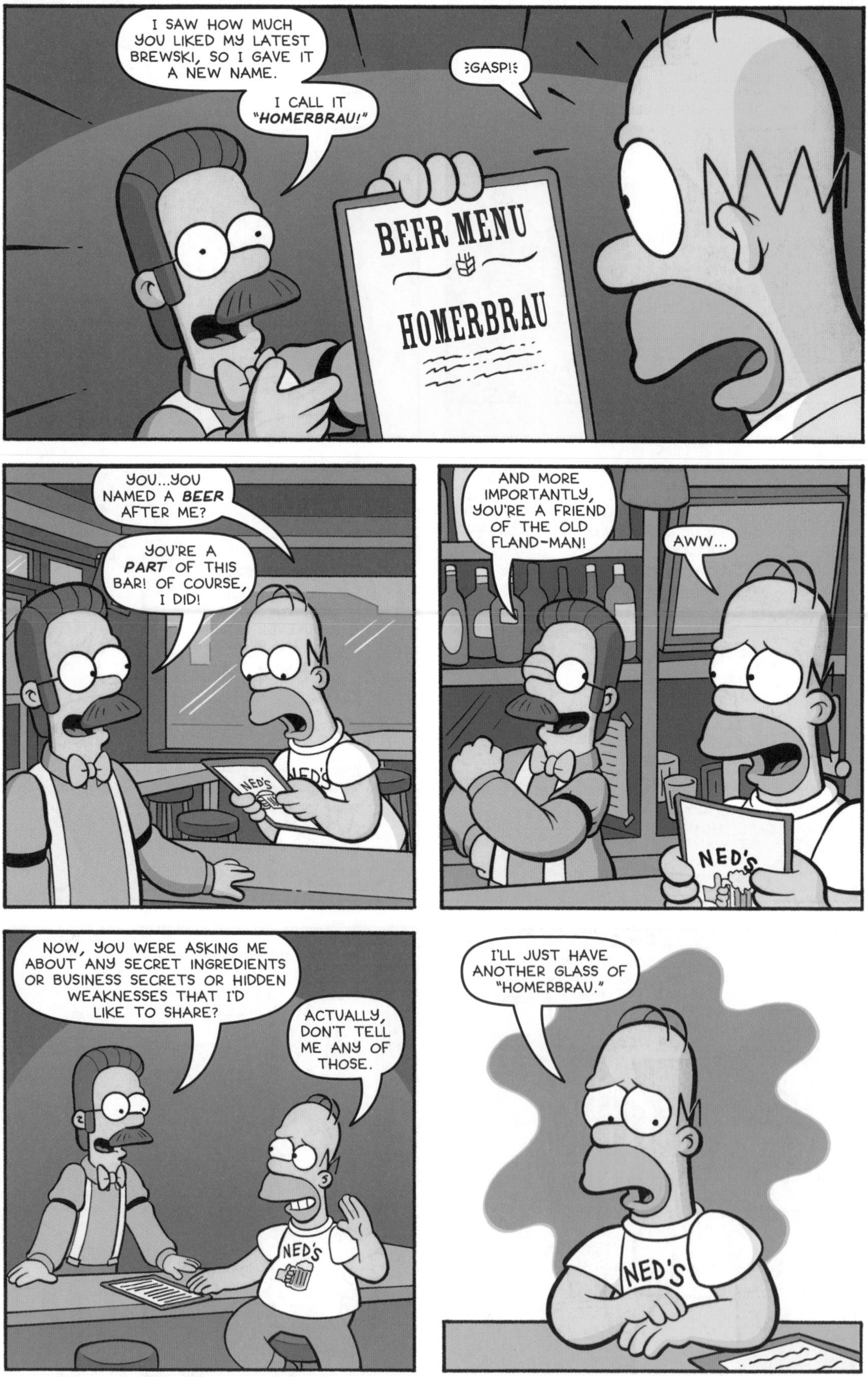
I SAW HOW MUCH YOU LIKED MY LATEST BREWSKI, SO I GAVE IT A NEW NAME.
I CALL IT "HOMERBRAU!"
GASP!
BEER MENU
HOMERBRAU
YOU...YOU NAMED A BEER AFTER ME?
YOU'RE A PART OF THIS BAR! OF COURSE, I DID!
NED'S
AND MORE IMPORTANTLY, YOU'RE A FRIEND OF THE OLD FLAND-MAN!
AWW...
NED'S
NOW, YOU WERE ASKING ME ABOUT ANY SECRET INGREDIENTS OR BUSINESS SECRETS OR HIDDEN WEAKNESSES THAT I'D LIKE TO SHARE?
ACTUALLY, DON'T TELL ME ANY OF THOSE.
NED'S
I'LL JUST HAVE ANOTHER GLASS OF "HOMERBRAU."
NED'S

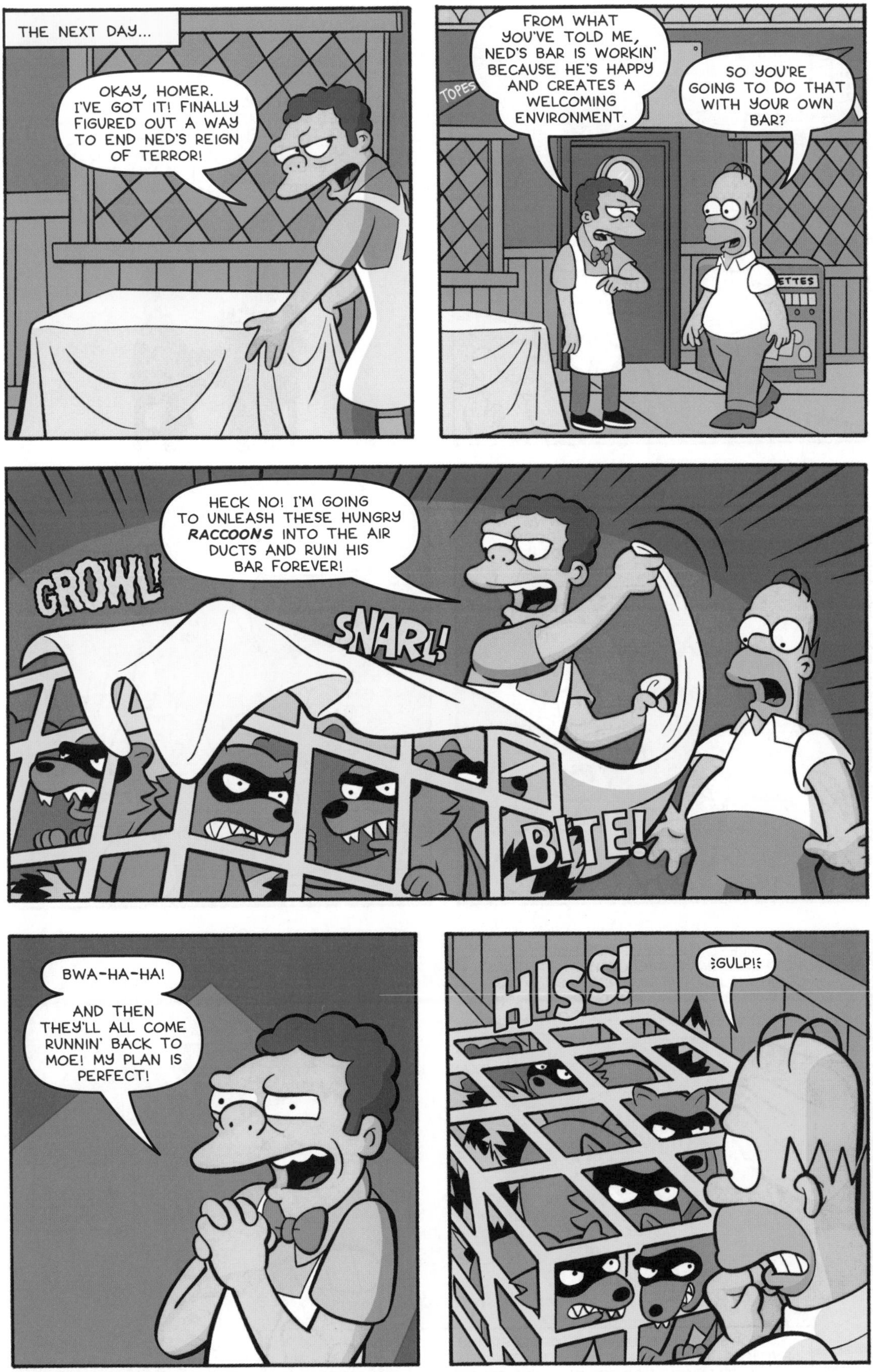
THE NEXT DAY...
OKAY, HOMER. I'VE GOT IT! FINALLY FIGURED OUT A WAY TO END NED'S REIGN OF TERROR!
FROM WHAT YOU'VE TOLD ME, NED'S BAR IS WORKIN' BECAUSE HE'S HAPPY AND CREATES A WELCOMING ENVIRONMENT.
SO YOU'RE GOING TO DO THAT WITH YOUR OWN BAR?
HECK NO! I'M GOING TO UNLEASH THESE HUNGRY *RACCOONS* INTO THE AIR DUCTS AND RUIN HIS BAR FOREVER!
GROWL!
SNARL!
BITE!
BWA-HA-HA!
AND THEN THEY'LL ALL COME RUNNIN' BACK TO MOE! MY PLAN IS PERFECT!
HISS!
GULP!

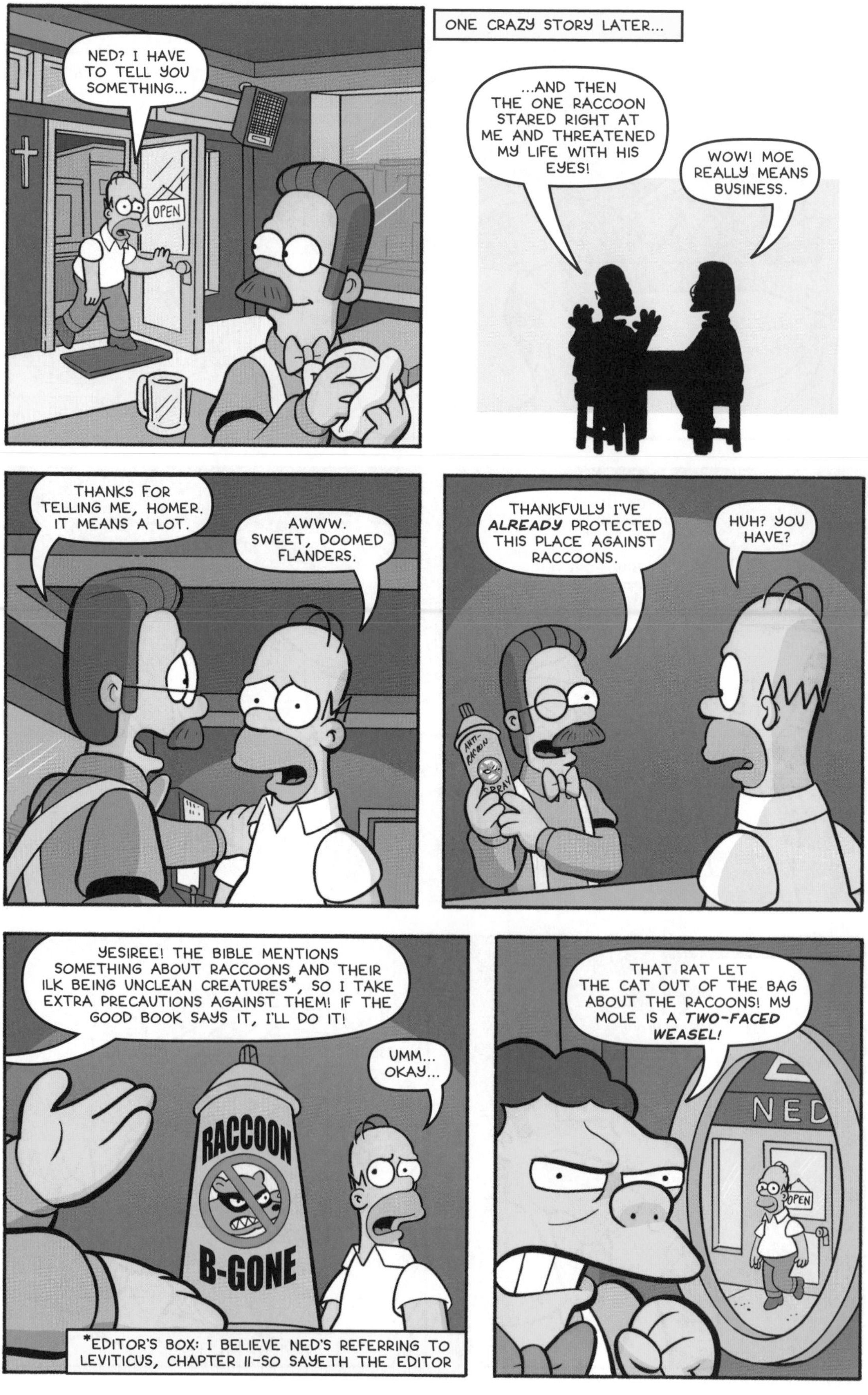
NED? I HAVE TO TELL YOU SOMETHING...
OPEN
ONE CRAZY STORY LATER...
...AND THEN THE ONE RACCOON STARED RIGHT AT ME AND THREATENED MY LIFE WITH HIS EYES!
WOW! MOE REALLY MEANS BUSINESS.
THANKS FOR TELLING ME, HOMER. IT MEANS A LOT.
AWWW. SWEET, DOOMED FLANDERS.
THANKFULLY I'VE ***ALREADY*** PROTECTED THIS PLACE AGAINST RACCOONS.
HUH? YOU HAVE?
YESIREE! THE BIBLE MENTIONS SOMETHING ABOUT RACCOONS AND THEIR ILK BEING UNCLEAN CREATURES*, SO I TAKE EXTRA PRECAUTIONS AGAINST THEM! IF THE GOOD BOOK SAYS IT, I'LL DO IT!
UMM... OKAY...
RACCOON B-GONE
*EDITOR'S BOX: I BELIEVE NED'S REFERRING TO LEVITICUS, CHAPTER 11–SO SAYETH THE EDITOR
THAT RAT LET THE CAT OUT OF THE BAG ABOUT THE RACOONS! MY MOLE IS A ***TWO-FACED WEASEL!***
NED
OPEN

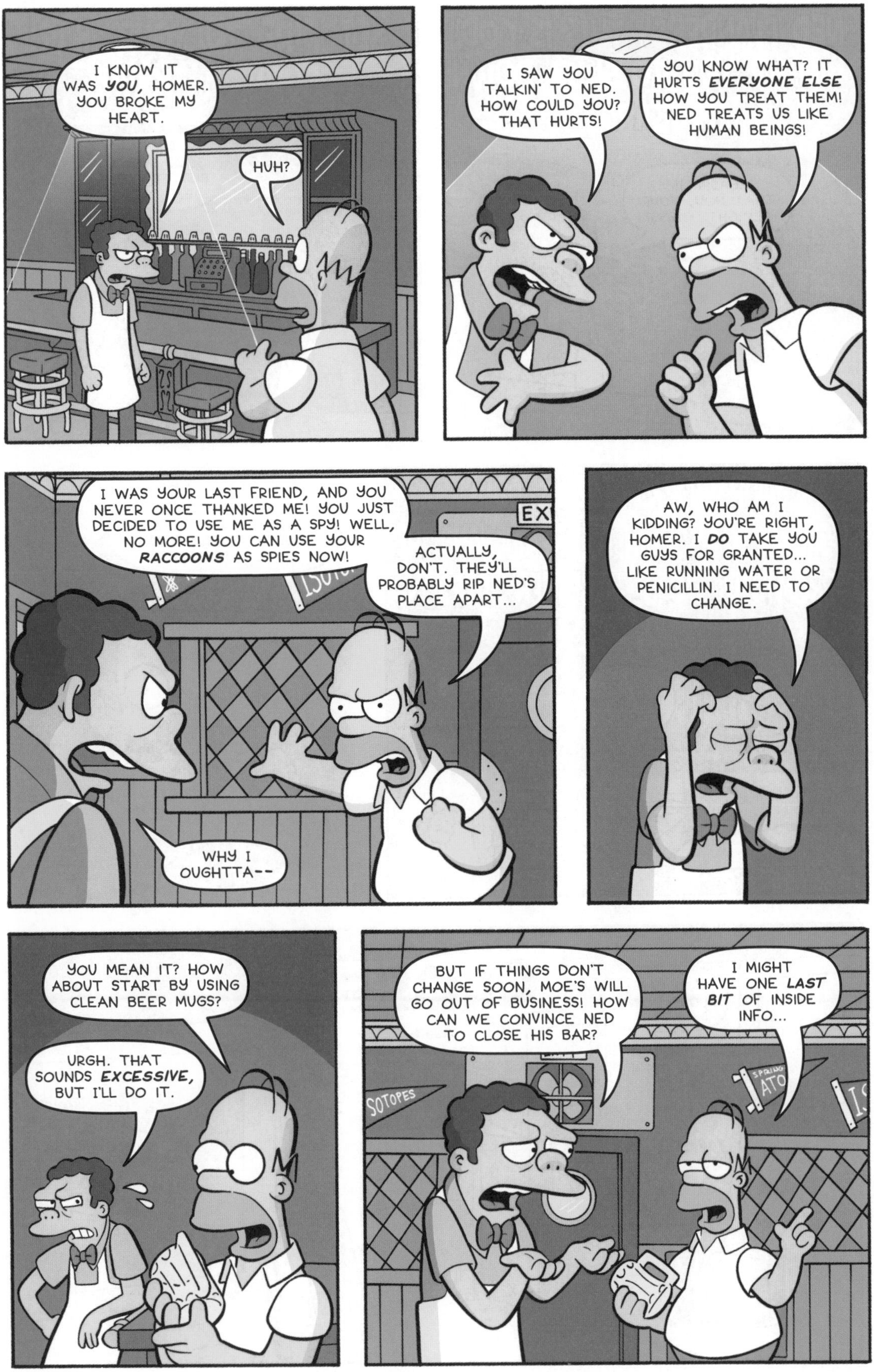
I KNOW IT WAS *YOU,* HOMER. YOU BROKE MY HEART.
HUH?
I SAW YOU TALKIN' TO NED. HOW COULD YOU? THAT HURTS!
YOU KNOW WHAT? IT HURTS *EVERYONE ELSE* HOW YOU TREAT THEM! NED TREATS US LIKE HUMAN BEINGS!
I WAS YOUR LAST FRIEND, AND YOU NEVER ONCE THANKED ME! YOU JUST DECIDED TO USE ME AS A SPY! WELL, NO MORE! YOU CAN USE YOUR *RACCOONS* AS SPIES NOW!
ACTUALLY, DON'T. THEY'LL PROBABLY RIP NED'S PLACE APART...
WHY I OUGHTTA--
AW, WHO AM I KIDDING? YOU'RE RIGHT, HOMER. I *DO* TAKE YOU GUYS FOR GRANTED... LIKE RUNNING WATER OR PENICILLIN. I NEED TO CHANGE.
YOU MEAN IT? HOW ABOUT START BY USING CLEAN BEER MUGS?
URGH. THAT SOUNDS *EXCESSIVE,* BUT I'LL DO IT.
BUT IF THINGS DON'T CHANGE SOON, MOE'S WILL GO OUT OF BUSINESS! HOW CAN WE CONVINCE NED TO CLOSE HIS BAR?
I MIGHT HAVE ONE *LAST BIT* OF INSIDE INFO...
SOTOPES

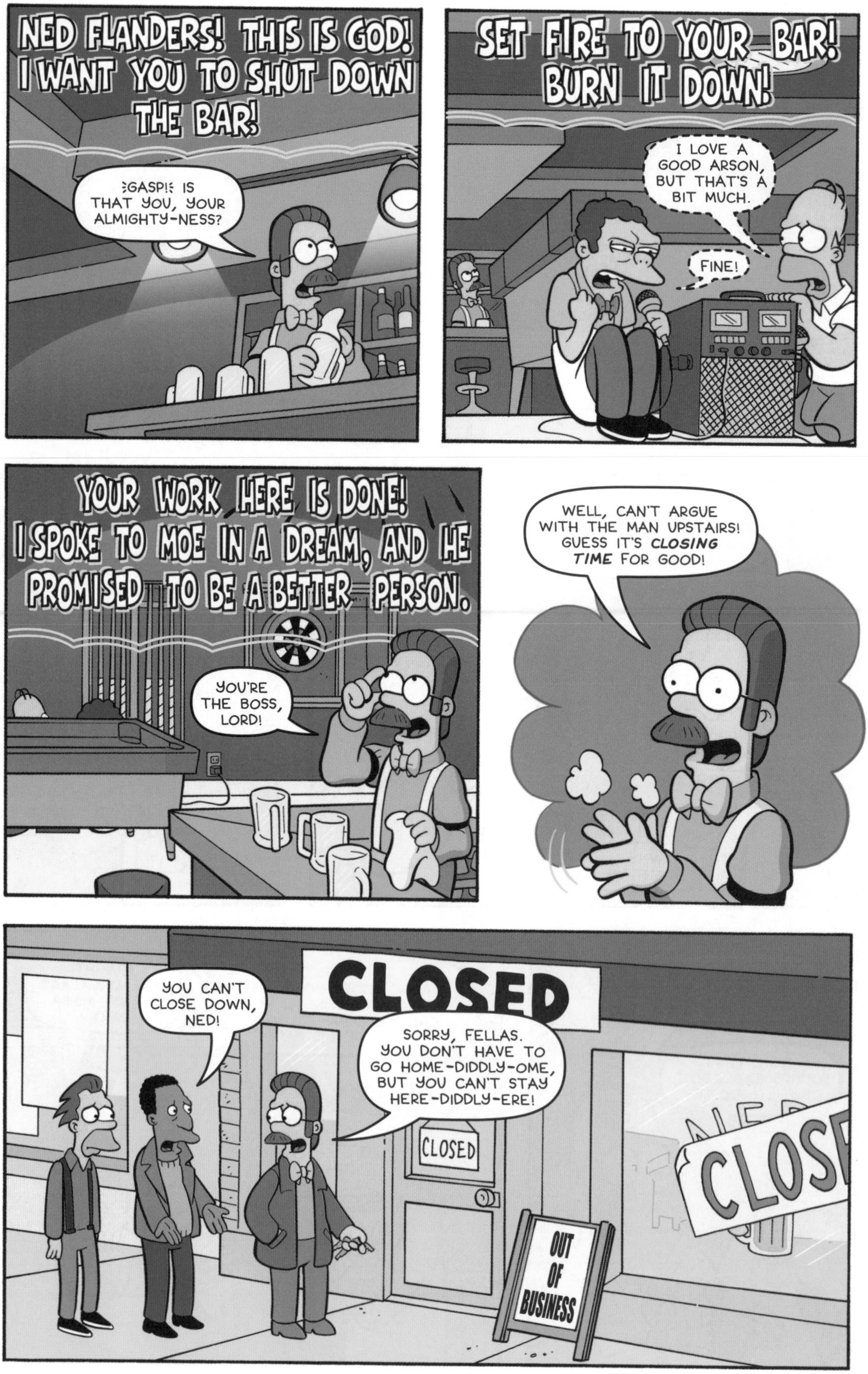
NED FLANDERS! THIS IS GOD! I WANT YOU TO SHUT DOWN THE BAR!
GASP! IS THAT YOU, YOUR ALMIGHTY-NESS?
SET FIRE TO YOUR BAR! BURN IT DOWN!
I LOVE A GOOD ARSON, BUT THAT'S A BIT MUCH.
FINE!
YOUR WORK HERE IS DONE! I SPOKE TO MOE IN A DREAM, AND HE PROMISED TO BE A BETTER PERSON.
YOU'RE THE BOSS, LORD!
WELL, CAN'T ARGUE WITH THE MAN UPSTAIRS! GUESS IT'S *CLOSING TIME* FOR GOOD!
CLOSED
YOU CAN'T CLOSE DOWN, NED!
SORRY, FELLAS. YOU DON'T HAVE TO GO HOME-DIDDLY-OME, BUT YOU CAN'T STAY HERE-DIDDLY-ERE!
CLOSED
OUT OF BUSINESS

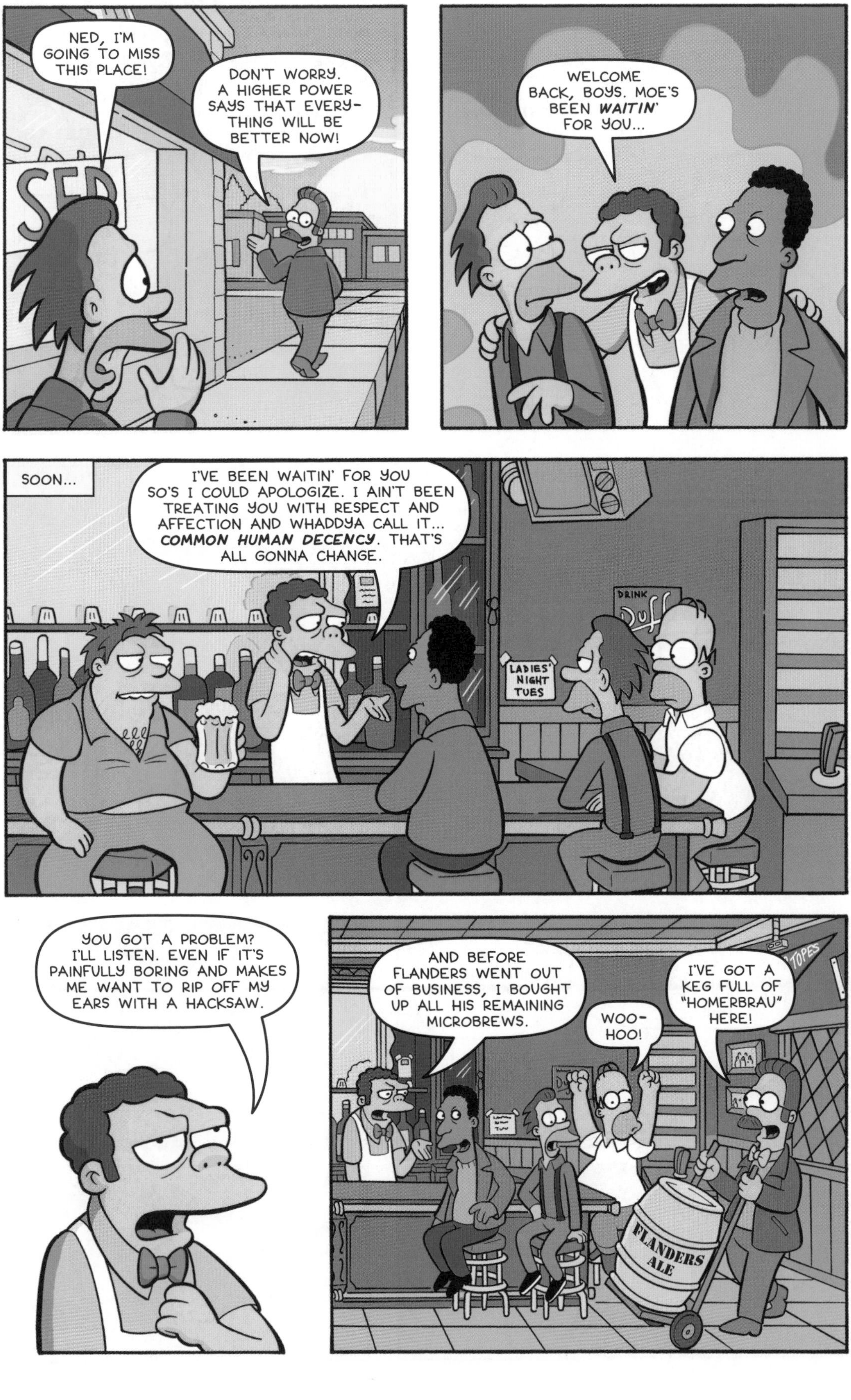
NED, I'M GOING TO MISS THIS PLACE!
DON'T WORRY. A HIGHER POWER SAYS THAT EVERY-THING WILL BE BETTER NOW!
WELCOME BACK, BOYS. MOE'S BEEN **WAITIN'** FOR YOU...
SOON...
I'VE BEEN WAITIN' FOR YOU SO'S I COULD APOLOGIZE. I AIN'T BEEN TREATING YOU WITH RESPECT AND AFFECTION AND WHADDYA CALL IT... ***COMMON HUMAN DECENCY***. THAT'S ALL GONNA CHANGE.
DRINK Duff
LADIES' NIGHT TUES
YOU GOT A PROBLEM? I'LL LISTEN. EVEN IF IT'S PAINFULLY BORING AND MAKES ME WANT TO RIP OFF MY EARS WITH A HACKSAW.
AND BEFORE FLANDERS WENT OUT OF BUSINESS, I BOUGHT UP ALL HIS REMAINING MICROBREWS.
WOO-HOO!
I'VE GOT A KEG FULL OF "HOMERBRAU" HERE!
FLANDERS ALE

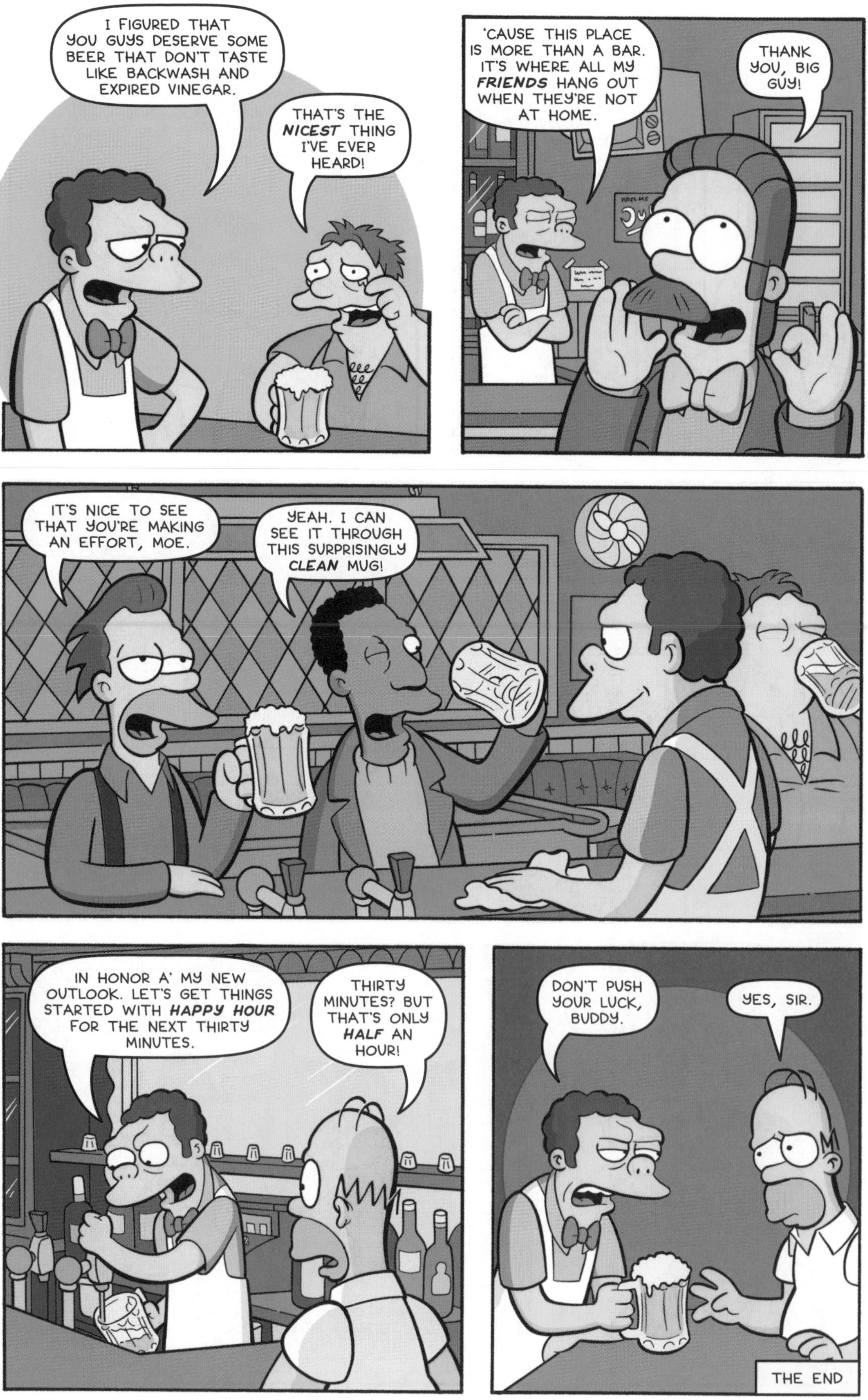
I FIGURED THAT YOU GUYS DESERVE SOME BEER THAT DON'T TASTE LIKE BACKWASH AND EXPIRED VINEGAR.
THAT'S THE NICEST THING I'VE EVER HEARD!
'CAUSE THIS PLACE IS MORE THAN A BAR. IT'S WHERE ALL MY FRIENDS HANG OUT WHEN THEY'RE NOT AT HOME.
THANK YOU, BIG GUY!
IT'S NICE TO SEE THAT YOU'RE MAKING AN EFFORT, MOE.
YEAH. I CAN SEE IT THROUGH THIS SURPRISINGLY CLEAN MUG!
IN HONOR A' MY NEW OUTLOOK. LET'S GET THINGS STARTED WITH HAPPY HOUR FOR THE NEXT THIRTY MINUTES.
THIRTY MINUTES? BUT THAT'S ONLY HALF AN HOUR!
DON'T PUSH YOUR LUCK, BUDDY.
YES, SIR.
THE END

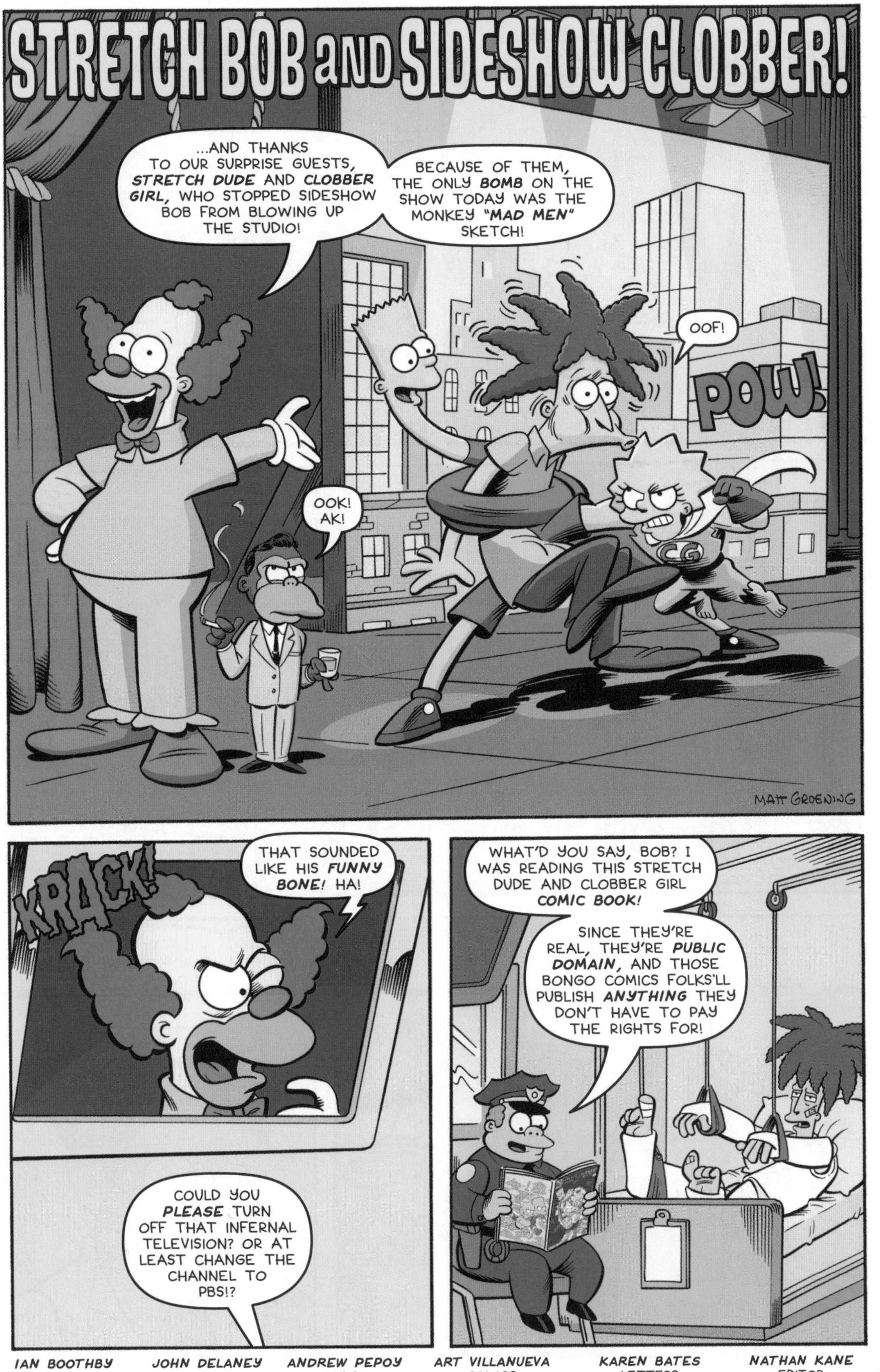
STRETCH BOB AND SIDESHOW CLOBBER!
...AND THANKS TO OUR SURPRISE GUESTS, *STRETCH DUDE* AND *CLOBBER GIRL*, WHO STOPPED SIDESHOW BOB FROM BLOWING UP THE STUDIO!
BECAUSE OF THEM, THE ONLY *BOMB* ON THE SHOW TODAY WAS THE MONKEY *"MAD MEN"* SKETCH!
OOK! AK!
OOF!
POW!
MATT GROENING
KRACK!
THAT SOUNDED LIKE HIS *FUNNY BONE!* HA!
COULD YOU *PLEASE* TURN OFF THAT INFERNAL TELEVISION? OR AT LEAST CHANGE THE CHANNEL TO PBS!?
WHAT'D YOU SAY, BOB? I WAS READING THIS STRETCH DUDE AND CLOBBER GIRL *COMIC BOOK!*
SINCE THEY'RE REAL, THEY'RE *PUBLIC DOMAIN,* AND THOSE BONGO COMICS FOLKS'LL PUBLISH *ANYTHING* THEY DON'T HAVE TO PAY THE RIGHTS FOR!

IAN BOOTHBY SCRIPT · *JOHN DELANEY* PENCILS · *ANDREW PEPOY* INKS · *ART VILLANUEVA* COLORS · *KAREN BATES* LETTERS · *NATHAN KANE* EDITOR

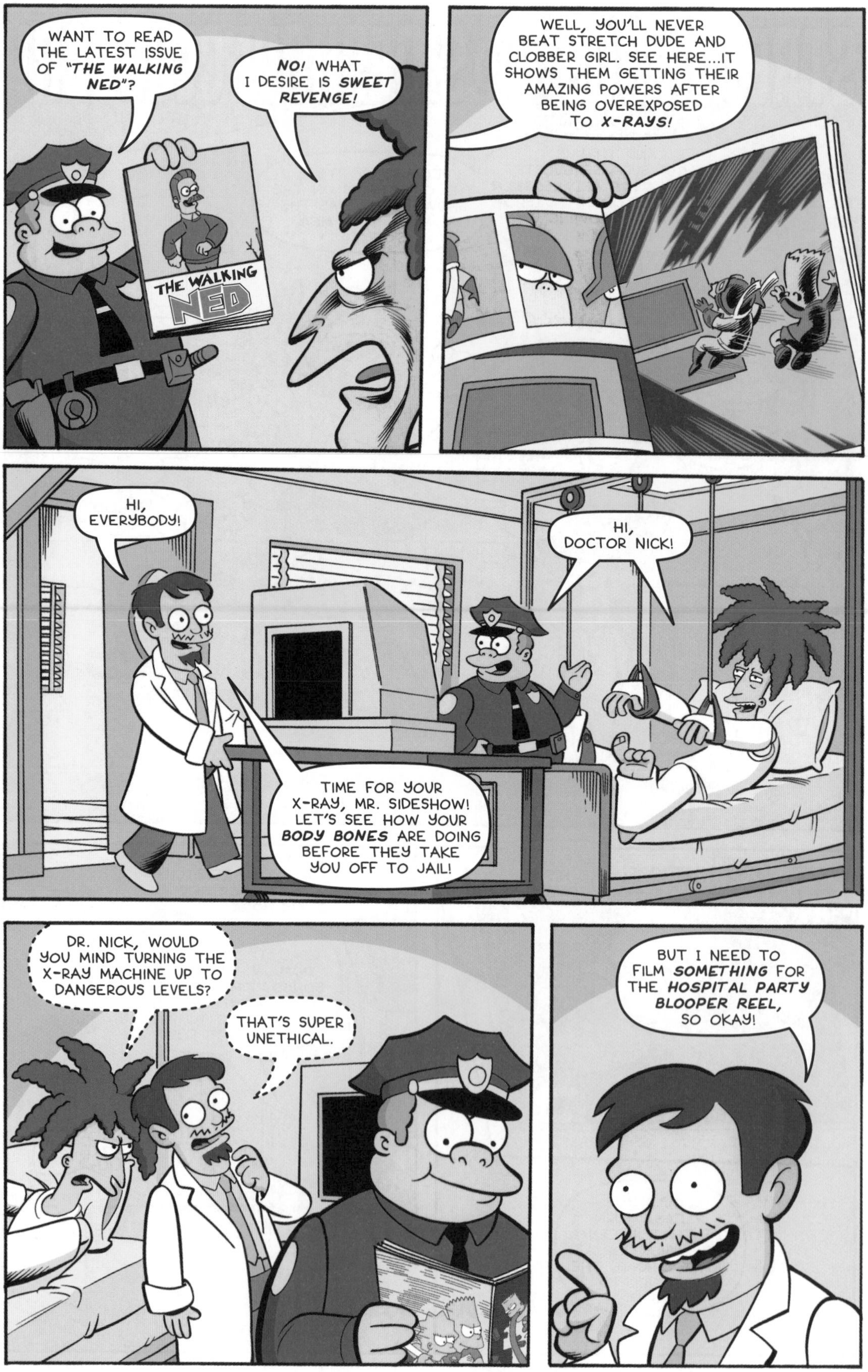
WANT TO READ THE LATEST ISSUE OF "THE WALKING NED"?
THE WALKING NED
NO! WHAT I DESIRE IS SWEET REVENGE!
WELL, YOU'LL NEVER BEAT STRETCH DUDE AND CLOBBER GIRL. SEE HERE...IT SHOWS THEM GETTING THEIR AMAZING POWERS AFTER BEING OVEREXPOSED TO X-RAYS!
HI, EVERYBODY!
HI, DOCTOR NICK!
TIME FOR YOUR X-RAY, MR. SIDESHOW! LET'S SEE HOW YOUR BODY BONES ARE DOING BEFORE THEY TAKE YOU OFF TO JAIL!
DR. NICK, WOULD YOU MIND TURNING THE X-RAY MACHINE UP TO DANGEROUS LEVELS?
THAT'S SUPER UNETHICAL.
BUT I NEED TO FILM SOMETHING FOR THE HOSPITAL PARTY BLOOPER REEL, SO OKAY!

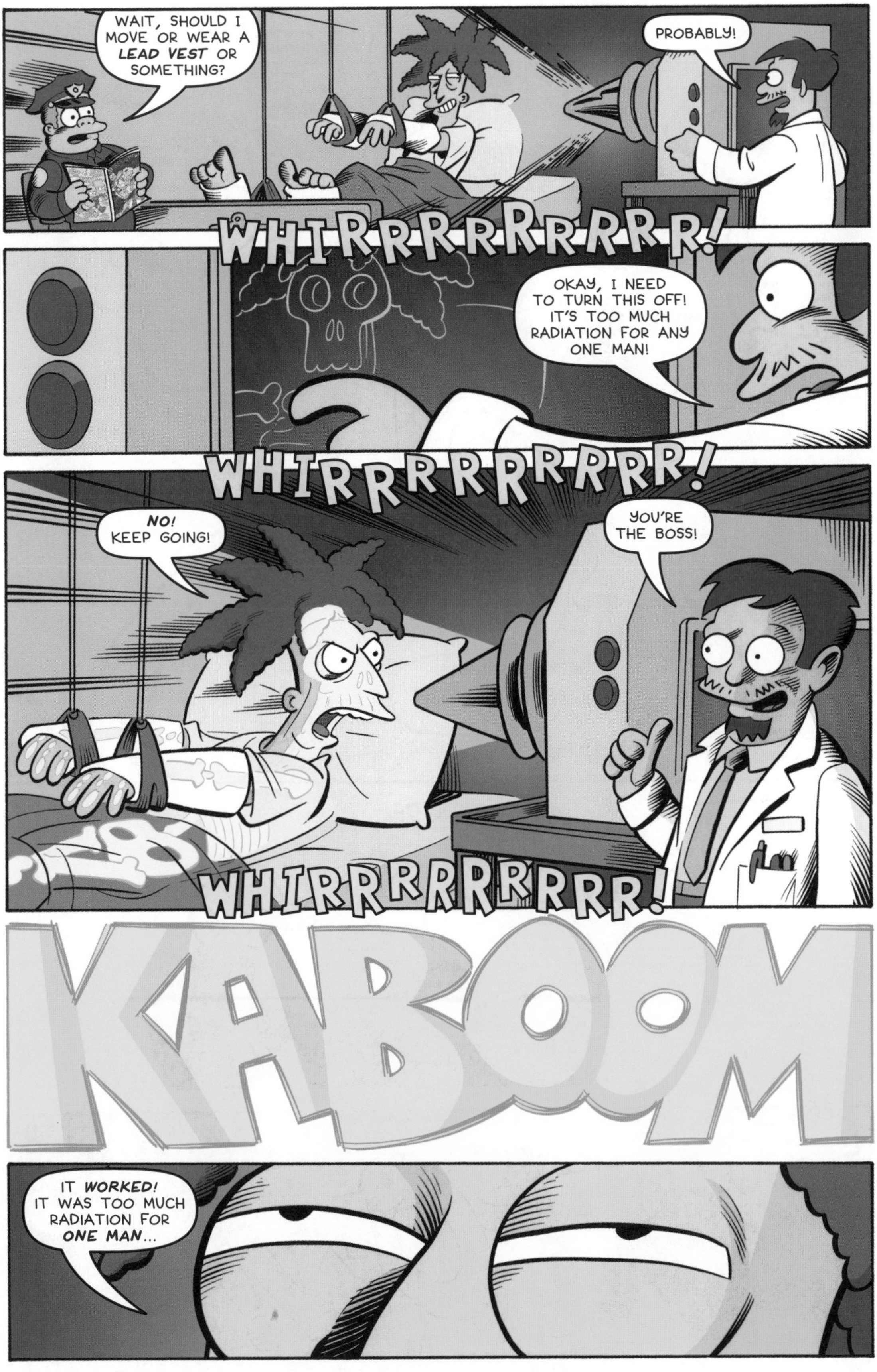
WAIT, SHOULD I MOVE OR WEAR A LEAD VEST OR SOMETHING?
PROBABLY!
WHIRRRRRRRRR!
OKAY, I NEED TO TURN THIS OFF! IT'S TOO MUCH RADIATION FOR ANY ONE MAN!
WHIRRRRRRRRR!
NO! KEEP GOING!
YOU'RE THE BOSS!
WHIRRRRRRRRR!
KABOOM
IT WORKED! IT WAS TOO MUCH RADIATION FOR ONE MAN...

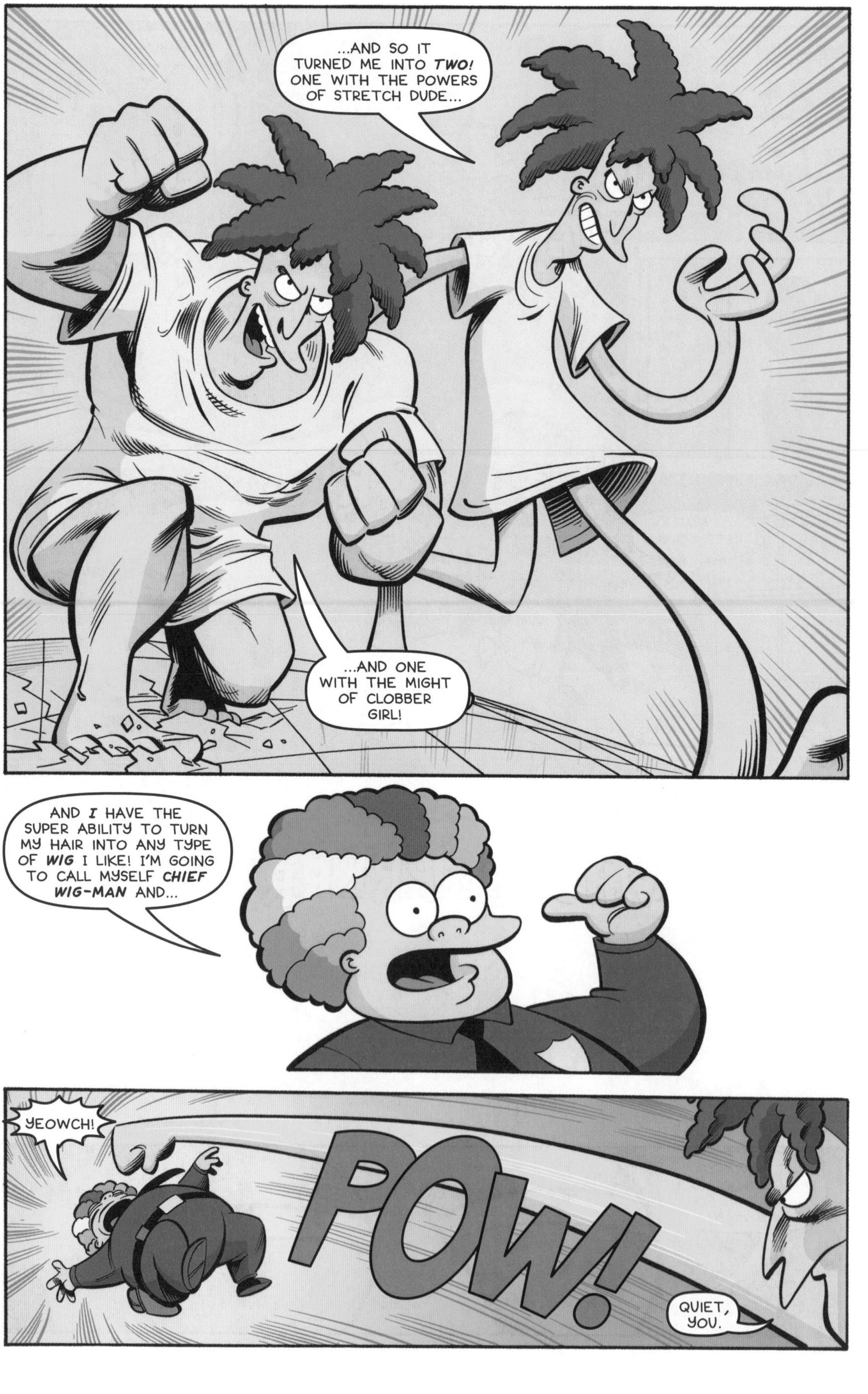
...AND SO IT TURNED ME INTO *TWO!* ONE WITH THE POWERS OF STRETCH DUDE...
...AND ONE WITH THE MIGHT OF CLOBBER GIRL!
AND *I* HAVE THE SUPER ABILITY TO TURN MY HAIR INTO ANY TYPE OF *WIG* I LIKE! I'M GOING TO CALL MYSELF *CHIEF WIG-MAN* AND...
YEOWCH!
POW!
QUIET, YOU.

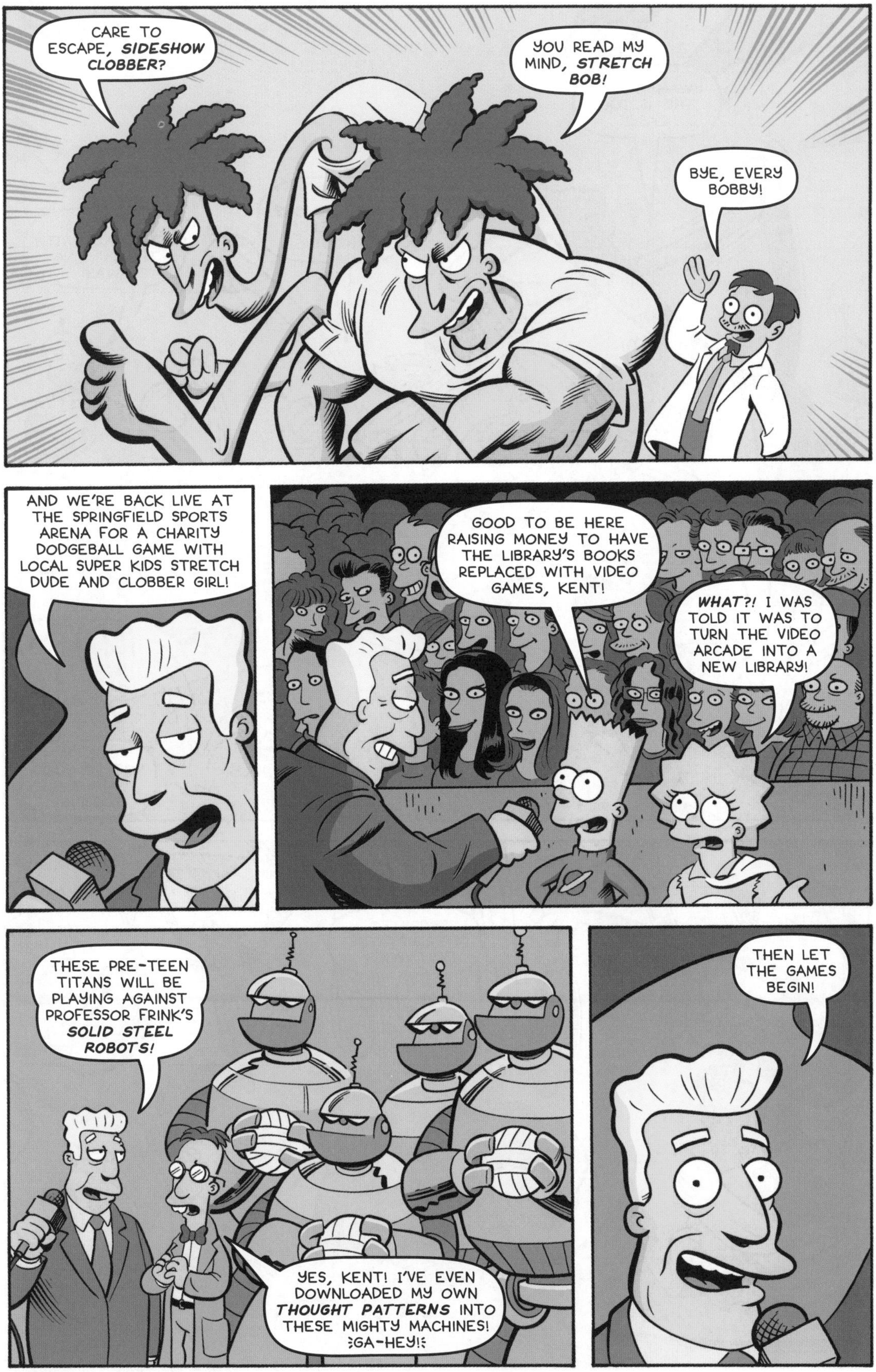
CARE TO ESCAPE, **SIDESHOW CLOBBER**?
YOU READ MY MIND, **STRETCH BOB**!
BYE, EVERY BOBBY!
AND WE'RE BACK LIVE AT THE SPRINGFIELD SPORTS ARENA FOR A CHARITY DODGEBALL GAME WITH LOCAL SUPER KIDS STRETCH DUDE AND CLOBBER GIRL!
GOOD TO BE HERE RAISING MONEY TO HAVE THE LIBRARY'S BOOKS REPLACED WITH VIDEO GAMES, KENT!
WHAT?! I WAS TOLD IT WAS TO TURN THE VIDEO ARCADE INTO A NEW LIBRARY!
THESE PRE-TEEN TITANS WILL BE PLAYING AGAINST PROFESSOR FRINK'S **SOLID STEEL ROBOTS**!
YES, KENT! I'VE EVEN DOWNLOADED MY OWN **THOUGHT PATTERNS** INTO THESE MIGHTY MACHINES! GA-HEY!
THEN LET THE GAMES BEGIN!

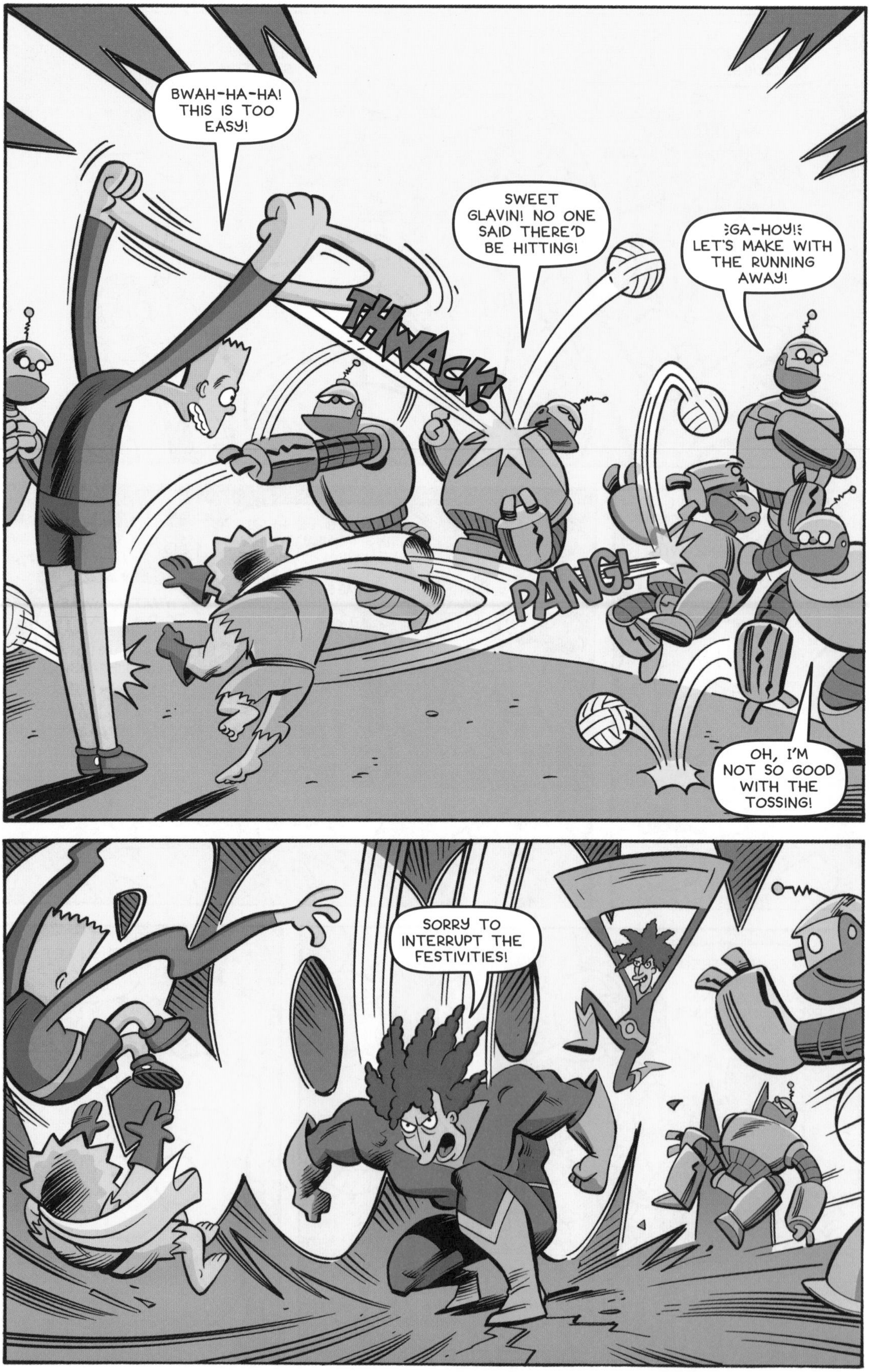
BWAH-HA-HA! THIS IS TOO EASY!
THWACK!
SWEET GLAVIN! NO ONE SAID THERE'D BE HITTING!
GA-HOY! LET'S MAKE WITH THE RUNNING AWAY!
PANG!
OH, I'M NOT SO GOOD WITH THE TOSSING!
SORRY TO INTERRUPT THE FESTIVITIES!

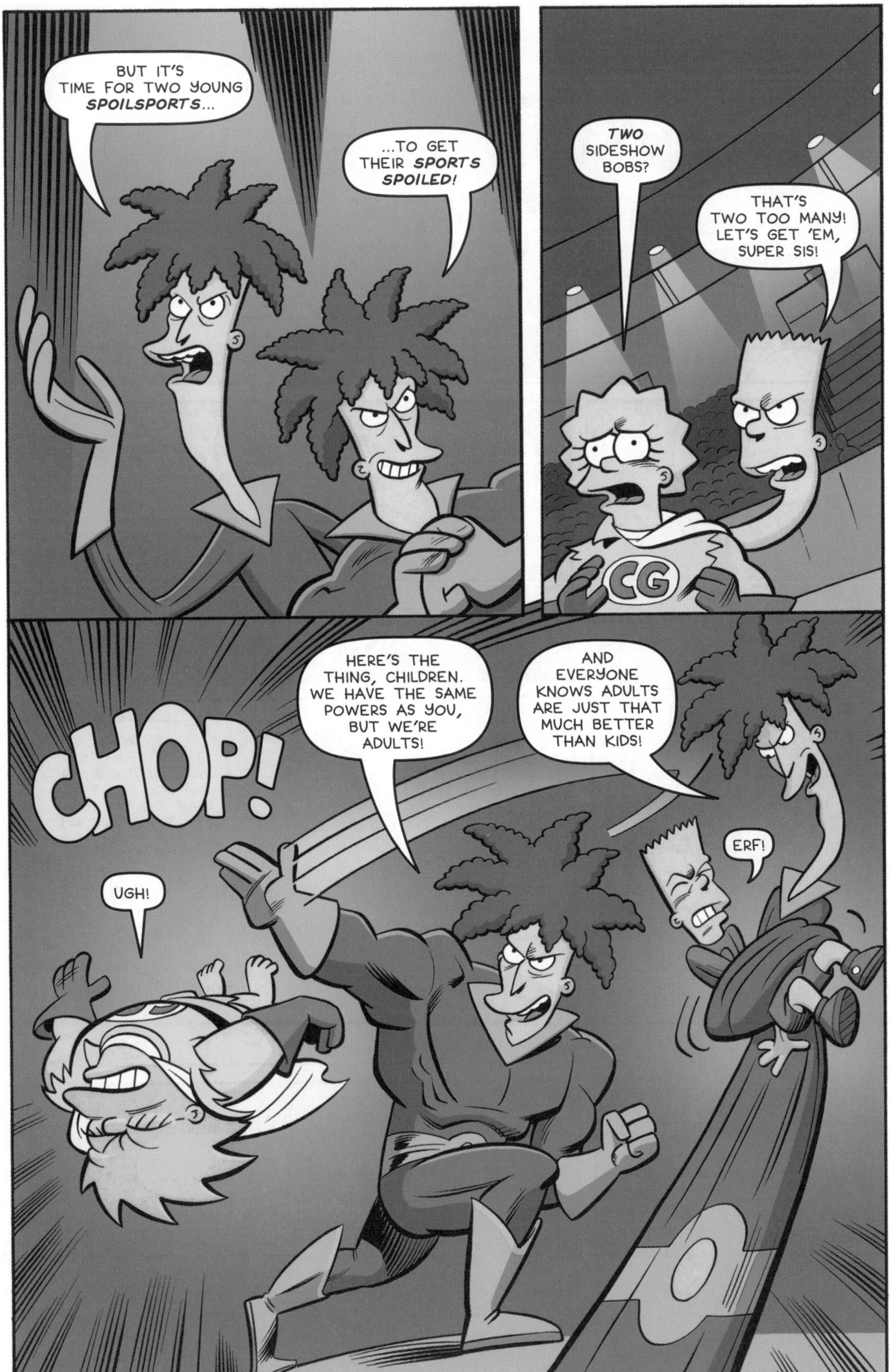
BUT IT'S TIME FOR TWO YOUNG SPOILSPORTS...
...TO GET THEIR SPORTS SPOILED!
TWO SIDESHOW BOBS?
THAT'S TWO TOO MANY! LET'S GET 'EM, SUPER SIS!
CHOP!
HERE'S THE THING, CHILDREN. WE HAVE THE SAME POWERS AS YOU, BUT WE'RE ADULTS!
AND EVERYONE KNOWS ADULTS ARE JUST THAT MUCH BETTER THAN KIDS!
UGH!
ERF!

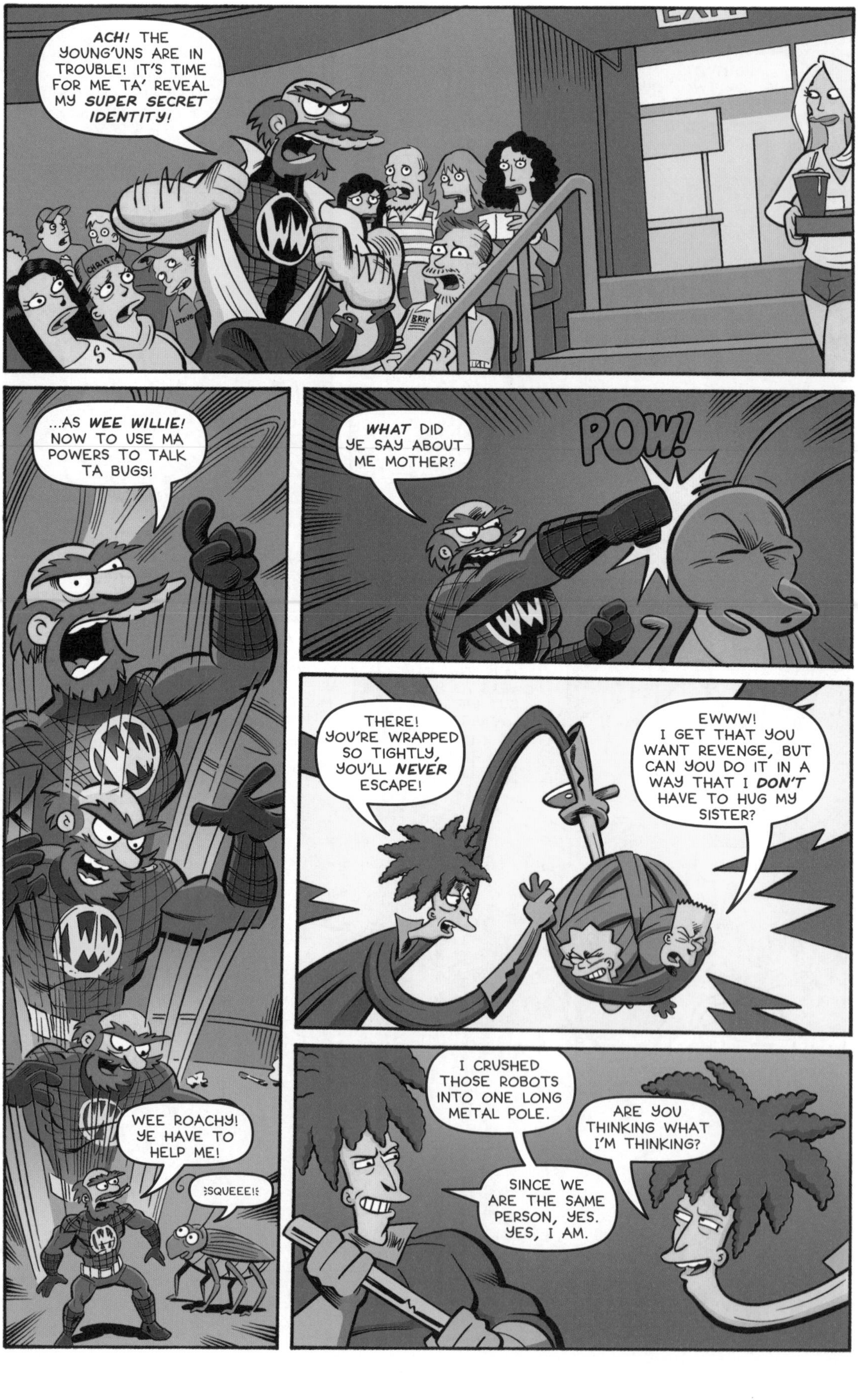
ACH! THE YOUNG'UNS ARE IN TROUBLE! IT'S TIME FOR ME TA' REVEAL MY SUPER SECRET IDENTITY!
...AS WEE WILLIE! NOW TO USE MA POWERS TO TALK TA BUGS!
WEE ROACHY! YE HAVE TO HELP ME!
SQUEEE!
WHAT DID YE SAY ABOUT ME MOTHER?
POW!
THERE! YOU'RE WRAPPED SO TIGHTLY, YOU'LL NEVER ESCAPE!
EWWW! I GET THAT YOU WANT REVENGE, BUT CAN YOU DO IT IN A WAY THAT I DON'T HAVE TO HUG MY SISTER?
I CRUSHED THOSE ROBOTS INTO ONE LONG METAL POLE.
ARE YOU THINKING WHAT I'M THINKING?
SINCE WE ARE THE SAME PERSON, YES. YES, I AM.

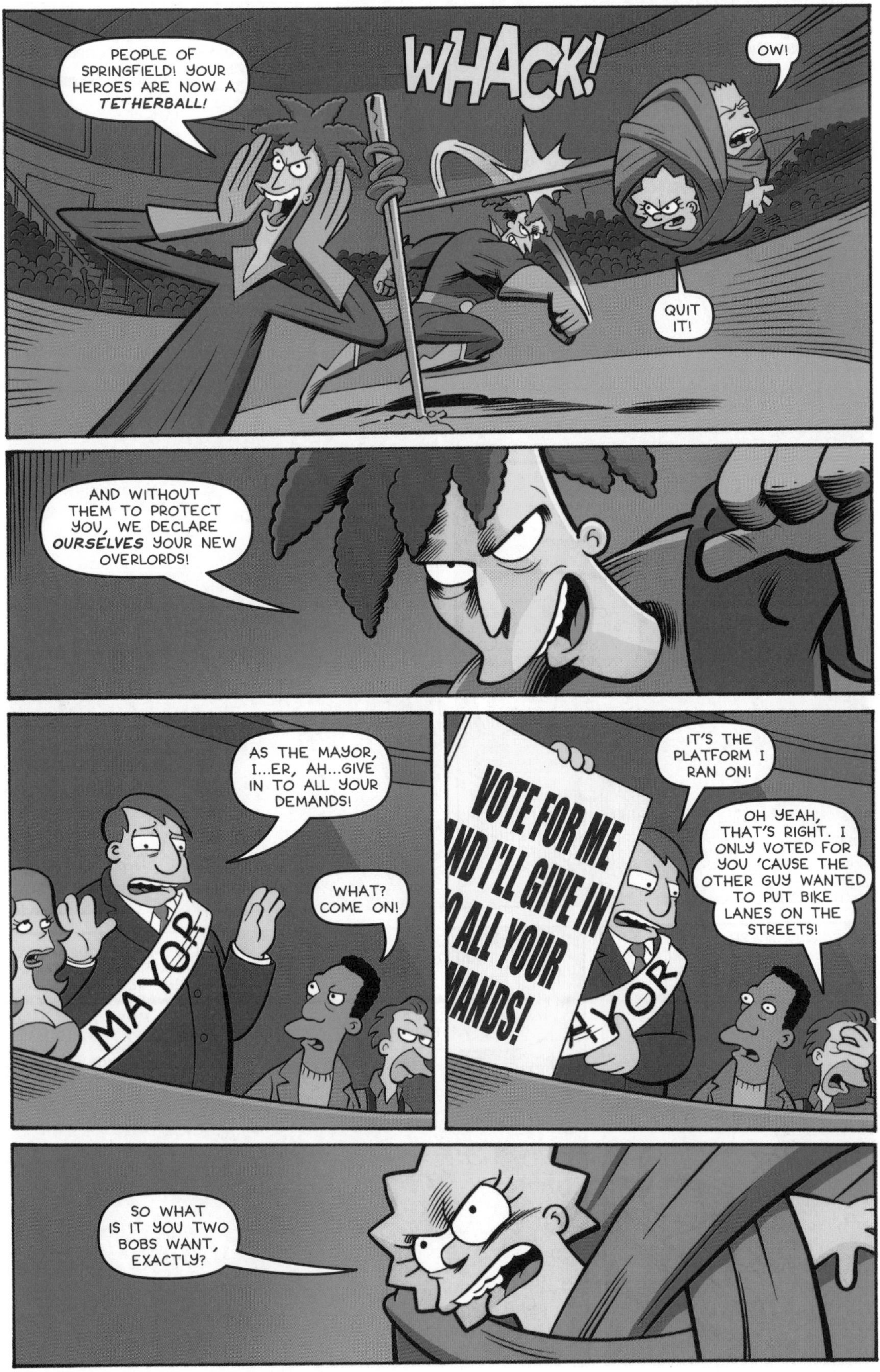
PEOPLE OF SPRINGFIELD! YOUR HEROES ARE NOW A *TETHERBALL!*
WHACK!
OW!
QUIT IT!
AND WITHOUT THEM TO PROTECT YOU, WE DECLARE *OURSELVES* YOUR NEW OVERLORDS!
AS THE MAYOR, I...ER, AH...GIVE IN TO ALL YOUR DEMANDS!
MAYOR
WHAT? COME ON!
VOTE FOR ME AND I'LL GIVE IN TO ALL YOUR DEMANDS!
IT'S THE PLATFORM I RAN ON!
OH YEAH, THAT'S RIGHT. I ONLY VOTED FOR YOU 'CAUSE THE OTHER GUY WANTED TO PUT BIKE LANES ON THE STREETS!
SO WHAT IS IT YOU TWO BOBS WANT, EXACTLY?

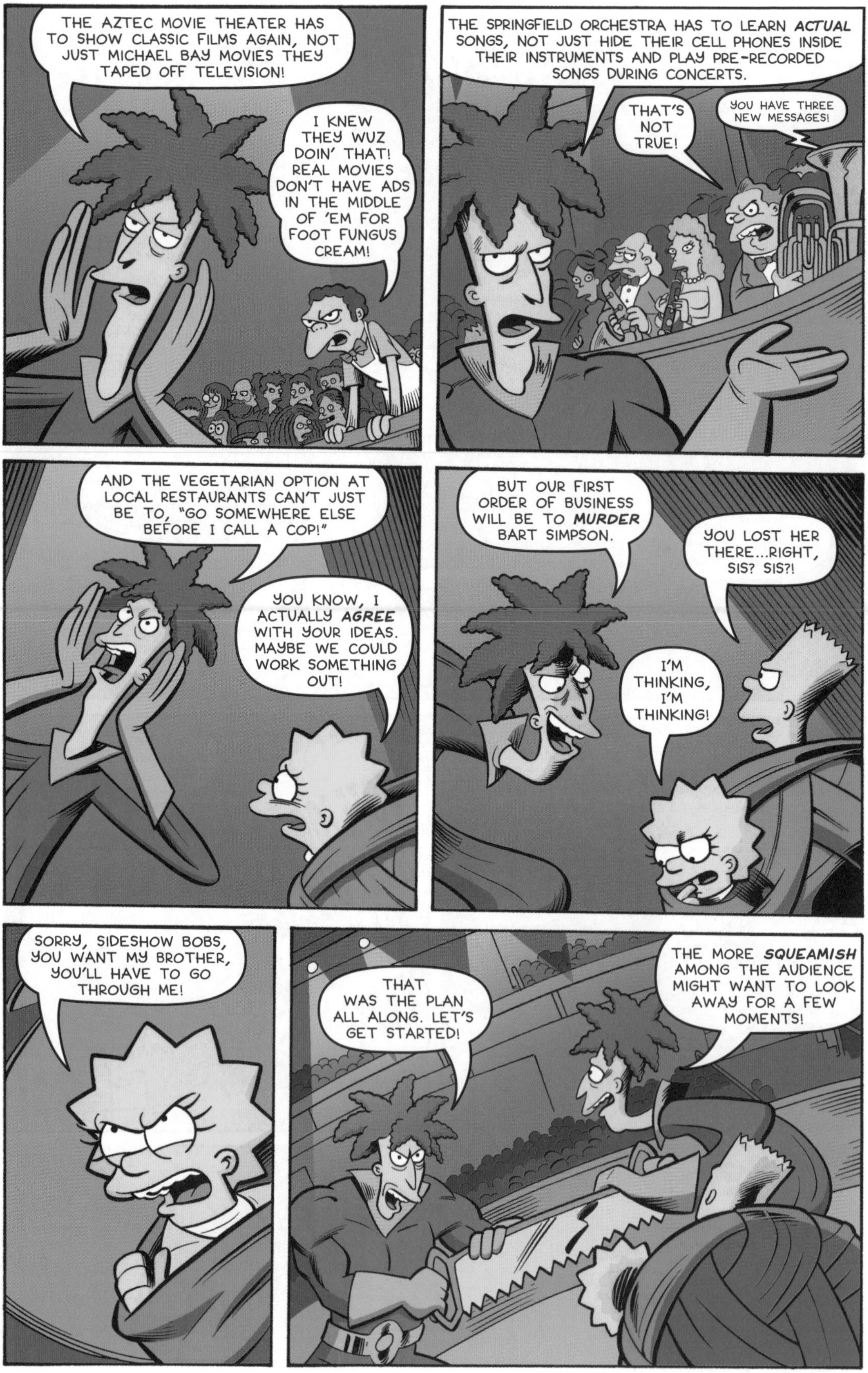
THE AZTEC MOVIE THEATER HAS TO SHOW CLASSIC FILMS AGAIN, NOT JUST MICHAEL BAY MOVIES THEY TAPED OFF TELEVISION!
I KNEW THEY WUZ DOIN' THAT! REAL MOVIES DON'T HAVE ADS IN THE MIDDLE OF 'EM FOR FOOT FUNGUS CREAM!
THE SPRINGFIELD ORCHESTRA HAS TO LEARN ACTUAL SONGS, NOT JUST HIDE THEIR CELL PHONES INSIDE THEIR INSTRUMENTS AND PLAY PRE-RECORDED SONGS DURING CONCERTS.
THAT'S NOT TRUE!
YOU HAVE THREE NEW MESSAGES!
AND THE VEGETARIAN OPTION AT LOCAL RESTAURANTS CAN'T JUST BE TO, "GO SOMEWHERE ELSE BEFORE I CALL A COP!"
YOU KNOW, I ACTUALLY AGREE WITH YOUR IDEAS. MAYBE WE COULD WORK SOMETHING OUT!
BUT OUR FIRST ORDER OF BUSINESS WILL BE TO MURDER BART SIMPSON.
YOU LOST HER THERE...RIGHT, SIS? SIS?!
I'M THINKING, I'M THINKING!
SORRY, SIDESHOW BOBS, YOU WANT MY BROTHER, YOU'LL HAVE TO GO THROUGH ME!
THAT WAS THE PLAN ALL ALONG. LET'S GET STARTED!
THE MORE SQUEAMISH AMONG THE AUDIENCE MIGHT WANT TO LOOK AWAY FOR A FEW MOMENTS!

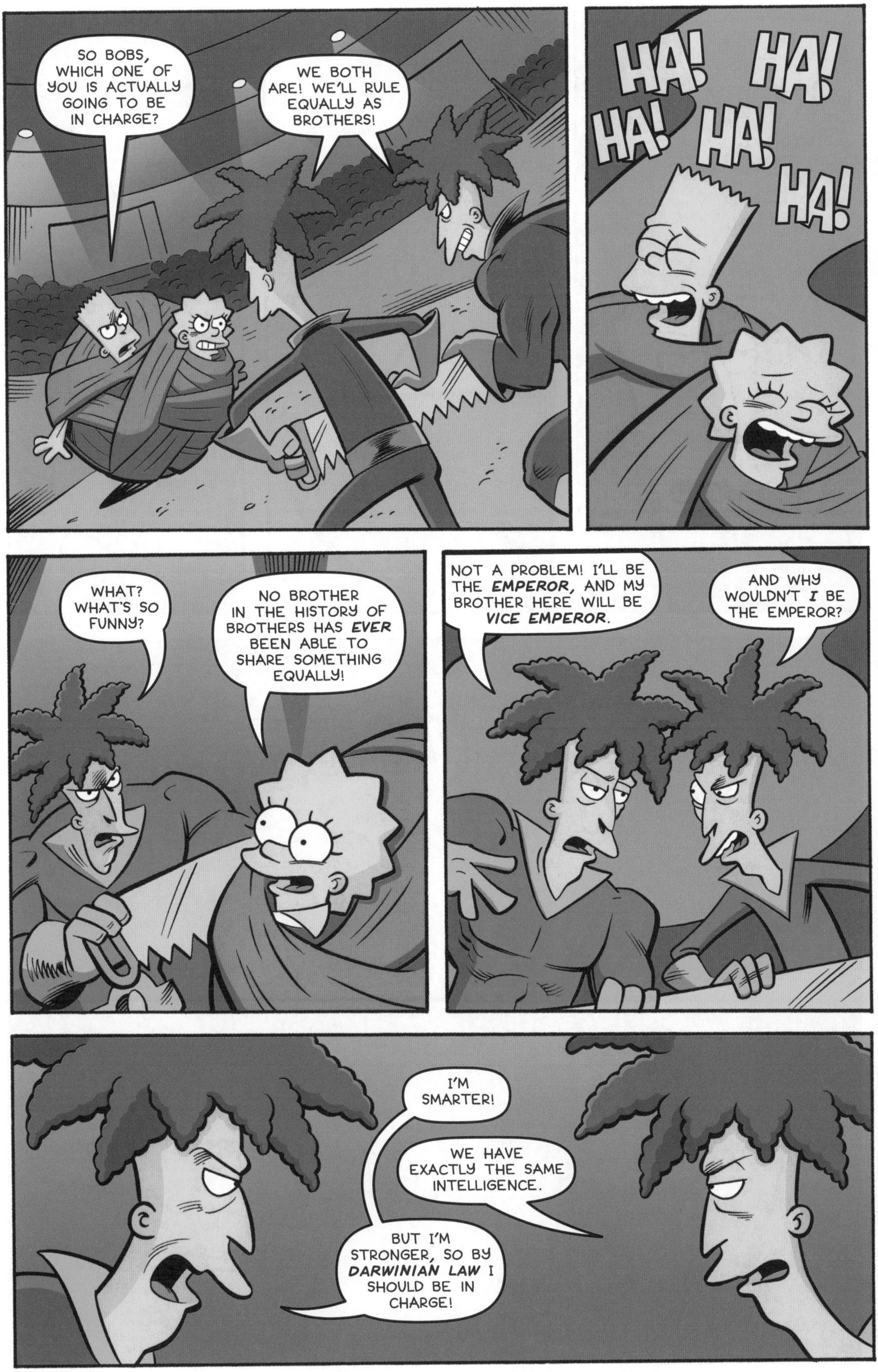
SO BOBS, WHICH ONE OF YOU IS ACTUALLY GOING TO BE IN CHARGE?
WE BOTH ARE! WE'LL RULE EQUALLY AS BROTHERS!
HA! HA! HA! HA! HA!
WHAT? WHAT'S SO FUNNY?
NO BROTHER IN THE HISTORY OF BROTHERS HAS **EVER** BEEN ABLE TO SHARE SOMETHING EQUALLY!
NOT A PROBLEM! I'LL BE THE **EMPEROR,** AND MY BROTHER HERE WILL BE **VICE EMPEROR**.
AND WHY WOULDN'T **I** BE THE EMPEROR?
I'M SMARTER!
WE HAVE EXACTLY THE SAME INTELLIGENCE.
BUT I'M STRONGER, SO BY **DARWINIAN LAW** I SHOULD BE IN CHARGE!

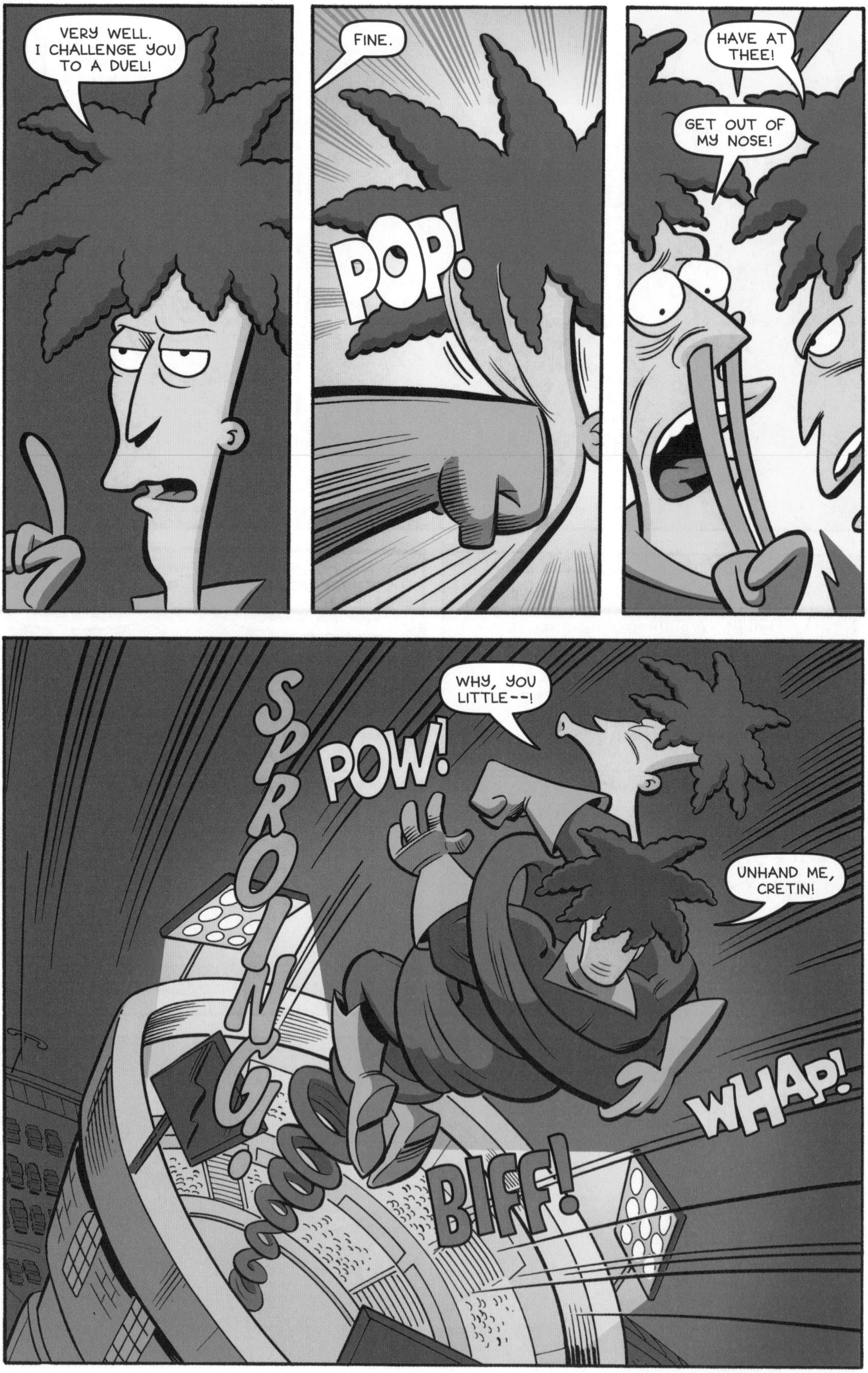
VERY WELL. I CHALLENGE YOU TO A DUEL!
FINE.
POP!
HAVE AT THEE!
GET OUT OF MY NOSE!
SPROING!
POW!
WHY, YOU LITTLE--!
UNHAND ME, CRETIN!
WHAP!
BIFF!

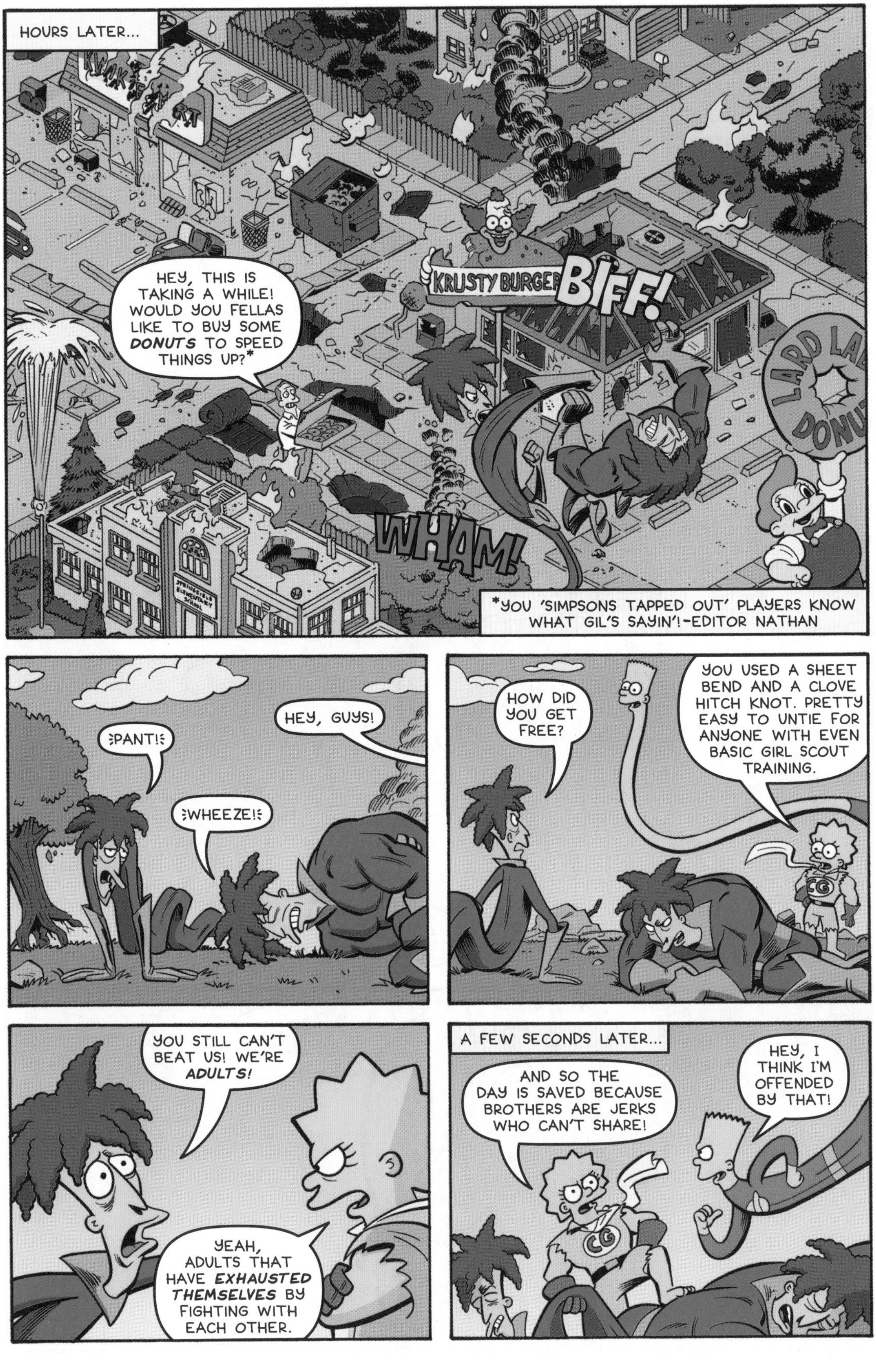
HOURS LATER...
HEY, THIS IS TAKING A WHILE! WOULD YOU FELLAS LIKE TO BUY SOME DONUTS TO SPEED THINGS UP?*
KRUSTY BURGER
BIFF!
LARD LAD DONUTS
WHAM!
*YOU 'SIMPSONS TAPPED OUT' PLAYERS KNOW WHAT GIL'S SAYIN'!-EDITOR NATHAN
PANT!
HEY, GUYS!
WHEEZE!
HOW DID YOU GET FREE?
YOU USED A SHEET BEND AND A CLOVE HITCH KNOT. PRETTY EASY TO UNTIE FOR ANYONE WITH EVEN BASIC GIRL SCOUT TRAINING.
YOU STILL CAN'T BEAT US! WE'RE ADULTS!
YEAH, ADULTS THAT HAVE EXHAUSTED THEMSELVES BY FIGHTING WITH EACH OTHER.
A FEW SECONDS LATER...
AND SO THE DAY IS SAVED BECAUSE BROTHERS ARE JERKS WHO CAN'T SHARE!
HEY, I THINK I'M OFFENDED BY THAT!

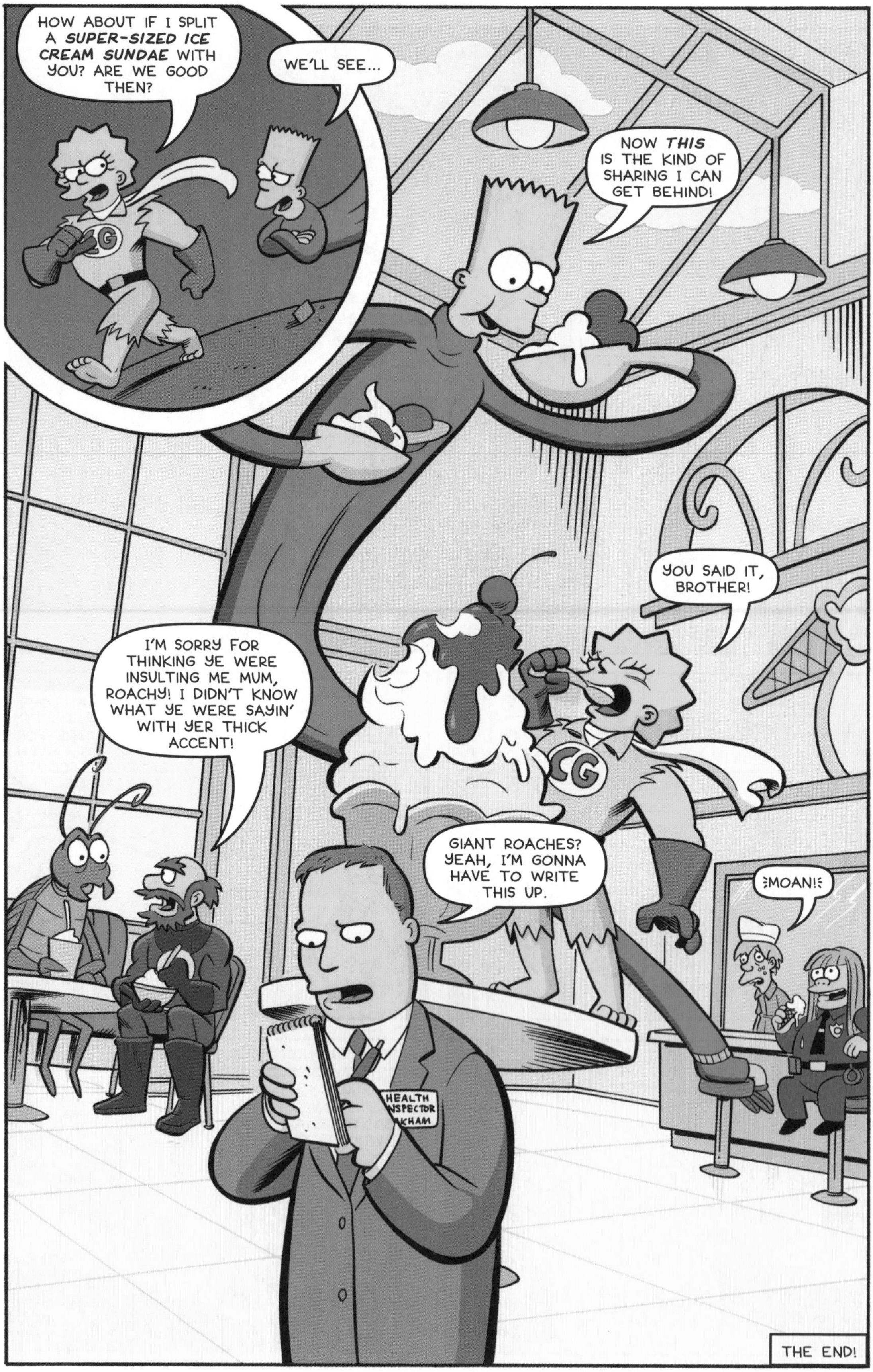
HOW ABOUT IF I SPLIT A SUPER-SIZED ICE CREAM SUNDAE WITH YOU? ARE WE GOOD THEN?
WE'LL SEE...
NOW THIS IS THE KIND OF SHARING I CAN GET BEHIND!
YOU SAID IT, BROTHER!
I'M SORRY FOR THINKING YE WERE INSULTING ME MUM, ROACHY! I DIDN'T KNOW WHAT YE WERE SAYIN' WITH YER THICK ACCENT!
GIANT ROACHES? YEAH, I'M GONNA HAVE TO WRITE THIS UP.
MOAN!
HEALTH INSPECTOR
THE END!

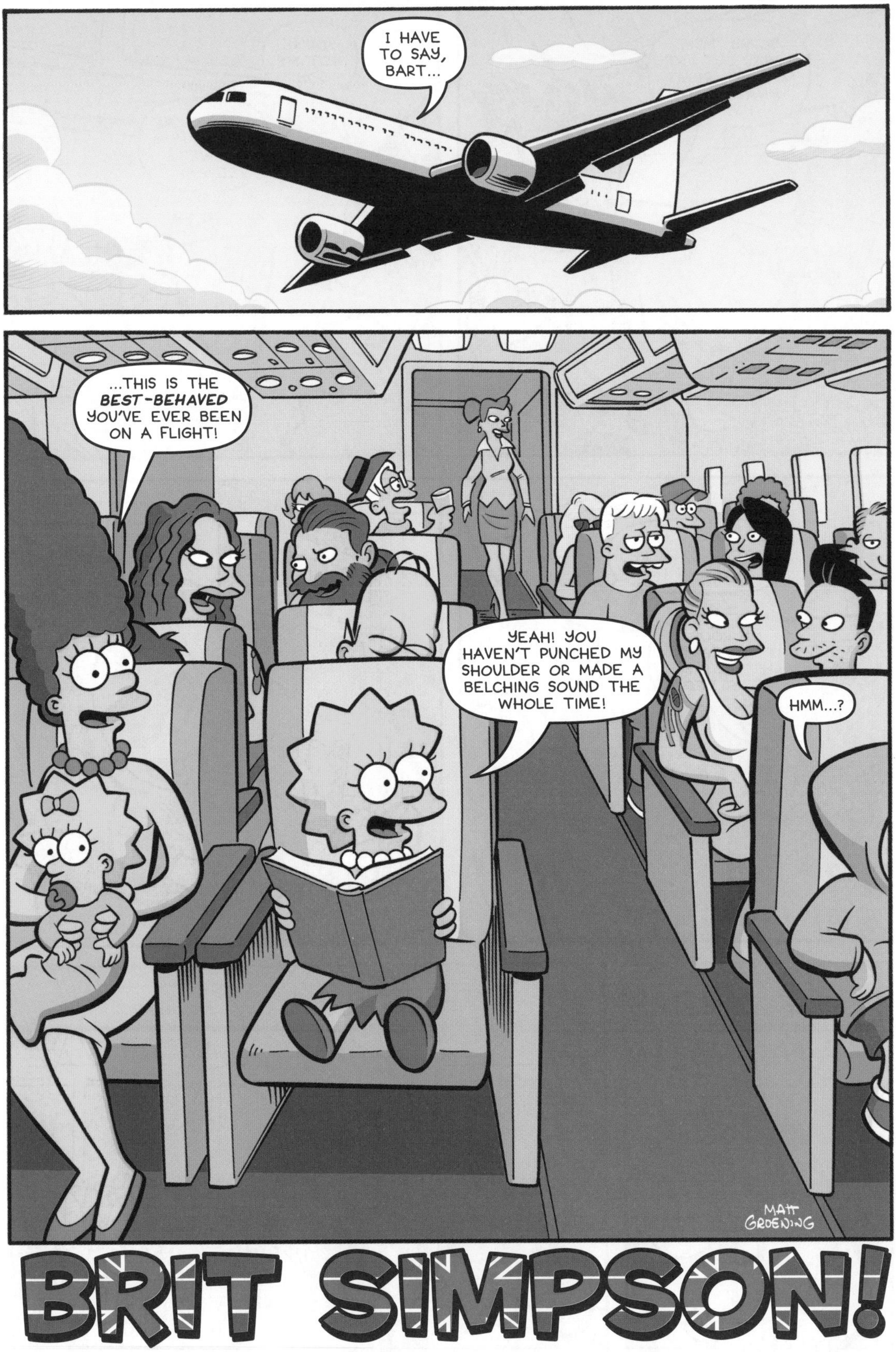
I HAVE TO SAY, BART...
...THIS IS THE BEST-BEHAVED YOU'VE EVER BEEN ON A FLIGHT!
YEAH! YOU HAVEN'T PUNCHED MY SHOULDER OR MADE A BELCHING SOUND THE WHOLE TIME!
HMM...?
MATT GROENING

BRIT SIMPSON!

IAN BOOTHBY WRITER | **JOHN DELANEY** PENCILS | **ANDREW PEPOY** INKS | **ART VILLANUEVA** COLORS | **KAREN BATES** LETTERS | **NATHAN KANE** EDITOR

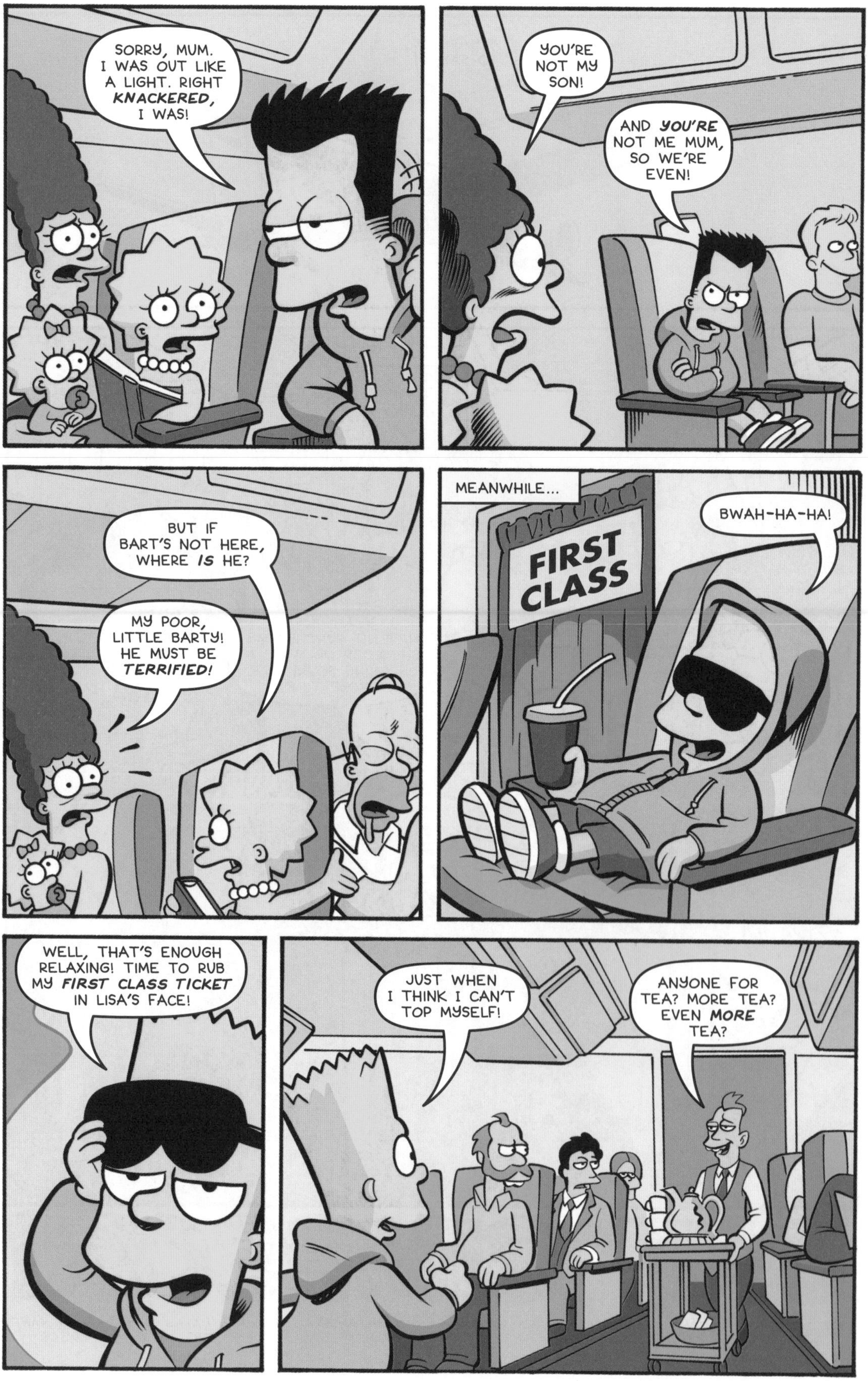
SORRY, MUM. I WAS OUT LIKE A LIGHT. RIGHT *KNACKERED,* I WAS!
YOU'RE NOT MY SON!
AND *YOU'RE* NOT ME MUM, SO WE'RE EVEN!
BUT IF BART'S NOT HERE, WHERE *IS* HE?
MY POOR, LITTLE BARTY! HE MUST BE *TERRIFIED!*
MEANWHILE...
FIRST CLASS
BWAH-HA-HA!
WELL, THAT'S ENOUGH RELAXING! TIME TO RUB MY *FIRST CLASS TICKET* IN LISA'S FACE!
JUST WHEN I THINK I CAN'T TOP MYSELF!
ANYONE FOR TEA? MORE TEA? EVEN *MORE* TEA?

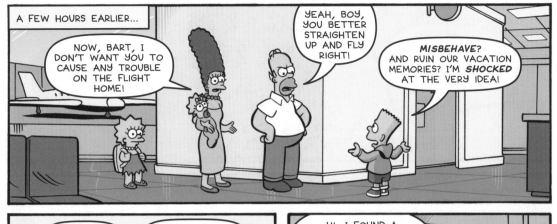

A FEW HOURS EARLIER...

NOW, BART, I DON'T WANT YOU TO CAUSE ANY TROUBLE ON THE FLIGHT HOME!

YEAH, BOY, YOU BETTER STRAIGHTEN UP AND FLY RIGHT!

MISBEHAVE? AND RUIN OUR VACATION MEMORIES? I'M *SHOCKED* AT THE VERY IDEA!

OBVIOUSLY, YOU'VE NEVER MET *YOU* BEFORE.

IF YOU'LL EXCUSE ME, I NEED TO FRESHEN UP!

HI, I FOUND A *COCKROACH* IN THE FREE BAG OF NUTS ON MY LAST FLIGHT AND WAS TOLD I COULD UPGRADE TO FIRST CLASS ON THIS ONE IF I KEPT MY MOUTH SHUT ABOUT IT.

WE DON'T HAVE A RECORD OF...

I HAVE THE NUTS HERE IF YOU'D LIKE TO LOOK INSIDE. I CAN SHOW EVERYONE!

AAAAH! NO! I HATE BUGS! JUST GIVE ME YOUR NAME!

SIMPSON.

YES, I SEE IT! GO RIGHT IN. WE'RE BOARDING OUR FIRST CLASS PASSENGERS ON FLIGHT 302 RIGHT NOW!

NOW BOARDING FLIGHT 203!

OKAY, SIMPSONS! THAT'S US! LET'S GO!

ZZZZ...

GRAB!

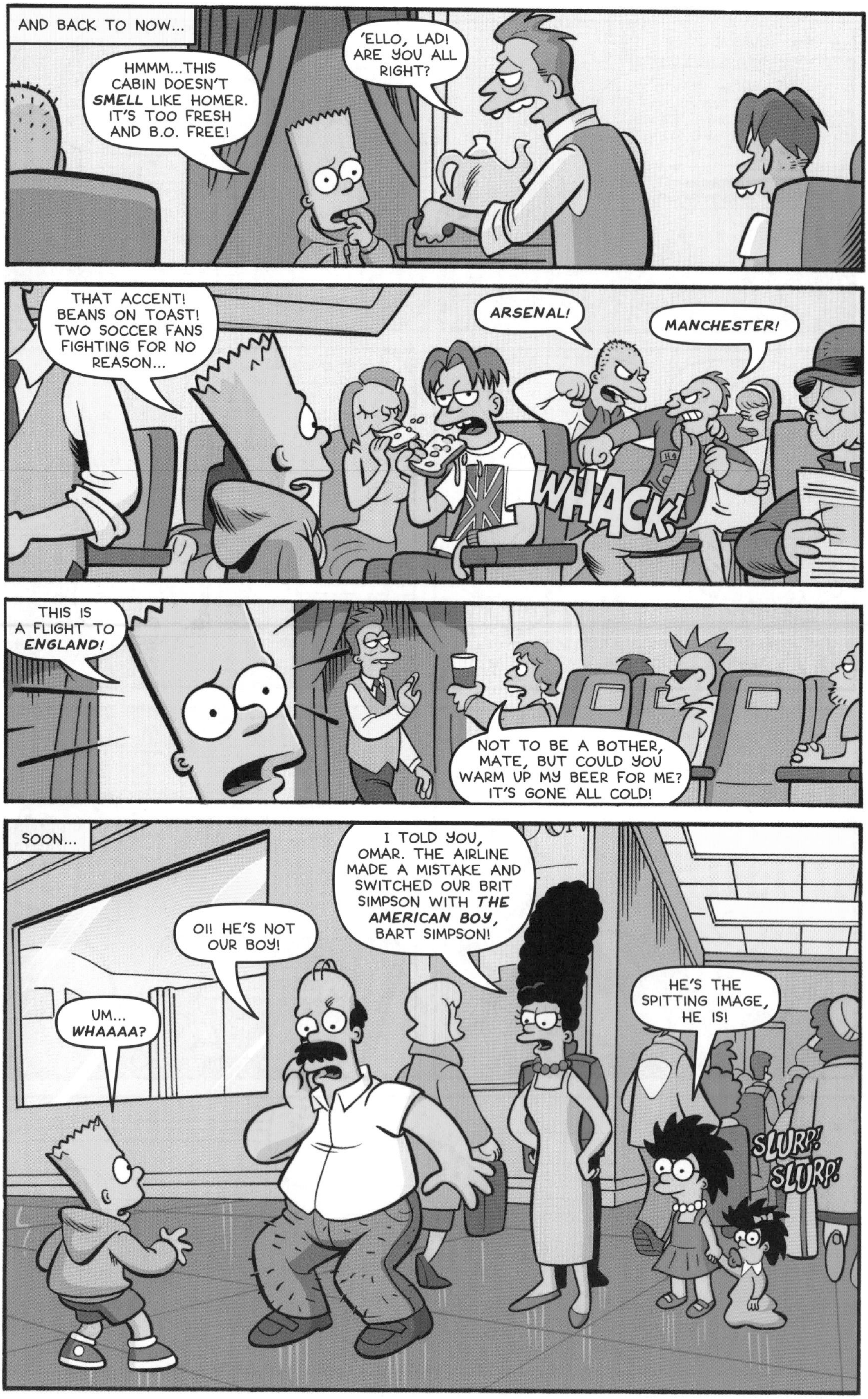
AND BACK TO NOW...
HMMM...THIS CABIN DOESN'T SMELL LIKE HOMER. IT'S TOO FRESH AND B.O. FREE!
'ELLO, LAD! ARE YOU ALL RIGHT?
THAT ACCENT! BEANS ON TOAST! TWO SOCCER FANS FIGHTING FOR NO REASON...
ARSENAL!
MANCHESTER!
WHACK!
THIS IS A FLIGHT TO ENGLAND!
NOT TO BE A BOTHER, MATE, BUT COULD YOU WARM UP MY BEER FOR ME? IT'S GONE ALL COLD!
SOON...
I TOLD YOU, OMAR. THE AIRLINE MADE A MISTAKE AND SWITCHED OUR BRIT SIMPSON WITH THE AMERICAN BOY, BART SIMPSON!
OI! HE'S NOT OUR BOY!
UM... WHAAAA?
HE'S THE SPITTING IMAGE, HE IS!
SLURP! SLURP!

HELLO, BART! I'M *MARNIE SIMPSON*, AND THIS IS MY HUSBAND, *OMAR*.

THE AIRLINE PUT ME IN TOUCH WITH YOUR MOTHER. SHE'S ON THE PHONE!

QUEEN

BART! I WAS SO WORRIED ABOUT YOU!

THE EARLIEST THE AIRLINE CAN SEND YOU HOME IS IN A WEEK! SO THE SIMPSONS OVER THERE HAVE SAID THEY'LL TAKE CARE OF YOU UNTIL THEN, AND *WE'LL* LOOK AFTER THEIR SON, BRIT!

I'M *LILY*, AND THIS IS *MAGPIE*!

I LOOKED UP YOUR GENEALOGY ONLINE AND IT TURNS OUT WE'RE ALL COUSINS! ISN'T THAT FASCINATING?

SLURP! SLURP!

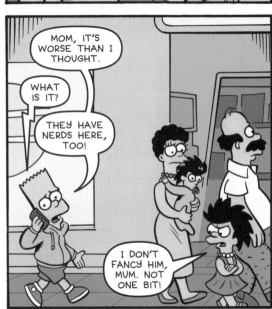

MOM, IT'S WORSE THAN I THOUGHT.

WHAT IS IT?

THEY HAVE NERDS HERE, TOO!

I DON'T FANCY HIM, MUM. NOT ONE BIT!

WELL, THE FIRST THING WE HAVE TO DO IS GET YOU HOME TO *SPRINGSHIRE*!

WHOA, OMAR! YOU'RE DRIVING ON THE WRONG SIDE OF THE ROAD!

I AM? THANKS FOR THE HEADS UP, LAD!

SPRINGSHIRE 25 km

SCREEEECH!

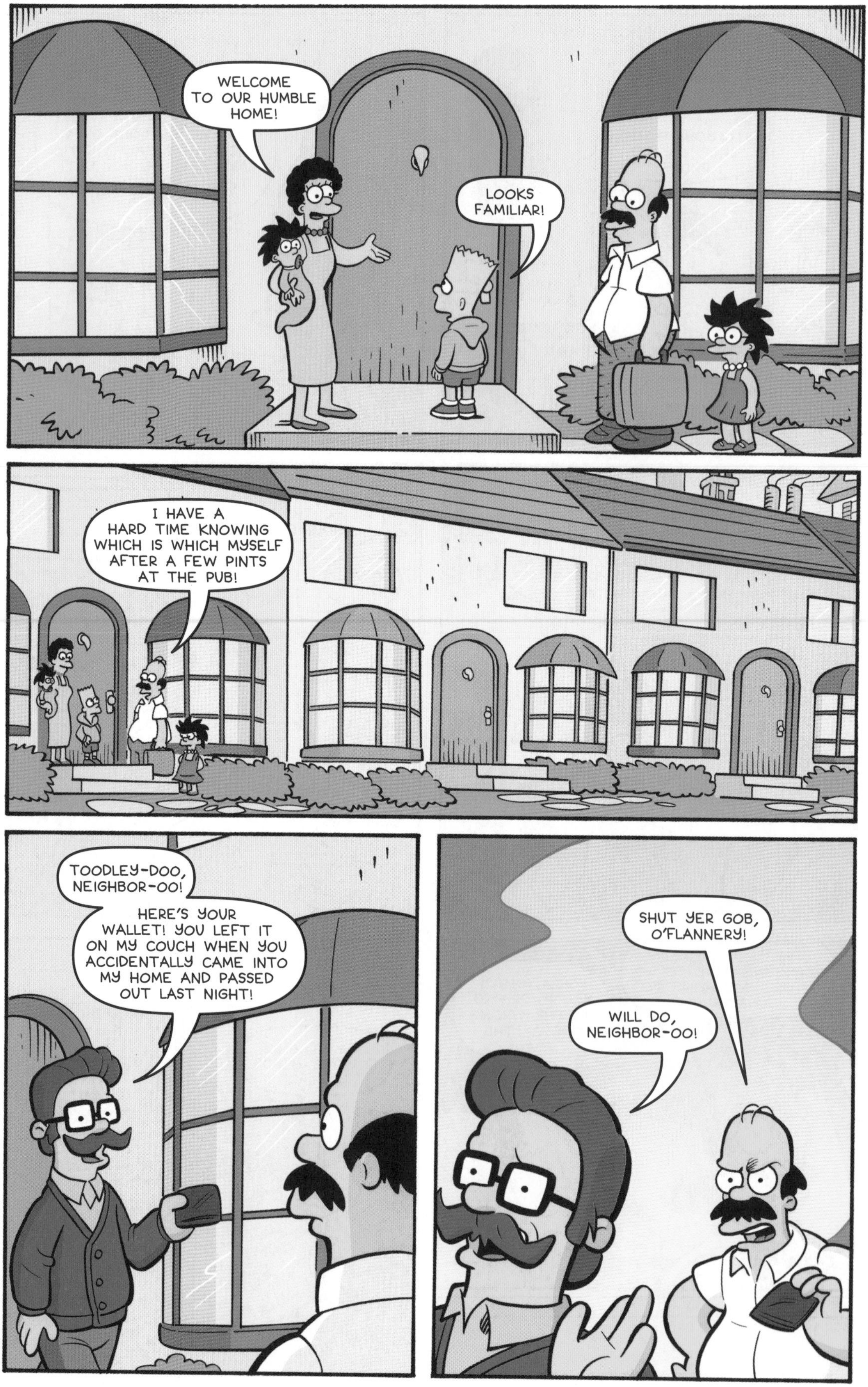
WELCOME TO OUR HUMBLE HOME!
LOOKS FAMILIAR!
I HAVE A HARD TIME KNOWING WHICH IS WHICH MYSELF AFTER A FEW PINTS AT THE PUB!
TOODLEY-DOO, NEIGHBOR-OO!
HERE'S YOUR WALLET! YOU LEFT IT ON MY COUCH WHEN YOU ACCIDENTALLY CAME INTO MY HOME AND PASSED OUT LAST NIGHT!
SHUT YER GOB, O'FLANNERY!
WILL DO, NEIGHBOR-OO!

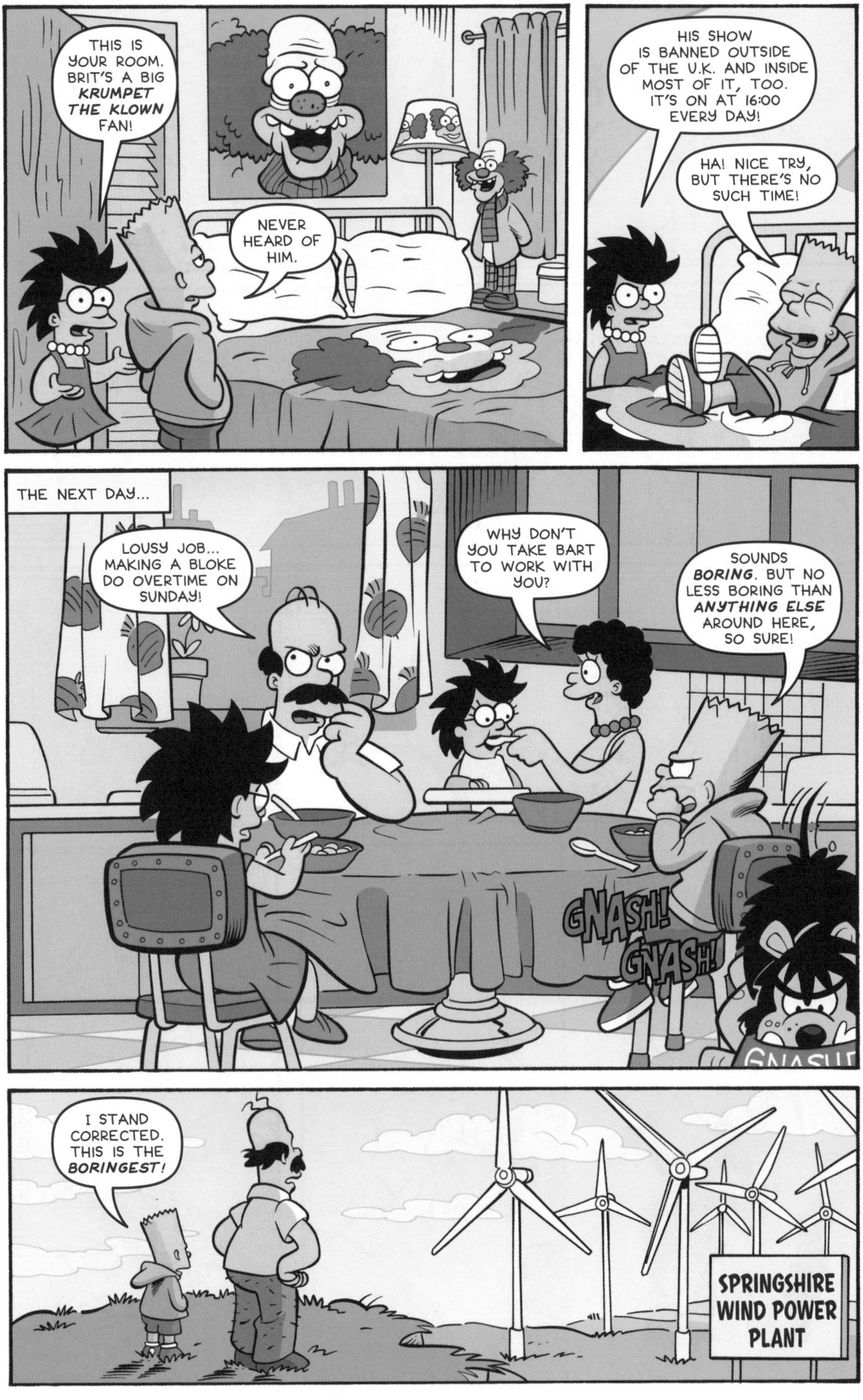
THIS IS YOUR ROOM. BRIT'S A BIG KRUMPET THE KLOWN FAN!
NEVER HEARD OF HIM.
HIS SHOW IS BANNED OUTSIDE OF THE U.K. AND INSIDE MOST OF IT, TOO. IT'S ON AT 16:00 EVERY DAY!
HA! NICE TRY, BUT THERE'S NO SUCH TIME!
THE NEXT DAY...
LOUSY JOB... MAKING A BLOKE DO OVERTIME ON SUNDAY!
WHY DON'T YOU TAKE BART TO WORK WITH YOU?
SOUNDS BORING. BUT NO LESS BORING THAN ANYTHING ELSE AROUND HERE, SO SURE!
GNASH! GNASH!
I STAND CORRECTED. THIS IS THE BORINGEST!
SPRINGSHIRE WIND POWER PLANT

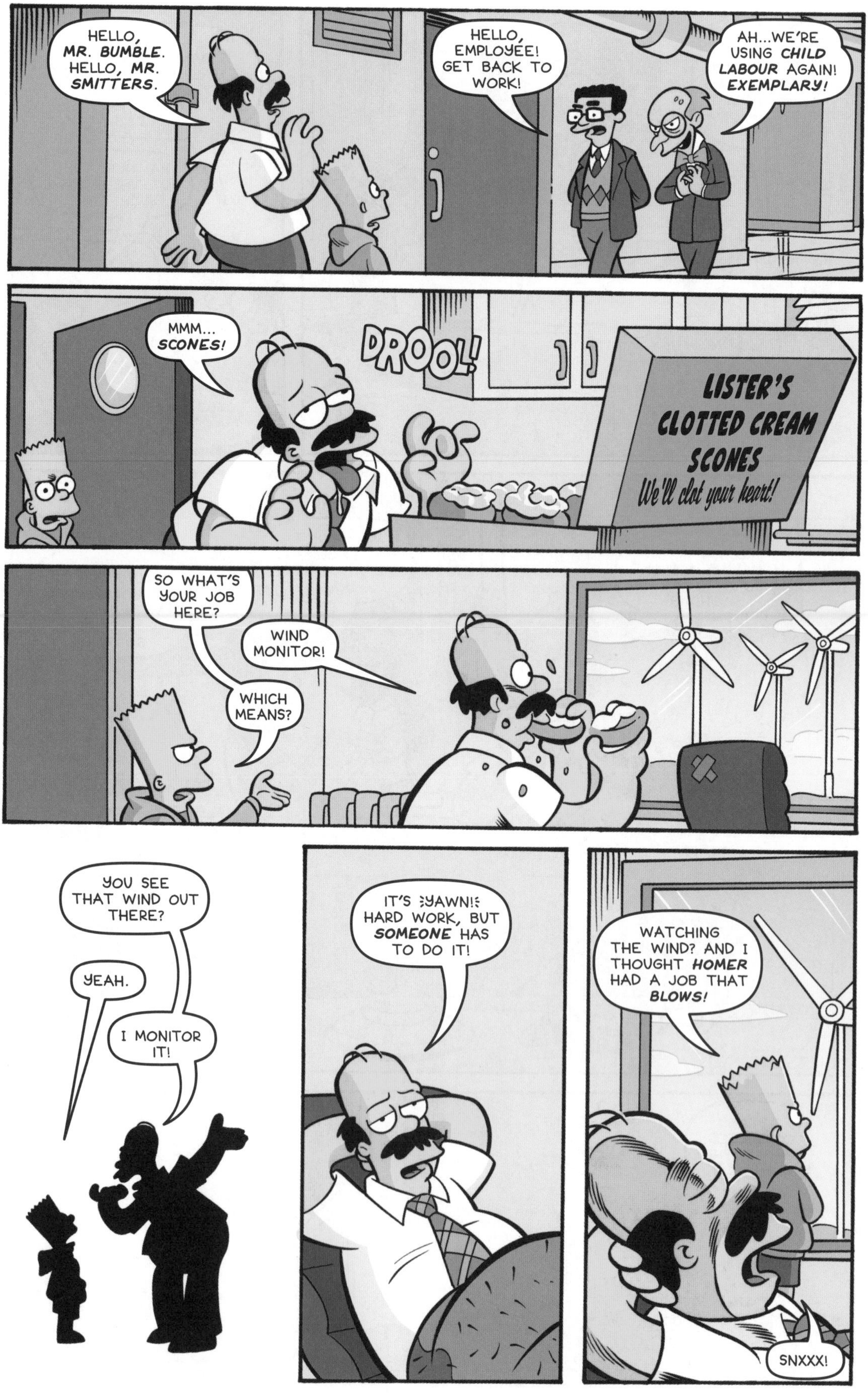
HELLO, MR. BUMBLE. HELLO, MR. SMITTERS.
HELLO, EMPLOYEE! GET BACK TO WORK!
AH...WE'RE USING CHILD LABOUR AGAIN! EXEMPLARY!
MMM... SCONES!
DROOL!
LISTER'S CLOTTED CREAM SCONES
We'll clot your heart!
SO WHAT'S YOUR JOB HERE?
WIND MONITOR!
WHICH MEANS?
YOU SEE THAT WIND OUT THERE?
YEAH.
I MONITOR IT!
IT'S YAWN! HARD WORK, BUT SOMEONE HAS TO DO IT!
WATCHING THE WIND? AND I THOUGHT HOMER HAD A JOB THAT BLOWS!
SNXXX!

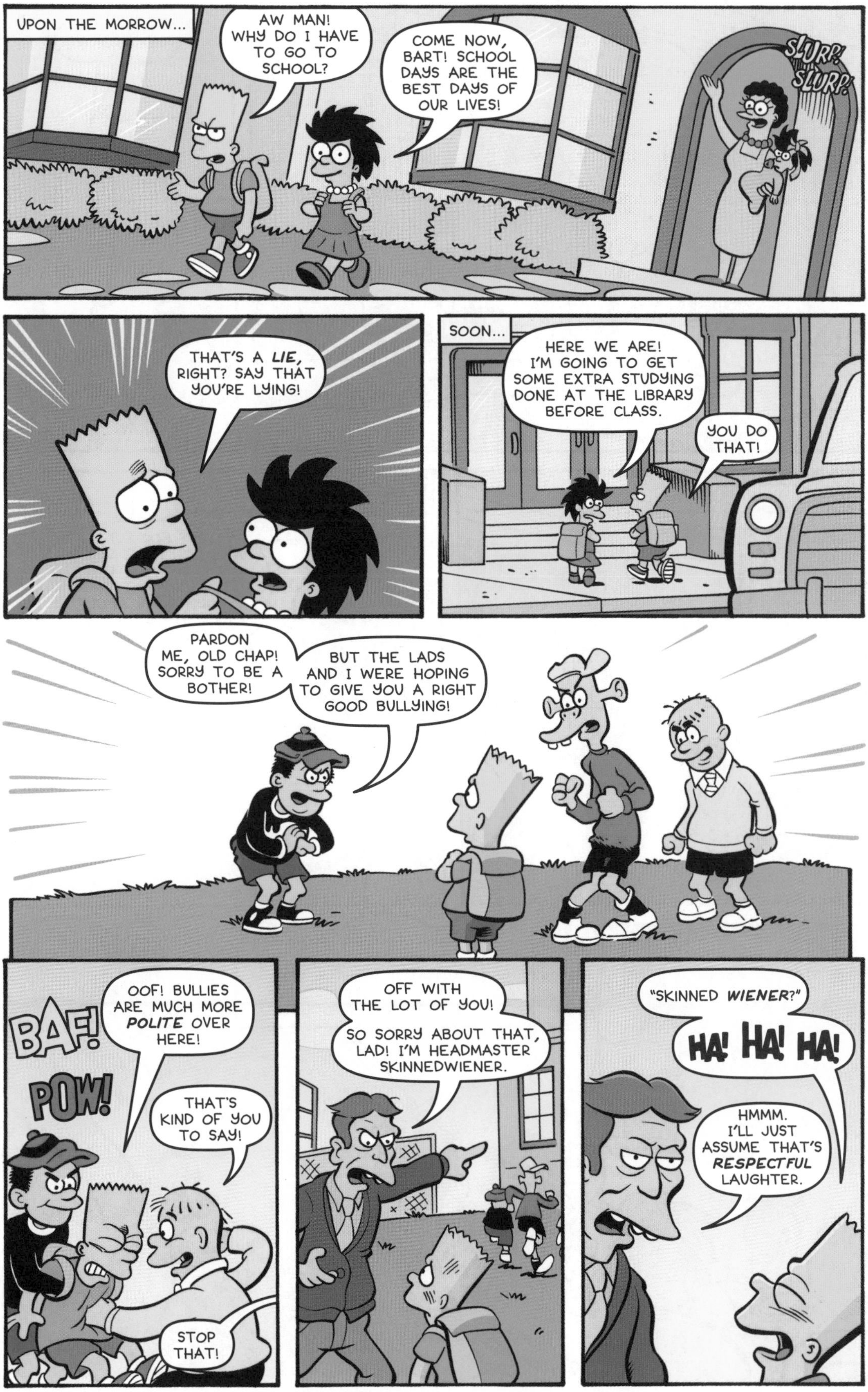
UPON THE MORROW...
AW MAN! WHY DO I HAVE TO GO TO SCHOOL?
COME NOW, BART! SCHOOL DAYS ARE THE BEST DAYS OF OUR LIVES!
SLURP! SLURP!
THAT'S A LIE, RIGHT? SAY THAT YOU'RE LYING!
SOON...
HERE WE ARE! I'M GOING TO GET SOME EXTRA STUDYING DONE AT THE LIBRARY BEFORE CLASS.
YOU DO THAT!
PARDON ME, OLD CHAP! SORRY TO BE A BOTHER!
BUT THE LADS AND I WERE HOPING TO GIVE YOU A RIGHT GOOD BULLYING!
BAF!
POW!
OOF! BULLIES ARE MUCH MORE POLITE OVER HERE!
THAT'S KIND OF YOU TO SAY!
STOP THAT!
OFF WITH THE LOT OF YOU!
SO SORRY ABOUT THAT, LAD! I'M HEADMASTER SKINNEDWIENER.
"SKINNED WIENER?"
HA! HA! HA!
HMMM. I'LL JUST ASSUME THAT'S RESPECTFUL LAUGHTER.

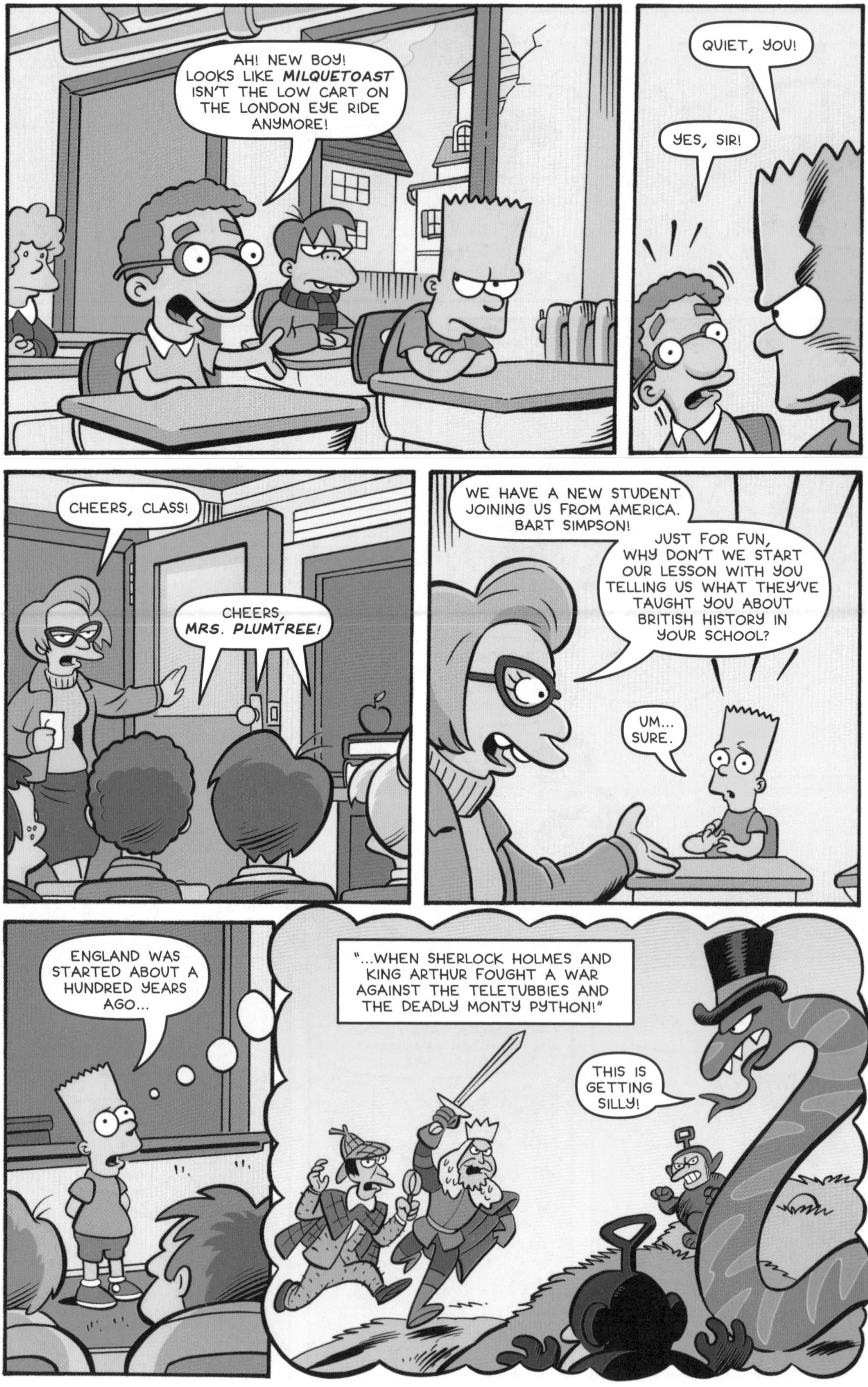
AH! NEW BOY! LOOKS LIKE MILQUETOAST ISN'T THE LOW CART ON THE LONDON EYE RIDE ANYMORE!
QUIET, YOU!
YES, SIR!
CHEERS, CLASS!
CHEERS, MRS. PLUMTREE!
WE HAVE A NEW STUDENT JOINING US FROM AMERICA. BART SIMPSON!
JUST FOR FUN, WHY DON'T WE START OUR LESSON WITH YOU TELLING US WHAT THEY'VE TAUGHT YOU ABOUT BRITISH HISTORY IN YOUR SCHOOL?
UM... SURE.
ENGLAND WAS STARTED ABOUT A HUNDRED YEARS AGO...
"...WHEN SHERLOCK HOLMES AND KING ARTHUR FOUGHT A WAR AGAINST THE TELETUBBIES AND THE DEADLY MONTY PYTHON!"
THIS IS GETTING SILLY!

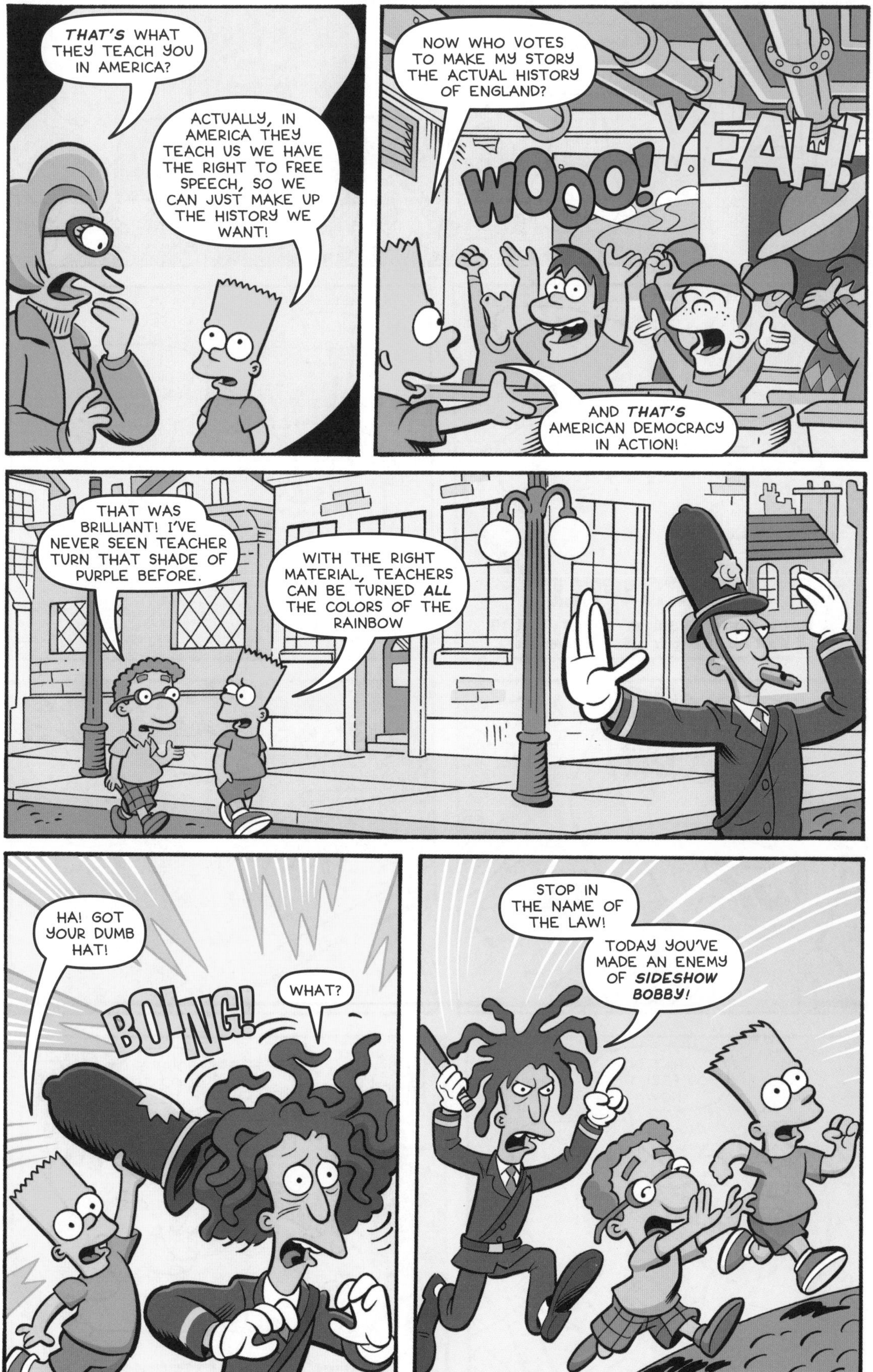
THAT'S WHAT THEY TEACH YOU IN AMERICA?
ACTUALLY, IN AMERICA THEY TEACH US WE HAVE THE RIGHT TO FREE SPEECH, SO WE CAN JUST MAKE UP THE HISTORY WE WANT!
NOW WHO VOTES TO MAKE MY STORY THE ACTUAL HISTORY OF ENGLAND?
WOOO!
YEAH!
AND THAT'S AMERICAN DEMOCRACY IN ACTION!
THAT WAS BRILLIANT! I'VE NEVER SEEN TEACHER TURN THAT SHADE OF PURPLE BEFORE.
WITH THE RIGHT MATERIAL, TEACHERS CAN BE TURNED ALL THE COLORS OF THE RAINBOW
HA! GOT YOUR DUMB HAT!
BOING!
WHAT?
STOP IN THE NAME OF THE LAW!
TODAY YOU'VE MADE AN ENEMY OF SIDESHOW BOBBY!

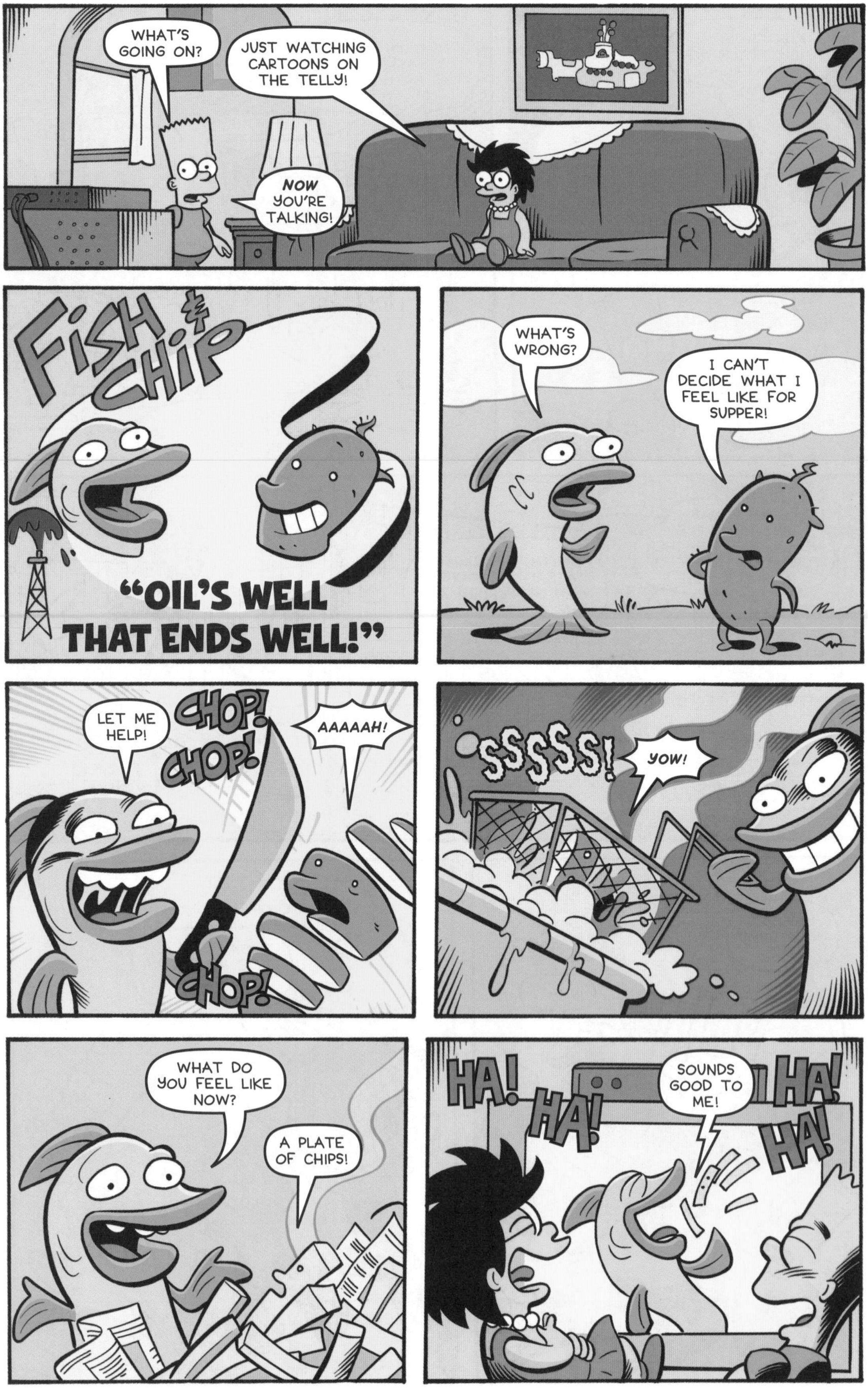
WHAT'S GOING ON?
JUST WATCHING CARTOONS ON THE TELLY!
NOW YOU'RE TALKING!
FISH & CHIP
"OIL'S WELL THAT ENDS WELL!"
WHAT'S WRONG?
I CAN'T DECIDE WHAT I FEEL LIKE FOR SUPPER!
LET ME HELP!
CHOP! CHOP!
AAAAAH!
CHOP!
SSSSS!
YOW!
WHAT DO YOU FEEL LIKE NOW?
A PLATE OF CHIPS!
HA! HA!
SOUNDS GOOD TO ME!
HA! HA!

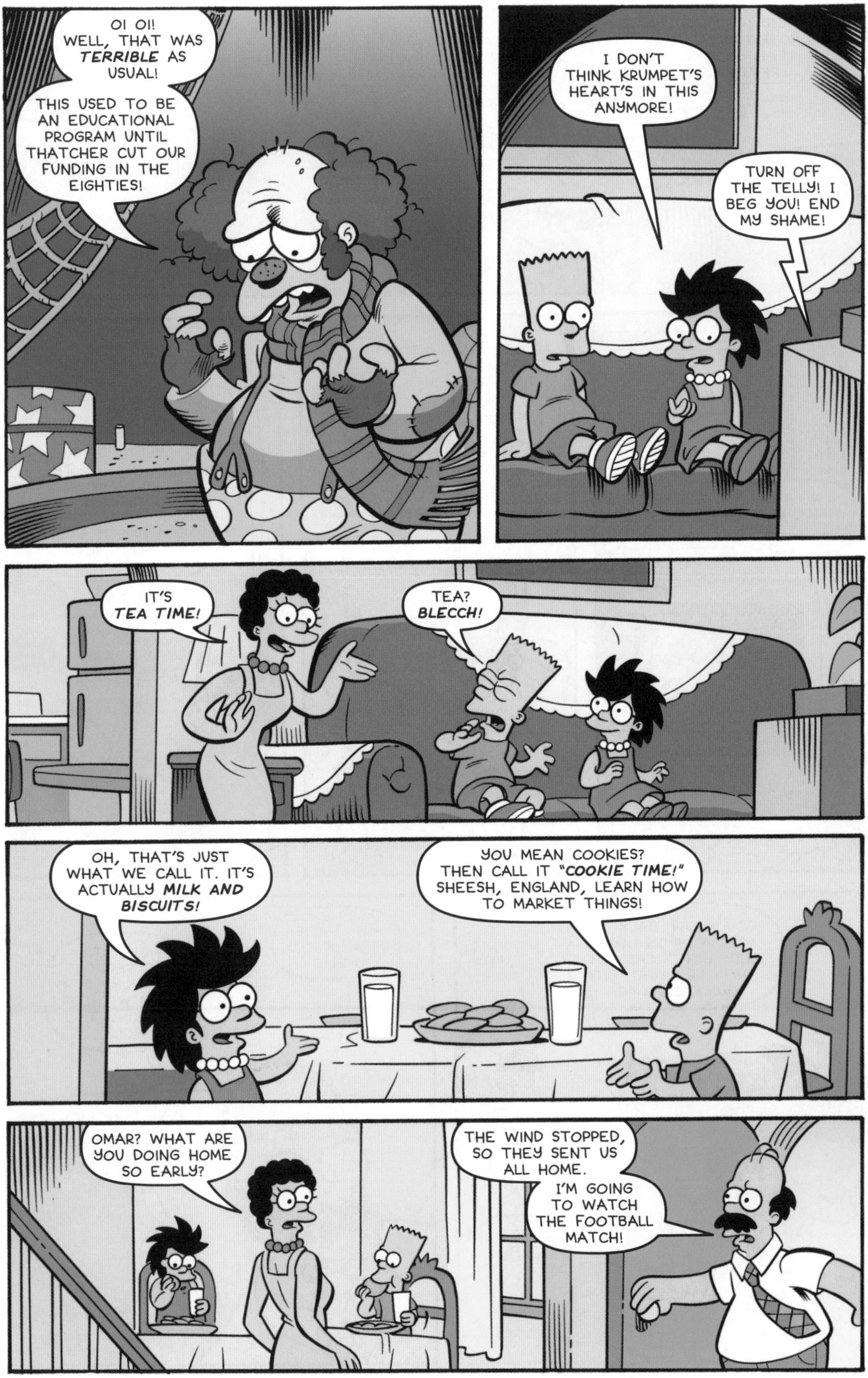
OI OI! WELL, THAT WAS *TERRIBLE* AS USUAL!
THIS USED TO BE AN EDUCATIONAL PROGRAM UNTIL THATCHER CUT OUR FUNDING IN THE EIGHTIES!
I DON'T THINK KRUMPET'S HEART'S IN THIS ANYMORE!
TURN OFF THE TELLY! I BEG YOU! END MY SHAME!
IT'S *TEA TIME!*
TEA? *BLECCH!*
OH, THAT'S JUST WHAT WE CALL IT. IT'S ACTUALLY *MILK AND BISCUITS!*
YOU MEAN COOKIES? THEN CALL IT "*COOKIE TIME!*" SHEESH, ENGLAND, LEARN HOW TO MARKET THINGS!
OMAR? WHAT ARE YOU DOING HOME SO EARLY?
THE WIND STOPPED, SO THEY SENT US ALL HOME.
I'M GOING TO WATCH THE FOOTBALL MATCH!

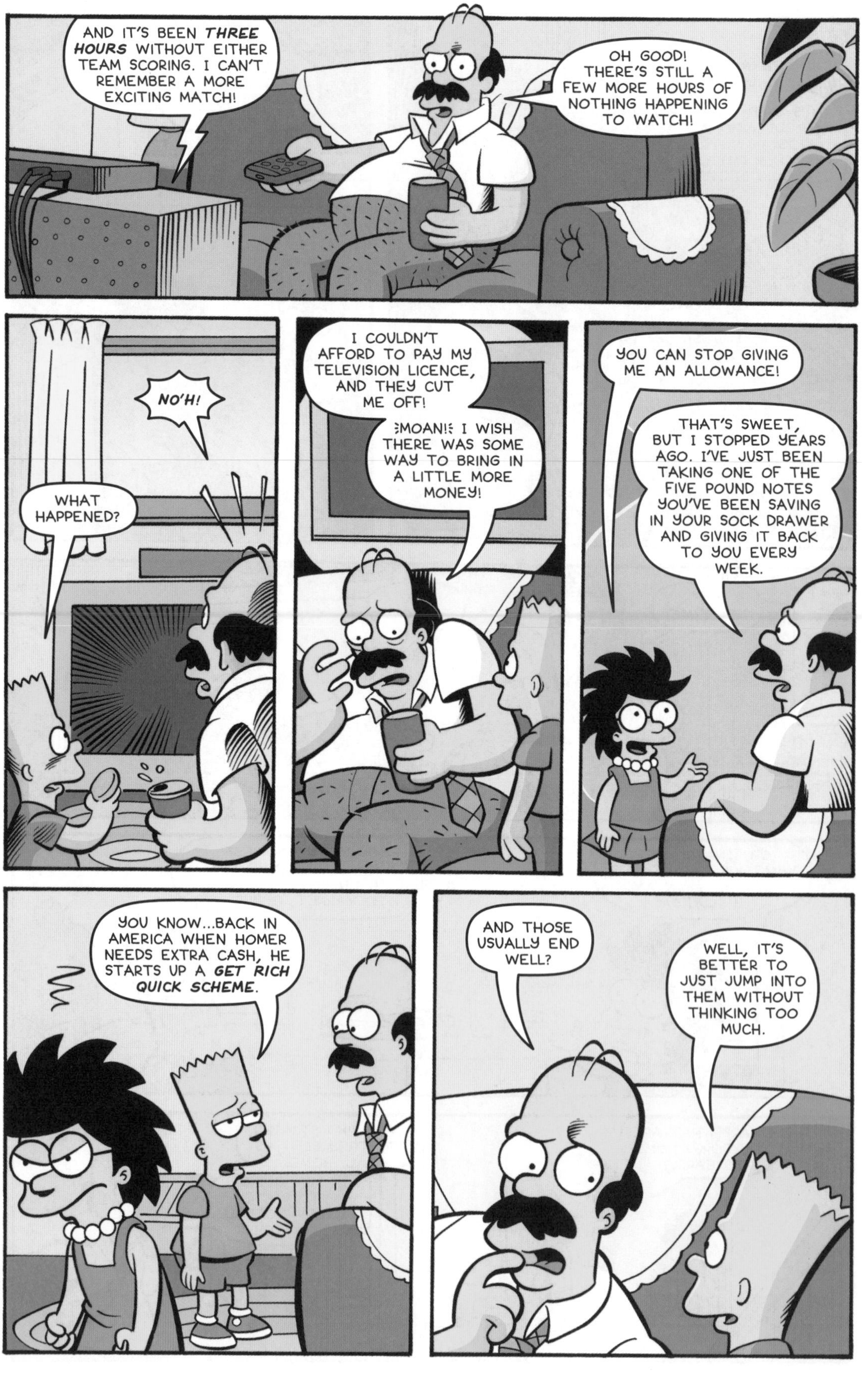
AND IT'S BEEN **THREE HOURS** WITHOUT EITHER TEAM SCORING. I CAN'T REMEMBER A MORE EXCITING MATCH!
OH GOOD! THERE'S STILL A FEW MORE HOURS OF NOTHING HAPPENING TO WATCH!
NO'H!
WHAT HAPPENED?
I COULDN'T AFFORD TO PAY MY TELEVISION LICENCE, AND THEY CUT ME OFF!
⁝MOAN!⁝ I WISH THERE WAS SOME WAY TO BRING IN A LITTLE MORE MONEY!
YOU CAN STOP GIVING ME AN ALLOWANCE!
THAT'S SWEET, BUT I STOPPED YEARS AGO. I'VE JUST BEEN TAKING ONE OF THE FIVE POUND NOTES YOU'VE BEEN SAVING IN YOUR SOCK DRAWER AND GIVING IT BACK TO YOU EVERY WEEK.
YOU KNOW...BACK IN AMERICA WHEN HOMER NEEDS EXTRA CASH, HE STARTS UP A **GET RICH QUICK SCHEME**.
AND THOSE USUALLY END WELL?
WELL, IT'S BETTER TO JUST JUMP INTO THEM WITHOUT THINKING TOO MUCH.

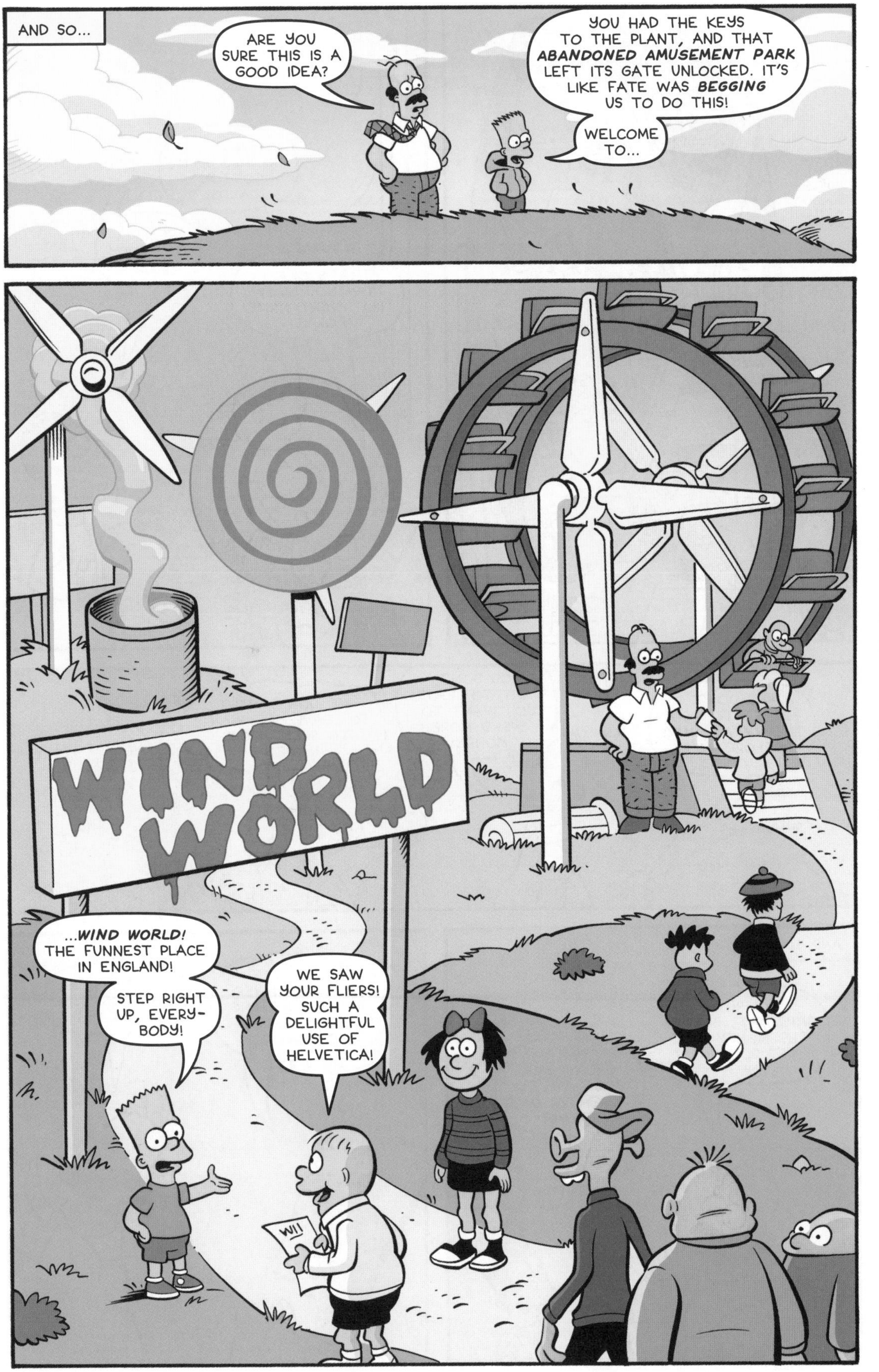
AND SO...
ARE YOU SURE THIS IS A GOOD IDEA?
YOU HAD THE KEYS TO THE PLANT, AND THAT ***ABANDONED AMUSEMENT PARK*** LEFT ITS GATE UNLOCKED. IT'S LIKE FATE WAS ***BEGGING*** US TO DO THIS!
WELCOME TO...
WIND WORLD
...***WIND WORLD!*** THE FUNNEST PLACE IN ENGLAND!
STEP RIGHT UP, EVERY-BODY!
WE SAW YOUR FLIERS! SUCH A DELIGHTFUL USE OF HELVETICA!

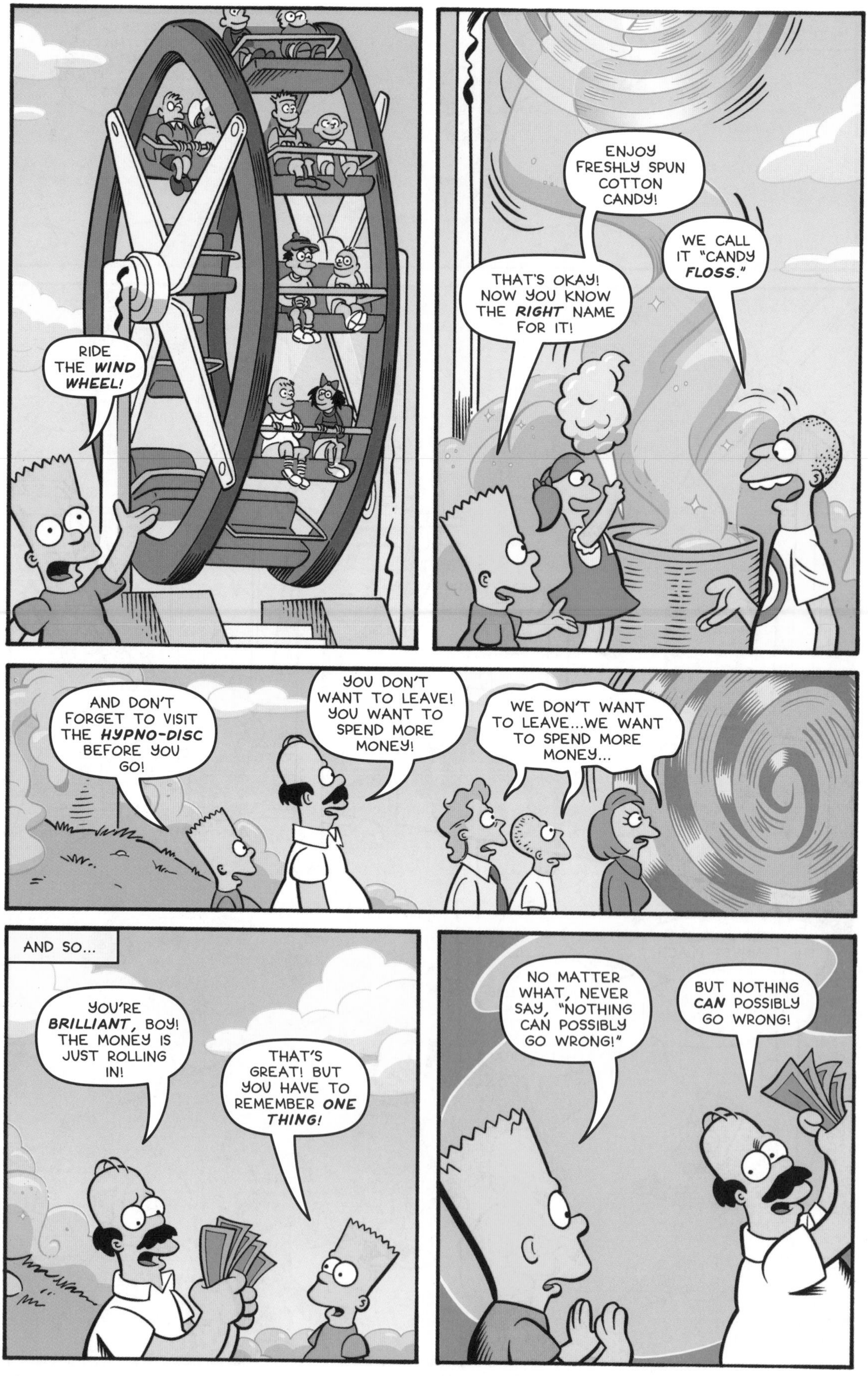

RIDE THE **WIND WHEEL!**
ENJOY FRESHLY SPUN COTTON CANDY!
WE CALL IT "CANDY **FLOSS**."
THAT'S OKAY! NOW YOU KNOW THE **RIGHT** NAME FOR IT!
AND DON'T FORGET TO VISIT THE **HYPNO-DISC** BEFORE YOU GO!
YOU DON'T WANT TO LEAVE! YOU WANT TO SPEND MORE MONEY!
WE DON'T WANT TO LEAVE...WE WANT TO SPEND MORE MONEY...
AND SO...
YOU'RE **BRILLIANT,** BOY! THE MONEY IS JUST ROLLING IN!
THAT'S GREAT! BUT YOU HAVE TO REMEMBER **ONE THING!**
NO MATTER WHAT, NEVER SAY, "NOTHING CAN POSSIBLY GO WRONG!"
BUT NOTHING **CAN** POSSIBLY GO WRONG!

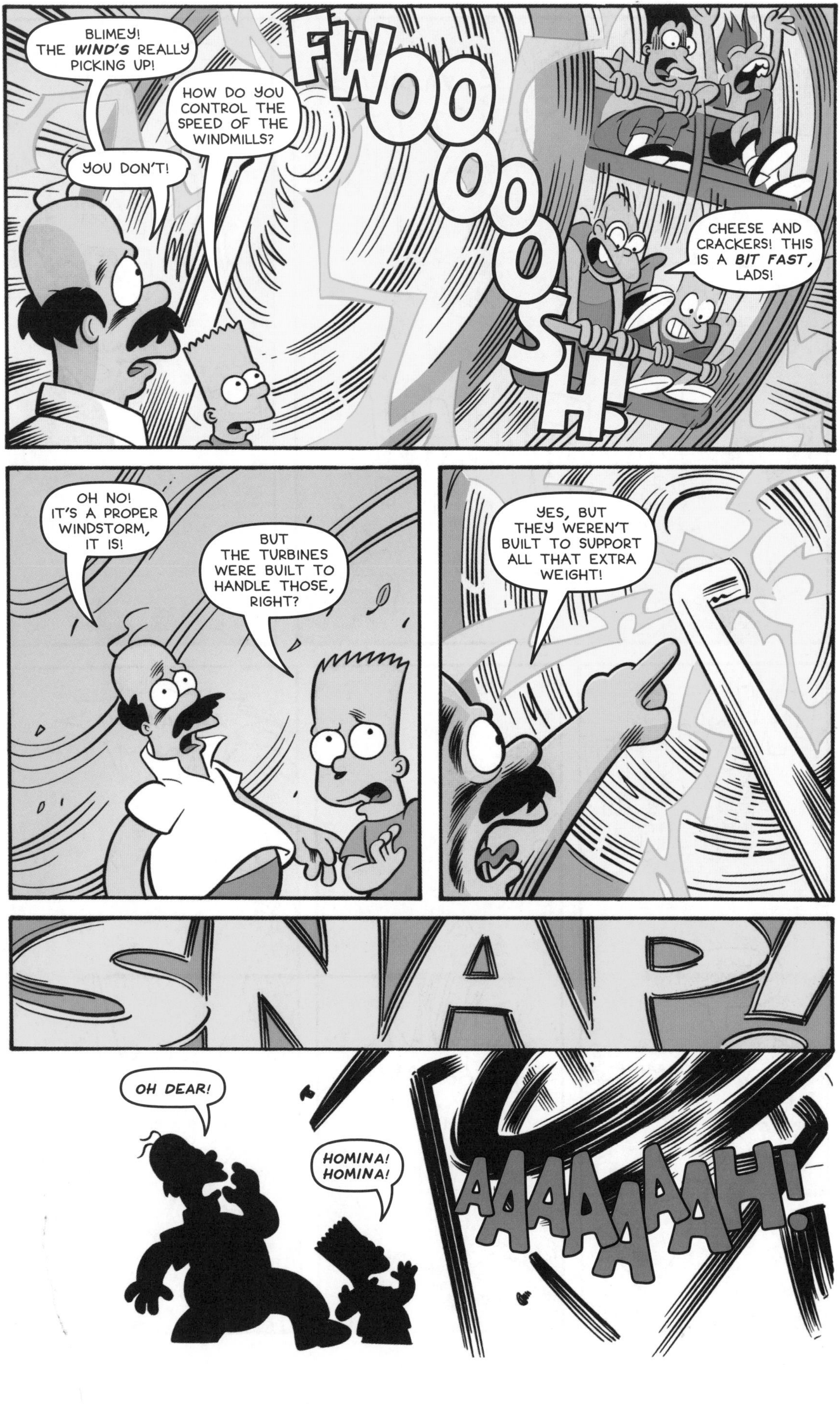
BLIMEY! THE WIND'S REALLY PICKING UP!
HOW DO YOU CONTROL THE SPEED OF THE WINDMILLS?
YOU DON'T!
FWOOOOOOSH!
CHEESE AND CRACKERS! THIS IS A BIT FAST, LADS!
OH NO! IT'S A PROPER WINDSTORM, IT IS!
BUT THE TURBINES WERE BUILT TO HANDLE THOSE, RIGHT?
YES, BUT THEY WEREN'T BUILT TO SUPPORT ALL THAT EXTRA WEIGHT!
SNAP!
OH DEAR!
HOMINA! HOMINA!
AAAAAAAH!

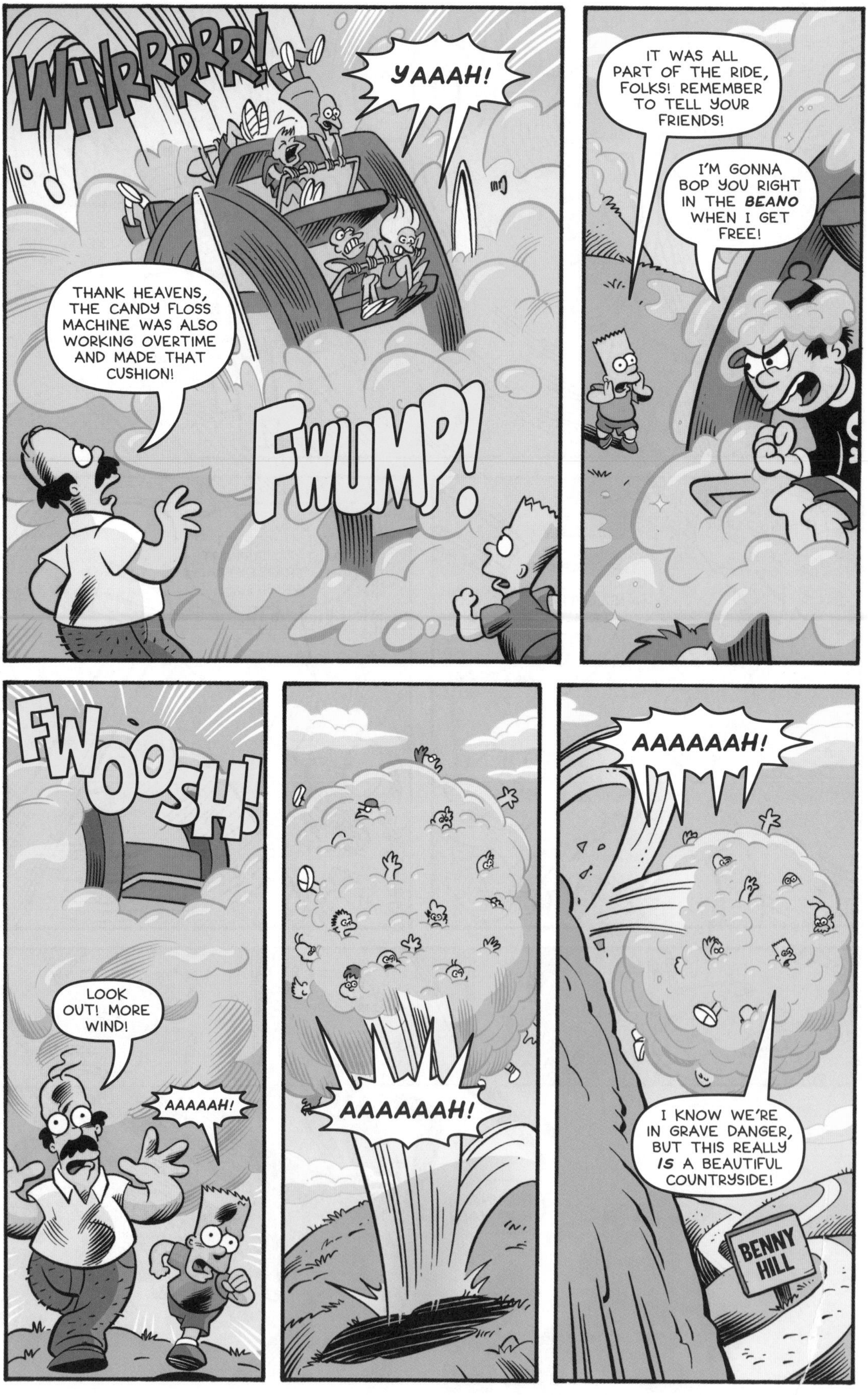
WHIRRRRR!
YAAAH!
THANK HEAVENS, THE CANDY FLOSS MACHINE WAS ALSO WORKING OVERTIME AND MADE THAT CUSHION!
FWUMP!
IT WAS ALL PART OF THE RIDE, FOLKS! REMEMBER TO TELL YOUR FRIENDS!
I'M GONNA BOP YOU RIGHT IN THE *BEANO* WHEN I GET FREE!
FWOOSH!
LOOK OUT! MORE WIND!
AAAAAH!
AAAAAAH!
AAAAAAH!
I KNOW WE'RE IN GRAVE DANGER, BUT THIS REALLY *IS* A BEAUTIFUL COUNTRYSIDE!
BENNY HILL

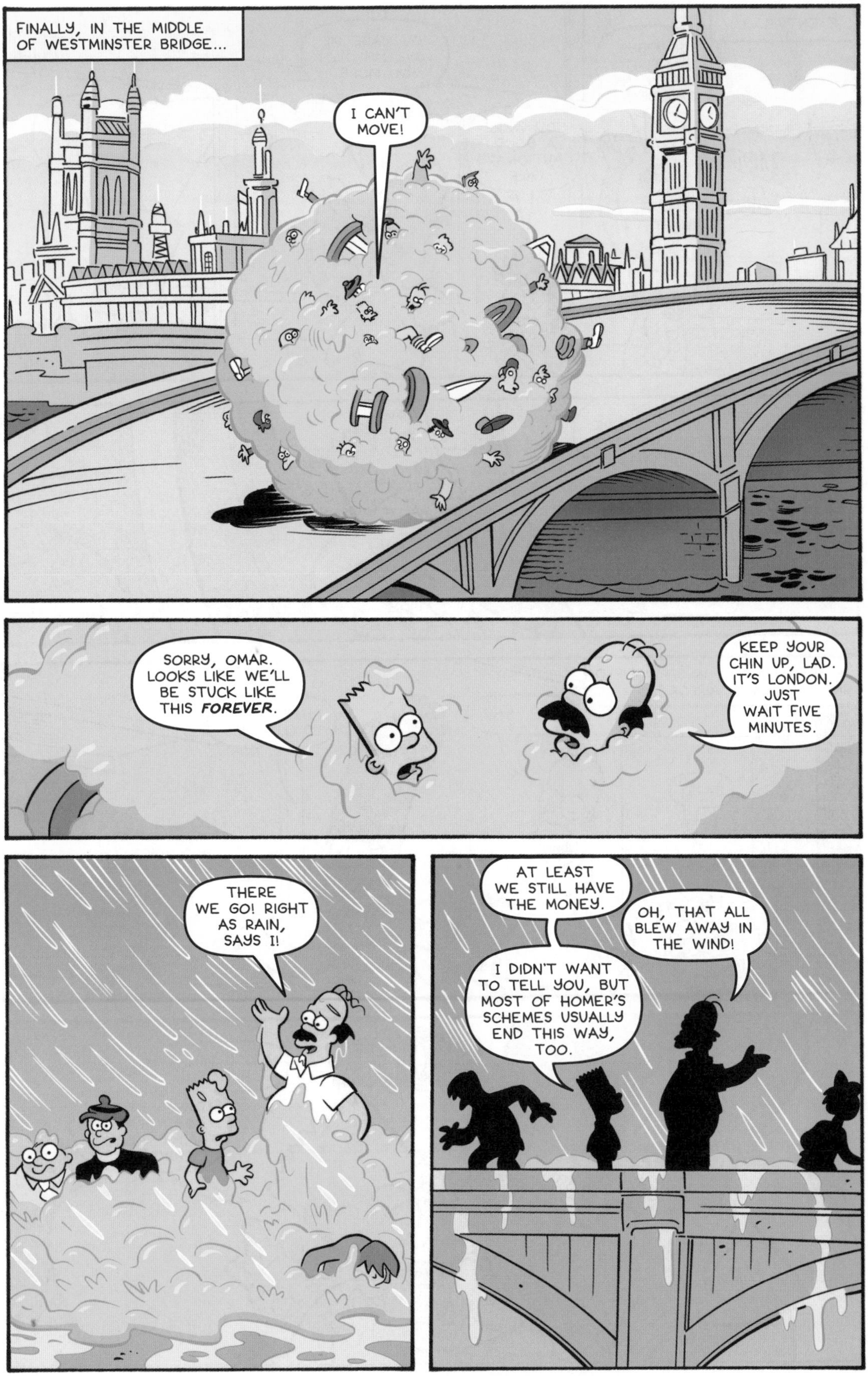
FINALLY, IN THE MIDDLE OF WESTMINSTER BRIDGE...
I CAN'T MOVE!
SORRY, OMAR. LOOKS LIKE WE'LL BE STUCK LIKE THIS *FOREVER*.
KEEP YOUR CHIN UP, LAD. IT'S LONDON. JUST WAIT FIVE MINUTES.
THERE WE GO! RIGHT AS RAIN, SAYS I!
AT LEAST WE STILL HAVE THE MONEY.
OH, THAT ALL BLEW AWAY IN THE WIND!
I DIDN'T WANT TO TELL YOU, BUT MOST OF HOMER'S SCHEMES USUALLY END THIS WAY, TOO.

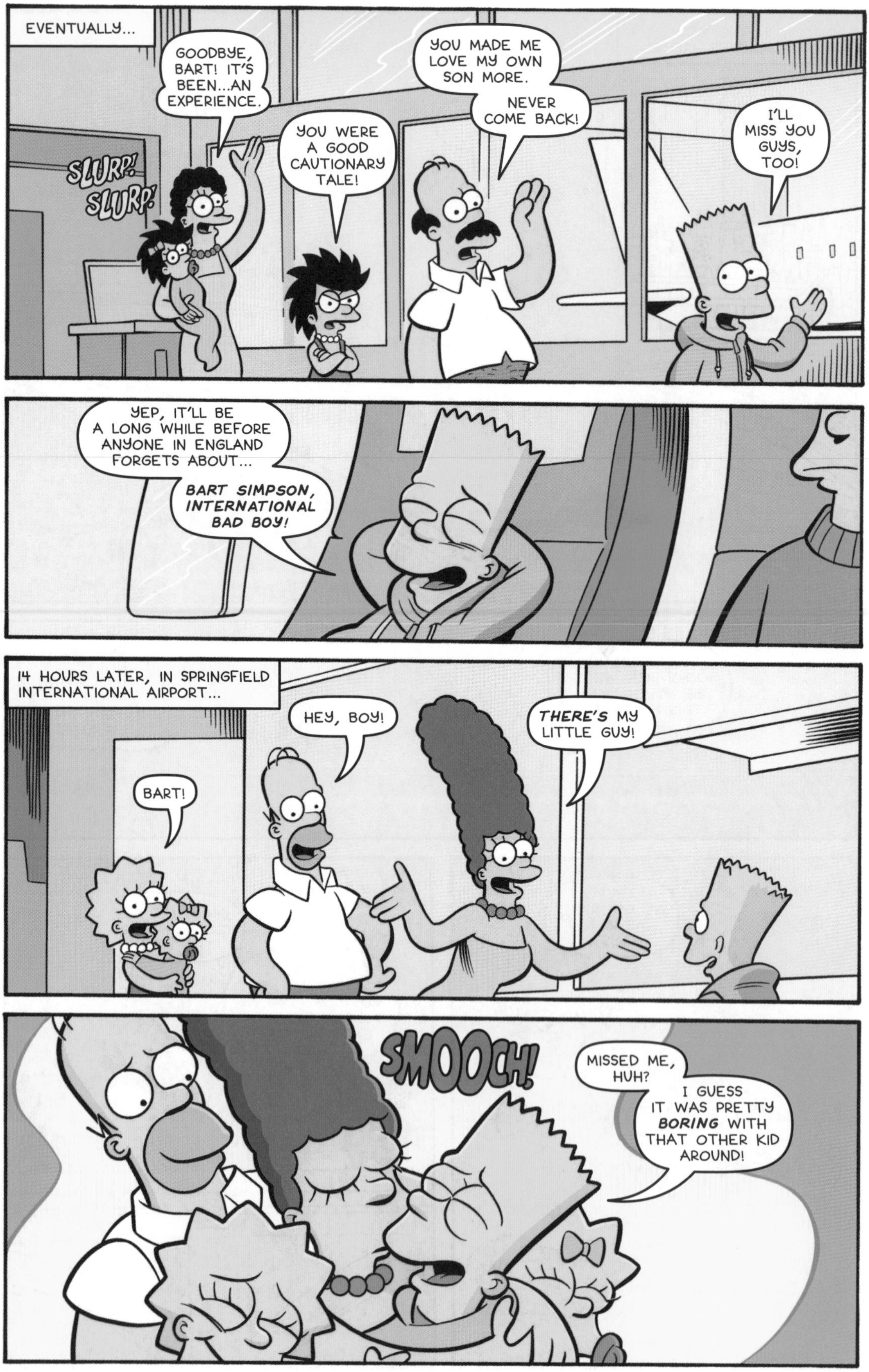
EVENTUALLY...
GOODBYE, BART! IT'S BEEN...AN EXPERIENCE.
SLURP! SLURP!
YOU WERE A GOOD CAUTIONARY TALE!
YOU MADE ME LOVE MY OWN SON MORE.
NEVER COME BACK!
I'LL MISS YOU GUYS, TOO!
YEP, IT'LL BE A LONG WHILE BEFORE ANYONE IN ENGLAND FORGETS ABOUT...
BART SIMPSON, INTERNATIONAL BAD BOY!
14 HOURS LATER, IN SPRINGFIELD INTERNATIONAL AIRPORT...
BART!
HEY, BOY!
THERE'S MY LITTLE GUY!
SMOOCH!
MISSED ME, HUH?
I GUESS IT WAS PRETTY BORING WITH THAT OTHER KID AROUND!

HEH.

WHAT?

WE NEVER KNEW HOW GOOD WE HAD IT WITH YOU, BOY!

BRIT WAS LIKE AN *EARTH-QUAKE* MADE OF MISCHIEF!

IT'S SO GOOD TO HAVE YOU HOME!

RIVALS

ATE 3

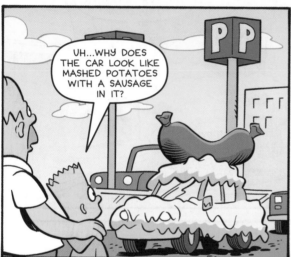

UH...WHY DOES THE CAR LOOK LIKE MASHED POTATOES WITH A SAUSAGE IN IT?

BRIT AND I OPENED A *BANGERS AND MASH* FOOD STAND OUT OF MY CAR.

HOW DID IT DO?

GREAT AT FIRST, THEN BARNEY OPENED THE *"EVERYONE'S A WIENER"* FLAME-BROILED HOT DOG WAGON.

BRIT DIDN'T LIKE THE COMPETITION AND REPLACED BARNEY'S HOT DOGS WITH FIRECRACKERS.

IT ALL GOT PRETTY CRAZY AFTER THAT.

THAT SOUNDS AMAZING!

IT WAS NEVER A DULL MOMENT WITH BRIT AROUND!

WHAT TH--?!

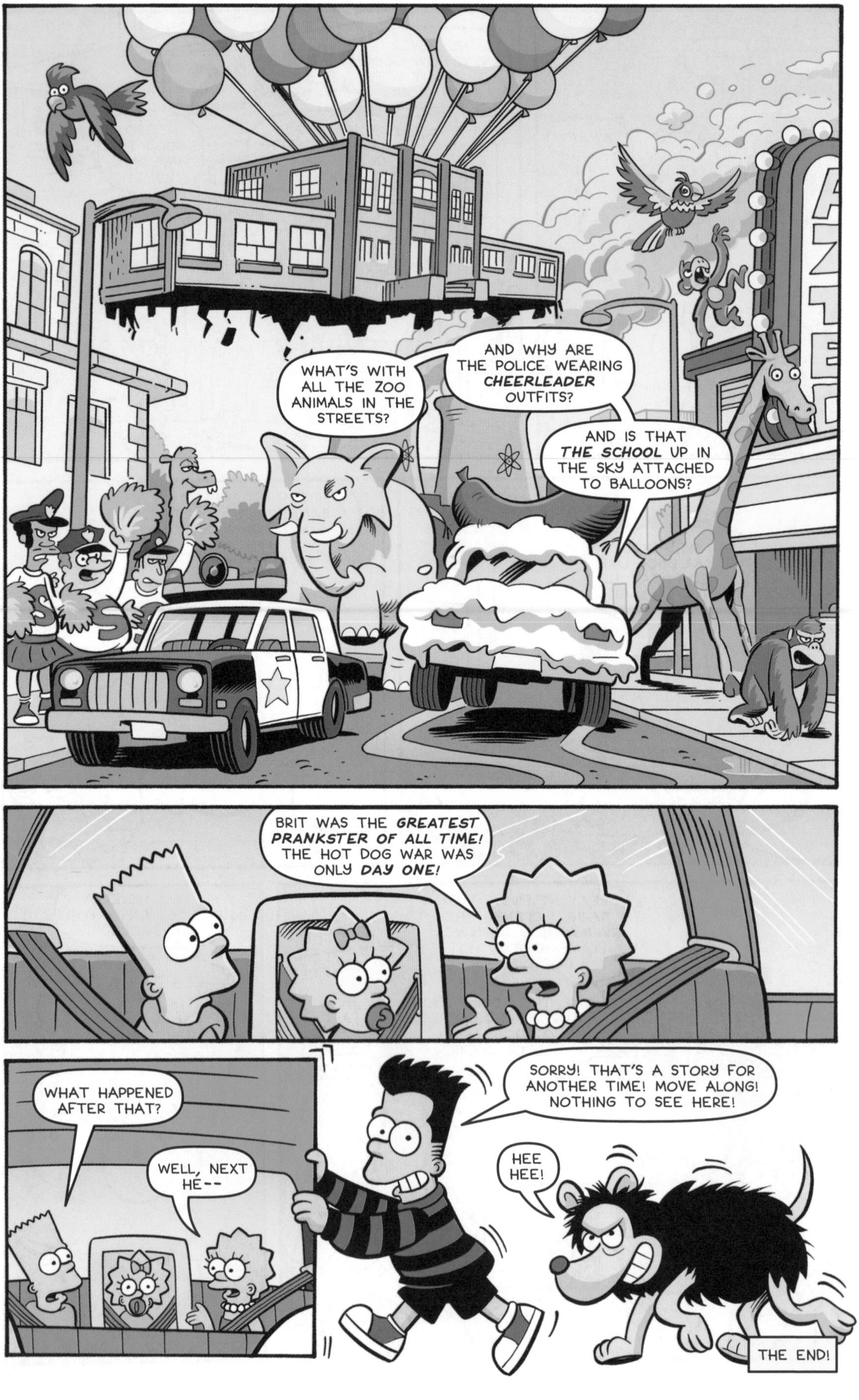
WHAT'S WITH ALL THE ZOO ANIMALS IN THE STREETS?
AND WHY ARE THE POLICE WEARING CHEERLEADER OUTFITS?
AND IS THAT THE SCHOOL UP IN THE SKY ATTACHED TO BALLOONS?
BRIT WAS THE GREATEST PRANKSTER OF ALL TIME! THE HOT DOG WAR WAS ONLY DAY ONE!
WHAT HAPPENED AFTER THAT?
WELL, NEXT HE--
SORRY! THAT'S A STORY FOR ANOTHER TIME! MOVE ALONG! NOTHING TO SEE HERE!
HEE HEE!
THE END!

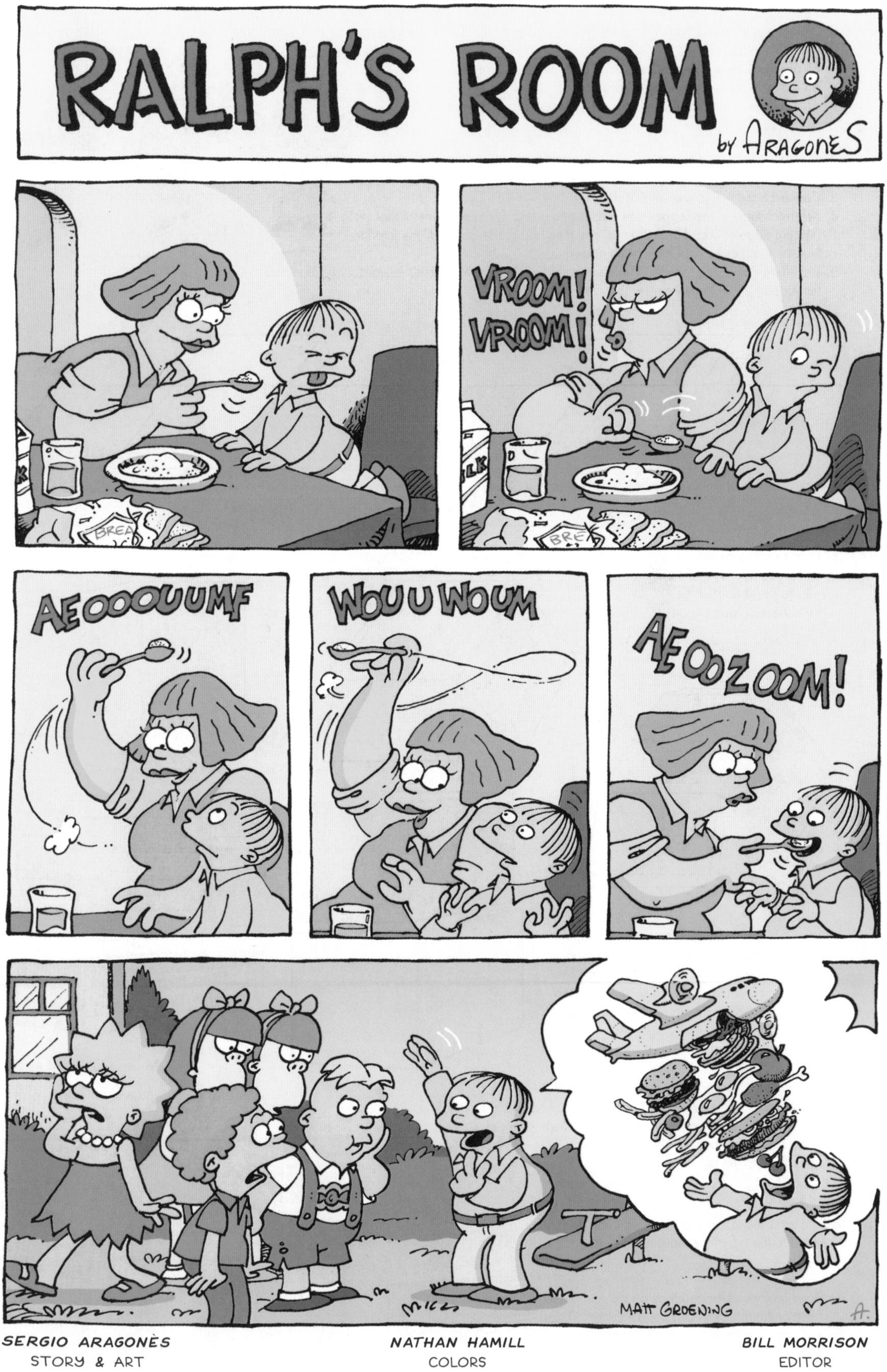
RALPH'S ROOM
by ARAGONES
VROOM! VROOM!
AEOOOUUMF
WOUUWOUM
AEOOZOOM!
MATT GROENING

SERGIO ARAGONÈS
STORY & ART

NATHAN HAMILL
COLORS

BILL MORRISON
EDITOR

BUSY HANDS PAPERCRAFT PROJECT!

WHAT YOU WILL NEED:

- Scissors, adhesive tape, and a straight edge (such as a ruler).
- An ability to fold along straight lines.
- An additional "mint condition" copy of this book secured elsewhere!

1. Cut out figures and bases.
2. Cut along the dotted line at the base of each figure and also the center of each curved base. (Be careful not to cut too far!)
3. Connect base to figure as shown (Fig. 1).
4. Before cutting out the shapes, use a ruler and a slightly rounded metal tool (like the edge of a key) to first score, and then fold lightly along all the interior lines (this will make final folds much easier).
5. Cut along the exterior shape. Make sure to cut all the way to where the walls, the roof, and the flap lines meet (Fig. 2).

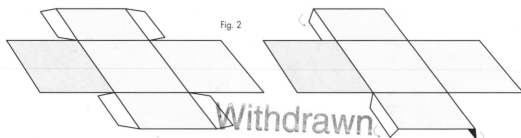

Fig. 1

Fig. 2

6. Form building by folding walls into place (Fig. 3) and secure all tabs to the interior of the building with tape (Fig. 4).

Fig. 3

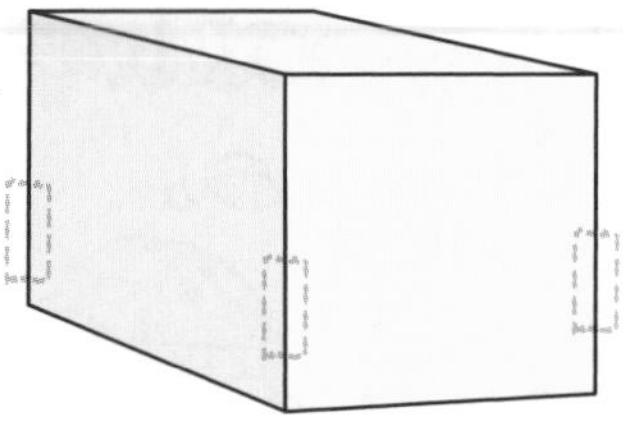

Fig. 4

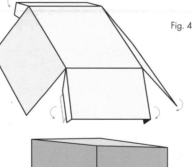

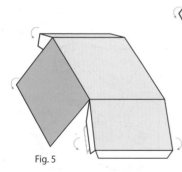

Fig. 5

7. Cut and fold second story shape as shown (Fig. 5), and secure with tape. See cutout page for instructions on placement of roof items. Then, place the second story on top of building and secure bottom flaps onto top of first story with tape (Fig. 6).

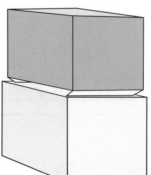

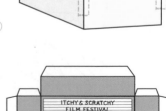

Fig. 6

ITCHY & SCRATCHY
FILM FESTIVAL
ITCHY & SCRATCHY
FILM FESTIVAL

Fig. 7

8. Cut and fold marquee into box-like shape as shown (Fig. 7), and secure with tape. Fold down the top rear tab and then fold in the two side tabs, taping them to the rear tab.

9. Fold back the tab on the Aztec sign and tape it to the top of the marquee (Fig. 8)

10. Place a piece of looped tape on the back of the marquee and press it firmly into place on the front of the building (Fig. 9).

AZTEC
ITCHY & SCRATCHY
FILM FESTIVAL

Fig. 8

AZTEC
ITCHY & SCRATCHY
FILM FESTIVAL

Fig. 9